> *L'amor che muove il sole e l'altre stelle.*
> *(Love which moves the sun and the other stars.)*
> —Dante.

Janeen
Marcelo
Singson

SAPPHIQUE

CATHERINE FISHER

SCHOLASTIC INC.
New York Toronto London Auckland
Sydney Mexico City New Delhi Hong Kong

Originally published in 2008 by Hodder Children's Books

ISBN 978-0-545-40036-7

12 11 10 9 8 7 6 5 4 3 2 1   11 12 13 14 15 16/0

Printed in the U.S.A.   75

First Scholastic printing, September 2011

Designed by Nancy R. Leo-Kelly
Text set in Adobe Garamond

THE ART MAGICKE

The alleyway was so narrow that Attia could lean against one wall and kick the other. She waited in the dimness, listening, her breath condensing on glistening bricks. A flicker of flames around the corner sent red ripples down the walls.

The shouts were louder now, the unmistakable roar of an excited crowd. She heard howls of delight, sudden gales of laughter. Whistles and stamping. Applause.

Licking a fallen drip of condensation from her lips, she tasted its salty grit, knowing she had to face them. She had come too far, searched too long, to back out now. It was useless feeling small and scared. Not if she ever wanted to Escape. She straightened, edged to the end of the alley, and peered out.

Hundreds of people were crammed into the small torch-lit square. They were squeezed together, their backs to her, the stench of sweat and bodies overpowering. Behind the mob a few old women stood craning to see. Halfmen crouched in shadows. Boys climbed on each other's shoulders, scrambling up onto the rooftops of squalid houses. Stalls of gaudy canvas sold hot food, the pungency of onions and spitting grease making her swallow with hunger. The Prison was interested too. Just above her, under the eaves of filthy straw, one of its tiny red Eyes spied curiously on the scene.

A howl of delight from the crowd made Attia set her shoulders; she stepped out deliberately. Dogs fought over scraps; she edged around them, past a shadowy doorway. Someone slipped out behind her; she turned, her knife already in her hand.

"Don't even try."

The cutpurse stepped back, fingers spread, grinning. He was thin and filthy and had few teeth.

"No problem, darling. My mistake."

She watched him slide into the crowd.

"It would have been," she muttered. Then she sheathed her knife and barged in after him.

Forcing a way through was tough. The people were tightly packed and eager to see whatever was going on up front; they groaned, laughed, gasped in unison. Ragged children crawled under everyone's feet, getting kicked and stepped on. Attia pushed and swore, slipped into gaps, ducked under elbows. Being small had its uses. And she needed to get to the front. She needed to see him.

Winded and bruised, she squirmed between two huge men and found air.

It was acrid with smoke. Firebrands crackled all around; before her, an area of mud had been roped off.

Crouched in it, all alone, was a bear.

Attia stared.

The bear's black fur was scabby, its eyes small and savage.

A chain clanked around its neck, and, well back in the shadows, a bear keeper held the end, a bald man with a long mustache, his skin glistening with sweat. Slung at his side was a drum; he beat it rhythmically and gave a sharp tug on the chain.

Slowly, the bear rose to its hind legs, and danced. Taller than a man, lumbering awkwardly, it circled, its muzzled mouth dripping saliva, its chains leaving bloody trails in its pelt.

Attia scowled. She knew just how it felt.

She put her hand up to her own neck, where the welts and bruises of the chain she had once worn were faded to faint marks.

Like that bear, she had been a manacled thing. If it hadn't been for Finn she still would be. Or, more likely, dead by now.

Finn.

His name was a bruise in itself. It hurt her to think of his treachery.

The drum beat louder. The bear capered, its clumsy dragging at the chain making the crowd roar. Attia watched grim-faced. Then, behind it, she saw the poster. It was plastered on the damp wall, the same poster that had been pasted up all over the village, everywhere she had looked. Ragged and wet, peeling at the corners, it invited gaudily.

COME ALL YOU GOOD PEOPLE

SEE **WONDERS!**

SEE THE LOST **FOUND!!**

SEE THE DEAD **LIVE!!!**

TONIGHT

SEE THE GREATEST **MAGICIAN**

IN **INCARCERON**

Wearing the DRAGON GLOVE of SAPPHIQUE!

THE DARK ENCHANTER

Attia shook her head in dismay. After searching for two months through corridors and empty wings, villages and cities, swampy plains and networks of white cells, for a Sapient, for a cell-born, for anyone who would know about Sapphique, all she'd found was a tacky sideshow in a back alley.

The crowd clapped and stamped. She was shoved aside.

When she'd pushed her way back she saw the bear had turned to face its handler; he was hauling it down, alarmed, prodding it away into the darkness with a long pole. The men around her roared with scorn.

"Try dancing with it yourself next time," one of them yelled. A woman giggled.

Voices from the back rose, calling for more, something new, something different, sounding impatient and scathing. Slow handclaps began. Then they faded, to silence.

In the empty space among the torches a figure was standing.

He came from nowhere, materializing into solidity from shadows and flamelight. He was tall, and wore a black coat that glistened with hundreds of tiny sparkles; as he raised his arms wide the sleeves fell open. The collar of the coat was high around his neck; in the gloom he looked young, with dark long hair.

No one spoke. Attia felt the crowd shock into stillness.

He was the image of Sapphique.

Everyone knew what Sapphique had looked like; there were a thousand pictures, carvings, descriptions of him. He was the Winged One, the Nine-Fingered, the One who had Escaped from the Prison. Like Finn, he had promised to return. Attia swallowed, nervous. Her hands were shaking. She clenched them tight.

"Friends." The magician's voice was quiet; people strained to hear him. "Welcome to my ring of wonders. You think you will see illusions. You think I will fool you with mirrors and false cards, with hidden devices. But I am not like other magicians. I am the Dark Enchanter, and I will show you true magic. The magic of the stars."

As one, the crowd gasped.

Because he raised his right hand and on it he was wearing a glove of dark fabric, and from it white flashes of light were sparking and crackling. The torches around the walls flared and sank low. A woman behind Attia moaned in terror.

Attia folded her arms. She watched, determined not to be overawed. How did he do it? Could that really be Sapphique's Glove? Could it have survived? Was there some strange power still lingering in it? But as she watched, her doubts began to slip from her grasp.

The show was astonishing.

The Enchanter had the crowd transfixed. He took objects, made them vanish, brought them back, plucked doves and Beetles out of the air, conjured a woman to sleep and made her rise slowly, unsupported, into the smoky acrid darkness. He drew butterflies from the mouth of a terrified child, conjured gold coins and threw them out to desperate, grabbing fingers, opened a door in the air and walked through it, so that the crowd bayed and howled for him to come back, and when he did it was from behind them, walking calmly through their frenzy so that they fell away, awed, as if afraid to touch him.

As he passed, Attia felt the brush of his coat against her arm;

her skin prickled, all the hairs on her skin standing up with a faint static. He gave one glance to the side, his eyes bright, catching hers.

From somewhere a woman screamed, "Heal my son, Wise One! Heal him."

A baby was lifted up, began to be passed forward over people's heads.

The Enchanter turned and held up his hand.

"That will be done later. Not now." His voice was rich with authority. "Now I prepare for the summoning of all my powers. For the reading of minds. For the entry into death and back to life."

He closed his eyes.

The torches flickered low.

Standing alone in the dark the Enchanter whispered, "There is much sorrow here. There is much fear." When he looked out at them again he seemed overwhelmed by the numbers, almost afraid of his task. Quietly he said, "I want three people to come forward. But they must be only those willing to have their deepest fears revealed. Only those willing to bare their souls to my gaze."

A few hands shot up. Women called out. After a moment of hesitation, Attia put her hand up too.

The Enchanter went toward the crowd. "That woman," he called, and one was shoved forward, hot and stumbling.

"Him." A tall man who had not even volunteered was

dragged out by those around him. He swore and stood awkwardly, as if transfixed by terror.

The Enchanter turned. His gaze moved inexorably across the massed faces. Attia held her breath. She felt the man's brooding stare cross her face like heat. He stopped, glanced back. Their eyes met, a dark second. Slowly he raised his hand and stabbed a long finger in her direction, and the crowd cried aloud because they saw that, like Sapphique, his right forefinger was missing.

"You," the Enchanter whispered.

She took a breath to calm herself. Her heart was hammering with terror. She had to force herself to push through into the dim, smoky space. But it was important to stay calm, to not show fear. Not show she was any different from anyone else.

The three of them stood in a line and Attia could feel the woman next to her trembling with emotion.

The Enchanter walked along, his eyes scrutinizing their faces. Attia met his stare as defiantly as she could. He would never read her mind; she was sure of that. She had seen and heard things he could never imagine. She had seen Outside.

He took the woman's hand. After a moment, very gently, he said, "You miss him."

The woman stared in amazement. A strand of hair stuck to her lined forehead. "Oh I do, Master. I do."

The Enchanter smiled. "Have no fear. He is safe in the peace of Incarceron. The Prison holds him in its memory. His body is whole in its white cells."

She shook with sobs of joy, kissed his hands. "Thank you, Master. Thank you for telling me."

The crowd roared its approval. Attia allowed herself a sardonic smile. They were so stupid! Hadn't they noticed this so-called magician had told the woman nothing?

A lucky guess and a few empty words and they swallowed it whole.

He had chosen his victims carefully. The tall man was so terrified he would have said anything; when the Enchanter asked him how his sick mother was he stammered that she was improving, sir. The crowd applauded.

"Indeed she is." The Enchanter waved his maimed hand for silence. "And I prophecy this. By Lightson her fever will have diminished. She will sit up and call for you, my friend. She will live ten more years. I see your grandchildren on her knee."

The man could not speak. Attia was disgusted to see tears in his eyes.

The crowd murmured. Perhaps they were less convinced, because when the Enchanter came to Attia, he turned to face them suddenly.

"It is easy, some of you are thinking, to speak of the future." He raised his young face and stared out at them.

"How will we ever know, you're thinking, whether he is right or wrong? And you are right to doubt. But the past, my friends, the past is a different thing. I will tell you now of this girl's past."

Attia tensed.

Perhaps he sensed her fear, because a slight smile curled his lips. He stared at her, his eyes slowly glazing, becoming distant, dark as the night. Then he lifted his gloved hand and touched her forehead.

"I see," he whispered, "a long journey. Many miles, many weary days of walking. I see you crouched like a beast. I see a chain about your neck."

Attia swallowed. She wanted to jerk away. Instead she nodded, and the crowd was silent.

The Enchanter took her hand. He clasped his own around it and his gloved fingers were long and bony. His voice was puzzled. "I see strange things in your mind, girl. I see you climbing a tall ladder, fleeing from a great Beast, flying in a silver ship above cities and towers. I see a boy. His name is Finn. He has betrayed you. He has left you behind and though he promised to return, you fear he never will. You love him, and you hate him. Is that not true?"

Attia's face was scorching. Her hand shook. "Yes," she breathed.

The crowd was transfixed.

The Enchanter stared at her as if her soul were transparent; she found she could not look away. Something was happening to him, a strangeness had come into his face, behind his eyes.

Small bright glints shone on his coat. The glove felt like ice around her fingers.

"Stars," he said breathlessly. "I see the stars. Under them a golden palace, its windows bright with candles. I see it through the keyhole of a dark doorway. It is far, far away. It is Outside."

Amazed, Attia stared at him. His grasp on her hand hurt but she couldn't move. His voice was a whisper. "There is a way Out. *Sapphique found it.* The keyhole is tiny, tinier than an atom. And the eagle and the swan spread their wings to guard it."

She had to move, break this spell. She glanced aside. People crowded the edges of the arena; the bear guard, seven jugglers, dancers from the troupe. They stood as still as the crowd.

"Master," she whispered.

His eyes flickered.

He said, "You search for a Sapient who will show you the way Out. I am that man." His voice strengthened; he swung to the crowd. "The way that Sapphique took lies through the Door of Death. I will take this girl there and I will bring her back!"

The audience roared. He led Attia by the hand out into the center of the smoky space. Only one torch guttered. There was a couch. He motioned her to lie on it. Terrified, she swung her legs up.

In the crowd someone cried out, and was instantly hushed.

Bodies craned forward, a stench of heat and sweat.

The Enchanter held up his black-gloved hand. "Death," he said. "We fear it. We would do anything to avoid it. And yet Death is a doorway that opens both ways. Before your eyes, you will see the dead live."

The couch was hard. She gripped the sides. This was what she had come for.

"Behold," the Enchanter said.

He turned and the crowd moaned, because in his hand was a sword. He was drawing it out of the air; slowly it was unsheathed from darkness, the blade glittering with cold blue light. He held it up, and unbelievably, miles above them in the remote roof of the Prison, lightning flickered.

The Enchanter stared up; Attia blinked.

Thunder rumbled like laughter.

For a moment everyone listened to it, tensed for the Prison to act, for the streets to fall, the sky to roll away, the gas and the lights to pin them down.

But Incarceron did not interfere.

"My father the Prison," the Enchanter said quickly, "watches and approves."

He turned.

Metal links hung from the couch; he fastened them around Attia's wrists. Then a belt was looped over her neck and waist. "Keep very still," he said. His bright eyes explored her face. "Or the danger is extreme."

He turned to the crowd. "Behold," he cried. "I will release her. And I will bring her back!"

He raised the sword, both hands on the grip, the point hovering over her chest. She wanted to cry out, gasp "No," but her body was chilled and numb, her whole attention focused on the glittering, razor-sharp point.

Before she could breathe, he plunged it into her heart.

This was death.

It was warm and sticky and there were waves of it, washing over her like pain. It had no air to breathe, no words to speak. It was a choking in her throat.

And then it was pure and blue and as empty as the sky she had seen Outside, and Finn was in it, and Claudia, and they were sitting on golden thrones, and they turned to look at her.

And Finn said, "I haven't forgotten you, Attia. I'm coming back for you."

She could only manage one word, and as she said it she saw his shock.

"Liar."

She opened her eyes.

Her hearing seemed to pop, to come back from somewhere far; the crowd was roaring and howling with joy, and the fastenings were undone. The Enchanter was helping her up. She stared down and saw that the blood on her clothes was shriveling, vanishing away; that the sword in his hand was clean; that she could stand. She took a great breath and her eyes cleared;

she saw that people were on the buildings and roofs, hanging on awnings, leaning out of windows, that the storm of applause went on and on, a screaming tide of adoration.

And the Dark Enchanter gripped her hand and made her bow with him, and his gloved fingers held the sword high above the crowd as the jugglers and dancers discreetly moved in to collect the rain of coins that showered like falling stars.

When it was all over, when the crowd was streaming away, she found herself standing in the corner of the square clutching her arms around herself. A low pain burned in her chest. A few women clustered at the door that the Enchanter had entered, their sick children already in their arms. Attia breathed out slowly. She felt stiff, and stupid. She felt as if some great explosion had deafened and stunned her.

Quickly, before anyone noticed, she turned and ducked under the awnings, past the bear pit, through the ragged camp of the jugglers. One of them saw her, but stayed sitting by the fire they had lit, cooking slivers of meat.

Attia opened a small door under an overhanging roof and slipped in.

The room was dark.

He was sitting in front of a smeared mirror lit only by a single guttering candle, and he looked up and saw her in the glass.

As she watched he took off the black wig, unfurled his

missing finger, wiped the smooth makeup from his lined face, tossed the ragged coat on the floor.

Then he leaned his elbows on the table and gave her a gap-toothed grin. "An excellent performance," he said.

She nodded. "I told you I could do it."

"Well, I'm convinced, sweetie. The job's yours, if you still want it." He slipped a wad of ket into his cheek and began to chew.

Attia glanced around. There was no sign of the Glove.

"Oh yes," she said. "I want it."

2

How could you betray me, Incarceron?
How could you let me fall?
I thought I was your son.
It seems I am your fool.
        —*Songs of Sapphique*

Finn flung the documents at the wall. Then he picked the inkwell up and hurled it after them. It exploded into a black, dripping star.

"Sire," the chamberlain gasped. "Please!"

Finn ignored him. He heaved the table over; it collapsed with a crash. Papers and scrolls cascaded everywhere, their seals and ribbons tangling. Grim, he stalked to the door.

"Sire. There are at least sixteen more—"

"Stuff them."

"Sire?"

"You heard. Burn them. Eat them. Feed them to the dogs."

"There are invitations which need your signature. The deeds of the Stygian Accord, the orders for the coronation robes."

Savagely, Finn turned on the thin figure scrabbling among the papers. "How many times do I have to say it? *There will be no coronation!*"

Leaving the man openmouthed he turned and hauled the doors wide. The guards outside stiffened to attention, but as they closed in behind him he swore at them. Then he ran, down the paneled corridor, through the curtains and across the Great Salon, vaulting the upholstered sofas, flinging the dainty chairs over, leaving the guards panting behind. With one quick leap onto the table he slithered over its polished surface, dodged silver candlesticks, jumped up onto the wide window seat, slid through the casement, and was gone.

Back in the doorway, breathless, the chamberlain groaned. He stepped discreetly into a small side chamber, closed the door, and hefted the pile of crumpled paper wearily under one arm. With a careful look around, he took out the minicom she had given him and pressed the button, with distaste, because he deplored this breach of Protocol. But he didn't dare not to, because she could be almost as ferocious as the Prince.

The device crackled. "What now?" a girl's voice snapped.

The chamberlain swallowed. "I'm sorry, Lady Claudia, but you asked me to tell you if it happened again. Well, I think it just did."

—◇◇◇—

FINN LANDED on all fours on the gravel outside the window and picked himself up. He stalked off across the grass. Parading groups of courtiers scattered as he passed, the women under their flimsy parasols dropping hurried curtsies, the men making elaborate bows and sweeping their hats off. Eyes fixed, Finn marched past. He scorned the pathways with their finely raked surfaces, cutting directly across the parterre, crunching the white seashells underfoot. An indignant gardener came out from behind a hedge, but as soon as he saw it was Finn he crumpled to one knee. Finn allowed himself a cold smile. Being the Prince in this pretty paradise had some advantages.

The day was perfect. Tiny fleecy clouds moved high in the sky, the amazingly blue sky he could never get used to.

A flock of jackdaws cavorted over the elms near the lake.

It was the lake he wanted.

That smooth blue expanse of water drew him like a magnet. He undid the stiff collar they made him wear, tearing it open, cursing everything over and over: the constricting clothes, the baffling rules of courtesy, the endless Protocol. Suddenly he broke into a run, past statues and classical urns planted with floral displays, making a gaggle of geese on the grass squawk and flutter and hiss away.

He was breathing more freely now. The sparks and dull pain behind his eyes were easing. The fit had been coming on him, back there in that stuffy unbearable room, behind that heaped desk. It had been growing inside him like anger. Maybe it *was* anger. Maybe he should have let it happen, fallen gratefully into it, the seizure that always waited for him somewhere like a black pit in the road.

Because whatever it made him see, however much it hurt,

after it was over he could sleep, deep and oblivious, without dreams of the Prison. Without dreams of Keiro, the oath-brother he had left there.

The lake water rippled under the faint breeze. He shook his head, angry at how perfectly judged the temperature was, how serene it all looked. At the jetty, rowboats bobbed and knocked at the end of their ropes, surrounded by flat green waterlily leaves, where tiny gnats danced.

He had no idea how much of it was real.

At least in the Prison he had known that.

Finn sat on the grass. He felt worn, and his anger was turning on himself. The chamberlain had only been doing his best. Throwing the ink had been stupid.

Lying on his stomach he buried his forehead under his arms and let the warm sun comfort him. It was so hot, and so bright. He could take it now, but for the first few days Outside he had been blinded, had had to wear dark glasses because his eyes wept and watered.

And then all those long weeks until his skin had lost that white pallor, those days of washing and delousing and the endless medication Jared had made him take. Weeks of patient lessons from Claudia in how to dress, how to talk, how to eat with knives and forks; the titles, the bows, how not to yell, spit, swear, fight.

Two months ago he had been a Prisoner without hope, a starved, ragged thief and liar. Now he was a Prince in paradise.

And yet he had never been more unhappy.

A shadow darkened the red light behind his eyelids. He kept them tight shut, but the scent of the perfume she wore came to him clearly; the rustle of her dress was loud as she sat beside him on the low stone parapet.

After a moment he said, "The Maestra cursed me, did you know that?"

Claudia's voice was cold. "No."

"Well, she did. The Maestra, the woman whose death was my fault? I took the crystal Key from her. Her dying words were *I hope it destroys you.* I think her curse is coming true, Claudia."

The silence went on so long that he raised his head and looked at her. She had her knees up under the peach silk dress and her arms hugged around them, and she was watching him with that concerned, annoyed look he had come to know. "Finn . . ."

He sat up. "Don't! Don't tell me I should forget the past. Don't tell me again that life here is a game, that every word you say and every smile, every gracious bow is a move in a game. I can't live like that! I won't."

Claudia frowned. She saw the strain in his eyes.

When the fits came he always had this look. She wanted to snap at him, but instead she made herself say quietly, "Are you all right?"

He shrugged. "It was coming. But it's gone. I thought . . . I thought when I Escaped there would be no more fits. All those stupid documents . . ."

Claudia shook her head. "Not them. It's Keiro again, isn't it?"

Finn stared ahead. After a while he said, "Are you always this sharp?"

She laughed. "I'm the pupil of Jared Sapiens. Trained in observation and analysis. And," she added bitterly, "I'm the daughter of the Warden of Incarceron. The game's finest player."

He was surprised she had even mentioned her father. He pulled a blade of grass and began to shred it. "Well, you're right. I can't stop thinking about Keiro. Keiro is my oath-brother, Claudia. We swore loyalty to each other, loyalty to death and beyond. You can't even guess what that means. In the Prison no one can survive alone; he looked after me when I didn't even know who I was. He watched my back in a hundred fights. That time in the cave of the Beast he came back for me, even though he had the Key, even though he could have gone anywhere."

Claudia was silent. Then she said, "I made him find you. Don't you remember?"

"He would have done it anyway."

"Would he?" She gazed over the lake. "From what I saw, Keiro was arrogant, ruthless, and incredibly vain. You were the one who seemed to take all the risks. He only cared about himself."

"You don't know him. You didn't see him fight our Winglord. He was amazing that day. Keiro is my brother. And I've left him in that hell, after I promised to get him Out."

A group of young men were strutting from the Archery Court. Claudia said, "It's Caspar and his cronies. Quick."

She jumped up and hauled one of the boats to shore; Finn stepped in and took the oars and she scrambled after him. With a few strokes they were safely out in the stillness of the lake, the prow rippling among the lily leaves. Butterflies danced in the warm air. Claudia lay back on the cushions and stared up at the sky. "Did he see us?"

"Yes."

"Good."

Finn watched the effete youths in disgust. Caspar's red hair and gaudy blue frockcoat were clear from here. He was laughing; he raised his bow and aimed it at the boat, twanging the empty string with a mocking grin. Finn stared back grimly. "Between him and Keiro I know which brother I'd choose."

Claudia shrugged. "Well, I'm with you there. Remember, I nearly had to marry him." She let the memory of that day come back to her; the cold deliberate pleasure she had felt in tearing the wedding dress, ripping its lace and white perfection apart, as if it had been her life she was tearing, or herself and her father. Herself and Caspar.

"You don't need to marry him now," Finn said quietly.

They were silent then, as the oars dipped and splashed in

the water. Claudia trailed her hand over the side, not looking at him. They both knew that she had been betrothed as a child to Prince Giles, and only when he had been presumed dead had Caspar, the younger prince, taken his place. But Finn was Giles now. She frowned.

"Look . . ."

They both said it together. Claudia was first to laugh. "You first."

He shrugged, not even smiling. "Look, Claudia, I don't know who I am. If you thought getting me out of Incarceron would bring my memory back, you were wrong. I can't remember any more than before—just flashes, visions that the fits bring. Jared's potions haven't made any difference." He stopped rowing suddenly, letting the boat drift, leaning forward. "Don't you see? *I may not be the real prince.* I may not be Giles, despite this." He held up his hand; she saw the faded tattoo of the crowned eagle.

"And even if I am . . . I've changed." He struggled to get the words out. "Incarceron has changed me. I don't fit in here. I can't settle. How can Scum like me be what you want? I keep looking behind me. I keep thinking that a small red Eye is spying on me up in the sky."

Dismayed, she watched him. He was right. She had thought it would be easy, had expected an ally, a friend. Not this tormented street fighter who seemed to loathe himself, who spent hours gazing at the stars.

His face was drawn, his voice a low mutter. "I can't be the King," he whispered.

Claudia sat up. "I've told you. You have to. If you want the power to get Keiro out you have to!" Angry, she turned and stared back at the lawns.

A gaudy gathering of courtiers was assembling. Two footmen carried a stack of gilt chairs, another was laden with cushions and croquet mallets. A sweating gang of underservants was propping a vast tasseled awning of yellow silk over trestle tables, and a procession of butlers and maids carried jellies, sweetmeats, cold capons, dainty pastries, and jugs of iced punch on silver trays.

Claudia groaned. "The Queen's buffet. I'd forgotten."

Finn looked over. "I'm not going."

"Yes you are. Take the boat back in." She gave him a fierce, hard look. "You have to keep it together, Finn. You owe me. I didn't wreck my life to get some thug onto the throne. Jared is working all hours on the Portal. We'll get it to work. We'll get Keiro out of the Prison. And that bitch Attia too, even though I notice you've been careful not to mention her. But you have to do your part!"

He scowled. Then he picked up the oars and rowed them back.

As they came close to the jetty, Claudia saw the Queen. Sia was wearing a dress of dazzling white, the elaborate skirts looped like a shepherdess's, showing small feet in glimmering slippers. Her pallid skin was protected from the sun by a wide hat, and a graceful wisp of shawl was tucked around her shoulders. She looked about twenty, but she must be four times that, Claudia thought sourly. And her eyes were strange, with pale irises. Witch's eyes.

The boat bumped.

Finn took a breath. He did up his collar, climbed out, and held out his hand. Formally, she took it and stepped elegantly onto the wooden boards. Together they walked toward the gathering.

"Remember," she breathed. "Use the napkins, not your fingers. Don't swear, don't scowl."

He shrugged. "What does it matter? She'd like us both dead anyway."

Claudia stepped away from him as the Queen hurried up.

"So here you both are! My dear boy, you look so much better today."

Finn bowed, awkward. Claudia dropped a low curtsy beside him. The Queen ignored her, took Finn's arm, and swept him away. "Come and sit by me. I have such a surprise for you."

She led Finn to the awning and made him sit beside her on the gilt thrones, clapped her hands for a servant to bring more cushions.

"I suppose he thinks he's King already." The slurred voice was right behind Claudia; she turned and saw Caspar, his doublet unlaced, a half-empty goblet in his hand. "My so-called stepbrother."

"You stink of wine," she muttered.

He winked sourly at her. "You like him better than me, don't you, Claudia? Your rough scabby thief. Well, don't get too close. Mama has her claws out for you. You're finished, Claudia. Without your father to protect you, you're nothing."

Furious, she stepped away from him but he came after her. "Just watch now. Watch Mama make her first move. The Queen is the strongest piece on the board. That could have been you, Claudia."

Queen Sia called for silence. Then she said in her silvery voice, "Dear friends. I have such good news. The Council of the Sapienti has sent word that everything is ready for the Proclamation of the Heir. All the edicts are drawn up and my dearest stepson Giles's right to the throne will be approved. I've decided to hold the ceremony tomorrow in the Crystal Court, and invite all the Ambassadors to the Realm and all the Court to witness it. And afterward, a masked ball for everyone!"

The courtiers applauded, the women whispering with delight. Claudia kept her face pleasant, though instantly she was alert. What was this? What was Sia up to? She loathed Finn. It had to be some sort of trap. Jared had always said the Queen would delay the Proclamation for months, let alone the coronation. Yet here she was announcing it. For tomorrow!

Sia's eyes met hers through the shimmering throng. She was laughing her tinkling laugh, making Finn stand, clasping his hand, lifting a thin glass of wine to toast him. Every nerve in Claudia's mind was tense with disbelief.

"Told you," Caspar smirked.

Finn looked furious. He opened his mouth but caught Claudia's glare and kept silent, simmering.

"He looks so cross." Caspar grinned. She turned on him but he jerked back at once, alarmed. "Yuck! Get the filthy thing off me!"

It was a dragonfly, a green glimmer of flickering wings; it darted at him and he swiped at it and missed. It landed, with a faint crackle, on Claudia's dress.

Before anyone else could see she took two steps toward the lake and turned, her voice a whisper. "Jared? This is not a good time."

No reply. The dragonfly flexed its wings. For a moment she thought she had made a mistake, that it was a real insect.

Then it breathed. "Claudia . . . Please. Come quickly . . ."

"Jared? What is it?" Her voice rose in anxiety. "What's wrong?"

No answer.

"Master?"

A faint sound. Glass falling, and smashing.

Instantly she turned and ran.

3

*Once Incarceron became a dragon, and a
Prisoner crawled into its lair. They made
a wager. They would ask each other riddles,
and the one who could not answer would
lose. If it was the man, he would give his
life. The Prison offered a secret way of
Escape. But even as the man agreed,
he felt its hidden laughter.*

*They played for a year and a day. The
lights stayed dark. The dead were not
removed. Food was not provided. The
Prison ignored the cries of its inmates.*

*Sapphique was the man. He had one
riddle left. He said, "What is the Key that
unlocks the heart?"*

*For a day Incarceron thought. For two
days. For three. Then it said, "If I ever
knew the answer, I have forgotten it."*

—Sapphique in the Tunnels of Madness

The showmen left the village early, before Lightson.

Attia waited for them outside the ramshackle walls,
behind a pillar of brick where gigantic shackles still hung, rust-

ing to red powder. When the Prison lights snapped on with their acrid flicker she saw seven wagons were already rumbling down the ramp, the bear cage strapped on one, the rest covered by contraptions of starry cloth. As they approached she saw the bear's small red eyes squint at her. The seven identical jugglers walked alongside, tossing balls to one another in complex patterns.

She swung up onto the seat and sat beside the Enchanter.

"Welcome to the troupe," he said. "Tonight's triumph is in a village two hours away, through the tunnels. A rat-haunted heap, but I hear they have a good stash of silver. You can get down well before we reach it. Remember, Attia, my sweetkin. You must never be seen with us. You do not know us."

She looked at him. In the harsh glare of the lights he had none of the youth of his stage disguise. His skin was pocked with boils, his coppery hair lank and greasy. Half his teeth were gone, probably in some fight. But his hands were powerful and delicate on the reins. A magician's dexterous fingers.

"What do I call you?" she muttered.

He grinned. "Men like me change their names like coats. I've been Silentio the Silent Seer, and Alixia the One-eyed Witch of Demonia. One year I was the Wandering Felon, the next, the Elastic Outlaw of the Ash Wing. The Enchanter is a new direction. Confers a certain dignity, I feel." He flicked the reins; the ox plodded patiently around a hole in the metallic track.

"You must have a real name."

"Must I?" He grinned at her. "Like Attia? Call that real?"

Annoyed, she dumped her bundle of possessions at her feet. "Real enough."

"Call me Ishmael," he said, and then laughed, a sudden throaty bark that startled her.

"What?"

"From a patchbook I once read. About a man obsessed with a great white rabbit. He chases it down a hole and it eats him and he's in its belly for forty days." He gazed out at the featureless plain of tilted metal, its few spiny shrubs. "Guess my name. Riddle me my name, Attia mine."

She scowled, silent.

"Is my name Adrax, or Malevin, or Korrestan? Is it Tom Tat Tot or Rumpelstiltsker? Is it—"

"Forget it," she said. There was a crazy glint in his eye now; he was staring at her in a way that she didn't like. To her alarm he leaped up and yelled out, "Is it Wild Edric who rides upon the wind?"

The ox strode on, unbothered. One of the seven identical jugglers ran alongside. "All right, Rix?"

The magician blinked. As if he had lost balance he sat down heavily. "Now you've told her. And it's Master Rix to you, fumblefingers."

The man shrugged and glanced at Attia. Discreetly he tapped his forehead, rolled his eyes, and walked on.

She frowned. She had thought he was high on ket, but maybe

she'd gotten herself mixed up with a lunatic. There were plenty of those in Incarceron. Half-brained or broken cell-borns. The thought made her think of Finn, and she bit her lip. But whatever this Rix was, there was something about him. Did he really have Sapphique's Glove, or was it just some stage prop? And if he did, how was she going to steal it?

He was silent now, gloomy all at once. His moods seemed to change swiftly. She didn't speak either, staring out at the grim landscape of the Prison.

In this Wing the light was a muted, fiery glow, as if something burned just out of sight. The roof here was too high to see, but as the wagons rumbled down the track they swerved around the end of a vast chain hanging down; she gazed up, but its top was lost in rusty wisps of cloud.

She had once sailed up there, in a silver ship, with friends, with a Key. But like Sapphique, she had fallen low.

Ahead, a range of hills rose up, their shapes odd and jagged.

"What are those?" she said.

Rix shrugged. "Those are the Dice. There's no way over them. The road goes under." He glanced at her sidelong. "So what brings an ex-slave to our little group?"

"I told you. I need to eat." She bit her nail and said, "And I'm curious. I'd like to learn a few tricks."

He nodded. "You and everyone else. But my secrets die with me, sister. Magician's Pledge."

"You won't teach me?"

"Only the Apprentice gets my secrets."

She wasn't that interested, but she needed to find out about the Glove. "That's your son?"

His bark of laughter made her jump. "Son! I probably have a few of those around the Prison! No. Each magician teaches his life's work to one person, his Apprentice. And that person comes once in a lifetime. It could be you. It could be anyone." He leaned closer and winked. "And I know them only by what they say."

"You mean, like a password?"

He swayed back in exaggerated respect. "That's exactly what I mean. A word, a phrase, that only I know. That my old master taught to me. One day, I will hear someone speak it. And that someone will be the one I teach."

"And pass your props on to?" she said quietly.

His eyes slid to her. He jerked the reins; the ox bellowed, hauled to a clumsy standstill.

Attia's hand shot to her knife.

Rix turned to her. Ignoring the shouts of the wagoners behind, he watched her with sharp, suspicious eyes. "So that's it," he said. "You want my Glove."

She shrugged. "If it was the real one . . ."

"Oh it's real."

She snorted. "Sure. And Sapphique gave it to you."

"Your scorn is meant to draw out my story." He flicked the

reins, and the ox lumbered on. "Well, I'll tell you, because I want to. It's no secret. Three years ago, I was in a Wing of the Prison known as the Tunnels of Madness."

"They exist?"

"They exist, but you wouldn't want to go there. Deep in one I met an old woman. She was sick, dying by the roadside. I gave her a cup of water. In return, she told me that when she was a girl, she had seen Sapphique. He had appeared to her in a vision, when she slept in a strange tilted room. He had knelt beside her, and taken from his right hand the Glove, and slid it under her fingers. *Keep this safe for me until I return*, he said."

"She was mad," Attia said quietly. "Everyone who goes there ends up mad."

Rix laughed his harsh bark. "Just so! I myself have never been quite the same. And I didn't believe her. But she drew from her rags a Glove, and closed my fingers over it. *I have hidden it for a lifetime,* she whispered, *and the Prison hunts for it, I know. You are a great magician. It will be safe with you.*"

Attia wondered how much was true. "And you've kept it safe."

"Many have tried to steal it." His eyes flicked sideways. "No one has succeeded."

He obviously had suspicions. She smiled and went on the attack. "Last night, in that so-called act of yours. Where did you get that stuff about Finn?"

"You told me, sweetkin."

"I told you I'd been a slave and that Finn . . . rescued me. But what you said about betrayal. About love. Where did you get that?"

"Ah." He made his fingers into a quick elaborate steeple. "I read your mind."

"Rubbish."

"You saw. The man, the sobbing woman."

"Oh, I saw!" She let a rich disgust enter her voice. "Tricking them with that junk! *He is safe in the peace of Incarceron.* How can you live with yourself?"

"The woman wanted to hear it. And you do both love and hate this Finn." The gleam was back in his eye. Then his face fell. "But the rumble of thunder! I admit that astonished me. That has never happened before. Is Incarceron watching you, Attia? Is it interested in you?"

"It's watching us all," she growled.

From behind, a shrill voice screeched, "Speed up, Rix!" The head of a giantess was peering from the starry cloth.

"And that vision of a tiny keyhole?" Attia had to know.

"What keyhole?"

"You said you could see Outside. The stars, you said, and a great palace."

"Did I?" His eyes were puzzled; she had no idea if it was pretense or not. "I don't remember. Sometimes when I wear the Glove I really think something takes over my mind." He shook the reins. She wanted to ask him more but he said, "I suggest you get down and stretch your legs. We'll be at the Dice soon, and then we all need to be on our guard."

It was a dismissal. Annoyed, Attia jumped from the cart.

"About time," the giantess snarled.

Rix smiled his toothless smile. "Gigantia, darling. Go back to sleep."

He whipped up the ox. Attia let the cart rumble ahead; in fact she let them all pass, the gaudy painted sides, the red and yellow spoked wheels, the pots and pans clattering underneath. Right at the back a donkey trailed on a long rope, and a few small children trudged wearily.

She followed, head down. She needed time to think. The only plan, when she had heard the rumors of a magician who claimed to own Sapphique's Glove, had been to find him and steal it. If she had been abandoned by Finn, she would try anything to find her own way Out. For a moment, as her feet tramped along the metal roadway, she allowed herself to relive the full misery of those hours in the cell at the world's end, Keiro's scorn and his pity and his "He's not coming back. Get used to it."

She had turned on him then. "He promised! He's your brother!"

Even now, two months later, his cold shrug and his answer chilled her.

"Not anymore." Keiro had paused at the door. "Finn's an expert liar. His specialty is getting people to feel sorry for him.

Don't waste your time. He's got Claudia now, and his precious kingdom. We'll never see him again."

"And where are you going?"

He had smiled. "To find my own kingdom. Catch me up." Then he had gone, shoving his way down the collapsed corridor.

But she had waited.

She had waited alone in the dingy silent cell for three days, until thirst and hunger drove her away. Three days of refusal to believe, of doubt, of anger. Three days to imagine Finn out in that world where the stars were, in some great marble palace with people bowing to him. Why hadn't he come back? It must have been Claudia. She must have persuaded him, put a spell on him, made him forget. Or the Key must have gotten broken, or lost.

But now it was harder to think like that. Two months was a long time. And there was another thought that hid in her mind, that crept out when she was tired or depressed. That he was dead. That his enemies out there had killed him.

Except that last night, in that moment of fake death, she had seen him.

A shout, ahead.

She looked up and saw, towering over her, the Dice.

That was exactly what they were. A great tumble of them, vaster than mountains, their sides white and faintly gleaming, as if a giant had tipped a pile of sugar cubes in the way, with smooth hollows that might be arranged in sixes and fives. In places, stunted stubby bushes struggled to grow; deep in the clefts and valleys a faint moss clung like grass. No roads led up there; the cuboid hills must be hard as marble, and smooth, impossible to climb. Instead the track ran into a tunnel hacked into the base.

The wagons halted. Rix stood up and said, "People."

Quite suddenly faces were peering out from the wagons, all the stunted, enormous, shriveled, dwarfish faces of the freak show. The seven jugglers clustered around. Even the bear guard ambled back.

"The rumor is that the gang that runs this road is greedy but thick." Rix took a coin from his pocket and spun it. It vanished into the air. "So we should get through without problems. If there are . . . obstructions, you all know what to do. Be alert, my friends. And remember, the Art Magicke is the art of illusion."

He made an elaborate bow and sat back down. Puzzled, Attia saw how the seven jugglers were distributing swords and knives, and small balls of blue and red. Then each of them climbed up by a driver. The carts closed together, a tight formation.

She climbed hastily behind Rix and his guard. "Are you seriously taking on some Scum gang with collapsible knives and fake swords?"

Rix didn't answer. He just grinned his gappy grin. As

the tunnel entrance loomed Attia loosened her own knife and wished desperately that she had a firelock. These people were crazy, and she didn't intend to die with them. Ahead, the tunnel's shadow loomed. Soon intense darkness closed over her.

Everything disappeared. No, not everything. With a wry smile she realized that if she leaned out she could see the lettering on the wagon behind; that it was picked out in glowing luminous paint—*The One, the Only, Traveling Extravaganza*— that its wheels were whirling spokes of green. There was nothing else. The tunnel was narrow; from its roof the noise of rumbling axles reverberated into an echoing thunder.

The farther in they went, the more worried she became. No road was without its owners; whoever held this one had a sure-fire ambush site. Glancing up she tried to make out the roof, whether anyone was up there on walkways or hanging from nets, but apart from the web of one uberspider she could see nothing.

Except, of course, the Eyes.

They were very obvious in the darkness. Incarceron's small red Eyes watched her at intervals, tiny starpoints of curiosity. She remembered the books of images she had seen, imagined how she must look to the curious Prison, tiny and grainy, gazing up from the wagon.

Look at me, she thought bitterly. *Remember, I've heard you speak. I know there is a way Out from you.*

"They're here," Rix muttered.

She stared at him. Then, with a crash that made her jump, a grid smashed down ahead in the darkness; and another, behind. Dust billowed up; the ox bellowed as Rix dragged it to a halt. The wagons creaked into a long straggling stillness.

"Greetings!" The shout came from the darkness ahead. "Welcome to the tollgate of Thar's Butchers."

"Sit tight," Rix whispered. "And follow my lead." He jumped down, a lanky shadow in the darkness.

Immediately a beam of light lit him. He shaded his eyes against it. "We're more than willing to pay great Thar whatever he wants."

A snort of laughter. Attia glanced up. Some of them were overhead, she was sure. Stealthily she drew her knife, remembering how the Comitatus had captured her with a flung net.

"Just tell us, great one, what's the fee?" Rix sounded apprehensive.

"Gold or women or metal. Whatever we choose, showman."

Rix bowed, and let relief creep into his voice. "Then come forward and take what you want, masters. All I ask is that the properties of our art are left us."

Attia hissed, "You're just going to let them—"

"Shut up," he muttered. Then, to a juggler, "Which one are you?"

"Quintus."

"Your brothers?"

"Ready, boss."

Someone was coming out of the dark. In the red glimmer of the Eyes, Attia saw him in flickers, a bald head, stocky shoulders, the glint of metal strapped all over him.

Behind, in a sinister line, other figures.

On each side, green lights flared with a sizzle.

Attia stared; even Rix swore.

The gang leader was a halfman.

Most of his bald skull was a metal plate, one ear a gaping hole meshed with filaments of skin.

In his hands he held a fearsome weapon, part ax, part cleaver. The men behind him were all shaven-headed, as if that was their tribemark.

Rix swallowed. Then he held up a hand and said, "We're poor folk, Winglord. Some thin silver coins, a few precious stones. Take them. Take anything. Just leave us our pathetic props."

The halfman reached out and gripped Rix by the throat. "You talk too much."

His henchmen were already climbing all over the wagons, pushing the jugglers aside, ducking under the canvas. Several of them came straight back out.

"Hell's teeth," one muttered. "These are beasts, not men."

Rix smiled wanly at the Winglord. "People will pay to see ugliness. It makes them feel human."

A stupid thing to say, Attia thought, watching Thar's grim face.

The Winglord narrowed his eyes. "So you'll pay us coins."

"Any amount."

"And women?"

"Indeed, lord."

"Even your children?"

"Take your pick."

The Winglord sneered. "What a stinking coward you are."

Rix pulled a rueful face. The man dropped him in disgust. He flicked a glance at Attia. "What about you, girl?"

"Touch me," she said quietly, "and I'll cut your throat."

Thar grunted. "Now that's what I like. Guts." He stepped forward and fingered the edge of his blade. "So tell me, coward. What are these . . . props?"

Rix paled. "Things we use in our act."

"And what makes them so precious?"

"They're not. I mean . . ." Rix stuttered. "To us, yes, but . . ."

The Winglord pushed his face close to the magician's. "Then you won't mind me looking at them, will you?"

Rix looked stricken. His own fault, Attia thought sourly. The Winglord pushed past him. He reached into the wagon, wrenched open the cavity that was hidden under the driver's footboard, and dragged out a box.

"No." Rix licked cracked lips. "Sir, please! Take anything we have, but not that! Without these trinkets we can't perform . . ."

"I have heard"—Thar smashed the hasp of the box thoughtfully—"tales about you. About a certain Glove."

Rix was silent.

The halfman tore the box lid off and looked inside.

Reaching in, he took out a small black object. Attia drew a breath. The glove was tiny in the man's paw; it was worn and had been mended, and the forefinger was marked with what might have once been bloodstains. She made a move; the man glanced at her and she froze. "So," he said greedily. "Sapphique's Glove."

"Please." Rix had lost all his bluster. "Anything but that."

The Winglord grinned. With mocking slowness, he began to pull the glove on over his fat fingers.

4

We have been most careful in setting the locks
of the Prison. No one can break in or out.
The Warden will hold the sole Key. Should
he die without passing on his knowledge, the
Esoterica must be opened. But only by his
successor. For these things are forbidden now.
—Project report; Martor Sapiens

"Jared?"

Breathless, Claudia burst through the door into her tutor's room and stared around.

It was empty.

The bed was neatly made, the spartan shelves lined with a few books. On the wooden floor sweet rushes were scattered, and a tray on the table had a plate with crumbs on it and an empty wineglass.

As she whirled to go the draft of her skirt lifted a paper.

She stared at it. It looked like a letter, on thick vellum, tucked under the glass. Even from here she could see the royal insignia on the back, the crowned Havaarna eagle, its raised talon holding the world. And the Queen's white rose.

She was in a hurry, she wanted to find Jared, but still she

stared at it. It had been opened, and read. He had left it lying around. It couldn't be a secret.

Still she hesitated. She would have read anyone else's letters without a scrap of remorse; in the Court everyone was a stranger, perhaps an enemy. They were part of the game. But Jared was her only friend. More than that. Her love for him was old and strong.

So when she crossed the room and opened the letter she told herself that it didn't matter, that he would only tell her about it anyway. They shared everything.

It was from the Queen. Claudia read it, her eyes widening.

> *My dear Master Jared,*
>
> *I write to you because I feel I need to make things clear between us. You and I have been enemies in the past; that really no longer need be the case. I know you are busy with your work of trying to reactivate the Portal. Claudia must be desperate to have news of her dear father. But I wonder if you might find time to wait on me? I will expect you in my private rooms, at seven.*
>
> *Sia, Regina*

And in small letters underneath: *We could be of great help to each other.*

Claudia frowned. She folded the note, jammed it back under the glass, and hurried out. The Queen was always plotting. But what did she want with Jared?

He had to be at the Portal.

As she grabbed a candle and shook it into life she tried not to feel so agitated. She opened the door in the paneling of the lavish corridor and pattered down the spiral staircase that led to the cellars, ducking cobwebs that regenerated themselves with irritating speed. The deep vaults were damp and chilly. Squeezing between the barrels and wine casks she hurried to the darkest corner where the high bronze doors reared to the roof and found to her horror that they were shut. The great snails that seemed to infest this place clung to the icy metal; their trails crisscrossed the damp surface.

"Master!" Claudia slammed her fist against the door. "Let me in!"

Silence.

For a moment she knew for sure that he couldn't, that he was lying unconscious, that the slow illness that had been consuming him for years had crumpled him in pain. Then another fear stabbed her even harder; that he had finally gotten the Portal to work and had trapped himself in Incarceron.

The door sprung open with a click.

She slipped in and stared.

And then she laughed.

On his hands and knees, trying to pick up hundreds and

hundreds of glistening blue feathers, Jared glanced up at her irritably. "This is not funny, Claudia."

She couldn't stop. She was silly with relief. She sat down in the single chair and let the giggles rise to a sort of hysteria that left her wiping her eyes with the silk of her skirt. Jared leaned back on his hands in the blue ocean of plumage and watched her. He wore a dark green shirt, the sleeves rolled up. His Sapient coat, flung over the chair, was buried in feathers. His long hair was tangled. But his smile, when it came, was rueful and real. "Well, all right. Perhaps it is."

The room that had always been so pure and white looked as if a thousand kingfishers had been plucked in it. Feathers lay on the metal desk and coated the sleek silver shelves with their unknowable devices. The floor was ankle deep. Clouds of them rose and settled at every movement. "Be careful. I knocked a flask over trying to grab them."

"Why feathers?" she managed to say at last.

Jared sighed. "One feather. I picked it up from the lawn. Small. Organic. Perfect for experimentation."

She stared at him. "One? Then . . ."

"Yes, Claudia. I finally managed to get something to happen. But not the right thing."

Amazed, she gazed around. The Portal was the way into Incarceron, but only her father knew its secrets, and he had sabotaged it in his escape Inside. He had sat in this very chair and disappeared, and she knew that he was lost somewhere within the miniaturized world that was the Prison. And since then nothing here had worked. Jared had spent months studying the controls of the desk, infuriating Finn with his care and delicate probing, but no switch or circuit had even lit.

"What happened?" She jumped up from the chair, suddenly afraid she might disappear.

Jared pulled a blue feather from his hair. "I placed it on the chair. For the last few days I've been experimenting with replacing broken components with various substitutes; the last was an illicit plastic I acquired from a trader in the market."

Claudia said immediately, "Did anyone see you?"

"I was well cloaked, so I trust not."

But they both knew that he had probably been followed.

"Well?"

"It must have worked. Because there was a flash and a . . . shiver. But the feather did not disappear, nor did it miniaturize. It multiplied. They're all perfectly identical." He looked around with a wan helplessness that suddenly struck Claudia. Quietly she said, "You mustn't work yourself too hard, Master."

He glanced up at her, his voice gentle. "I am aware of that."

"I know Finn is always prowling here, bothering you."

"You should call him Prince Giles." He stood, wincing slightly. "Soon to be King."

They looked at each other. Claudia nodded. Glancing around, she found a sack that held tools; she emptied them out and began to stuff the feathers in, handful by handful.

Jared sat on the chair and leaned forward. "Can Finn cope with such a pressure?" he asked quietly.

She paused. He saw how her hand hesitated; then she worked harder and faster.

"He'll have to. We brought him out of Incarceron to be King. We need him." She looked up. "It's strange. All I cared about when this started was not marrying Caspar. And getting the better of my father. All my life I've plotted and planned, been obsessed with those things . . ."

"And now you've achieved them, you are not satisfied." He nodded. "Life is a series of stairs up which we climb, Claudia. You've read Zelon's Philosophies. Your horizons have moved."

"Yes, but Master, I don't know . . ."

"You do." He reached out his delicate hand and gripped hers, stopping her. "What do you want of Finn, when he becomes King?"

For a long moment she was still, as if thinking. But she said exactly what he knew she would. "I want him to overturn the Protocol. Not the way the Steel Wolves want, by killing the Queen. I want to find a way peacefully, so we can start time again, live naturally without this stagnation, this stifling false history."

"Is that possible? We have few reserves of energy."

"Yes, and they're all wasted on palaces for the rich, and keeping the sky blue, and trapping the poor and forgotten in a Prison run by a tyrannical machine." Savagely she swept up the last feathers and stood. "Master, my father is gone. I never thought it possible, but I feel like half of me is gone with him. But I am his successor, and if anyone is Warden of Incarceron now, it's me. So I'm going to the Academy. I'm going to read the Esoterica."

She turned, not wanting to see the alarm on his face. Jared said nothing. He gathered up his coat and followed her out, and as they crossed the threshold of the door they both felt again that strange shift, as if the room straightened itself out behind them. Turning, Claudia stared at its white purity, the place that existed both here and at home, as her father's study.

Jared swung the gates closed and fastened the chains across. He clipped a small device to the bronze. "This is just a safeguard. Medlicote was down here this morning."

Claudia was surprised. "My father's secretary?"

Jared nodded, preoccupied.

"What did he want?"

"He had a message for me. He took a good look around. I think he's as curious as everyone else in the Court."

Claudia had always disliked the tall, silent man who worked for her father. But now she said quietly, "What message?"

They had reached the stairs. She dumped the sack of feathers for some servant to clear; Jared stepped back with perfect Protocol to let her go first. For a moment, as she swished up under the cobwebs, a sliver of fear came to her, a fear that he would lie or evade her question. But his voice was normal. "A message from the Queen. I'm not sure what it's about. She wants to meet with me."

Claudia smiled sweetly into the dimness. "Well, you should go. We need to know what she's up to."

"I have to say I find her terrifying. But yes, you're right."

She waited for him at the top; as he emerged from the doorway he caught the frame and breathed in sharply for a moment, as if a spark of pain had stung him. Then he caught her eye and straightened. They walked along the paneled corridor in silence, turning in to a long hallway lined with hundreds of blue and white vases each as high as a man, filled with ancient potpourri that moldered mustily. Under their feet the wooden boards creaked.

"The Esoterica are kept at the Academy," Jared said.

"Then I'll have to go there."

"You'll need the Queen's permission. And we both know she does not really want the Portal reopened."

"Master, I'll go, whatever she says. And you'll have to come with me, because I won't understand any of what I find."

"That will mean leaving Finn here on his own."

She knew that. She had been thinking about that for days. "We'll need to find a bodyguard for him."

They had reached the Honeysuckle Court. The sweet scent of its tangling flowers was like a wave of summer; it made her feel happier. As they walked out into the maze of formal paths, the evening sun lit the cloisters of twisted crystal and gold; tiny mosaic pieces glittered, and a few bees hummed in the clipped rosemary and lavender.

Far off, the clock on the high tower began to chime a quarter to seven. Claudia frowned. "You'd better go. Sia doesn't like to be kept waiting."

Jared took out the watch from his pocket and checked it.

Claudia said, "You always carry that now."

"Your father gave it to me. I think of myself as its guardian."

The timepiece was digital and accurate. Inside its gold case it was purely non-Era, and that had always amazed her, because her father had been meticulous about detail.

Gazing now at the fine silver chain, the tiny cube that hung from it, she wondered how the Warden was coping with the filth and poverty of the Prison. But then, he knew it well enough. He had been there many times.

Jared clicked the watch shut. He held it still a moment. Then, his voice very soft, he said, "Claudia, how did you know I was to meet the Queen at seven?"

She froze.

For a moment she couldn't say anything. Then she glanced at him. She knew her face was flushed.

"I see," he said.

"Master, I . . . I'm sorry. The note was lying there. I picked it up and read it." She shook her head. "I'm sorry!" She felt ashamed. And somewhere, annoyed at her slip.

"I won't say I'm not a little hurt," he said, buttoning his coat. Then he looked up and his green eyes were fixed on her. Urgently he said, "We must never doubt each other, Claudia. They will try to divide us, try to turn us against each other, you and me and Finn. Never let them do that."

"I never will." She was fierce. "Jared, are you angry with me?"

"No." He smiled ruefully. "I have long known you are your father's daughter. Now, I'll ask the Queen to let us ride to the Academy. Come to the tower later, and I'll tell you all about it."

She nodded, and watched him walk away, bowing as he passed two ladies-in-waiting who curtsied and watched his slim dark shape appreciatively. They turned, and saw Claudia. She fixed them with a cold stare; they hurried away.

Jared was hers. But however much he tried to hide it, she knew she had hurt him.

―◁◦◦◦▷―

AT THE corner of the cloister Jared waved back at Claudia and turned in to the archway. As soon as he was out of her sight, he stopped. Leaning his hand on the wall he took deep breaths. Before seeing the Queen he would need his medication. He took a handkerchief out and wiped his forehead, letting the sharp spasm subside, quietly counting the pulse rate under his finger.

He should not be so upset. Claudia was right to be inquisitive. And after all, he had one secret even from her.

He took out the watch and held it till the metal grew warm in his hand. For a moment back there, he had been about to tell her, until she had given herself away about the Queen. And what had stopped him? Why shouldn't she know that he held between his fingers the tiny cube that was Incarceron, the place where her father, and Keiro, and Attia were imprisoned?

He let it rest on his palm, remembering the Warden's voice, mocking his horror. *You are like a god, Jared. You hold Incarceron in your hands.* Beads of sweat smeared it; he wiped them away. He shut the watch up and plunged it into his pocket, and hurried to his room.

⋖◦◦◦▻

CLAUDIA STARED gloomily at her feet. For a moment she had almost hated herself; now she told herself not to be stupid.

She had to get back to Finn. The news of the Proclamation would be hard for him. As she walked quickly through the cloister she sighed. Sometimes in these last few weeks, when they had been out hunting, or riding in the woods, she had had the feeling that he was on the brink of fleeing, of turning his horse's head and galloping away into the woods of the Realm, away from the Court and the burden of being the Prince who had come back from the dead. He had wanted so hard to Escape, to find the stars. And all he had found was a new prison.

Beyond the cloister were the mews; on a sudden impulse Claudia ducked under the low archway into the dusty hall.

She needed time to think and this was her favorite place in the crowded Court. Sunlight fell through a high window at the far end of the building; the air smelled of old straw and dust, and the birds.

They sat, tethered to posts, all the noble hawks and falcons of the Court. Some wore tiny red hoods that covered their eyes; as they tossed their heads or preened, small bells rang, a miniature plume rippled. Others stared at Claudia as she passed down the aisle between their enclosures, the great owls with their wide eyes, twisting their necks soundlessly, the sparrowhawks with a fierce tawny gaze, the merlin sleepily. At the far end, tethered by leather jesses, a great eagle glared arrogantly at her, its beak yellow and cruel as gold.

She took a gauntlet down and pulled it on; tugging a fragment of meat from a hanging bag, she held it out. The eagle turned its head. For a moment it was as still as a statue, watching her intently. Then its beak snatched; it tore the sinewy flesh between its talons.

"A true symbol of the Royal house."

Claudia jumped.

Someone was standing in the shadows behind a stone screen. She could see his hand and arm in the slant of sunlight, where dust motes floated. For a moment she almost thought it was her father, and a stab of feeling she couldn't guess at jerked her hand into a fist.

Then she said, "Who is that?"

A rustle of straw.

She had no weapon. No one was here. She took one step back.

The man came forward, slowly. The sunlight slashed on his tall, thin shape, his greasy hair hanging scraggily, the small half-moons of his glasses.

She breathed out angrily. Then she said, "Medlicote."

"Lady Claudia. I hope I didn't startle you."

Her father's secretary made a stiff bow and she dropped a brief, cold curtsy. It struck her that though she had seen the man nearly every day of her life when her father was home, she had probably hardly ever spoken to him before. He was gaunt and had a slightly hunched look, as if the hours spent laboring over a desk had begun to bend him.

"Not at all," she lied. Then, hesitantly, "Actually, I'm glad to have the chance to speak to you. My father's affairs—"

"Are in perfect order." The interruption astounded her; she stared at him. He stepped closer. "Lady Claudia, forgive my discourtesy, but we have little time. Perhaps you may recognize this."

He held out ink-stained fingers and dropped something small and cold into the gauntlet she wore. The slash of sunlight fell across it. She saw a small metal token; a running beast, its mouth open and snarling. She had never seen it before. But she knew what it meant.

It was a steel wolf.

5

"I could breathe fire on you," the wirewolf growled.
"Do it," said Sapphique. "Just don't throw me into
the water."
"I could gnaw your shadow away."
"That's nothing, compared with the black water."
"I could crush your bones and sinews."
"I fear the terrible water more than you."
The wirewolf flung him angrily into the lake.
So he swam away, laughing.
      —The Wirewolf Returns

The glove was too small.

Horrified, Attia watched how the material stretched, how small tears opened at its seams. She glanced at Rix; his eyes were fixed in fascination on the Winglord's fingers.

And he was smiling.

Attia breathed in; suddenly she understood. All that pleading for them not to touch the props—*he had wanted this all along!*

She glanced at Quintus. The juggler held a red ball and a blue ball, alert. Behind, in the gloom, the troupe waited.

Thar held up his hand. In the darkness the black glove was almost invisible, as if his limb had been severed at the wrist. He barked a harsh laugh. "So now. If I snap my fingers do gold coins tumble from them? If I point at a man does he fall dead?"

Before anyone could answer he had tried it, turning and jabbing his forefinger at one of the bulky men behind him.

The thug's face went white. "Why me, chief?"

"Scared, Mart?"

"I just don't like it, that's all."

"More fool you." Thar swung back and stared at Rix contemptuously. "I've seen better props under a wagon wheel. You must be some showman to make anyone believe in this junk."

Rix nodded. "So I am. The greatest showman in Incarceron."

He raised his hand.

Instantly, Thar's scorn flicked off; he glanced down at his gloved fingers.

Then he howled in agony.

Attia jumped. The echo of the cry rang in the tunnel; the Winglord was yelping and clutching the glove. "Get it off me! It's burning me!"

"How very unfortunate," Rix murmured.

Thar's face was red with fury. "Kill him," he roared.

His men moved but Rix said, "Do that and you'll never get it off." He folded his arms, his thin face unmoved. If it was a performance, Attia thought, it was masterly. Slowly, so no one noticed, she slipped over into the driver's seat.

Thar was swearing, tearing desperately at the glove. "Acid! It's eating into my skin!"

"If you will misuse the things of Sapphique, what can you expect?" There was an edge in Rix's voice that made Attia glance at him. The gap-toothed grin was gone; he had that hard look of obsession that had alarmed her before. Behind her the juggler Quintus made a nervous click with his tongue.

"Kill the others then!" Thar was gasping now.

"No one will be hurt." Rix fixed the gang with a level stare. "You will allow us to pass, right out of the Dice hills, and then I take the spell off. Any treachery, and the anger of Sapphique will burn him for all eternity."

Their eyes flickered at one another.

"Do it," Thar howled.

It was a moment of danger. Attia knew that everything depended on the fear the gang had of their leader. If one of them ignored him or killed him or took command, Rix was finished. But they looked cowed and uneasy. First one, then the rest, shuffled back.

Rix jerked his head.

"Move," Quintus said.

Attia grabbed the reins.

"Wait!" Thar screamed. His gloved fingers twitched, as if electric sparks were jerking through them. "Stop it. Stop it doing that."

"I'm not making it do anything," Rix said, interested.

The black fingers clutched, convulsed. The halfman lurched forward, snatched a brush from the bucket of gilt paint hanging under the wagon. Gold drips splattered the tunnel floor.

"What now?" Quintus muttered.

Thar staggered to the wall. With a huge splashing movement, his gloved hand drew five shining letters on the curved metal.

ATTIA.

Everyone stared in astonishment. Rix looked at her.

Then he swung to Thar. "What are you doing?"

"I'm not doing it!" The man was almost choking with terror and fury. "The filthy Glove is alive!"

"You can write?"

"Of course I can't write. I don't know what it says!"

Attia was breathless with awe. She scrambled down from the wagon and ran to the wall. The letters dripped and ran, long spindly streaks of gold.

"What?" she gasped. "What next?"

With a jerk, as if it dragged him, Thar's hand whipped the brush up and wrote.

THE STARS EXIST, ATTIA. FINN SEES THEM.

"Finn," she breathed.

SOON, SO WILL I. BEYOND SNOW AND STORM.

Something brushed her skin. She caught it; a small, soft object, it drifted down from the dark roof.

A blue feather.

And then they were falling all around, soft as laughter, a snow of tiny blue feathers, each identical, falling on the wagons and the war band and the road, a muffling, impossible storm, feathers hissing and crackling in the flames, snuffled away and trampled by the oxen, falling in eyes and on shoulders, on the canvas roofs, on the blades of axes, sticking in the clots of paint.

"The Prison is doing this!" Rix's voice was a whisper of awe. He caught her arm. "Quickly. Before—"

But it was too late.

With a roar the tempest came out of the dark and flattened him against her; she staggered, but he hauled her up. The wrath of Incarceron raged, a scream of hurricane that scoured the tunnel and smashed down the gates. The war band was scattered; as Rix dragged Attia away she saw how Thar crumpled, how the black glove shriveled and split on his hand, dissolving to a network of holes, skeins of raw, bloody skin.

Then she was scrambling aboard; Rix yelled and whipped at the oxen and they were moving, rumbling on blindly through the blizzard. Attia covered her head with her arms as the feathers gusted at her, and above them she saw the thrown spheres of the jugglers light the eerie storm with green and red and purple.

It was hard going. The oxen were tough, but even they staggered with the force of the wind, putting their heads down and plodding on. Beside her, Attia heard a faint, wind-snatched hysteria; glancing up she saw that Rix was laughing softly to himself, blue feathers snagged in his hair and clothes.

It was too hard to talk, but Attia managed a look back. There was no sign of Thar's Butchers. After twenty minutes the tunnel became lighter; the wagon came around a long bend and she saw light ahead, a jagged entrance through the feather-storm.

As they plodded toward it the storm died, as suddenly as it had come.

Slowly, Attia took her arms down and drew breath. At the tunnel entrance Rix said, "Anyone following?"

She tried to see. "No. Quintus and his brothers are at the back."

"Excellent. A few stunballs will stop pursuit."

Her ears stung from the icy wind. Huddling her coat around her she picked feathers from her sleeves, spat out blue fluff. Then she said, appalled, "The Glove was destroyed!"

He shrugged. "What a pity."

The deadpan words, the smug grin made her stare. Then she looked past him at the landscape.

It was a frozen world.

Below them the road ran down between great banks of ice, head high, and she could see that this whole Wing was an open tundra, abandoned and windswept, stretching far into the gloom of the Prison. There was a great moat blocking their way, with a bridge fortified with a portcullis of black metal worn thin by the abrasions of sleet. An entrance had been jaggedly cut through it; the ends of steel bars bent back. Oily slush showed where traffic had passed, but to Attia the sudden cold seared like fear.

"I've heard of this place," she whispered. "This is the Ice Wing."

"How clever of you, sweetkin. So it is."

As the oxen slipped and clattered down the slope she was silent. Then she said, "So it wasn't the real Glove?"

Rix spat to one side. "Attia, if he'd opened any box or hidden compartment on this wagon he'd have found a glove. A small black glove. I never said it was Sapphique's. None of them are, in fact. Sapphique's Glove is too close to my heart to be stolen."

"But . . . it burned him."

"Well, he was right about the acid. As for not being able to take it off, he was perfectly able to. But I made him believe he could not. That is magic, Attia. To take a man's mind and twist it to believe the impossible." For a moment he concentrated on guiding the ox around a jutting girder. "Once he had let us go he would have believed the spell to be ended."

She watched him sideways. "And the writing?"

Rix's eyes slid to hers. "I was going to ask you about that."

"Me?"

"Even I can't make an illiterate man write. The message was for you. Odd things have been happening, Attia, since we met you."

She realized she was biting her nails. She wrapped her hands hastily in her sleeves. "It's Finn. It must be Finn. He's trying to speak to me. From Outside."

Rix's voice was quiet. "And you think the Glove will help?"

"I don't know! Perhaps . . . if you let me just see it . . ."

He stopped the wagon so abruptly that she almost fell off. "*No.* It's dangerous, Attia. Illusions are one thing, but this is a real object of power. Even I wouldn't dare wear it."

"You've never even been tempted?"

"Maybe. But I'm crazy, not stupid."

"But you wear it in the act."

"Do I?" He grinned.

"You're infuriating," she said.

"My life's ambition. Now. This is where you get down."

She stared around. "Here?"

"The settlement is about two hours ahead. Remember, you don't know us, we don't know you." He fished in his pocket and put three brass coins into her hand. "Get yourself something to eat. And tonight, sweetkin, remember to tremble a bit more when I raise the sword. Look scared stiff."

"I don't need to act." She climbed down, then stopped halfway. "How do I know that you're not just dumping me here and heading on?"

Rix winked and whipped up the ox. "I wouldn't dream of such a thing."

She watched them all pass. The bear was hunched in misery, its cage floor blue with feathers. One of the jugglers waved at her, but no one else even put his head out.

Slowly, the troupe rolled into the distance.

Attia tugged her pack onto her back and stamped life into her cold feet. She walked quickly at first, but the track was treacherous, a frozen metalway greasy with oil. As she descended into the plain, the walls of ice slowly rose on each side; soon they were higher than her head, and as she picked her way past them she saw objects and dust embedded deep inside. A dead dog, its jaws wide. A Beetle. In one place, small round black stones and grit. In another, so deep among blue bubbles she could barely see it, the bones of a child.

It grew bitterly cold. Her breath began to cloud around her. She hurried, because the wagons were already out of sight, and only by walking fast could she keep warm.

Finally, at the bottom of the slope, she reached the bridge. It was stone, and it arched over the moat, but as she slipped along in the cart ruts she saw that the moat was frozen solid, and leaning over the side made her shadow darken its dirty surface. Debris was strewn across it. Chains led from the cutwaters, disappearing deep into the ice.

The portcullis, when she came to it, was black and ancient. The ends of the bent bars glittered with icicles, and on the very top a solitary long-necked bird perched, white as snow. For a moment she thought it was a carving, until suddenly it spread its wings and flew, with a mournful *cark*, high into the iron-gray sky.

Then she saw the Eyes.

There were two, one on each side of the iron gate. Tiny and

red, they stared down at her. Icicles hung from them like frozen tears.

Attia stopped, breathless, holding her side. She stared up. "I know you're watching me. Was it you that sent the message?"

Silence. Only the low cold whisper of snow.

"What did you mean, that you would see the stars soon? You're the Prison. How can you see Outside?"

The Eyes were steady points of fire. Did she imagine that one had winked?

She waited until she was too cold to stand there any longer. Then she climbed through the gap in the portcullis and trudged on.

Incarceron was cruel, they all knew that. Claudia had said that it wasn't meant to be, that the Sapienti had made the Prison as a great experiment, a place of light and warmth and safety. Attia laughed aloud, bitterly. If so, it had failed. The Prison kept its own council. It rearranged its landscapes and struck down troublemakers with laserfire, if it felt like it. Or it let its inmates fight and prey on each other and laughed to see them struggle. It knew nothing of mercy. And only Sapphique—and Finn—had ever Escaped it.

She stopped and raised her head. "I suppose that makes you angry," she said. "I suppose that makes you jealous, doesn't it?"

There was no answer. Instead the snow became real. It fell gently and relentlessly, and she shouldered her pack and walked wearily through it, a noiseless cold that chilled her fingers and toes, chapped her lips and cheeks, made her breath a frosted cloud that did not disperse.

Her coat was threadbare, her gloves had holes. She cursed Rix as she stumbled in frozen potholes, tripped over broken mesh.

The track was covered already, the ruts of the wagons hidden. A pile of ox dung was a frozen mound.

But when she looked up, her lips blue with cold, she saw the settlement.

It seemed to be a collection of low round mounds, as white as their surroundings. They rose out of the tundra, all but invisible except for the smoke escaping from vents and chimneys. Tall poles soared above them; she saw a man at the top of each, as if they were lookouts.

The track branched off and she saw how the troupe's wagons had crushed snow here, how wisps of straw and a few feathers had fallen at the turn. Walking cautiously on, she peered around the ice wall and saw that the road ended in a barrier of wood. On one side of it a plump woman sat knitting before a brazier of hot coals.

Was this their security?

Attia bit her lip. Tugging her hood closer down on her face, she trudged through the snow and saw the woman look up, hands knitting rhythmically.

"Got any ket?"

Surprised, Attia shook her head.

"Good. Need to see your weapons."

She took out her knife and held it up. The woman dumped the knitting and took it, opened a chest, and shoved it in. "Any more?"

"No. So what do I defend myself with?"

"No weapons in Frostia. Rules of the town. Need to search you now."

Attia watched her bag being rummaged. Then she spread her arms and the woman frisked her efficiently and stepped away. "Fine. Go ahead." She picked up the knitting and clacked away.

Bewildered, Attia climbed over the frail barrier. Then she said, "Will I be safe?"

"Plenty of empty rooms now." The woman glanced up. "You can get a room at the second dome, if you ask."

Attia turned away. She wanted to know if just one old woman had searched all of Rix's wagons, but couldn't ask, since she wasn't supposed to know them. Still, just before she ducked into the dome entrance, she said, "Do I get the knife back when I leave?"

No one answered. She gazed back.

And stood still in astonishment.

The stool was empty. A pair of knitting needles clattered by themselves in midair.

Red wool trailed on the snow, like a bloodstain. "No one leaves," it said.

73

6

> *If one is lost, another will take his place.*
> *The Clan will endure until Protocol dies.*
> *—The Steel Wolves*

Claudia took a deep breath, dismayed and astonished. Her fingers closed on the tiny metal wolf.

"I see you understand," Medlicote said.

The eagle stirred at his voice, turning its cruel head and glaring at him.

She didn't want to. "This was my father's?"

"No, my lady. It belongs to me." His gaze behind the small half-moon glasses was calm. "The Clan of the Steel Wolf has many secret members, even here at Court. Lord Evian is dead and your father has vanished, but others of us remain. We hold to our purpose. To overthrow the Havaarna dynasty. To end Protocol."

All she could think of was that this was a new threat to Finn. She held out the Steel Wolf and watched him take it back.

"What do you want?"

He took his glasses off and rubbed them. His face was gaunt, his eyes small. "We want to find the Warden, my lady. As you do."

Did she? The remark shook her. Her eyes swerved to the

doorway, down the sun-slashed hall beyond the brooding hawks. "We shouldn't talk here. We may be watched."

"It is important. I have information."

"Well, tell me."

He hesitated. Then he said, "The Queen plans to install a new Warden of Incarceron. It will not be you, my lady."

She stared at him. "*What!*"

"Yesterday she held a private meeting of her advisors, the Privy Council. We believe the purpose was to—"

She couldn't believe this. "I'm his heir! I'm his daughter!"

The tall secretary paused. When he resumed, his voice was dry. "But you are not his daughter, my lady."

It silenced her. She found she was clutching her dress; she let go and drew a deep breath. "So. That's it."

"Of course your origin as a baby brought from Incarceron is known to the Queen. She told the members of the Council that you had no rights in blood to the Wardenship, or the house and lands of the Wardenry . . ."

Claudia gasped.

". . . and that there were no official documents of adoption— in fact the Warden had committed a serious crime by releasing you, an inmate and the daughter of inmates."

She was so angry now, she felt it like a chilly sweat on her skin. She stared at the man, trying to work out where he stood in this. Was he really from the Wolves, or was he working for the Queen?

As if he sensed her doubt he said, "Madam, you must know I owed everything to your father. I was merely a poor scrivener; he advanced me and I respected him greatly. I feel, in his absence, that his interests must be protected."

She shook her head. "My father is an outlaw now. I don't even know if I want him back." She paced over the stone floor, her skirt sending dust swirling up into the light. But the Wardenry! She certainly wanted that. She thought of the beautiful old house where she had lived all her life, its moat and rooms and corridors, Jared's precious tower, her horses, all the green fields and woods and meadows, the villages and rivers. She could never let the Queen take them. And leave her penniless.

"You're agitated," Medlicote said. "It is hardly surprising. My lady, if—"

"Listen to me." She turned on him sharply. "Tell these Wolves that they must do nothing. Nothing! Do you understand?" Ignoring his surprise she said, "You mustn't think Finn . . . Prince Giles . . . is your enemy. He may be the Havaarna heir, but I assure you he is as determined to abolish Protocol as you are. I insist you stop any plots against him."

Medlicote stood still, looking at the stone floor. When he looked up she realized her show of temper had had no effect on him.

"Madam, with respect, we too thought that Prince Giles might be our savior. But this boy, if he is indeed the Prince, is not what we expected. He is melancholy, indeed sullen, and rarely appears in public. When he does his manner is awkward. He seems to brood on those he has left behind in Incarceron . . ."

"Isn't that understandable?" she snapped.

"Yes, but he is far more interested in finding the Prison than about what happens here. Then there are the fits he has, the loss of memory . . ."

"*All right!*" She was furious with him. "All right. But leave him to me. I mean that. I order you."

Far off the stable clock chimed seven. The eagle opened its beak and made a harsh cry; the merlin, far down on its perch, flapped its wings and screeched.

A shadow darkened the mews door.

"Someone's coming," she said. "Go. Quickly."

Medlicote bowed. As he stepped back into the shadows only the half-moons of his glasses glittered. He said, "I will report your order to the Clan, my lady. But I can give no assurances."

"You will," she said, "or I'll have you arrested."

His smile was grim. "I do not think you would do that, Lady Claudia. Because you too would do anything to change this Realm. And the Queen needs only a small excuse to remove you."

She swept away from him and marched toward the door, tossing down the gauntlet. Her anger burned her, but she knew it was not just at him. She was angry with herself, because he had said what she thought, what she had been secretly thinking for months, only she had never allowed herself to realize it. Finn was a disappointment to her.

Medlicote's judgment had been coldly accurate.

"Claudia?"

She looked up and saw Finn was standing in the doorway. He looked hot and agitated. "I've been looking everywhere. Why did you run off like that?"

He stepped toward her but she swept past him, as if irritated. "Jared called me."

Finn's heart leaped. "Has he got the Portal to work? Has he found the Prison?" He grabbed her arm. "Tell me!"

"Let go of me." She shook him off. "I suppose you're in a panic because of this Proclamation. It's nothing, Finn. It means nothing."

He scowled. "I keep telling you, Claudia. I won't be King till I can find Keiro—"

Something snapped in her. Suddenly all she wanted to do was hurt him. "You never will," she said. "Don't you realize that? Are you so stupid? And you can forget all your maps and searches because the Prison isn't like that, Finn. It's a world so small that you could crush it between your fingers like an ant and not even notice!"

"What do you mean?" He stared at her. There was a warning itch behind his eyes, a prickle of sweat on his back, but he ignored it. He caught her arm again and knew he was hurting her; furious, she flung him away.

He couldn't breathe. "*What do you mean?*"

"It's true! Incarceron is only huge from Inside. The Sapienti miniaturized it to some zillionth of a nanometer! That's why no one comes or goes. That's why we have no idea where it is. And you'd better get it into your head, Finn, because that's why Keiro and Attia and the thousands of Prisoners in there will never come out. Never! There's not enough power left in the whole world to do it, even if we knew how."

Her words were dark black spots that flew at him. He beat them away. "It can't be . . . You're lying . . ."

She laughed harshly. The silk of her dress crackled in the sun. Its brilliance stabbed him like a bright dagger. He rubbed a hand down his face and his skin was dry as paper.

"Claudia," he said. But no sound came out.

She was talking. She was saying something hard and scathing and storming away from him, but it was all too far for him to hear now. It was behind the sparkling itchy shimmer that was rising around him, the familiar, dreaded heat that crumpled his knees and turned the world black, and all he could think of as he fell was that the cobbles were stone and that his forehead would smack against them and that he would lie in his own blood.

And then there were hands, grabbing him.

There was a forest and he fell from his horse into it.

And then there was nothing.

JARED SAID softly, "I believe the Queen is expecting me."

The guardsman outside the Royal Apartments barely nodded. He turned and gave a smart rap on the door; it opened instantly, and a footman in a coat as blue as the feathers stepped out.

"Master Sapient. Please follow me."

Jared obeyed, wondering at the amount of powder on the man's wig. There was so much that it had dusted his shoulders with a faint grayness like ash. Claudia would have been amused. He tried to smile about it, but his nervousness tightened the muscles of his face, and he knew he was pale and scared. A Sapient should be calm. In the Academy they had taught techniques of detachment. He wished he could concentrate on them now.

The Royal Apartments were vast. He was led down a corridor frescoed on each side with murals of fish, so lifelike that it was like walking underwater. Even the light through the high windows was a filtered green. After that came a blue room painted with birds and a room with a carpet as yellow and soft as desert sand, with palm trees growing out of it in elaborate urns. To his relief he was ushered past the entrance of the Great State Chamber; he had not been in there since the terrible morning of Claudia's non-wedding, and he didn't want to. It brought back memories of how the Warden had looked at him through the crowd. He shivered even now to think of it.

The footman paused before a padded door and opened it, bowing low. "Please wait here, Master. Her Majesty will be with you shortly."

He stepped in. The door closed with a soft click. Like a muffled trap.

The room was small and intimate. Upholstered sofas faced each other across a wide stone hearth where an enormous bowl of roses stood, flanked by sconces in the shape of eagles. Sunlight poured through the high windows.

Jared wandered to one of them.

Wide lawns lay beyond. Bees buzzed in archways of honeysuckle. The voices of croquet players laughed from the nearby gardens. He wondered if the game was quite in Era. The Queen tended to pick and choose what pleased her. Threading his hands together nervously, he turned away and walked to the fireplace.

The room was warm and faintly stuffy, as if rarely used.

The furniture smelled musty.

Wishing he could loosen his collar, he made himself sit down.

At once, as if she had been waiting for just that, the door opened and the Queen glided in. Jared jumped up.

"Master Jared. Thank you so much for coming."

"My pleasure, Madam."

He bowed, and she made a graceful curtsy. She still wore the shepherdess costume; he noticed a wilting bunch of violets tucked in her belt.

Sia missed nothing, including his glance. She gave her silvery laugh and dropped the flowers onto the table. "Dear Caspar. Always so thoughtful to his mama." She lounged on one sofa and pointed to the other. "Please sit, Master. Let's not be too formal."

He sat, his back upright.

"A drink?"

"No. Thank you."

"You look a little too pale, Jared. Are you getting enough fresh air?"

"I'm quite well, thank you, Your Majesty." He kept his voice steady. She was playing with him. He thought of her as a cat, a mischievous white cat toying with the mouse it will eventually kill with one clawed blow. She smiled. Her curiously light eyes gazed at him.

"I'm afraid that isn't quite true, is it? But let's talk about your search. What progress have you made?"

He shook his head. "Very little. The Portal is badly damaged. I fear it may be beyond repair." He did not say anything about the Warden's study at home, nor did she ask. Only he and Claudia knew that the Portal was identical in both places. He had ridden there weeks ago to check it. It was exactly the same as here. "However, something happened today that I did not expect."

"Oh?"

He told her about the feather. "The replication was extraordinary. But I have no way of knowing whether anything happened in the Prison. Since the Warden took both Keys with him we have no communication with the inmates."

"I see. And have you come any closer to finding Incarceron's actual location?"

He moved slightly, feeling the watch's heavy tick against his chest. "I'm afraid not."

"Such a pity! We know so little."

What would she do if she knew he carried it in his pocket? Stamp on it with her white-heeled shoes?

"Lady Claudia and I have decided we must visit the Academy." He surprised himself by his assured tone. "The records of the making of the Prison may be there among the Esoterica. Perhaps there will be diagrams, equations."

He paused, aware that he was perilously close to infringing Protocol. But Sia's gaze was on her neat fingernails.

"You will go," she said. "But not Claudia."

Jared frowned. "But . . ."

She lifted her eyes and smiled at him sweetly, full in his face. "Master, how many more years does your physician think you will live?"

He breathed in sharply. He felt as if she had stabbed him, a bitter resentment that she could ask him, a cold dread of answering. His hands shook.

Glancing down, he tried to speak steadily, but his voice sounded strange to himself.

"Two years. At most."

"I am so very sorry." She did not take her eyes off him. "And you agree with him?"

He shrugged, hating her pity. "I think he is a little optimistic."

She made a small pout with her red lips. Then she said, "Of course, we are all the victims of fate and destiny. For example, if there had never been the Years of Rage, the great war, the Protocol, a cure for even your rare condition would certainly have been available years ago. Research then was extensive. Or so I gather."

He stared at her, his skin prickling, sensing danger.

The Queen sighed. She poured out wine into a crystal cup and settled back with it, curling her legs under her up on the sofa. "And you are so young, Master Jared. Barely thirty, I understand?"

He managed to nod.

"And a brilliant scholar. Such a loss to the Realm. And dear Claudia! How will she bear it?"

Her cruelty astounded him. Her voice was silken and sad; she ran one long finger thoughtfully around the rim of the cup. "And the pain you will have to bear," she said softly. "Knowing that soon no medicine will help, that you will lie helpless and ill, day after long day sinking further from what you were, until not even Claudia will be able to bring herself to see you. Until death will be welcome."

He stood abruptly. "Madam, I don't know what—"

"You do know. Sit down, Jared."

He wanted to walk to the door, open it, storm out, away from the horror she faced him with. Instead, he sat. His forehead was damp with sweat. He felt defeated.

She eyed him calmly. Then she said, "You will go and examine the Esoterica. The collection is vast, the remnants of a world's wisdom. I'm sure you will find some medical research that can help you. The rest will be up to you. You will need to experiment, to test, to do whatever it is you Sapienti do. I suggest you remain at the Academy; the medical facilities there are the best we have. A blind eye will be turned to any infringements of Protocol; you can do as you wish. You can spend your remaining time as it should be spent, in the research that will cure you." She leaned forward, her skirts rustling. "I offer it to you, Jared. The forbidden knowledge. The chance of life."

He swallowed.

In the stuffy room every sound seemed magnified, the voices outside worlds away.

"What do you want in return?" he said, hoarse.

She leaned back, smiling. As if she had won. "I want nothing. Literally, nothing. The Portal must never open again. The gates of Incarceron, wherever that place is, must be found to be impassable. All attempts must fail."

Over the top of the crystal glass, her eyes met his.

"And Claudia need never know."

7

*Sapphique leaped up, overjoyed. "If you cannot
answer, then I've won. Show me a way Out."*

*Incarceron laughed in its million halls. It
raised a claw and the skin of the claw split and
the dragonskin Glove curled off and lay on the
ground.*

*Sapphique was alone. He picked the shining
thing up and cursed the Prison.*

*But when he put his hand into Incarceron's
he knew its plans.*

He dreamed its dreams.

—Sapphique in the Tunnels of Madness

That evening's show was packed.

The troupe had erected their creaking wooden stage in
the central space of one of the snow-domes, a smoky hollow of
hewn iceblocks, melted and refrozen over so many years that
the roof was twisted and seamed, gnarled with gloops and pinnacles of ice, black with soot.

Watching Rix stand before the two chosen volunteers next
to her, Attia tried to keep her face rapt and wondering, but
she knew he was very tense. The crowd here had been quiet

all evening. Too quiet. Nothing seemed to impress them.

And things hadn't gone well. Perhaps it was the bitter cold, but the bear had refused to dance, crouching mournfully on the stage, despite all prodding. The jugglers had dropped their plates twice, and even Gigantia had only managed to draw a few spatters of applause by lifting a man on a chair with one of her huge hands.

But when the Dark Enchanter had appeared, the silence had grown deeper, more intense. The people stood in attentive rows, their eyes fixed in fascination on Rix as he faced them, young and dark, the black glove on his right hand, its forefinger pinned back to show the maiming. It was more than fascination. It was hunger. From this close, Attia saw the sweat on his forehead.

The things he had said to the two women had been greeted with silence too. Neither of them had wept or clasped his hands with joy or given any indication of recognizing anything, even though he had managed to pretend they had. Their rheumy eyes just gazed imploringly at him. Attia had had to do the sobbing and cries of amazement; she thought she hadn't overplayed it, but the stillness had cowed her. The applause had been a mere ripple.

What was wrong with them all?

As she gazed out she saw they were dirty and sallow, their mouths and noses muffled and scarved against the cold, their eyes sunken with hunger. But that was nothing new.

There seemed to be few old people, hardly any children. They stank of smoke and sweat and some sweet herbal tang. And they stood apart; they did not crowd together. Some sort of commotion caught her eye; to one side a woman swayed and fell. Those nearby stepped away. No one touched her, or bent over her. They left a space around her.

Maybe Rix had seen it too.

As he turned Attia caught a flash of panic under his makeup, but his voice was as smooth as ever.

"You search for an Enchanter of power, a Sapient who will show you the way out of Incarceron. All of you search for that!" He swung on them, challenging, daring them to deny it.

"I am that man! The way that Sapphique took lies through the Door of Death. I will take this girl through that door. And I will bring her back!"

She didn't have to pretend. Her heart was thudding hard.

There was no roar from the crowd, but the silence was different now. It had become a threat, a force of such desire it scared her. As Rix led her to the couch she glanced out at the muffled faces and knew that this was no audience happy to be fooled. They wanted Escape like a starving man craves food. Rix was playing with fire here.

"Pull out," she breathed.

"Can't." His lips barely moved. "Show must go on."

Faces pressed forward to see. Someone fell, and was trampled. A soft ice thaw dripped from the roof, on Rix's makeup, on her hands gripping the couch, on the black glove. The crowd's breath was a frosted contagion.

"Death," he said. "We fear it. We would do anything to avoid it. And yet Death is a doorway that opens both ways. Before your eyes, you will see the dead live!"

He drew the sword out of the air. It was real. It gleamed with ice as he held it up.

This time there was no rumble, no lightning from the roof. Maybe Incarceron had seen the act too often. The crowd stared at the steel blade greedily. In the front row a man scratched endlessly, muttering under his breath.

Rix turned. He fastened the links around Attia's hands. "We may have to leave fast. Be ready."

The loops went around her neck and waist. They were false, she realized, and was glad.

He turned to the crowd and held up the sword. "Behold! I will release her. And I will bring her back!"

He'd switched it. It was fake too. She only had seconds to notice, before he plunged it into her heart.

This time there was no vision of Outside.

She lay rigid, unbreathing, feeling the blade retract, the cold damp of fake blood spread on her skin.

Rix was facing the silent mob. Now he turned; she sensed him come near, his warmth bending over her.

He tugged the sword away. "Now," he breathed.

She opened her eyes. She felt unsteady, but not like the first time. As he helped her stand and the blood shriveled miraculously on her coat she felt a strange release; she took his hand and was shown to the crowd and she bowed and smiled in relief, forgetting for a moment that she was not supposed to be part of the act.

Rix bowed too, but quickly. And as her euphoria drained away, she saw why.

No one was applauding.

Hundreds of eyes were fixed on Rix. As if they waited for more.

Even he was thrown. He bowed again, lifted the black glove, stepped backward on the creaking boards of the stage.

The crowd was agitated; someone shouted. A man shoved himself forward, a thin gangly man muffled up to the eyes; he tore himself out from the crowd and they saw he held one end of a thick chain. And a knife.

Rix swore briefly; out of the corner of her eye Attia saw the seven jugglers scurrying for weapons backstage.

The man climbed up on the boards. "So Sapphique's Glove brings men back to life."

Rix drew himself up. "Sir, I assure you—"

"Then prove it again. Because we need it."

He hauled on the chain, and a slave fell forward onto the boards, an iron collar around his neck, his skin raw with hideous sores. Whatever the disease was, it looked terrible.

"Can you bring him back? I've already lost—"

"He's not dead," Rix said.

The slave owner shrugged. Then quickly, before anyone could move, he cut the man's throat. "He is now."

Attia gasped, her hands over her mouth.

The red slash overflowed, the slave fell choking and writhing. All the crowd murmured. Rix did not move.

For a moment Attia had the sense he was frozen with horror, but when he spoke his voice had not a tremor. "Put him on the couch."

"I'm not touching him. You touch him. You bring him back."

The people were shouting. Now they were crying out and crawling up the sides of the stage, all around, closing in.

"I've lost my children," one cried.

"My son is dead," another screamed.

Attia looked around, backing away, but there was nowhere to go. Rix grabbed her hand with his black-gloved fingers. "Hold tight," he whispered. Aloud he said, "Stand well back, sir."

He raised his hand, clicked his fingers.

And the floor collapsed.

Attia fell through the trapdoor with a suddenness that knocked the breath out of her, and crashed on a mat stuffed with horsehair.

"Move!" Rix yelled. He was already on his feet; hauling her up, he ran, crouched under the planking of the stage.

The noise above them was a fury; running footsteps, shouts

and wails, a clash of blades. Attia scrambled over the joists; there was a curtain at the back and Rix dived under it, tugging off wig and makeup, false nose, fake sword.

Gasping, he whipped his coat off, turned it inside out, and put it back on, tied it with string, became a bent, hunched beggar before her eyes.

"They're all bloody mad!"

"What about me?" she gasped.

"Take your chance. Meet outside the gate, if you make it."

And he was gone, hobbling into a snow tunnel.

For a moment she was too furious to move. But a head and shoulders came down the trapdoor behind her. She hissed with fear and ran.

Dodging into a side cavern she saw that the wagons were gone, their tracks deep in the snow. They hadn't waited for the end. She scrambled after them, but there were too many people down that way, people surging out of the dome, some fleeing, some a mob smashing everything within reach. She turned back, cursing. To have come all this way and then to lose the Glove to a baying crowd!

And in her mind the red slash of the slave's throat opened over and over.

The tunnel led out between the snow-domes. The settlement was in chaos; strange cries echoed, the sickly smoke burned everywhere. She ducked into a quiet alley and ran down it, wishing desperately for her knife.

The snow here was thick, but hard-packed, as if from many feet. At the end of the lane was a large dark building; she ducked inside.

It was dim, and icy cold.

For a while she just crouched behind the door, breathing hard, waiting for pursuers. Distant shouts came to her. Her face against the frozen wood, she stared through a crack. Nothing but darkness came down the lane . . . And a light, falling snow.

Finally, she stood, stiff, brushing ice from her knees, and turned.

The first thing she saw was the Eye.

Incarceron gazed at her from the roof, its small curious scrutiny. And under it, on the ground, were the boxes.

She knew what they were as soon as she saw them.

A stack of coffins, hastily built, stinking of disinfectant.

Kindling was piled all around them.

She stopped breathing, flung her arm over nose and mouth, gave a wail of horror.

Plague!

It explained everything: the people falling, the cowed and muffled silence, the desperation for Rix's magic to be real.

She stumbled out backward, sobbing with dread, grabbing snow, scrubbing her hands, her face, her mouth and nose. Had she caught it? Had she breathed it in? *Oh god, had she touched anyone?*

Breathless, she turned to run.

And saw Rix.

He was stumbling toward her. "No way out," he gasped. "Can we hide in there?"

"No!" She caught his arm. "This is a plague village. We have to get out of here."

"So that's it!" To her amazement he laughed in relief. "Just for a minute there, sweetie, I thought I was losing my touch. But if it's just—"

"We could already be infected! Come on!"

He shrugged, turned.

But as he faced the darkness he stopped.

A horse stepped out from the smoky shadows of the lane, a horse dark as midnight, its rider tall, wearing a tricorn hat. He wore a black mask with narrow eyeholes. His coat was long and his boots supple and fine. He carried a firelock, and now he pointed it with practiced skill straight at Rix's head.

Rix froze.

"The Glove," the shadow whispered. "Now."

Rix wiped his face with one black hand, then spread his fingers. His voice adopted its cringing whine. "This, lord? It's just a prop. A stage prop. Take anything from me, sir, but please, not—"

"Cut the act, Enchanter." The highwayman's voice was amused and cold. Attia watched, alert. "I want the real Glove. Now."

Reluctant, Rix slowly took a small black bundle from his inside pocket.

"Give it to the girl." The firelock edged slightly toward her. "She brings it to me. You make any move and I kill both of you."

Attia surprised herself, and both of them, by her harsh laugh. The masked man glanced quickly at her, and she caught his blue eyes. She said, "That's not the Glove either. The real one he keeps in a small pouch under his shirt. *Close to his heart.*"

Rix hissed with fury. "What is this? Attia!"

The masked man clicked the trigger back. "Then get it."

Attia grabbed Rix, tugged the robe open, and dragged the string from around his neck. His face close to hers, he whispered, "So you were a plant all along."

The pocket was small, of white silk.

She stepped back, thrust it into her coat. "I'm sorry, Rix, but—"

"I believed in you, Attia. I even thought you might turn out to be my Apprentice." His eyes were hard; he stabbed a bony finger at her. "And you've betrayed me."

"The Art Magicke is the art of illusion. You said it."

Rix's face contorted in white fury. "I won't forget this. You've made a mistake crossing me, sweetie. And believe me, I'll have my revenge on you."

"I need the Glove. I need to find Finn."

"Do you? *Keep it safe*, Sapphique said. Is he safe, your thief friend? What does he want it for, Attia? What harm will he do with it?"

"Maybe I'll wear it." The highwayman's eyes were cold through his mask.

Rix nodded. "Then you will control the Prison. And the Prison will control you."

"Take care of yourself, Rix," Attia said. She put up her arm, and Keiro leaned down and pulled her up behind him.

They turned the horse in a circle of sparks. Then they galloped away into the icy dark.

The Boy in
the Yellow Coat

8

*Our Realm will be splendid. We will live as
men should live, and the land will be tilled
for us by a million yeomen. Above us the
ruined moon will be our emblem of the Years
of Rage. It will flicker through the clouds like
a lost memory.*

— *King Endor's Decree*

Finn lay deep in a softness of pillows so comfortable that
his whole body was relaxed. Sleep was a drowsy content;
he wanted to slip back into it, but already it was receding, with-
drawing from him like a shadow from the sun.

The Prison was quiet. His cell was white and empty, and
only a small red Eye watched him from the ceiling.

"Finn?" Keiro's voice came from somewhere close.

Behind it the Prison remarked, "He looks younger when he
sleeps."

Bees hummed through an open window. There was a sweet
scent of flowers he had no name for.

"Finn? Can you hear me?"

He turned, licked dry lips.

When he opened his eyes the sun dazzled him.

The figure bending over him was tall and fair, but it was not Keiro.

Claudia sat back with relief. "He's awake."

Finn felt all the knowledge of where he was flood him like a wave of despair. He tried to sit, but Jared's hand came down gently on his shoulder. "Not yet. Take your time."

He lay in an enormous four-poster bed, on soft white pillows. Above him the dusty canopy was embroidered with suns and stars and intricate twining briar roses.

Something sweet smoldered in the hearth. Servants moved discreetly around, bringing water, a tray.

"Get them out," he croaked.

Claudia said, "Stay calm." She turned. "Thank you all. Please tell the Queen's Majesty that His Highness is quite recovered. He will attend the Proclamation."

The chamberlain bowed, ushered the footmen and maids out, and closed the double doors.

At once Finn struggled up. "What did I say? Who saw me?"

"Don't distress yourself." Jared sat on the bed. "Only Claudia. When the seizure ended she summoned two of the groundsmen. They brought you up the back stairs. No one saw."

"But they all know." He felt sick with anger and shame.

"Drink this." The Sapient poured a cordial into a crystal glass; he held it out and Finn took it quickly. His throat was parched with thirst. It always was, afterward.

He didn't want to meet Claudia's eyes, but she seemed unembarrassed; when he looked up she was pacing impatiently at the foot of the bed.

"I wanted to wake you, but Jared wouldn't let me. You slept all night and half the morning! The ceremony is in less than an hour."

"I'm sure they can wait for me." His voice was sour. Then, slowly, he gripped the empty glass and looked at Jared. "Is it true? What she told me? That the Prison . . . that Keiro . . . are so small?"

"It's true." Jared refilled the glass.

"It's not possible."

"It was only too possible for the Sapienti of old. But Finn, listen to me. I want you to try not to think of it, not now. You have to prepare yourself for the ceremony."

Finn shook his head. Astonishment was like a trapdoor inside him; it had opened under him and he could not stop falling into it. Then he said, "I remembered something."

Claudia stopped. "*What?*" She came around the bed. "What was it?"

He lay back and glared at her. "You sound just like Gildas. All he ever cared about were the visions. Not about me."

"Of course I care." She made a real effort to calm her voice. "When I saw you were ill I—"

"I'm not ill." He swung his feet out of bed. "I'm a Starseer." They were silent. Then Jared said, "The seizures have an epileptic nature but I suspect they were triggered by whatever drug they gave you to forget your past."

"They? You mean the Queen."

"Or the Warden. Or indeed the Prison itself. If it's any consolation, I do think the fits will become less severe with time."

Finn scowled. "Fine. Meanwhile the Crown Prince of the Realm collapses into a twitching cripple every few weeks."

"This is not the Prison," Jared said quietly. "Illness is not a crime here." His voice was sharper than usual. Claudia frowned, annoyed at Finn's clumsiness.

Finn put the glass on the table and his head in his hands, dragging his fingers through his tangled hair. After a moment he said, "I'm sorry, Master. I'm always thinking only of myself."

"But what did you remember?" Claudia was impatient. She leaned against the bedpost, staring at him, her face tense with expectation.

Finn tried to think. "The only things I've ever been sure of as memories have been blowing out the candles on the cake, and the boats on the lake . . ."

"Your seventh birthday. When we were betrothed."

"So you say. But this time, it was different." He wrapped his arms around his chest; Claudia took the silk robe from the chair and brought it quickly. He put it on, concentrating. "I think . . . I'm sure really, that I was older this time. I was certainly riding a horse. A gray horse. There was undergrowth whipping against my legs . . . bracken, very high. The horse crashed through it. There were trees."

Claudia took a breath; Jared's hand came up to keep her silent. Calmly he said, "The Great Forest?"

"Maybe. Bracken and brambles. But there were Beetles too."

"Beetles?"

"They're in the Prison. Small metal things; they clear away rubbish, eat metal and plastic and flesh. I don't know if this was a forest here, or Inside. How could they have been here . . . ?"

"You just might be mixing things up." Claudia couldn't keep quiet any longer. "But that doesn't mean it wasn't a real memory. What happened?"

Jared took a small scanner from his pocket and placed it on the bedclothes. He made an adjustment to it, and it beeped. "The room is almost certainly full of listening devices. This will give us some protection, if you speak quietly."

Finn stared at it. "The horse jumped. There was a pain in my ankle. I fell."

"A pain?" Claudia came and sat next to him. "What sort of pain?"

"Sharp. Like a sting. It was . . ." He paused, as if the memory was flickering, just beyond reach. "Orange. Orange and black. Small."

"A wasp? A bee?"

"It hurt. I looked down at it." He shrugged. "Then nothing."

Hurriedly he pulled up his ankle and examined it. "Just here. It went through the boot leather."

There were many old marks and scars. Claudia said, "Could it have been some sort of tranquilizer? Like your false insects, Master."

"If it was," Jared said slowly, "the maker was skillful, and unbothered by Protocol."

Claudia snorted. "The Queen uses Protocol to control others, not herself."

Jared fingered the collar of his robe. "But Finn, you have ridden in the forest many times since you left the Prison. This may not be an old memory. It may not even be a memory at all." He paused, seeing the defiance come into the boy's face. "I say this because others may say it. They'll say you dreamed it."

"I know the difference." Finn's voice was angry. He stood up, tying the robe around him. "Gildas always said the visions came from Sapphique. But this was memory. It was so . . . sharp. It happened, Jared. I fell. I remember falling." His eyes held Claudia's. "Wait for me. I'll get ready."

They watched him walk into the wood-paneled dressing room and slam the door.

Bees hummed peacefully in the honeysuckle outside.

"Well?" Claudia whispered.

Jared got up and crossed to the window. He opened the

casement wider and sat on the sill, leaning his head back.

After a moment he said, "In the Prison, Finn had to survive. He learned the power of lies."

"You don't believe him?"

"I didn't say that. But he is skillful at telling the stories his listeners want to hear."

She shook her head. "Prince Giles was hunting in the forest when he fell. What if this is that memory? What if he was drugged then, and taken to wherever they wiped his mind?" Excited, she jumped up, came over to him. "What if it's all coming back to him?"

"Then that's good. But do you remember his story of the Maestra, Claudia? The woman who gave him the Key? We have heard several versions of that. Each time, he tells it differently. Who knows which if any is the truth?"

They were silent a moment. Claudia smoothed the silk of her dress, trying not to feel deflated. She knew Jared was right, that at least one of them had to keep a clear head. It was the method he had always taught her, to weigh up arguments, to probe them without favor. But she so wanted Finn to remember, to change, to become suddenly the Giles they needed. She wanted to be sure of him.

"You don't resent my skepticism, Claudia?" Her tutor's voice was wistful; she looked up, surprised, and saw he was looking at her closely.

"Of course not!" Caught by some sadness in his eyes she

came over and sat by him, gripping his arm. "Are you well, Master? All this worry over Finn . . ."

"I am quite well, Claudia."

She nodded, not wanting to know if he was lying. "But I haven't asked you about the Queen. What did she have to say that was so urgent?"

He looked away, out at the green lawns. "She wanted to know how the efforts to open the Portal went. I told her about the feathers." He smiled his rare smile. "I don't think it impressed her."

Claudia said, "No."

"And I broached the subject of the Academy."

"Don't tell me. She won't let me go."

It was his turn to be surprised. "Correct. You think it is because of what Medlicote told you? That she plans to disinherit you?"

"She can try," she said fiercely. "She'll have a battle on her hands."

"Claudia, there is more. She . . . is happy for me to go. Alone."

She opened her eyes wider. "To search for the way In? But why? We both know she doesn't want it found."

He nodded, gazing down at his thin fingers.

"It's some sort of plot. She wants to get you out of Court." Claudia bit her nails, thinking hard. "Out of the way. Perhaps she knows you won't find anything, that you'll be wasting your time. Maybe she already knows where Incarceron is . . ."

"Claudia, I have to tell you . . ." He looked up and turned, but at that moment the tower clock began to strike, and the dressing room door opened.

Finn ran out. "Where's my sword?"

"Here." Claudia took the foil from the chair and watched him buckle it on. "You should have a servant to do that."

"I can do it myself."

She looked at him. His hair had grown longer since his Escape; now it was hastily tied back in a black ribbon. His frockcoat was a rich midnight blue, and though the sleeves were edged with gold, it had none of the laced and ruffled extravagance of the other courtiers. He wouldn't wear powder, or bright colors, or any of the perfumed sashes and stars and plumed hats the Queen had sent him. It was as if he was in mourning. The austerity reminded her of her father.

He stood there nervously. "Well?"

"You look fine. But you should have more gold lace. We have to show these people—"

"You look every inch the Prince," Jared said, coming and opening the door.

Finn didn't move. His hand gripped the sword hilt as if it were the only familiar thing there. "I don't know if I can do this," he said.

Jared stepped back. "Yes you can, Finn." He moved closer

and his voice was so quiet Claudia barely caught the words. "You will do it for the Maestra's sake."

Startled, Finn stared at him. But then the bell rang again, and Claudia slipped her arm firmly in his and led him from the room.

All the corridors of the Court were lined with people. Well-wishers, servants, soldiers, secretaries, they gathered in hallways and peered from doors and galleries to see the Crown Prince of the Realm going to his Proclamation.

Preceded by a guard of thirty men-at-arms, sweating in their shining cuirasses, ceremonial swords upright in their hands, Claudia and Finn walked quickly toward the State Apartments. Flowers were thrown at Finn's feet, applause rippled from doorways and stairs. But it was muted, and Claudia knew that, and she wanted to frown under the gracious smile she had to keep on her face. Finn wasn't popular enough. People didn't know him. Or they thought he was surly and remote. It was all his own fault.

But she smiled and nodded and waved at them, and Finn walked stiffly, bowing here and there at faces he recognized, and she knew Jared was reassuringly behind her, his Sapient coat swirling the dust on the floor. They were escorted through the myriad apartments of the Silver Wing, and the Gold Rooms, and the Turquoise Ballroom, massed with staring crowds, and the Mirrored Salon, where the walls of looking glass made the gathering seem overwhelmingly huge. Under glittering chandeliers they walked, through air that was hot and cloying with perfume and sweat and pomander oils, through whispers and polite cheers and curious scrutiny. Music tinkled from viols and cellos on a high balcony; rose petals were tossed in showers from the ladies-in-waiting. Finn looked up and managed a smile; the pretty women tittered and hid their faces behind fans.

His arm was hot and tense in Claudia's; she squeezed his wrist in reassurance. And as she did so she realized how little she really knew of him, of the agony of his memory loss, of the life he had lived.

As they came to the entrance of the Crystal Court two liveried footmen bowed and flung the doors back.

The vast room shimmered. Hundreds of people turned their heads.

Claudia loosened her arm and stepped back beside Jared. She saw how Finn gave her one glance; then he drew himself up and marched on, one hand on his sword. She followed, wondering what terrors of the Prison had taught him such cold bravado.

Because the room was full of danger.

As the crowd fell back she walked between their sweeping bows and elegant curtsies and wondered how many secret weapons were concealed here, how many assassins lurked, how many spies pushed close. A silken flock of smiling women, Ambassadors in full regalia, Countesses and Dukes and all the ermine robes of the Privy Council opened to show the scarlet carpet that led the length of the room, and the tiny birds in bright cages that sang and fluttered in the high arches of the roof. And everywhere, like a bewildering maze, the thousand crystal pillars that gave the room its name reflected and twisted and entwined from the vaulted ceiling.

On each side of the dais ranks of Sapienti stood, their iridescent robes catching the light. Jared joined them, quietly moving to the end of the line.

The dais itself was raised on five wide marble steps, and on the top of it were two thrones. Queen Sia rose from one.

She wore a hugely looped gown of white satin, a cloak trimmed with ermine, and the crown. It was oddly small on her elaborate hair, Claudia thought, stopping at the front row of courtiers next to Caspar. He glanced at her and grinned, and the hulking bodyguard named Fax stood close behind him. Claudia turned away, frowning.

She watched Finn.

He climbed the steps swiftly, his head slightly bowed. At the top he turned to face the crowd and she saw his chin go up, the steady defiant stare he sent out at them all. But for the first time she thought, *If he tried, he could look like a prince.*

The Queen held up her hand. The murmuring crowd fell silent; only the hundreds of finches cheeped and warbled high above.

"Friends. This is a historic day. Giles, who was once lost from us, has returned to take up his inheritance. The Havaarna Dynasty welcomes its Heir. The Realm welcomes its King."

It was a pretty speech. Everyone applauded it. Claudia caught Jared's eye and he blinked slowly. She tried not to smile.

"And now we will hear the Proclamation."

As Finn stood rigidly beside Sia, the First Lord Sapient, a thin, austere man, stood and handed his silver wand tipped with its crescent moon to a footman. From another he took a parchment scroll, unrolled it, and began to read from it in a firm, sonorous voice. It was long and tedious, full of clauses and titles and legalese, but Claudia realized it was essentially an announcement of Finn's intention to be crowned, and the assertion of his rights and fitness. When the phrase "sane in mind and whole in body and in spirit" rolled out she stiffened, sensing rather than seeing Finn's tension. Beside her, Caspar made a small tutting noise. She glanced at him. He still wore the stupid smirk.

Suddenly a cold fear sprang up in her. Something was wrong. They had something planned. She moved, agitated; Caspar's hand caught hers.

"I hope you're not going to interrupt," he breathed in her ear, "and ruin Finn's lovely day."

She stared at him.

The Sapient ended, rolling the scroll. ". . . Thus it is Proclaimed. And unless there be any who cry out against it, I affirm and announce here and before these witnesses, before the Court and the Realm, that the Prince Giles Alexander Ferdinand of the Havaarna, Lord of the Southern Isles, Count of—"

"*I object.*"

The Sapient faltered, fell silent. The crowd turned, astonished.

Claudia whipped her head around.

The voice had been quiet but firm, and it came from a boy. He pushed his way through and past her, and she saw he was tall and had brown hair and there was a clear, purposeful look in his eyes. He wore a coat of fine golden satin. And his resemblance to Finn was astonishing.

"I object."

He looked up at the Queen and Finn and they stared back, and the First Sapient made a sharp gesture, and the soldiers lifted their weapons quickly.

"And who are you, sir, that you think you may object?" the Queen said in amazement.

The boy smiled and held out his hands in a curiously regal gesture. He stood on the step and bowed low.

"Madam Stepmother," he said, "don't you know me? I am the real Giles."

9

So he rose up and sought the hardest way,
the road that leads inward. And all the time
he wore the Glove he did not eat or sleep
and Incarceron knew all his desires.
                              —*Legend of Sapphique*

The horse was tireless, its metal legs deep in snow.
Attia held tight to Keiro, because the cold made her stiff and her hands numb, and several times she almost felt she would fall.

"We have to get far enough away," Keiro said over his shoulder.

"Yes. I know."

He laughed. "You're not a bad little operator. Finn would be proud."

She didn't answer. The plan of how they should steal the Glove had been hers and she had known she could do it, but she felt a curious shame at betraying Rix. He was crazy, but she'd liked him and his ramshackle troupe. As they rode she wondered what he would be doing now, what story he would be spinning them. But he'd never used the real Glove in the act, so they should be able to carry on. And she shouldn't feel sorry for him. There was no place for pity in Incarceron. But as she thought that, she thought of Finn, who had pitied her, once, and rescued her. She frowned.

The Ice Wing glittered in the darkness. It was as if the artificial light of the Prison had been stored deep in its frozen strata, so that even now, in darkness, the vast tundra was pale and phosphorescent, its pitted surface swept by cold winds. Shimmers of aurora rippled in the sky, as if Incarceron amused itself with strange effects in the long hours of the arctic night.

They rode for over an hour, the land becoming more and more contorted, the air colder. Attia grew tired, her legs aching, her back an agony.

Finally, Keiro slowed the beast. His back was damp with sweat. He said, "This will have to do."

It was a great overhang of ice, sheened with a frozen waterfall.

"Great," she muttered.

Slowly, the horse picked its way in, among boulders furred with frost. Attia swung both feet over and slid gratefully down. Her legs almost gave way; she grabbed one of the rocks, then stretched, groaning.

Keiro jumped down. If he was stiff, he was far too proud to show it. He took off the hat and mask and she saw his face.

"Fire," he muttered.

There was nothing to burn. Finally he found an ancient tree stump; there was still some bark that could be snapped off, and with some kindling from the pack and a great deal of impatient swearing, he managed to get it alight. The heat was paltry, but Attia was glad to stretch out her hands and shiver over it.

She crouched, watching him. "We said a week. You were lucky I'd managed to guess . . ."

"If you think I was going to hang around a stinking plague-heap, you were wrong." He sat opposite. "Besides, things were getting rough back there. That mob might have gotten to it first."

Attia nodded.

Keiro watched ice drip into the fire. The damp wood hissed and crackled. His face was edged with shadows, his blue eyes red-rimmed with weariness, but his old arrogance was still there, his effortless sense of superiority. "So how was it?"

She shrugged. "The magician's name was Rix. He was . . . strange. Maybe a little mad."

"His act was rubbish."

"You would think that." She remembered the lightning in the sky, the dripping letters painted by the man who could not write. "A few odd things happened. Perhaps because of the Glove. I thought I saw Finn."

Keiro lifted his head sharply. "Where?"

"It was . . . a sort of dream."

"A vision?" He groaned. "Oh, fantastic! That's all I need! Another Starseer." Dragging the pack nearer, he took out some bread, tore it open, and tossed her the smaller part. "So what did you see my precious oathbrother doing? Sitting on his golden throne?"

Exactly, she thought, but instead she said, "He looked lost."

Keiro snorted. "Sure. Lost in his luxurious corridors and throne rooms. His wine and women. I suppose he's got them all eating out of his hand, Claudia and his stepmother, the Queen, and whoever else is soft enough to listen to him. I taught him how to do that. I taught him how to survive, when he was a stunned kid sobbing at every loud bang. And this is how he repays me."

Attia swallowed the last of the bread. She had heard all this before. "It wasn't Finn's fault you couldn't Escape."

He glared at her. "I don't need you to remind me."

She shrugged, trying not to glance at his hand. He always seemed to wear gloves now, even when it wasn't so cold.

But under the dirty and embroidered red gauntlet was Keiro's secret, the thing that haunted him and of which he never spoke, the single metal fingernail that told him that he was not entirely human. And that he had no idea how much of his body Incarceron had made.

Now he muttered, "Finn swore he'd try to find some way to get me Out. All the Sapienti of his pathetic kingdom would work at it. But I don't intend to wait around. He forgot the Outside, so maybe he's forgotten us now. All I know is if I ever find him again he'll regret it."

"Unlikely to happen," Attia said heartlessly.

He glanced at her, his handsome face flushed. "And what about you? Always had a soft spot for poor old Finn, didn't you?"

"He saved my life."

"Twice. Once with my magic ring. Which I should still have, instead of it being wasted on you."

She was silent. She was used to his scorn, and his moods. He tolerated her because she was useful, and she stayed with him because if Finn came back, it would be to find Keiro. She had no illusions about that.

Gloomily, Keiro sank a mouthful of sour beer. "Look at me. Skulking in the Ice Wing, when I should have been leading the old gang now, out on some raid, taking the chief's share of the plunder. I beat Jormanric in a fair fight! I destroyed him. I had everything in my hands, and I let Finn persuade me to leave it. And what happens? He Escapes and I don't."

His disgust was real; Attia didn't bother to remind him that she had tripped his opponent at the critical moment and won the fight for him. Instead she said, "Stop moping. We've got the Glove. At least let's take a look at it."

He was still a moment, then brought out the silk pouch from his pocket. He dangled it from one finger. "What a pretty little thing. I won't ask how you found out where he kept it."

She shuffled closer. If her guess had been wrong . . .

Carefully, Keiro opened the drawstring, tipped out a small,

dark, crumpled object. He spread the thing out on his palm and they stared at it in fascination.

It was extremely old. And very different from the gloves Rix had worn in his act.

For a start it was not made of fabric, but of some glistening, scaly skin, very soft and supple. Its color was difficult to define; it seemed to shimmer and change between dark green and black and metallic gray. But it was certainly a glove.

The fingers were worn and stiff, and the thumb had been repaired with a patch, sewn by ragged stitches. On the gauntlet were pinned a few metal objects, tiny images of a beetle and a wolf, and two swans linked by a fine chain. But most unexpected of all, the fingers of the Glove were tipped with ancient, ivory-yellow claws.

Keiro said wonderingly, "Is it really dragonskin?"

"Could be snake." But she had never seen scales so fine and tough.

Slowly, Keiro took his own glove off. His hand was muscular and dirty.

"Don't," she said.

Sapphique's Glove looked too small for him. It seemed to be made for a fine, delicate hand.

"I've been waiting a lifetime."

She knew he thought it would somehow change things, that wearing it might negate the components that were part of him, that if Finn came back through the Portal to fetch him he could follow, by wearing this. But Rix's warning haunted her.

"Keiro . . ."

"Shut up, Attia." He opened the Glove. It crackled slightly and she smelled its fusty, ancient smell. But before he could slide his fingers in, the horse raised its head and gave a sharp snort. Keiro froze.

Beyond the rigid waterfall the Ice Wing seemed dark and silent, deserted in its black night. As they listened they heard the low moan of the wind that gusted out there, a cold echo in the meltholes and glaciers of the abandoned landscape.

And then something else.

A chink of metal.

Keiro stamped on the fire, Attia dived behind a rock. There was no way of hiding the horse, but it stood quietly, as if it too sensed the danger.

With the flames gone the Prison's night was blue and silver; the seamed currents of the waterfall twisted like grotesque marble.

"See anything?" Keiro squeezed in beside her, shoving the Glove into his shirt.

"I thought so. Yes. There."

A glint, out on the tundra. Aurora reflecting on steel. A flicker of torchlight.

Keiro swore. "Is it Rix?"

"I don't see how it can be." Rix could never have caught up

with them, not with the clumsy wagons. She narrowed her eyes and stared.

There was something out there. It lurched in the shadows. As the light it carried flared up she glimpsed a creature, lumpy, as if it had many heads. It clanked, as if its body was made of chains. A thread of dread touched her spine. *"What is that?"*

Keiro was very still. "Something I hoped never to run into." His voice was drained of all bravado; glancing at him she saw only a flicker of his eyes.

It was making straight for them. Perhaps it could smell the horse, or sense the frozen water. The chinking became regular, as if the thing marched with military precision. As if its centipede legs were a legion.

Keiro said, "Get on the horse. Leave everything."

The fear in his voice made her move without question. But the horse sensed it too, and it whinnied, loud in the silence.

The creature stopped. It whispered. It had many voices, and its heads turned, hydra-like, to one another. Then it began to lope raggedly, awkwardly, parts of it falling, being dragged, staggering up. It yelled and swore at itself, bunched in a dark bristling mass. Sword blades and flames gleamed in its hands. Green aurora flickered over it.

It was a Chain-gang.

⊸◦◦◦⊶

CLAUDIA STARED at the boy. He straightened, saw her, and smiled warmly. "Claudia! You've grown up so much. You look wonderful!" He stepped toward her and before she could move or the guards could stop him, he had taken her hand and kissed it formally.

Astonished, she said, "Giles?"

Instantly there was an uproar. The crowd buzzed with excitement, the soldiers looked to the Queen. Sia was standing absolutely still, as if thunderstruck; with an elegant movement she recovered, lifted her hand, and waited for silence.

It came slowly. A guard banged his halberd on the floor. The crowd hushed, but there were still whispers. The Sapienti glanced at one another; Claudia saw Finn stride forward and stare at the newcomer angrily. "What do you mean, 'the real Giles'? I'm Giles."

The stranger turned and looked at him as if he were dirt. "You, sir, are an escaped Prisoner and an imposter. I don't know what malice lies behind your claims, but I can tell you they are certainly not true. I am the rightful Heir." He turned to the crowd. "And I've come to claim my inheritance."

Before anyone else could speak the Queen said, "Enough! Whoever you are, sir, you are certainly far too bold. I will hear this matter in private. My lords, please join us." Her pale eyes glanced at Finn. "You too are entitled to hear."

She turned regally, and the Ambassadors and courtiers bowed low. Claudia grabbed Finn as he came past. He shook her off.

"It can't be him," she whispered. "Keep calm."

"Then why did you say that name? Why did you say that, Claudia!" He sounded furious. She had no real answer.

"I was . . . it was just the shock. He has to be a pretender."

"Does he?" Finn's glare was hard. Then he turned and was striding swiftly through the crowd, one hand on his sword.

The room was in confusion. Claudia felt Jared grab her sleeve. "Come on," he said.

They hurried to the door of the Privy Chamber, pushing through the perfumed and bewigged mass of bodies, Claudia gasping breathlessly, "Who is he? Has the Queen set this up?"

"If so, she's an excellent actress."

"Caspar hasn't got the brains."

"Certain metal animals then?"

She stared at him for a second, wide-eyed. Then the spears of the door-guards clashed in front of her.

Astonished, she said, "Let me through."

A flustered footman murmured, "I'm sorry, my lady. Sapienti and Privy Council only." He glanced at Jared. "You can enter, Master."

Claudia drew herself up. For a moment Jared almost felt sorry for the man.

"I am the Warden of Incarceron's daughter," she said in a voice that dripped ice. "You will stand aside now, before I ensure your transfer to the most rat-ridden keep in this Realm."

The footman was young. He swallowed. "Madam . . ."

"Not a word." She stared at him, impassive. "Just move."

For a moment Jared wondered if it would work. And then an amused murmur came from behind them. "Oh let her in. What harm can it do? I wouldn't want you to miss all the fun, Claudia."

Faced with a grinning Caspar, the footman shrank. The guards stood back.

Instantly Claudia swept past them and through the door. Jared waited, and bowed, and the Prince hurried after her, his bodyguard close as a shadow. Walking behind, the Sapient felt the door click shut at his back.

The Privy Chamber was small and smelled musty. The seats were of ancient red leather, arranged in a horseshoe, the Queen's in the center with her coat of arms suspended over it. The Councilors sat, the Sapienti gathered behind them.

Not knowing where to go, Finn stood near the Queen, trying to ignore Caspar's grin, the way he leaned over and said something in his mother's ear, the way she tinkled a laugh.

Claudia came and stood next to him, her arms folded. They said nothing to each other.

"Well?" The Queen leaned forward graciously. "You may approach."

The boy in the yellow coat came and stood within the horseshoe. Every eye was on him, but he seemed completely at his ease. Finn looked him over with instinctive dislike. The same height as himself. Brown, wavy hair. Brown eyes. Smiling. Confident.

Finn scowled.

The stranger said, "Your Majesty. My lords. I have made a serious claim, and I understand the gravity of it. But I intend to prove to you that what I say is true. I am indeed Giles Alexander Ferdinand of the Havaarna, Lord of the Southern Isles, Count of Marly, Crown Prince of this Realm."

He was talking to all of them, but his eyes were on the Queen. And just for a bright second, on Claudia.

"Liar," Finn snarled.

The Queen said, "I will have silence."

The Pretender smiled. "I was brought up among you until my fifteenth year. Many of you will remember me. You, Lord Burgogne. You will remember the times I borrowed your fine horses, the time I lost your goshawk in the Great Forest."

The Councilor, an elderly man in a black furred robe, looked startled.

"My lady Amelia will remember the day when her son and I fell out of a tree dressed as pirates and nearly landed on top of her." His smile was warm. One of the Queen's ladies of the Chamber nodded. Her face was white. "It was so," she whispered. "How we laughed!"

"Indeed we did. I have many such memories." He folded his arms. "My lords, I know all of you. I can tell you where you live, the names of your ladies. I have played with your children. I can answer any question you ask me about my tutors; my dear bodyservant, Bartlett; my father, the late King; and my mother,

Queen Argente." For a moment then, a shadow crossed his face. But he smiled and shook his head. "Which is more than this Prisoner, with his oh-so-convenient memory loss, can do."

Beside her, Claudia felt Finn's stillness like a threat.

"So where have I been all this time, you will be asking. Why was my death faked? Or perhaps you will already have heard from my gracious stepmother, the Queen, how my supposed fall from my horse at the age of fifteen was . . . arranged, as a protection for my own safety."

Claudia bit her lip. He was using the truth and twisting it. He was very clever. Or had been well taught.

"It was a time of great danger. There is a secret and sinister organization, gentlemen, of which you may have heard. It is known as the Clan of the Steel Wolves. Their plans have only recently been foiled, with the failure of their attempt on Queen Sia's life, and the exposure of their leader, the disgraced Warden of Incarceron."

Now he was not looking at Claudia. He was playing the audience like an expert, his voice clear and steady. "Our spies have been aware of them for years, and it was known that they planned my death. My death, and the revoking of the Edict. The end of Protocol. They would return us to the terrors and chaos of the Years of Rage. And so I disappeared. Not even the Queen knew of my plans. I realized that the only way to be safe was to make them think I was already dead. And to await my time." He smiled. "Now, my lords, that time has come."

He beckoned, his gesture regal, and natural, and a footman brought a package of paper to him.

Claudia chewed her lip anxiously.

"I have here documentary evidence of what I say. My royal line, my birth deeds, many letters I have received, invitations—many of you wrote them. You will recognize them. I have the portrait of my fiancée as a child, given by her to me at our engagement."

Claudia drew in a sharp breath. She glanced up at him, and he looked steadily back.

"Above all, lords and masters, I have the evidence of my own flesh."

He held up his hand, drew back the lacy ruffle of his sleeve, turned slowly so that the whole room could see.

On his wrist, tattooed deep into the skin, was the crowned Eagle of the Havaarnas.

10

Hand to hand, skin to skin,
Twin in a mirror, Incarceron.
Fear to fear, desire to desire,
Eye to eye. Prison to prison.
　　　　　—Songs of Sapphique

It had heard them.

"Move!" Keiro yelled.

Attia grabbed the reins and saddle, but the horse was terrified; it circled and whickered, and before she could scramble up Keiro had jumped back, swearing. She turned.

The Chain-gang waited. It was male, twelve-headed, helmeted, the bodies fused at hand and wrist and hip, linked with umbilical skin-chains from shoulder to shoulder or waist to waist. Beams of light shone from some of its hands; in others were weapons; blades, cleavers, a rusted firelock.

Keiro had his own firelock out. He leveled it at the center of the huddled thing. "No nearer. Keep well away."

Torch beams focused on him. Attia clung to the horse, its sweaty flank hot and trembling under her hand.

The Chain-gang opened and its bodies moved apart; it became a line of shadows, the movement making her think stupidly of paper chains she had made as a child, cutting a man and then pulling wide a line of them.

"I said keep back!" Keiro swiveled the weapon along the line. His hand was steady, but he could only fire at one part of it, and then surely the rest would attack. Or would they?

The Chain-gang spoke.

"We want food."

Its voice was a ripple of repetitions, one over another.

"We've nothing to give you."

"Liar. We smell bread. We smell flesh."

Was it one, or many? Did it have one brain, controlling its bodies like limbs, or was each of them a man, eternally and horribly joined? Attia stared at it, fascinated.

Keiro swore. Then he said, "Throw it the bag."

Carefully, Attia took the food bag off the horse and threw it onto the ice. It skittered over the ground. A long arm reached down and gathered it up. It disappeared into the creature's misshapen darkness.

"Not enough."

"There's no more," she said.

"We smell the beast. Its hot blood. Its sweet meat."

She glanced at Keiro in alarm. Without the horse they were trapped here. She stood beside him. "No. Not the horse."

Faint crackles of static lit the sky. She prayed the lights would come on. But this was the Ice Wing, eternally dark.

"Leave," Keiro said savagely. "Or I blow you away. I mean it!"

"Which of us? The Prison has joined us. You cannot divide us."

It was moving in. Out of the corner of her eye Attia saw movement; she gasped, "It's all around." She backed off, terrified, suddenly sure that if one of its hands touched her, the fingers would grow into hers.

Clinking with steel the Chain-gang had almost surrounded them. Only the frozen falls behind offered some protection; Keiro backed up against the seamed ice and snapped, "Get on the horse, Attia."

"What about you?"

"Get on the horse!"

She hauled herself up. The linked men lurched forward.

Instantly the horse reared.

Keiro fired.

A blue bolt of flame drilled the central torso; the man vaporized instantly, and the Chain-gang screamed in unison, eleven voices in a howl of rage.

Attia forced the horse around; leaning down to grab Keiro, she saw the thing reunite, its hands joining, the skin-chains slithering, regrowing tight.

Keiro turned to leap up behind her, but it was on him. He yelled and kicked out, but the hands were greedy. They had him around the neck and the waist; they tugged him from the horse. He struggled, swearing viciously, but there were too many of them, they were all over him, and their knives flashed in the blue ice-light. Attia fought the panicking horse, leaned down, snatched the firelock from him, and aimed it.

If she fired she'd kill him.

Skin-chains were wrapping him like tentacles. It was absorbing him; he would take the place of the dead man.

"Attia!" His yell was muffled. The horse reared; she struggled to keep it from bolting.

"Attia!" For a moment his face was clear; he saw her.

"Fire!" he screamed.

She couldn't.

"Fire! *Shoot me!*"

For a moment she was frozen in terror.

Then she brought the weapon up and fired.

⊰◦◦◦⊱

"HOW CAN this have happened?" Finn stormed across the room and flung himself into the metal chair. He stared around at the humming gray mystery that was the Portal. "And why meet here?"

"Because it's the only place in the entire Court that I'm certain isn't bugged." Jared closed the door carefully, feeling the strange effect the room had, the way it straightened out, as if adapting to their presence. As it must do, if, as he suspected, it was some halfway stage to the Prison.

Feathers still littered the floor. Finn kicked at them.

"Where is she?"

130

"She'll be here."

Jared watched the boy; Finn stared back. Quieter, he said, "Master, do you doubt me too?"

"Too?"

"You saw him. And Claudia . . ."

"Claudia believes you are Giles. She always has, from the moment she first heard your voice."

"She hadn't seen him then. She said his name." Finn got up, walked restlessly to the screen. "Did you see how polished he was? How he smiled and bowed and held himself like a prince? I can't do that, Master. If I ever knew how, I've forgotten. The Prison has scoured it out of me."

"A skilled actor . . ."

Finn spun around. "Do you believe him? Tell me the truth."

Jared linked his delicate fingers together. He shrugged slightly. "I am a scholar, Finn. I am not so easily convinced. These so-called proofs will be examined. There will certainly be a process of questioning, for both him and you, before the Council. Now that there are two claimants to the throne, every-thing has changed." He glanced sidelong at Finn. "I thought you weren't eager to take up your inheritance."

"I am now." Finn's voice was a growl. "Keiro always says what you fought for, you should keep. I only ever talked him out of anything once."

"When you left the gang?" Jared watched him. "These things

you've told us about the Prison, Finn. I need to know they are true. About the Maestra. About the Key."

"I told you. She gave me the Key, and then she was killed. She fell into the Abyss. Someone betrayed us. It wasn't my fault." He was resentful. But Jared's voice was pitiless.

"She died because of you. And this memory of the forest, of falling from the horse. I need to be sure that it's real, Finn. Not just what you think Claudia needs to hear."

Finn's head jerked up. "A lie, you mean!"

"Indeed."

Jared knew he was taking a risk. He kept his gaze level. "The Council will want to hear it too, in every detail. They will question you over and over. It will be them you have to convince, not Claudia."

"If anyone else said this, Master, I'd . . ."

"Is that why your hand is on your sword?"

Finn clenched his fingers. Slowly, he wrapped both arms around himself and went and slumped in the metal chair.

They were silent awhile, and Jared could hear the faint hum of the tilted room, a sound he had never succeeded in isolating. Finally Finn said, "Violence was our way of life in the Prison."

"I know. I know how hard it must be . . ."

"Because I'm not sure." He turned. "I'm not sure, Master, who I am! How can I convince the Court when I'm not even convinced myself!"

"You have to. Everything depends on you." Jared's green eyes were fixed on him. "Because if you are supplanted, if Claudia loses her inheritance, and I am . . ." He stopped.

Finn saw his pale fingers fold together. "Well, there will be no one to care about the injustices of Incarceron. And you will never see Keiro again."

The door opened, and Claudia swept in. She looked hot and flustered; there was dust on her silk dress. She said, "He's staying in Court. Would you believe it! She's given him a suite of rooms in the Ivory Tower."

Neither of them answered. Feeling the tension in the room, she glanced at Jared, then took the blue velvet pouch out of her pocket and crossed the room with it.

"Remember this, Master?"

Undoing the drawstring, she tipped it up and a miniature painting slid out, a masterly work in its frame of gold and pearls, the back engraved with the crowned eagle.

She gave it to Finn and he held it in both hands. It showed a boy smiling, his eyes dark in the sunlight. His gaze was shy, but direct and open.

"Is it me?"

"Don't you recognize yourself?"

When he answered, the pain in his voice shocked her.

"No. Not anymore. That boy had never seen men killed for scraps of food, had never tormented an old woman to show where her few coins were hidden. He'd never wept in a cell with his mind torn away, never lain awake at night hearing the screams of children. He's not me. He's never been taunted by the Prison."

He thrust the image back at her and rolled up his sleeve. "Look at me, Claudia."

His arms were pocked with old scars and burns. She had no idea how he had gotten them. The mark of the Havaarna Eagle was faded and indistinct.

She made her voice strong. "Well, he's never seen the stars, then, not like you've seen them. This was you." She held it alongside him, and Jared came to see.

The resemblance was unquestionable. And yet she knew that the boy down there in the hall looked like this too, and without the haunted pallor Finn still had, without the thinness of face and that lost something in the eyes.

Not wanting him to sense her doubt she said, "Jared and I found this in the cottage of an old man named Bartlett. He looked after you when you were small. He left a document, about how much he loved you, how he thought of you as his son."

Hopelessly, Finn shook his head.

She went on fiercely. "I have paintings too, but this is better than all of them. I think you must have given it to him. He was the one who knew after the accident that the body wasn't yours, that you were still alive."

"Where is he? Can we get him here?"

She caught Jared's eye and he said quietly, "Bartlett is dead, Finn."

"Because of me?"

"He knew. They got to him."

Finn shrugged. "Then I'm sorry. But the only old man I loved was called Gildas. And he's dead too."

Something crackled.

The screen on the desk spat light. It flickered.

Jared ran straight to it, Claudia close behind. "What was that? What happened?"

"Some connection. Maybe . . ."

He turned. Something had changed in the hum of the room. It seemed to draw back, to ratchet up the scale. With a screech Claudia ran and hauled Finn out of the chair with such a jerk that they both almost fell over. "It's working! The Portal! But how!"

"From Inside." White with tension Jared watched the chair. They all stared at it, not knowing what to expect, who might come. Finn snatched out his sword.

Light flashed, the blinding brilliance Jared remembered.

And on the chair was a feather.

It was as big as a man.

∞∞∞∞

THE FIRELOCK spat flame. It sliced through the ice under the feet of the Chain-gang and the creature howled, toppling and sliding down the collapsed floe. Its bodies tangled, grabbing at one another. Attia fired again, targeting the smashed plates of ice, yelling, "Come on!"

Keiro struggled to get clear. He fought and bit and kicked with furious energy, but his feet too were slipping into the slush, and there was still a hand gripping his long coat. Then the fabric tore and for a moment he was free.

He reached up and she leaned and grabbed him; he was heavy, but the terror of being pulled back and smothered made him scramble over the horse's back behind her.

Attia shoved the weapon under her arm, struggling with the reins. The horse was panicking; as it reared a great crack split the night. Glancing down Attia saw that all the ice was breaking up; from the crater she had made, black crevasses were zigzagging out. Icicles snapped off the waterfall, smashing in jagged heaps.

The firelock was snatched from her. Keiro yelled, "Keep it still!" but the horse tossed its head in fear, its hooves clattering and sliding down the frozen slabs.

The Chain-gang was struggling, half in meltwater. Some of its bodies lay under the others, its chains of sinew and skin iced with frost.

Keiro raised the weapon.

"NO!" Attia screamed. "We can get away." And then, when he didn't lower it, "They were men once!"

"If they remember they'll thank me." Keiro's voice was grim. The blast scorched them. He fired three, four, five times, coldly and efficiently, until the weapon sputtered and coughed and was useless. Then he threw it down into the charred crater.

Attia's hands were sore on the leather reins. She fought the horse to a standstill.

In the eerie silence the faintest whisper of wind crusted the snow. She could not look down at the dead men; instead she gazed up at the distant roof and felt a shiver of wonder, because for a moment she thought she saw thousands of tiny points of shimmering light in that black firmament, as if the stars that Finn had told her of were there.

Keiro said, "Let's get out of this hellhole."

"How?" she muttered.

The tundra was a web of crevasses. Under the broken ice, water was rising, an ocean of metallic gray. And the glistening specks were not stars, they were the outlying skeins of a silver fog, slowly circling down from Incarceron's heights.

The fog came down into their faces. It said, *You should not have killed my creatures, halfman.*

<hr />

CLAUDIA STARED at the huge central stalk of the feather, the great blue barbs linked stiffly with each other. Carefully she reached out and touched the fluffy plumes at the end. The feather was identical to the tiny one Jared had picked up from the lawn. But gross, swollen. Wholly wrong.

Amazed, she whispered, "What does it mean?"

An amused voice answered her. "It means, my dear, that I am returning your little gift."

For a moment she couldn't move. Then she said, "Father?"

Finn took her arm and turned her. She saw, appearing on the screen very slowly, pixel by pixel, the image of a man. As the picture completed itself she recognized him, the severity of his dark coat, the brushed perfection of his hair, tied elegantly back. The Warden of Incarceron, the man she still thought of as her father, was looking down at her.

"Can you see me?" she gasped.

There it was. His old, cold smile.

"Of course I can see you, Claudia. I think you would be surprised what I can see." His gray eyes turned to Jared. "Master Sapient, I congratulate you. I had thought the damage I had done to the Portal would be enough. It seems, as ever, that I underestimated you."

Claudia linked her hands in front of her. She straightened up, the way she always stood rigidly upright before him, as if she were a small child again, as if his clear gaze diminished her.

"I return the materials of your experiment," the Warden said drily. "As you can see, the problems of scale remain. I would advise you strongly, Jared, not to send anything living through the Portal. The results might be fatal to all of us."

Jared frowned. "But the feathers arrived there?"

The Warden smiled and did not answer.

Claudia couldn't wait any longer. The words burst out of her. "Are you really in Incarceron?"

"Where else?"

"But where is it? You never told us!"

A flicker of surprise crossed his face. He leaned back, and she saw he was in some dark place, because a glimmer like flamelight reflected briefly in his eyes. A soft pulsing sound came from somewhere in the darkness. "Didn't I? Well I'm afraid, Claudia, that you must ask your precious tutor about that."

She glanced at Jared. He seemed embarrassed, not meeting her eyes.

"Can you really not have told her, Master?" The mockery in her father's voice was clear. "And I thought you had no secrets in your little partnership. Well, it seems you should be careful, Claudia. Power corrupts all men. Even Sapienti."

"Power?" she snapped.

His hands opened elegantly, but before she could demand more Finn elbowed her aside.

"Where's Keiro? What's happening to him?"

The Warden said coldly, "How should I know?"

"When you were Blaize you had a tower full of books! The Prison's records of everyone. You could find him . . ."

"Do you really care?" The Warden leaned forward. "Well then, I'll tell you. At this moment he is fighting for his life with a monstrous creature of many heads."

Catching Finn's shocked stillness, he laughed. "And you're not there to watch his back. That must hurt. But this is where he belongs. This is Keiro's world, without friendship, without love. And you, Prisoner, belong here too."

The screen flickered and spat.

"Father . . ." Claudia said quickly.

"So you still call me that?"

"What else can I call you?" She stepped forward. "You're the only father I know."

For a moment he gazed at her, and she noticed in the disintegrating image that his hair was a little grayer than it had been, his face more lined. Then he said quietly, "I am a Prisoner too now, Claudia."

"You can Escape. You have the Keys . . ."

"Had." He shrugged. "Incarceron has taken them."

The image was rippling. Desperately she said, "But why?"

"The Prison is consumed with desire. Sapphique began it, because when he wore the Glove, he and the Prison became one mind. He infected it."

"With a disease?"

"A desire. And desire can be a disease, Claudia." He was watching her, his face shivering and dissolving and re-forming. "You are to blame too, for describing it all so well. And so Incarceron burns with longing. For all its thousand eyes there is one thing it has never seen, and it will do anything to see."

"What?" she breathed, already knowing.

"Outside," he whispered.

For a moment no one spoke. Then Finn leaned forward. "What about me? Am I Giles? Did you put me in the Prison? *Tell me!*"

The Warden smiled at him.

Then the screen went blank.

There is a growing terror in speaking with the Prison. My secrets seem small and pitiful. My dreams seem foolish. I begin to fear it can see even into my mind.

—Lord Calliston's Diary

The fog slid between them. It was icy. A mist of millions of droplets. Attia felt it chill her skin, condense on her lips.

"Remember me, Attia?" it whispered.

She scowled. "I remember."

"Ride," Keiro muttered.

She urged the horse on gently. But it slithered and the ground tilted, and she knew Incarceron had them trapped here, because the temperature was rising fast and the whole Wing was melting around them.

Keiro must have felt it too. He snapped, "Leave us alone. Go and torture some other inmates."

"I know you, halfman." The voice was close, in their ears, against their cheeks. *"You are part of me, my atoms beat in your heart, itch in your skin. I should kill you now. I should melt the ice and let you drown here."*

Suddenly Attia slid down from the horse. She stared up into

the gray night. "But you won't. You've been watching me all the time. You wrote that message on the wall!"

"That I would see the stars? Yes, I used the fool's hand. Because I will see them, Attia, and you will help me."

Light was gathering. It showed her that through the fog two great red Eyes were being lowered on cables. They gleamed like rubies, one so close to Keiro, its hot glare scorched him. He slid down hastily, close behind her.

"I have spent centuries longing to Escape, but who can escape themselves? The Warden tries to tell me it won't work, but my plan had only one flaw and you have solved that."

"What do you mean, the Warden?" Keiro snapped. "He's out there with his precious daughter and her Prince."

The Prison laughed. Its amusement was a rumble that split the ice; floes splashed into the rising sea of meltwater. The berg they were standing on tipped; lumps fell from its edge.

The fog opened a cavernous mouth. *"I see you don't know. The Warden is Inside now, and forever, because both the Keys are mine. I have used their energy to build my body."*

The ice was unsteady. Attia grabbed the horse. "Your body?" she whispered.

"In which I will Escape."

Keiro said, "That's not possible."

They both knew somehow that they had to keep it talking, that one whim of the Prison's fickle cruelty could tip them into the icy water, that it could open ducts that would sweep them away, deep into the endless drains and tunnels of its metallic heart.

"You would say that." Incarceron's voice was rich with contempt. *"You who cannot leave here because of your imperfections. But Sapphique's dream of the stars is mine now, and there is a way. A secret way, a way no one expects. I am building myself a body. Like a man's but greater, a winged creature. It will be tall and beautiful and perfect. Its eyes will be of emerald and it will walk and run and fly, and in it I will put all my personality and power and leave the Prison an empty shell. You have the final piece that I need to complete it."*

"Do we?"

"You know you do. I have sought my son's lost Glove for centuries; it has been kept secret, even from me." It laughed, amused. *"But that fool Rix found it. And you have it here."*

Keiro gave Attia a stare of alarm. The ice platform was floating now, and on each side the fog swirled so thickly, they could see nothing of the tundra. She felt that the Prison had indeed swallowed them, that they were traveling deep inside its vast belly, like the man in the whale in Rix's patchbook.

Rix. His words flared in her memory. *The Art Magicke is the art of illusion.*

Waves lifted under the thinning ice. Far off in the fog she saw the links of a vast chain, hanging down. They were being washed toward it. Rapidly she said, "You want it?"

"It will be my right hand."

Keiro's eyes were blue and bright. She saw at once what he was planning. He said, "You'll never get it."

"My son, I could kill you now and take it . . ."

The Glove was in Keiro's hands. "Not before I put it on. Not before I know everything about you."

"No."

"Watch me."

"NO!" Lightning flickered. The fog poured in, over the horse, hiding them from each other. Attia gripped Keiro's elbow, felt his heat through the coat.

"Perhaps it's time we made a few conditions then." Keiro was invisible, but his voice was steely. "I have the Glove. I could wear it. I could tear it apart in seconds. But if you want it, I could bring it to you."

The Prison was silent.

She felt Keiro shrug. "It's up to you. It seems to me this is the only thing in this Hell you can't control. The Glove was Sapphique's. It has strange power. Spare our lives and show us the way, and it's yours. Otherwise I put it on. And what will that make me?"

She could see him now. The fog retreated, drew back. In a moment of horror she realized that they were alone on a berg of ice in a wide sea of water, a greasy metallic ocean. It stretched as far as she could see in every direction, and the two Eyes of the Prison slid into it and stared up at her thoughtfully through its slow, turgid ripples.

"Your arrogance is surprising."

"I've had a lot of practice," Keiro said.

"You cannot know what the Glove does."

"You don't know what I know." He stared down, defiant. "There are no little red Eyes in my brain, tyrant."

Lights came on. High in the roof Attia glimpsed walkways and suspended roads, a whole Wing miles above them, where tiny dots that must be people clustered and looked down.

"Ah, but what if there are, halfman? What if I see even there?"

Keiro laughed. It was hollow, but if the Prison had just named his own darkest dread, he covered it well. "You don't scare me. Men made you, men can unmake you."

"Indeed." The voice was dry and angry. *"Then very well, we will make a deal. Bring me the Glove and I will reward you with Escape. But should you ever attempt to put it on I will burn you and it to a cinder. I will have no rivals."*

The chain hung before them. It was huge and heavy and it fell into the sea with a splash, the molten water sending up a thick spray that Attia could taste on her lips. As the metal rattled down, they saw that a transitway was dragged behind it, a track that unrolled on the sea's heaving surface, vanishing into the remnants of mist.

Keiro hauled himself back onto the horse, but before he could ride Attia said, "Don't even think about leaving me here."

"I don't need you. I've got the Glove now."

"You need an oathbrother."

"I've got one of those too."

"Yes," she said sourly. "But he's busy."

Keiro stared down at her. His hair was long and damp; it gleamed in the light. His eyes were cold and calculating; for a moment she knew he would ride away. And then he leaned down and hauled her up.

"Only till I find someone better," he said.

⁂

THE QUEEN held a State dinner that evening in the Claimants' honor.

As Claudia sat at the long table licking the last traces of lemon syllabub from her spoon, she thought of her father. Seeing him had shaken her. He had looked thinner, his contempt less assured. She hadn't been able to stop thinking about what he'd said. But surely Incarceron, the very intelligence the Sapienti had created, could never leave the Prison, because if it did all that would be left would be a dark shell of metal. Millions of Prisoners would die, without light, air, food. It had to be impossible.

Trying not to think of it, she watched Finn anxiously through the candles and wax fruit and hothouse arrangements. He had been placed next to the Countess of Amaby, one of the teasing, mincing women of the Court who were fascinated by his moodiness, and who would gossip maliciously about him afterward. He seemed to be barely answering her endless chat, staring into his wine cup, and drinking too much, Claudia thought.

"Poor Finn. He looks so unhappy," the Pretender murmured.

Claudia frowned. Queen Sia had placed the two Prince Gileses opposite each other, halfway down the table, and now from her throne was watching them both.

"Yes. Well, that's your fault." Claudia put the spoon into her dish and looked straight at him. "Who *are* you? Who's put you up to this?"

The boy who called himself Giles smiled sadly. "You know who I am, Claudia. You just won't admit it to yourself."

"Finn is Giles."

"No, he isn't. It was convenient for you to believe that once. I don't at all blame you. If I'd had to face marrying Caspar, I'd have done something as drastic, and I'm sorry for leaving you to such a fate . . . But you know you'd already started to doubt Finn even before I came back from the dead. Hadn't you?"

She watched him in the candlelight and he leaned back and smiled. Close to, his resemblance to Finn was astonishing, but it was as if they were strange twins—one bright, the other dark, one easy, the other tormented. Giles—she didn't know what else to call him—wore a silk coat of peach satin, his dark hair perfectly groomed and tied in a black ribbon. His fingernails, she noticed, were manicured, the hands of someone who had never worked. He smelled of lemon and sandalwood. His table manners were exquisite.

"You're so sure of yourself," she murmured. "But you have no idea what I think."

"Don't I?" He leaned forward as the footmen cleared the dishes and set small gilt-edged plates. "We were always alike, Claudia. I used to say to Bartlett—"

"Bartlett?" She stared at him, uneasy.

"A dear old man who was my chamberlain. He was the one I talked to most, after Father died, about us, about our marriage. He said you were a haughty little thing, but he liked you."

She sipped her wine, barely tasting it. The things he said, his casual memories, disturbed her. *A haughty little thing.* The old man had written something almost identical in the secret testament she and Jared had found. And surely only they knew of its existence.

As small dishes of strawberries were served she said, "If Giles was locked in Incarceron, the Queen was part of the plot. So she must know Finn is the real Prince."

He smiled, shaking his head, eating the fruit.

"She doesn't want Finn to be King," Claudia went on, stubborn. "But if he died, it would be far too suspicious. So she decides to discredit him. First she needs to find someone who's the same age, and who looks like him."

Giles said, "These strawberries are really wonderful."

"Did she send out messengers through the Realm?" Claudia dipped a finger in the bowl of rosewater. "They must have been delighted when they found you. A real look-alike."

"You really should try them." His smile was warm.

"A bit too sweet for me."

"Then let me." He swapped his dish for hers, politely. "You were saying?"

"Only two months to train you. Not enough, but you're clever. You'd learn fast. First they'd use a skinwand, get the likeness exact. Then they'd drill you in etiquette, family history, what Giles ate, rode, liked, who he played with, what he studied. They'd teach you to ride and dance. They'd make you memorize his whole childhood." She glanced at him. "They must have a few Sapienti in their pay. And they must have promised you a fortune."

"Or be holding my poor dear mother in a dungeon, maybe."

"Or that."

"But I'm to be King, remember?"

"They'll never let you be King." Claudia glanced over at Sia. "They'll kill you, when you've served your purpose."

For a moment he was silent, dabbing his mouth with a linen napkin, and she thought she'd scared him. Then she saw he was gazing at Finn through the haze of candle smoke, and when he answered, his light humor had vanished. "I came back to save the Realm from being ruled by a thief and a murderer." He turned. "And to save you from him too."

150

Startled, she glanced down. His fingers touched hers on the white tablecloth.

Carefully, she drew her hand away. "I don't need saving."

"I think you do. From that barbarian, and from my evil stepmother. We should stand together, Claudia. We should watch each other's back, and think of the future." He turned the crystal glass carefully. "Because I will be King. And I will need a Queen I can trust."

Before she could answer, a loud rapping came from the high end of the table. The majordomo was beating the floor with his staff. "Your excellencies. Lords, ladies, Masters. The Queen will speak."

The babble of chatter hushed. Claudia caught Finn's dark glare, fixed on her; she ignored it and looked at Sia. The Queen was standing, a white figure, her pale neck glistening with a diamond necklace that caught the flamelight in its rainbow brilliants. She said, "Dear friends. Let me give you a toast."

Hands went to glasses. Down the table Claudia saw the peacock-bright coats of the men, and the women's satins shimmer. Behind, in the shadows, rows of silent footmen waited.

"To our two Claimants. To dear Giles." She raised her glass archly to the Pretender, then turned to Finn. "And dear Giles."

Finn glowered. Someone tittered a nervous laugh. In the moment of tension no one seemed to breathe.

"Our two Princes. Tomorrow the investigation will begin

into their stories." Sia's voice was light; she smiled coyly. "This . . . rather unfortunate situation will be resolved. The true Prince will be discovered, I do assure you. As for the other, the Impostor, I'm afraid he will pay dearly for the inconvenience and anxiety he has caused our Realm." Her smile was icy now. "He will be shamed and tortured. And then he will be executed."

Utter silence.

Into it she said lightly, "But with a sword, not an ax. As befits royalty." She raised her glass. "To Prince Giles of the Havaarna."

Everyone stood, in a rattle of chairs. "Prince Giles," they murmured.

As she drank, Claudia tried to hide her shock, tried to catch Finn's eye, but it was too late. He stood slowly, as if the long tension of the meal had broken, glaring across at the Pretender. His stillness made the buzz and chatter subside into quiet curiosity.

"I am Giles," he said, "and Queen Sia knows it. She knows my memory was lost in Incarceron. She knows I have no hope of answering any of the Council's questions." The bitterness of his voice made Claudia's heart thump. She put down her glass hurriedly and said, "Finn," but he stormed on as if he hadn't heard her, his gaze hard on the courtiers.

"What should I do, ladies and gentlemen? Do you want me to take a DNA test? I'll do it. But then, that wouldn't be Protocol, would it? That would be forbidden! The technology for that is hidden and only the Queen knows where. And she's not saying."

The guards at the door edged forward. One drew his sword.

If Finn saw, he didn't care. "There's only one way to solve this, the way of honor, the way we'd do it in Incarceron."

He pulled a glove from his pocket, a studded gauntlet, and before Claudia realized what it meant he had shoved the dishes aside and flung it between the candles and flowers. It struck the Pretender full in the face; a shocked murmur rippled down the table.

"Fight me." Finn's voice was thick with anger. "I challenge you. Any weapons. Your choice. Fight me for the Realm."

Giles's face was white, his control icy. He said, "I would be most happy to kill you, sir, at any hour and with any weapon I can find."

"Absolutely not." The Queen's voice was sharp. "There will be no dueling. I totally forbid it."

The two Claimants glared at each other, like reflections in a smoky mirror. From down the table Caspar's drawl rose. "Oh let them, Mama. It would save so much bother."

Sia ignored him. "There will be no duel, gentlemen. And the investigation will begin tomorrow." She held Finn with her ice-pale eyes. "I will not be disobeyed."

He bowed stiffly and then thrust back his chair and stalked out, the guards moving hastily aside. Claudia stood, but Giles said softly, "Don't go, Claudia. He's nothing, and he knows it."

For a moment she paused. Then she sat. She told herself it was because Protocol forbade anyone leaving before the Queen, but Giles smiled at her, as if he knew something else.

Furious, she fidgeted for twenty minutes, her fingers tapping her empty glass, and when finally the Queen rose and she could slip away, she raced up to his room and knocked on the door.

"Finn. Finn, it's me."

If he was there, he would not answer.

Finally, she walked down the paneled corridor to the casement at its end and gazed out at the lawns, leaning her forehead on the cool glass. She wanted to storm and yell at him. What was he thinking of? How would fighting help! It was just the sort of stupid, arrogant thing Keiro would have done.

But he wasn't Keiro.

And biting her nail, she recognized, deep inside herself, the sickening doubt that had been growing in her mind for two months. That perhaps she had made a terrible mistake.

That perhaps he wasn't Giles either.

12

*He opened the window and looked out at
the night. "The world is an endless loop,"
he said. "A Möbius strip, a wheel in which
we run. As you have discovered, who have
traveled so far just to find yourself where
you started from."*

*Sapphique went on stroking the blue cat.
"So you can't help me?"*

He shrugged. "I didn't say that."

—Sapphique and the Dark Enchanter

The trackway undulated over the leaden sea.

At first Keiro let the horse gallop, and whooped at
the speed and the freedom, but that was dangerous, because the
metal trackway was slippery, slushy water washing right over it.
The mist hung close, so that Attia felt they were riding through
cloud with only glimpses now and then of distant dark shapes,
which might have been islands or hills.

Once, a jagged chasm gaped to one side.

Finally the horse was so weary, it could barely run.

After nearly three hours Attia came back from drowsiness to
realize that the sea was gone. Around them the mist was shredding, to reveal a jungle of spiny cacti and aloes, head high, the

great leaves blade-sharp. A path ran straight into it, the plants at each side curled and crisp, smoking blackly, as if Incarceron had drilled this road only minutes ago.

"It's not going to let us get lost, is it?" Keiro muttered.

They dismounted and made an uncomfortable camp in the fringe of the forest. Gazing in, Attia smelled the scorched soil, saw the skeletons of leaves like cobwebs of fine metal.

Though neither of them said anything, she saw Keiro eyeing the undergrowth uneasily, and as if the Prison mocked their fear, it put the lights out, abruptly.

There was little left to eat—some dried meat and a cheese that Attia sliced the mold from, and two apples stolen from Rix's stores for the horse. As she chewed, she said, "You're crazier than Rix."

He looked at her. "Am I?"

"Keiro, you can't make deals with Incarceron! It will never let you Escape, and if we bring it the Glove . . ."

"Not your problem." He threw the apple core away, lay down, and wrapped a blanket around him.

"Of course it is." She glared at his back furiously. "Keiro!"

But he didn't answer, and she had to sit, nursing her anger, until the change in his light breathing told her he was asleep.

They should have taken turns to keep watch. But she was too tired to care, and so they both slept at once, curled in musty blankets while the tethered horse snuffled hungrily.

Attia dreamed of Sapphique. Sometime in the night he

came out of the forest and sat down next to her, stirring up the glowing ashes of the fire with a stick, and she rolled over and stared at him. His long dark hair shadowed his face. The high collar of his robe was worn and frayed. He said, "The light is going."

"What?"

"Can't you feel it being used up? Fading away?" He glanced at her sideways. "The light is slipping through our hands."

She glanced at the hand holding the charred stick. The right forefinger was missing, its stump seamed white with scars. She whispered, "Where is it going, Master?"

"Into the Prison's dreams." He stirred the fire, and his face was narrow and strained. "This is all my fault, Attia. I showed Incarceron that there is a way Out."

"Tell me how." Her voice was urgent; she shuffled up close to him. "How you did it. How you Escaped."

"Every Prison has a crack."

"What crack?"

He smiled. "The tiniest, most secret way. So small, the Prison does not even know it exists."

"But where is it? And does the Key open it, the Key the Warden has?"

"The Key unlocks only the Portal."

She suddenly felt cold with fear, because he replicated before her, a whole line of him like images in a mirror, like the Chaingang in its manacles of flesh.

She shook her head, bewildered. "We have your Glove. Keiro says—"

"Don't put your hand into that of a beast." His words whispered through the spiny undergrowth. "Or you will be made to do its work. Keep my Glove safe for me, Attia."

The fire crackled. Ashes shifted. He became his own shadow, and was gone.

She must have slept again, because it seemed hours later when the clink of metal woke her, and she sat up and saw Keiro saddling the horse. She wanted to tell him about the dream, but it was already hard to remember. Instead she yawned and stared up at the Prison's distant ceiling.

After a while she said, "Do the lights seem different to you?"

Keiro tugged the girth straps. "Different how?"

"Weaker."

He glanced at her, then up. For a minute he was still. Then he went on loading the horse. "Maybe."

"I'm sure they are." Incarceron's lights were always powerful, but now there seemed a faint flicker to them. She said, "If the Prison is really building a body for itself it must be using enormous reserves of power to do it. Draining energy from its systems. Maybe the Ice Wing isn't the only Wing shut down. We haven't seen anyone since that. . . creature back there. Where are they all?"

Keiro stood back. "Can't say I care."

"You should."

He shrugged. "Rule of the Scum. Care for no one but your brother."

"Sister."

"I told you, you're temporary."

Later, climbing up behind him onto the horse, she said, "What happens when we get to wherever Incarceron is taking us? Are you just going to hand over the Glove?"

She felt Keiro's snort of laughter through his gaudy scarlet jerkin. "Watch and learn, little dog-slave."

"You haven't got a clue. Keiro, listen to me! We can't help it do this!"

"Not even for a way Out?"

"For you, maybe. But what about the others? What about everyone else?"

Keiro urged the horse to a run. "No one in this hellhole has ever cared for me," he said quietly.

"Finn . . ."

"Not even Finn. So why should I care for them? They're not me, Attia. They don't exist for me."

It was useless arguing with him. But as they rode into the dim undergrowth she let herself think of the terror of it, of the Prison shutting down, the lights going off and never coming back on, the cold spreading. Systems would seize up, foodslots shut down. Ice would form quickly and unstoppably, through whole Wings, down corridors, over bridges. Chains would become masses of rust. Towns would freeze, the houses cold and deserted, the market stalls collapsed under howling snowdrifts. The air would turn to poison. And the people! There was no way to imagine them, the panic, the fear and loneliness, the trampling savagery such a collapse would unleash, the bloody struggle for survival. It would be the destruction of a world.

The Prison would withdraw its mind, and leave its children to their fate.

Around them, light faded to a green gloom. The path was cindery and silent, the horse's hooves muffled in the incinerated dust. Attia whispered, "Do you believe that the Warden is in here?"

"If so, things are not going smoothly for my princely brother." He sounded preoccupied.

"If he's still alive."

"I told you, Finn can bluff his way out of anything. Forget him." Keiro peered into the gloom. "We've got our own troubles."

She scowled. The way he talked about Finn annoyed her, his pretense of not caring, of not being hurt. Sometimes she wanted to scream her anxiety at him, but that would be useless, would only draw the grin, the cool shrug. There was an armor around Keiro. He wore it flamboyantly and invisibly. It was as much a part of him as his dirty yellow hair, his hard blue eyes. Only once, when the Prison had cruelly shown them his imperfection, had she ever glimpsed through it. And she knew he would never forgive Incarceron for that, or for what he felt he was.

The horse stopped.

It whickered. Its ears flattened.

Alert, Keiro said, "See anything?"

Great briars wreathed round them, barbed with spines. "No," she said.

But she could hear something. A small sound, very far off, like a whisper from a nightmare.

Keiro had heard it too. He turned, listening. "A voice? What's it saying?"

Faint, repeated over and over, a tiny breath of triple syllables. She kept very still. It seemed crazy, impossible. But.

"I think it's calling my name," she said.

⊲◦◦◦⊳

"Attia! Attia, can you hear me?"

Jared adjusted the output and tried again. He was hungry, but the bread roll on the platter was hard and dry. Still, it was better than feasting upstairs with the Queen. Would she notice he wasn't there? He prayed not, and the anxiety made his fingers tremble on the controls. Over his head the screen was a stripped-down mass of wires and circuitry, cables rigged into and out of its connectors. The Portal was silent, apart from its usual hum.

Jared had grown to like its silence. It soothed him, so that even the pain that pushed its jagged edge into his chest seemed blunted down here. Somewhere high above, the labyrinth of the Court teemed with intrigue, tower on tower, chamber within chamber, and beyond the stables and gardens lay the countryside of the Realm, wide and perfect in its beauty under the stars.

He was a dark flaw in the heart of that beauty. He felt the guilt of it, and it made him work with agitated concentration. Since the Queen's silken blackmail, her offer of the Academy's hidden lore, he had barely been able to sleep, lying awake in his narrow bed, or pacing the gardens so deep in hope and fear that it had taken hours for him to notice how closely she was having him followed.

So, just before the banquet, he had sent her a brief note.

I accept your offer. I leave for the Academy tomorrow at dawn.
Jared Sapiens

Every word had been a wound, a betrayal. That was why he was here now.

Two men had followed him to the Sapients' Tower, he had made sure of that, but Protocol meant that they had not been able to enter. The Tower here at Court was a great stone keep full of the apartments of the Queen's Sapienti, and unlike his own at home at the Wardenry, this was a model of Era, a maze of orreries and alchemical alembics and leather-bound books, a mockery of learning. But it was a true labyrinth, and in his first days here he had discovered passageways and covered vaults that led discreetly out to the stables, the kitchens, the laundry rooms, the stills.

Losing the Queen's men had been almost too easy.

But he had made sure. For weeks now the staircase down to the Portal had been guarded by his own devices. Half of the spiders that hung on plastic webs in the dirty cellars were his observers.

"Attia. Attia. Can you hear me? This is Jared. Please answer."

This was his last chance. The Warden's appearance had shown him that the screen still worked. That artful flickering out had not fooled Jared—Claudia's father had switched off rather than answer Finn's question.

At first he had thought of searching for Keiro, but Attia was safer. He had sampled the recordings of her voice, the images of her he and Claudia had seen through the Key; using the finding mechanism he had once seen the Warden use, he had experimented for hours with the complicated imputs. Suddenly, when he had been almost ready to give up, the Portal had sparked and crackled into life. He hoped it was searching, pinpointing the girl in the vastness of the Prison, but it had been humming all night now and in his weariness he could no longer keep out the feeling that it wasn't really achieving anything at all.

He drank the last of the water, then reached into his pocket and brought out the Warden's watch and put it on the desk. The tiny cube clicked on the metal surface.

The Warden had told him that this cube was Incarceron.

He spun it gently, with his little finger.

So small.

So mysterious.

A prison you could hang on your watch chain.

He had subjected it to every analysis he knew, and there were no readings. It had no density, no magnetic field, no whisper of power. No instrument he possessed had been able to penetrate its silvery silence. It was a cube of unknown composition, and inside it was another world.

Or so the Warden had told him.

It struck Jared now that they had only John Arlex's word for that. What if it had just been his last taunting legacy to his daughter? What if it had been a lie?

Was that why he, Jared, hadn't told her yet?

He had to do it now. She should know. The thought that she should also know about his arrangement with the Queen rose up at once and tormented him.

He said, "Attia, Attia. Answer me. Please!"

But all that answered was a sharp beep in his pocket. He whipped out the scanner and swore softly. Maybe the watchers had gotten tired of snoring on the Tower doorstep and come looking for him.

Someone was creeping through the cellars.

⊲◌◌◌⊳

"WE SHOULD stay on the path," Keiro snapped down at her; she was staring intently into the undergrowth.

"I tell you I heard it. My name."

Keiro scowled and slid down from the horse. "We can't ride in there."

"Then we crawl." She had crouched, was on hands and knees. In the green gloom a tangle of roots sprawled under the high leaves. "Underneath. It has to be fairly close!"

Keiro hesitated. "If we turn aside, the Prison will think we're double-crossing it."

"Since when are you scared of Incarceron?" She looked up at him and he stared back hard, because she always seemed to know just how to needle him. Then she said, "Wait here. I'll go on my own," and crawled in.

With a hiss of irritation Keiro tethered the horse tight and crawled in after her. The leaf-litter was a mass of tiny brittle foliage; he felt it crunch under his knees, stab through his gloves. The roots were vast, a snaky smooth mesh of metal. After a while he realized they were great cables, snaking out into the Prison's soil, supporting the foliage like a canopy. There was hardly room to raise his head, and over his bent back briars and thorns and brambles of steel tore and snagged his hair.

"Keep lower," Attia muttered. "Lie flat."

Keiro swore long and viciously as his scarlet coat ripped at the shoulder. "For god's sake, there's nothing—"

"Listen." She stopped, her foot in his face. "Hear it?"

A voice.

A voice of static and crackle, as if the spiny branches themselves had picked up its repeated syllables.

Keiro rubbed his face with a dirty hand. "Go on," he said quietly.

They crawled under the razor-sharp tangle. Attia dug her fingers in the litter and pulled herself along. Pollen made her sneeze; the air was thick with micro-dust. A Beetle scurried, clicking, through her hair.

She wriggled past a thick trunk and saw, as if it was wreathed in the forest of thorn and razorwire, the wall of a dark building.

"It's like Rix's book," she gasped.

"Another one?"

"A beautiful princess sleeps for a hundred years in a ruined castle."

Keiro grunted, dragging his hair from thorns. "So?"

"A thief breaks in and steals a cup from her treasure. She turns into a dragon and they fight."

Keiro wriggled up next to her. He was breathless, his hair lank with dirt and sweat. "I must be thick even to listen to you. Who wins?"

"The dragon. She eats him, and then . . ."

Static crackled.

Keiro hauled himself into a dusty space. Vines sprawled up a wall of dark glossy brick. In its base a very tiny wooden door was smothered with ivy.

Behind it, the voice sparked and crackled.

"Who's there?" it whispered.

13

> *I fooled the Prison*
> *I fooled my father.*
> *I asked a question*
> *It could not answer.*
> —*Songs of Sapphique*

"It's me! I've been looking everywhere for you!"

Jared closed his eyes in relief. Then he opened the door and let Claudia dart in. Her evening dress was covered with a dark cloak. She said, "Is Finn here?"

"Finn? No . . ."

"He's challenged the Pretender to a duel. Can you believe that?"

Jared went back to the screen. "I'm afraid I can, Claudia."

She stared beyond him at the mess. "Why are you here in the middle of the night?" Coming closer, she looked at him closely. "Master, you look so drained. You should sleep."

"I can sleep at the Academy." There was a bitter note in his voice that she didn't recognize.

Worried, she crouched on the workbench, pushing the fine tools aside. "But I thought . . ."

"I leave tomorrow, Claudia."

"So soon?" It shook her. She said, "But . . . you're getting so close to success. Why not take a few more days . . ."

"I can't."

He was never so short with her. She wondered if it was the pain, driving him on. And then he sat, folding his long thin fingers together on the desk, and said sadly, "Oh Claudia, how I wish we were safely at home at the Wardenry. I wonder how my fox cub is doing, and the birds. And I miss my observatory, Claudia. I miss looking out at the stars."

Gently she said, "You're homesick, Master."

"A little." He shrugged. "I'm sick of the Court. Of its stifling Protocol. Of its exquisite meals and endlessly sumptuous rooms where each door hides a watcher. I should like a little peace."

It silenced her. Jared was rarely gloomy; his grave calm was always there, a safe presence at her back. She fought down her alarm. "We'll go home then, Master, as soon as Finn is safely on the throne. We'll go home. Just you and me."

He smiled, nodding, and she thought he looked wistful. "That may be a long time. And a challenge won't help."

"The Queen's forbidden them to fight."

"Good." His fingers tapped together on the desk. She realized that the systems were all live, the Portal humming with distorted energy.

He said, "I have something to tell you, Claudia. Something important." Leaning forward, he didn't look at her. "Something I should have told you before, that I shouldn't have kept from you. This journey to the Academy. There is a reason that . . . the Queen has allowed me to go . . ."

"To search the Esoterica, I know," she said impatiently, pacing up and down. "I know! I just wish I could come. Why let you and not me? What's she up to?"

Jared raised his head and watched her. His heart was hammering; he felt almost too ashamed to speak. "Claudia . . ."

"But then perhaps it's just as well I'm staying. A duel! He's got no idea how to behave! It's as if he's forgotten all he ever was . . ."

Catching her tutor's eye she stopped and laughed an awkward laugh. "Sorry. What were you going to say?"

There was an ache in him that was not caused by his illness. Dimly he recognized it as anger, anger and a deep, bitter pride. He had not known he was proud. *You are her tutor, her brother, and more her father than I have ever been.* The Warden's scorching words of jealousy came back to him; for a moment he savored them, gazing at Claudia as she waited, so unsuspecting. How could he destroy the trust between them?

"This," he said. He tapped the watch that lay on the desk. "I think you ought to have it."

Claudia looked relieved, then surprised. "My father's watch?"

"Not the watch. This."

She came closer. He was touching the silver cube that hung on the chain. It had been so familiar in her father's hands that she barely noticed it, but now a sudden wonder swept her that her father—so austere a man—should have worn a charm.

"Is it for good luck?"

Jared did not smile. "It's Incarceron," he said.

⊰◦◦◦⊱

FINN LAY in the long grass looking up at the stars.

Through the dark blades the distant brilliance of their light brought him a sort of comfort. He had come here with the hot jealousy of the banquet still burning in him, but the silence of the night and the beauty of the stars were easing it away.

He shuffled his arm behind his head, feeling the prickle of grass down his neck.

They were so far away. In Incarceron he had dreamed of them, his symbol of Escape; now he realized they were still that, that he was still imprisoned. Perhaps he always would be. Perhaps it would be best just to disappear, to ride away into the forest and not come back. It would mean abandoning Keiro, and Attia.

Claudia wouldn't care. He moved uncomfortably as he thought it, but the thought stayed. She wouldn't. She'd end up marrying this Pretender and being Queen, as she'd always meant to be.

Why not?

Why not just go?

Where, though? And how would he feel riding through the endless Protocol of this stifled world and dreaming every night of Keiro in the metallic, livid hell of Incarceron, not knowing if he was alive or dead, maimed or insane, killing or already dead?

He rolled over, curling up. Princes were supposed to sleep in golden beds with damask canopies, but the Palace was a nest of enemies; he couldn't breathe there. The familiar prickle behind his eyes had gone, but the dryness in his throat warned him that the fit had been near. He had to be careful. He had to have more control.

And yet the angry moment of the challenge was dear to him. He relished it, over and over again, seeing the Pretender jerking aside, the slap of redness on his face. He'd lost his cool then, and Finn smiled in the dark, his cheek resting on the damp grass.

A rustle, behind him.

He rolled swiftly and sat up. The wide lawns were gray in the starlight. Beyond the lake the woods of the estate raised black heads against the sky. The gardens smelled of roses and honeysuckle, sweet in the warm summer air.

He lay back again, staring up.

The moon, a ruined hollow, hung like a ghost in the east. Jared had told him that it had been attacked in the Years of Rage, that now the ocean tides were altered, that the fixed orbit had changed the world.

And after that they had stopped all change altogether.

When he was King, he would change things. People would

be free to do or say what they wanted. The poor wouldn't have to slave on great estates for the rich. And he would find Incarceron, he would release them all . . . But then he was going to run away.

He stared up at the white stars.

Finn Starseer doesn't run. He could almost hear Keiro's sarcasm.

He turned his head, sighed, stretched out.

And touched something cold.

With a shiver of steel his sword was in his hand; he had leaped up, was alert, his heart thudding, a prickle of sweat on his neck.

Far off in the lighted Palace a drift of music echoed.

The lawns were still empty. But there was something small and bright stuck in the grass just above where his head had been.

After a moment, listening intently, he bent down and picked it up. And as he stared at it, a shiver of fear made his hand shake.

It was a small steel knife, wickedly sharp, and its handle was a wolf, stretched thin, jaws open and savage.

Finn drew himself up and looked all around, his hand tight on the sword hilt.

But the night was silent.

—◁◦◦◦▷—

THE DOOR gave at the third kick. Keiro dragged a cable of bramble away and ducked his head inside. His voice came back, muffled. "Corridor. Have you got the handlight?"

172

She handed it to him.

He scraped in, and she waited, hearing only muffled movement. Then he said, "Come on."

Attia crawled through, and stood up beside him.

The interior was dark, and filthy. It had obviously been abandoned years ago, maybe centuries. A lumber of junk lay in heaps under cobwebs and grime.

Keiro shoved something aside and maneuvered himself between a heaped desk and a broken cupboard. He wiped the dust off with his gloved hand and stared down at the litter of broken crockery. "Just what we need."

Attia listened. The corridor led into darkness, and nothing moved down there but the voices. There were two of them now, and they faded oddly in and out of hearing.

Keiro had his sword ready. "Any trouble, we're out of here. One Chain-gang is enough for any lifetime."

She nodded, and made to move past him, but he grabbed her and shoved her behind him. "Watch my back. That's your job."

Attia smiled sweetly. "And I love you too," she whispered.

They walked warily down the dim space. At the end a great door stood ajar, fixed immovably half open, and when she slipped through behind Keiro, Attia saw why; furniture had been piled and heaped against it, as if in some last desperate attempt to keep it closed.

"Something went on here. Look there." Keiro flashed the handlight at the floor. Dark stains marred the paving. Attia guessed it might once have been blood. She looked closer at the junk, then around at the galleried hall. "It's all toys," she whispered.

They stood in the wreckage of a sumptuous nursery. But the scale was all wrong. The dollhouse that she stared at was enormous, so that she could almost have crawled in, her head squashed against the ceiling of the kitchen, where plaster hams hung and a joint had fallen from its spit. The upstairs windows were too high to see into. Hoops and tops and balls and skittles were littered across the room's center; walking over to them she felt an amazing softness under her feet, and when she knelt and felt it, it was carpet, black with grime.

Light grew. Keiro had found candles; he lit a few and stuck them around.

"Look at this. A giant, or dwarves?"

The toys were bewildering. Most were too big, like the huge sword and ogre-sized helmet that hung from a hook. Others were tiny—a scatter of building blocks no bigger than salt grains, books on a shelf that started as vast folios at one end and went down to minuscule locked volumes at the other. Keiro heaved open a wooden chest and swore to find it overflowing with dressing-up clothes of all sizes. Still, he rummaged in there and found a leather belt with gilt trappings. There was a pirate's coat too, of scarlet leather. Immediately he tugged off his own and put the new one on, strapping the belt tight around it.

"Suit me?"

"We're wasting time." The voices had faded. Attia turned, trying to identify where the sound came from, edging between the vast rocking horse and a row of dangling puppets that hung, broken-necked and tangle-limbed, on the wall, their small eyes watching her, red as Incarceron's.

Beyond them were dolls. They lay tumbled, princesses with golden hair, whole armies of soldiers, dragons of felt and cambric with long, forked tails. Teddies and pandas and stuffed animals Attia had never seen lay in a heap as high as the ceiling.

She waded in and heaved them aside.

"What are you doing?" Keiro snapped.

"Can't you hear them?"

Two voices. Small and crackling. As if the bears spoke, the dolls conversed. Arms and legs and heads and blue glass eyes tumbled apart.

Under them was a small box, the lid inlaid with an ivory eagle.

The voices were coming from inside it.

<hr />

FOR A long moment Claudia said nothing. Then she came close, picked up the watch, and let the cube hang on its chain and turn so that it glittered in the light.

Finally she whispered, "How do you know?"

"Your father told me."

She nodded, and he saw the fascination in her eyes.

"You hold a world in your hands. That's what he said to me."

"Why didn't you tell me before?"

"I wanted to try some tests on it. None of them worked. I suppose I wanted to make sure he was telling the truth."

The screen crackled. Jared looked at it absently.

Claudia watched the cube turn. Was this really the hellish world she had entered, the Prison of a million Prisoners?

Was this where her father was?

"Why would he lie? Jared?"

He wasn't listening. He was at the controls, adjusting something, so that the hum in the room modulated. She felt a sudden nausea, as if the world had shifted, and she put the watch down hurriedly.

"The frequency's changed!" Jared said. "Maybe . . . Attia! Attia! Can you hear me?"

Only silence crackled. Then, to their astonishment, faint and far away, they heard music.

"What is that?" Claudia breathed.

But she knew what it was. It was the high, silly tinkle of a musical box.

—◁◦◦◦▷—

Keiro held the box open. The tune seemed too loud; it filled the cluttered hall with an eerie, menacing jollity. But there was no mechanism, nothing to produce it. The box was wooden and completely empty but for a mirror inside its lid. He turned it upside down and examined the underside. "Doesn't seem possible."

"Give it to me."

He glanced at her, then handed it over.

She held it tight, because she knew the voices lay here, behind the music. "It's me," she said. "It's Attia."

<hr/>

"There was something." Jared ran his delicate fingers over the controls, jabbing quickly. "There. There! Hear it?"

A crackle of words. So loud that Claudia winced, and he reduced the volume instantly.

"*It's me. It's Attia.*"

"We've got her!" Jared sounded hoarse with joy. "Attia, this is Jared! Jared Sapiens. Tell me if you can hear me."

A minute of static. Then her voice, distorted, but intelligible. "Is it really you?"

Jared glanced at Claudia, but her face made his triumph die. She looked oddly stricken, as if the girl's voice had brought back dark memories of the Prison.

Quietly he said, "Claudia and I are both here. Are you well, Attia? Are you safe?"

Crackle. Then another voice, sharp as acid. "Where's Finn?"

Claudia breathed out slowly. "Keiro?"

"Who bloody else. Where is he, Claudia? Where's the Prince? Are you there, oathbrother? Are you listening to me, because I'm going to break your filthy neck."

"He's not here." Claudia moved closer to the screen. It was rippling frantically. Jared made a few adjustments.

"There," he said quietly.

She saw Keiro.

He looked just the same. His hair was long and he'd tied it back; he wore some flashy coat with knives in his belt.

There was a fierce anger in his eyes. He must be able to see her too, because instant scorn broke over his face. "Still in the silks and satins then."

Behind him, she saw Attia, in the shadows of some cluttered room. Their eyes met. Claudia said, "Listen, have you seen my father?"

Keiro let his breath out in a silent whistle. Glancing at Attia he said, "So it's true? He's Inside?"

Her voice sounded small. "Yes. He took both Keys, but the Prison has them now. It's got this fanatical plan . . . It wants to build—"

"A body. We know." Keiro enjoyed the brief silence of their astonishment, but Attia snatched the box back and said, "Is Finn all right? What's happening there?"

"The Warden sabotaged the Portal." Jared looked strained, as if time was short. "I've made some repairs, but . . . we can't get you Out yet."

"Then . . ."

"Listen to me. The Warden is the only one who can help you. Try and find him. How are you seeing us?"

"Through a musical box."

"Keep it with you. I might—"

"Yes, but Finn!" Attia was pale with anxiety. "Where's Finn?"

Around her the nursery suddenly rippled. Keiro yelled in alarm. "What was that?"

Attia stared. The whole fabric of the world had thinned.

She had a sudden terror that she might somehow fall through it, down, like Sapphique, into the eternal blackness. And then the grimy carpet was firm under her feet and Keiro was saying, "The Prison must be furious. We have to go."

"Claudia!" Attia shook the box, seeing only herself in the mirror. "Are you still there?"

Voices, arguing. Noise, movement, a door opening. And then a voice said, "Attia. This is Finn." The screen lit, and she saw him.

She couldn't speak.

Words eluded her; there were so many of them to say.

She managed his name. "Finn . . . ?"

"Are you both all right? Keiro, are you there?"

She felt Keiro standing close behind her. His voice, when it came, was dark and mocking.

"Well," he said. "Look at you."

14

None of us know who we are anymore.
                                        —The Steel Wolves

Finn and Keiro stared at each other.

Years of reading his oathbrother's moods told Finn this one was savage. Knowing Claudia and Jared were watching, he rubbed his flushed face. "Are you all right?"

"Oh, I'm just as you'd expect. My oathbrother's Escaped. I have no gang, no Comitatus, no food, no home, no followers. I'm an outcast in every Wing, a thief who steals from thieves. I'm the lowest of the low, Finn. But then, what else do you expect from a halfman?"

Finn closed his eyes. The dagger of the Steel Wolves was in his belt; he felt its edge against his ribs.

"It's not all paradise out here."

"Oh really?" Arms folded, Keiro surveyed him. "You look well set up to me, brother. Hungry, are you?"

"No, but—"

"Sore? Dead-beat? Bleeding from fighting off a chain of monsters?"

"No."

"Well, I am, Prince Finn!" Keiro exploded into rage. "Don't

stand there in your golden palace asking for my sympathy. What happened to your plans to get us Out!"

Finn's heart was beating too loud; his skin prickled. He felt Claudia close up behind him. As if she knew he couldn't answer she said firmly, "Jared is doing everything he can. It's not easy, Keiro. My father saw to that. You'll have to be patient."

There was a snort of scorn from the screen.

Finn sat on the metal chair. He leaned forward, both hands on the desk, toward them. "I haven't forgotten you. I haven't abandoned you. I think about you all the time. You must believe me."

But it was Attia who answered. "We do. We're all right, Finn. Please don't worry about us. Do you still get the visions?"

The concern in her eyes warmed him a little. "Some. They're trying medicines, but nothing helps."

"Attia." It was Jared who interrupted, his voice intrigued. "Tell me, are you near any object that might be emitting power? Any part of the Prison's systems?"

"I don't know . . . We're in some sort of . . . nursery."

"Did she say nursery?" Claudia whispered.

Finn shrugged. All he was watching was Keiro's silence.

"It's just . . ." Jared was puzzled. "There are some peculiar readings coming in. As if some potent source of energy was very close to you."

Attia said, "It must be the Glove. The Prison wants—"

Her voice stopped abruptly. There was a scuffle and a mutter, and the screen tilted and flickered and went black. Jared said, "Attia! Are you all right?"

Muffled and angry, Keiro's voice hissed, "Shut up!" Then, louder, "The Prison's unstable. We're getting out of here."

A muffled yelp. A whiplash of steel.

"Keiro?" Finn leaped up. "He's drawn his sword. Keiro! What's going on there?"

A clatter. Distinctly they heard Attia's hiss of fear. "The puppets," she breathed.

Then nothing but static.

She'd bitten Keiro's hand; now he jerked it away from her mouth and she gasped. "Look. Look!"

He turned and saw. The puppet on the end of the row was moving. The strings that worked it were taut from the roof's darkness, and its head was lifting, turning smoothly to look at them.

One lank hand rose and pointed. The jaw clacked.

"I told you not to betray me," it said.

Attia backed up, holding the musical box tight, but it gave a broken clank in her hands and the mirror cracked into pieces. She threw it down.

The puppet jerked upright, knock-kneed, rickety as a skeleton. Its face was some ancient harlequin, the nose hooked and hideous. It wore a striped jester's cap and bells. Its eyes were red.

"We haven't," Keiro said rapidly. "We heard a voice and came to find out what it was. We've got the Glove safe and we're still bringing it to you. I didn't let her tell them about it. You saw that."

Attia scowled at him. Her mouth was sore where he had clamped his hand over it.

"*I saw.*" The wooden jaw opened and closed, but its voice, with its faint echo, came from nowhere. "*You interest me, Prisoner. I could destroy you and yet you defy me.*"

"What's new?" Keiro's drawl was sarcastic. "You could destroy us all, anytime." He stepped up to the puppet, his handsome face to its ugliness. "Or is there some twisted remnant of your programming left? He says, the Sapient out there, that you were made to be a Paradisc. We should have had everything. So what went wrong? What did you do, Prison? What turned you into a monster?"

Attia stared at him, appalled.

The puppet raised its hands and feet and danced, a slow, macabre caper.

"*Men went wrong. Men like you, who seem so bold and are in fact riddled with fears. Crawl back to your horse and ride on my road, Prisoner.*"

"I'm not afraid of you."

"*No? Shall I tell you then, Keiro, the answer to what torments you? It would end the pain forever, because you'd know.*" The puppet's face bobbed mockingly before him. "*You'd know how far the circuitry and plastic reaches into your body, how much of you is flesh and blood, how much of you belongs to me.*"

"I already know."

Attia was shocked at the whisper his voice had become.

"No you don't. None of you know. To find out you must open up your heart, and die. Unless I tell you. Shall I tell you, Keiro?"

"No."

"Let me tell you now. Let me end the uncertainty."

Keiro looked up. His eyes were blue and blazing with anger. "We'll go back to your stinking road. But I swear one day it'll be me doing the tormenting."

"I can see you want to know. Very well. In fact, you are—"

The sword slashed. With a yell of fury Keiro sliced through the strings and the puppet collapsed, a heap of splinters and a mask.

Keiro stamped on them; the face cracked under his boot. He raised his face, eyes blazing. "Do you see that! Having a body will make you vulnerable, Prison-puppet. If you have a body you can die!"

The dark nursery was silent.

Breathing hard, he whirled around and saw Attia's face.

He scowled. "I suppose that stupid grin is because Finn is alive."

"Not entirely," she said.

⊂◯◯◯⊃

CLAUDIA RAN down the stairs the next morning, slipping past the retainers carrying the Queen's breakfast. Probably the Pretender's too, she thought. She glanced up at the Ivory Tower,

184

wondering how he was enjoying his splendor. If he was some farm boy, it would all be new to him. And yet his manner had been so assured. His hands so smooth!

Quickly, before the doubts came back, she turned in to the stables, past the rows of cybersteeds to the real horses at the end.

Jared was adjusting his saddle.

"You haven't got much baggage," she muttered.

"The Sapient carries all he needs in his heart. Which is from where, Claudia?"

"Martor Sapiens. The Illuminatus. Book One." She watched Finn lead out his horse, surprised. "Are you coming too?"

"You suggested it."

She had forgotten that. It rather annoyed her now; she wanted to see Jared on his way by herself, to say good-bye to him privately. He might be away for days, and the Court would be even more hateful in his absence.

If Finn noticed, he said nothing, turning and swinging himself up into the saddle expertly. Riding had come naturally to him, though he had no memory of doing it before the Prison. He waited while Claudia's horse was saddled and the groom held her foot while she mounted.

"Is that outfit in Era?" he asked quietly.

"You know very well it isn't."

She wore a boy's riding coat and trousers under her skirt. Watching Jared turn his horse she said suddenly, "Change your plans, Master, don't go. After what happened last night . . ."

"I have to go, Claudia." His voice was strained and low; he rubbed the horse's neck gently. "Please don't make me feel worse than I do about it."

She didn't see why. It would mean work on the Portal would pause, just when they were having success. But he was her tutor, and though he rarely exercised it, his authority was real. Besides, she sensed he had his own reasons for going. The Sapienti returned yearly to the Academy; perhaps his superiors had summoned him.

"I'll miss you."

He looked up, and for a moment she thought there was a desolation in his green eyes. Then he smiled and it was gone. "And I you, Claudia."

They rode slowly through the courtyards and quadrangles of the vast palace. Servants drawing water and hauling in wagonloads of kindling stared, their eyes on Finn. It made him ride proudly, trying to look like a prince.

Housemaids shaking sheets outside the laundry stopped to watch. At the corner of the scrivener's offices Claudia saw Medlicote come out of the door. As she rode past he bowed elaborately.

Jared raised an eyebrow. "That looks meaningful."

"Leave him to me."

"I don't like leaving you with that problem, Claudia."

"They won't try anything, Master. Not if the Pretender is their candidate."

Jared nodded, the breeze lifting his dark hair. Then he said, "Finn, what did Attia mean by the Glove?"

Finn shrugged. "Sapphique made a wager with the Prison once. Some say they played dice, but Gildas had a version where they told riddles. Anyway, the Prison lost."

"So what happened?" Claudia asked.

"If you were a Prisoner you'd have guessed. Incarceron never loses. It shed the skin from its claw and vanished. But Sapphique took the skin and made a glove and used it to cover his maimed hand. The story says when he put it on he knew all the Prison's secrets."

"Including the way Out?"

"Presumably."

"So why did Attia mention it?"

"Why did Keiro try to stop her mentioning it, rather?"

Jared's voice was thoughtful. He glanced at Finn. "Keiro's anger troubles you."

"I hate him like that."

"It will pass."

"I'm more worried about what happened to cut them off." Claudia glanced at Jared, who nodded.

As they reached the cobbled entrance the noise of the clattering hooves drowned talk. They rode under three gateways and through the vast Barbican with its murder-holes and portcullis. The vaguely medieval arrowslits were not Era, of course, but the Queen thought them picturesque.

They had always made the Warden tut with displeasure.

Beyond, the green fields of the Realm stretched out in their morning beauty. Claudia breathed a sigh of relief. She grinned at Finn. "Let's gallop."

He nodded. "Race you up the hill."

It was a joy to be riding, and free of the Court. She urged the horse on, and the breeze lifted her hair, and the sky was blue and sunlit. On all sides in the golden fields birds sang among the corn; as the lanes divided and narrowed vast hedges rose on each side, the deep tracks hollowed with apparent age. She had no idea how much of this landscape was real—certainly some of the birds, and the hosts of butterflies . . . surely they were real. In truth, if they weren't, she didn't want to know. Why not accept the illusion, just for one day?

The three of them slowed on the top of a small hill and gazed back at the Court. Its towers and pinnacles gleamed in the sun. Bells were ringing, and the glass roof shone like a diamond.

Jared sighed. "It's strange how beguiling illusion can be."

"You always told me to beware of it," Claudia said.

"So you should. As a society we have lost the ability to tell the real from the fake. Most of the Court, at least, don't even care which is which. It concerns the Sapienti greatly."

"Maybe they should enter the Prison," Finn muttered. "We never had any trouble."

Jared glanced at Claudia, and they both thought of the watch, which she wore now, safe in her deepest pocket.

It was two leagues to the fringes of the Forest, and almost midday when they approached it.

The road to this point had been broad and well-used—traffic between the Court and the western villages was steady, and the ruts of wheels had cut deep in the baked mud.

But once under the green canopy the trees gradually closed in, and vast deer-nibbled boughs of mighty oaks gave way to the tangled undergrowth of the wildwood. Branches hung heavily overhead, the sky barely seen through their meshed leaves.

Finally they came to the crossroads and the track that branched off to the Academy. It ran downhill through a green clearing, crossed a stream on a clapperbridge, and wound its way up the other side into the wood again.

Jared stopped. "I'll go on from here alone, Claudia."

"Master . . ."

"You need to get back. Finn must be there for the investigation."

"I don't see the point," Finn growled.

"It's vital. You have no memories, so you must impress them by your personality. By the strength you have, Finn."

Finn gazed at him. "I don't know I have any, Master."

"I believe you do." Jared smiled calmly. "Now, I ask you to look after Claudia, while I'm gone."

Finn raised an eyebrow and Claudia snapped, "I can look after myself."

"And you must look after him. I depend on both of you."

"Don't worry about us, Master." Claudia leaned over and kissed him. He smiled and turned the horse, but she saw how under his calm there was a tension as if this separation meant more than she knew.

"I'm sorry," he said.

"Sorry?"

"For going."

She shook her head. "You'll only be a few days."

"I did what I could." His eyes were dark in the forest shadows. "Remember me kindly, Claudia."

She suddenly had nothing to say. A chill struck her; she wanted to stop him, to call after him, but he had urged the horse and it was already striding away down the lane.

Only when he had reached the bridge did she stand in the stirrups and yell, "Write to me!"

"He's too far," Finn muttered, but Jared turned and waved his hand.

"His hearing is excellent," she said, foolishly proud.

They watched until the dark horse and its slim rider disappeared under the eaves of the wood. Then Finn sighed. "Come on. We should get back."

They rode slowly and silent. Claudia was moody; Finn barely spoke. Neither of them wanted to think about the Pretender, or what decision the Council would come to.

Finally Finn looked up. "It's darker. Isn't it?"

The slants of sunlight that had lit the forest earlier had gone. Instead clouds had gathered, and the breeze had become a wind, threshing high branches.

"There's no storm ordered. Wednesday's the Queen's archery day."

"Well, it looks like a storm to me. Maybe it's real weather."

"There is no real weather, Finn. This is the Realm."

But in ten minutes rain began. It came as a pattering and was suddenly a torrent, lashing with tremendous noise through the leaves. Claudia thought of Jared and said, "He'll be soaked."

"So will we!" Finn glanced around. "Come on. Hurry!"

They galloped. The ground was already soft; the hooves splashed into puddles that spilled over the track. Branches whipped at Claudia's face; her hair flew out across her eyes and plastered itself to her cheek. She shivered, unused to the cold and the wet.

"This is all wrong. What's going on?"

Lightning spat; from overhead the low, heavy grumble of thunder rolled down the sky. For a moment Finn knew it was the voice of Incarceron he heard, its terrible, cruel mockery, knew he had never Escaped at all. He turned and yelled, "We shouldn't be under the trees. Hurry!"

They whipped the horses up and raced. Claudia felt the rain like blows in her chest; as Finn pulled ahead she shouted at him to wait, to slow down.

Only his horse replied. With a high whinny it reared, hooves kicking the air, and then to her horror it fell, crashing on one side, and he rolled from it, slamming into the ground.

"Finn!" she screamed.

Something slashed past her, whipping into the wood, thudding into a tree.

And then she knew it wasn't rain, or lightning.

It was a hail of arrows.

Ruined,
Like the Moon

15

> *Each man and woman will have their*
> *place and be content with it. Because*
> *if there is no change, what will disturb*
> *our peaceful lives?*
> —*King Endor's Decree*

"Claudia!"

Finn rolled over as a firelock blazed; the tree next to him was scorched with diagonal fire. "Get down!"

Did she have no idea how to act in an ambush? Her horse was panicking; he took a deep breath and ran from cover, grabbing it by the bridle. "Get down!"

She jumped, and they both fell. Then they were squirming into the bushes, lying flat, breathless. Around them the forest roared with rain.

"Hurt?"

"No. You?"

"Bruised. Nothing serious."

Claudia dragged soaked hair from her eyes. "I can't believe this. Sia would never order it. Where are they?"

Finn was watching the trees intently. "Over there, behind that thicket, maybe. Or high in the branches."

That alarmed her. She twisted to see, but rain blinded her. She wriggled farther back, her hands deep in leaf-litter, the stink of decaying foliage rich in her face.

"Now what?"

"We regroup." Finn's voice was steady. "Weapons? I've got a sword and knife."

"There's a pistol in my saddlebag." But the horse had already bolted. She glanced sidelong at Finn. "Are you enjoying this?"

He laughed, a rare event. "It livens things up. But back in Incarceron we used to be the ones doing the ambushing."

Lightning blinked. Its brilliance lit the wood and the rain came down harder, hissing through the bracken.

"I could try and crawl to that oak," Finn muttered in her ear. "And get around . . ."

"There might be an army out there."

"One man. Maybe two, no more." He squirmed back, the bushes rustling. Instantly two arrows thwacked into the bole of the tree above them. Claudia gasped.

Finn froze. "Well, maybe not."

"This is the Steel Wolves," she hissed.

Finn was silent a moment. Then he said, "Can't be. They could have killed me last night."

She stared at him through the downpour. "What?"

"They left this next to my head." He held up the dagger, the snarling wolf's head dripping in his fingers.

Then as one, they turned. Voices were approaching through the hissing forest.

"See them?"

"Not yet." She eased forward.

"I think our enemy has." Finn watched the small movements of branches. "I think they're pulling out."

"Look." A wagon was rumbling along the track, precariously laden with mown hay, the loose cover flapping in the wind. A brawny man walked beside it and another drove, sackcloth hoods covering their faces, their boots thick with mud.

"Peasants," Claudia said. "Our only chance."

"The archers might still be—"

"Come on." Before he could stop her she scrambled out. "Wait! Please, stop!"

The men stared. The big one swung a heavy cudgel up as he saw Finn behind her, sword in hand. "What's this?" he said sourly.

"Our horses were frightened and ran off. By the lightning." Claudia shivered in the rain, pulling her coat around her.

The big serf grinned. "Bet you had to hold each other tight then?"

She drew herself upright, aware that she was soaked and her hair dripped in a tangled mess, made her voice cold and imperious. "Look, we need someone to go and find our horses, and we need—"

"The rich always need." The cudgel tapped against the raw

red hands. "And we all have to jump, but it won't always be like that. One day soon . . ."

"Enough, Rafe." The voice came from the wagon, and Claudia saw that the driver had pushed back his hood. His face was wrinkled, his body bent. He seemed old, but his voice was strong enough. "Follow us, missy. We'll get you to the cottages, and then we'll find your horses."

With a low *hup!* he whipped up the ox, and the heavy beast lumbered past. Claudia and Finn kept close under the shelter of the towering load of hay, wisps slipping off and drifting down on them. Above the trees the sky had begun to clear; the rain ended quite suddenly, and a shaft of sunlight broke through, lighting the distant aisles of the forest. The storm was passing as quickly as it had come.

Finn glanced back. The muddy track was empty. A black-bird began to sing in its stillness.

"They've gone," Claudia muttered.

"Or they're following." Finn turned. "How far are these cottages?"

"Just here, lad, just here. Don't you fret. I won't let Rafe rob you, even if you are Court folk. The Queen's people, are you?"

Claudia opened her mouth indignantly, but Finn said, "My girl works for the Countess of Harken. She's a lady's maid."

She fixed him with a stare of astonishment, but the wizened driver nodded. "And you?"

He shrugged. "A groom in the stables. We borrowed the

horses, it was such a fine day . . . We'll get into terrible trouble now. Beaten, probably."

Claudia watched him. His face was as doleful as if he believed the story himself; something about him had changed in a moment to an apprehensive servant, his best livery ruined by the mud and rain.

"Ah well. We were all young once." The old man winked at Claudia. "Wish I was young again."

Rafe guffawed with mirth.

Claudia set her lips tight but tried to look miserable. She was cold and wet enough for it.

When the wagon clattered through a broken gateway she muttered quietly to Finn, "What are you up to?"

"Keeping them on our side. If they knew who we were . . ."

"They'd jump to help! We could pay . . ."

He was watching her strangely. "Sometimes, Claudia, I think you don't understand anything at all."

"Such as what?" she snapped.

He nodded ahead. "Their lives. Look at this."

Cottages was hardly a word for them. Two lopsided, squalid buildings squatted at the edge of the track. Their thatch was in holes, wattle and daub walls patched with hurdles. A few ragged children ran out and stared, silent, and as Claudia came closer she saw how thin they were, how the youngest coughed and the oldest was bow-legged with rickets.

The wagon rumbled into the lee of the buildings. Rafe yelled at the children to find the horses and they scattered, and then he ducked under one of the low doorways.

Claudia and Finn waited for the older man to climb down. His hunched back was even more evident when he stood, no taller than Finn's shoulder.

"This way, lord's groom and lady's maid. We don't have much, but we do have a fire."

Claudia frowned. She followed him down the steps under the wooden lintel.

At first she saw nothing but the fire. The interior was black. Then the stink rose up and hit her with its full force, and it was so bad she gasped and stopped dead, and only Finn's shove in her back made her stumble on. The Court had its share of bad smells, but there was nothing like this; a stench of animal dung and urine and sour milk and the fly-buzzed remnants of bones that cracked in the straw under her feet. And above all, the sweet smell of damp, as if the whole hovel was settling deep into the earth, tilting and softening, its wooden posts rotten and beetle-bored.

As her eyes became used to the gloom she saw sparse furnishings—a table, joint-stools, a box-bed built into the wall. There were two windows, small and wood-slatted, a branch of ivy growing in through one.

The old man dragged up a stool for her. "Sit, missy, and dry yourself. You too, lad. They call me Tom. Old Tom."

She didn't want to sit. There were certainly fleas in the straw.

The miserable poverty of the place sickened her. But she sat, holding out her hands to the paltry fire.

"Put some kindling on." Tom shuffled to the table.

"You live here alone?" Finn asked, tossing on dry sticks.

"My wife died these five years. But some of Rafe's young ones sleep here. He has six, and his sick mother to care for . . ."

Claudia noticed something in a dim doorway; she realized after a moment that it was a pig, snuffling the straw of the adjoining room. That would be the byre.

She shivered. "You should glass the windows. The draft is terrible."

The old man laughed, pouring out thin ale. "But that wouldn't be Protocol, would it? And we must abide by the Protocol, even as it kills us."

"There are ways around it," Finn said softly.

"Not for us." He pushed the pottery cups toward them. "For the Queen maybe, because them that make the rules can break them, but not for the poor. Era is no pretense for us, no playing at the past with all its edges softened. It's real. We have no skinwands, lad, none of the precious electricity or plastiglas. The picturesque squalor the Queen likes to ride past is where we live. You play at history. We endure it."

Claudia sipped the sour beer. She realized she had always known this. Jared had taught her, and she had visited the poor of the Wardenry, ruled over by her father's strict regime. Once, in a snowy January, seeing beggars from the coach, she had asked him if more couldn't be done for them. He had smiled his remote smile, smoothed his dark gloves. "They are the price we pay, Claudia, for peace. For the tranquility of our time."

A small cold flame of anger burned in her now, remembering. But she said nothing. It was Finn who asked, "Is there resentment?"

"There is." The old man drank and rapped his pipe on the table. "Now, I have little food but . . ."

"We're not hungry." Finn hadn't missed the evasion, but Claudia's voice interrupted him.

"May I ask you, sir. *What is that?*"

She was staring at a small image in the darkest corner of the room. A slant of sunlight caught it; showed a crude carving of a man, his face shadowy, his hair dark.

Tom was still. He seemed dismayed; for a moment Finn was sure he would yell for the brawny neighbor. Then he went on knocking dust from his pipe. "That is the Nine-Fingered One, missy."

Claudia put down her cup. "He has another name."

"A name to be spoken in whispers."

She met his eye. "Sapphique."

The old man looked at her, then Finn. "His name is known in the Court then. You surprise me, miss lady's maid."

"Only among the servants," Finn said quickly. "And we know very little of him. Except that he Escaped from Incarceron." His hand shook on the cup. He wondered what the old man would say if he knew that he, Finn, had spoken to Sapphique in visions.

"Escaped?" The old man shook his head. "I know nothing about that. Sapphique appeared from nowhere in a flash of blinding light. He possessed great powers of magic—they say he turned stones into cakes, that he danced with the children. He promised to renew the moon and free the Prisoners."

Claudia glanced at Finn. She was desperate to know more, but if they asked too much the old man would stop. "Where exactly did he appear?"

"Some say the forest. Others a cave, far to the north, where a charred circle is still burned on the mountainside. But how can you pin down such a happening?"

"Where is he now?" Finn asked.

The old man stared. "You don't know? They tried to silence him, of course. But he turned himself into a swan. He sang his final song and flew away to the stars. One day he will return and end the Era forever."

The fetid room was silent. Only the fire crackled. Claudia didn't look at Finn. When he spoke again his question shocked her.

"So what do you know of the Steel Wolves, old man?"

Tom paled. "I know nothing of them."

"No?"

"I don't talk of them."

"Because they plan revolution, like your loose-tongued neighbor? Because they want to murder the Queen and the Prince, and destroy Protocol?" Finn nodded. "Wise to keep silent then. I suppose they tell you that when that happens the Prison will be opened and there will be no more hunger. Do you believe them?"

The hunchback stared back evenly at him across the table. "Do you?" he whispered.

A tense silence. It was broken by the stamp and rattle of hooves, a child's shout.

Tom rose slowly. "Rafe's boys have found your horses."

He looked at Claudia, then back at Finn and said, "I think perhaps too much has been said here. You're no groom, lad. Are you a prince?"

Finn smiled ruefully. "I'm a Prisoner, old man. Just like you."

They mounted and rode back as quickly as they could.

Claudia had given all the coins she had to the children.

Neither spoke. Finn was alert for another ambush, Claudia still brooding over the injustice of Era, her own unthinking acceptance of riches. Why should she be rich? She had been born in Incarceron. If it hadn't been for the Warden's ambitions she would be there still.

"Claudia, look," Finn said.

He was staring through the trees, and glancing up at the alarm in his voice, she saw a tall plume of smoke rising ahead.

"It looks like a fire."

Anxious, she urged her horse on. As they emerged from the forest and clattered under the barbican, the acrid smell grew.

Smoke filled the inner courtyards of the Palace and as they galloped in, the wind was crackling. A frenzied army of ostlers and grooms and servants were running, dragging out horses and squawking hawks, hauling pumps, buckets of water.

"Where is it?" Claudia swung down.

But she could already see where it was. The whole ground floor of the East Wing was ablaze, furniture and hangings being tossed out of windows, the great bell ringing, flocks of disturbed doves flapping in the hot air.

Someone came up beside her and Caspar's voice said, "Such a pity, Claudia. After all dear Jared's hard work."

The cellars. *The Portal.* She gasped and raced after Finn. He was already at one of the doorways, black smoke billowing out into his face, flames flickering deep in the building. She grabbed him and he shook her away. Then she grabbed him again and hauled him back and he turned, his face white with shock. "Keiro! It's our only way to him!"

"It's finished," she said. "Don't you see? The ambush was to keep us away. They've done this."

Following her gaze, he looked behind.

Queen Sia stood on the balcony, a white lace handkerchief to her face. Behind her, calm and unconcerned, his eyes on the collapsing crash of stone and flame, was the Pretender.

"They've sealed the Portal," Claudia said bleakly. "And it's not only Keiro. They've trapped my father Inside."

16

A great Fimbulwinter will close down on the world.
Darkness and cold will spread from Wing to Wing.
There will come one called the Unsapient, from far
away, from Outside.
He will plot and scheme with Incarceron.
They will make the Winged Man.
　　　　—Sapphique's Prophecy of the World's End

Attia, holding tight to Keiro on the horse, stared past his shoulder.

They had finally reached what seemed the end of the spiny jungle, because the road led out and downhill. The horse stood wearily, snorting frosty breath.

Framing the road was a black archway. It bristled with spikes, and on its top perched a long-necked bird.

Keiro frowned. "I hate this. Incarceron is leading us by the nose."

She said, "Maybe it'll lead us to some food then. We've eaten nearly everything."

Keiro kicked the horse on.

As they neared it, the black arch seemed to grow, its massive shadow stretching out toward them until they entered its darkness. Here the road glittered with frost; the horse's hooves rang with metallic clarity on the iron paving. Attia stared up. The bird on the summit was enormous, dark wings spread wide, and just as she rode under it she realized it was a statue, and not of a bird but a man with great wings, as if he was ready to leap, and fly.

"Sapphique," she whispered.

"What?"

"The statue . . . It's Sapphique."

Keiro snorted. "What a surprise." His voice doubled, echoing. They were well under the vault; it smelled of urine and damp, and green slime ran down its walls. She was so stiff she wanted to stop, to climb down and walk, but Keiro was in no mood to linger. Since they had spoken to Finn he had been silent and moody, his answers viciously sharp.

Or he had ignored her altogether.

But then she hadn't wanted to talk much either. Hearing Finn's voice had been a sudden joy, but almost at once it had soured, because he had sounded so different, so full of anxiety.

I haven't abandoned you. I think about you all the time.

Was that true? Was his new life really not the paradise he'd expected?

In the darkness of the vault she said angrily, "You should have let me tell them about the Glove. The Sapient knew there was something. It might have helped . . ."

"The Glove is mine. Don't forget it."

"Ours."

"Don't push me too far, Attia." He was silent a moment, then muttered, "Find the Warden, Jared said. Well, that's just what we're doing. If Finn's failed us, we have to look out for ourselves."

"So it wasn't that you were scared to tell them," she said acidly.

His shoulders tightened. "No. It wasn't. The Glove is none of Finn's business."

"I thought oathbrothers shared everything."

"Finn has freedom. He isn't sharing that."

Suddenly they rode out from the archway, and the horse stopped, as if in astonishment.

In this Wing the light was a dull red. Below them was a hall larger than any Attia had ever seen, its distant floor crisscrossed by transitways and tracks. They were high in its roof, and from their feet a great curving viaduct carried the road across, so that Attia could see its arches and tapering columns disappearing into the mirk. Fires burned like tiny Eyes on the floor of the hall.

"I'm stiff."

"Get down then."

She slid from the horse and the road felt unsteady under her feet. She crossed to the rusty railing and looked over.

There were people down there, thousands of them. Great migrations of people, pushing trucks and wagons, carrying children. She saw flocks of sheep, a few goats, some precious cattle, the herders' armor gleaming in the coppery light.

"Look at this. Where are they all going?"

"The opposite way to us." Keiro didn't dismount. He sat tall, gazing down. "People are always moving in the Prison. They always think there's somewhere better. The next Wing, the next level. They're fools."

He was right. Unlike the Realm, Incarceron was always in a state of change; Wings were reabsorbed, doors and gates sealed themselves, steel bars sprang up in tunnels. But she wondered what cataclysm had caused such numbers to travel, what force drove them on. Was this the result of the dying light? The growing cold?

"Come on," Keiro said. "We have to cross this thing, so let's get on with it."

She didn't like the idea. The viaduct was barely wide enough for a wagon. It had no parapets, just a surface potholed with rust and a gulf of air on each side. It was so high faint wisps of cloud hung unmoving across it.

"We should lead the horse. If it panics . . ."

Keiro shrugged and dismounted. "Fine. I'll lead, you come behind. Stay alert."

"No one's going to attack us up here!"

"That remark shows why you were a dog-slave and I was . . . almost . . . Winglord. This is a track, right?"

"Yes . . ."

"Then someone owns it. Someone always does. If we're lucky there'll be a toll to pay at the far end."

"And if we're unlucky?"

He laughed, as if the danger had cheered him. "We make a quick descent. Though maybe not, because the Prison's on our side now. It has reasons to keep us safe."

Attia watched him lead the horse onto the viaduct before she said quietly, "Incarceron wants the Glove. I don't suppose it cares who brings it."

He heard her, she was sure. But he didn't look back.

Crossing the rusting structure was precarious. The horse was nervous; it whickered and once sidestepped, and Keiro soothed it continuously in a low irritated mutter, swear words merging seamlessly with comfort. Attia tried not to look to either side. There was a strong wind that nudged slyly against her; she braced her body, aware that with one gust Incarceron could topple her over the edge. There was nothing to hold on to. She paced in terror, foot before foot.

The surface was corroded. Debris lay on it, scraps of metal, abandoned filth, snags of cloth caught from the wind and fluttering like ragged flags. Her feet crunched the frail bones of a bird.

She concentrated on walking, barely lifting her head. Gradually she became aware of empty space, a giddiness of air. Small dark tendrils began to sprawl across the track.

"What's that?"

"Ivy." Keiro's mutter was tight with tension. "Growing up from below."

How could it grow this far? She glanced briefly to the right and giddiness swept her like sweat. Tiny people moved beneath, the sound of wheels and voices faint on the wind. Her coat flapped against her.

The ivy thickened. It became a treacherous tangle of glossy leaves. In places it was impassable; Keiro had to coax the terrified horse along the very edge of the viaduct, its hooves clanging on metal. His voice was a low mutter.

"Come on, you scrawny nag. Come on, you useless beggar."

Then he stopped.

His voice was snatched by the wind. "There's a big hole here. Be careful."

When she came to it she saw its charred edge first, crumbling with rust. Wind howled up through it. Below, iron girders corroded, old bird's-nests in their joists. A heavy chain looped into emptiness.

Soon there were other holes. The track became a yielding nightmare, creaking ominously wherever the horse trod. After a few minutes, she realized Keiro had stopped.

"Is it blocked?"

"As good as." His voice was tight, oddly breathless. His breath frosted as he looked back at her. "We should go back. We'll never cross this."

"We've come too far!"

"The horse is on the edge of panic."

Was he scared? His voice was low, his face set. For a moment she sensed weakness, but then his hissed anger reassured her. "Back up, Attia!"

She turned.

And saw the impossible.

Masked figures were swarming up over the sides of the viaduct, through holes, up chains and bines of ivy. The horse gave a whinny of fear and reared. Keiro dropped the reins and leaped back.

She knew it was over. The horse plunged in terror; it would fall, and far below, the starving people would butcher its body.

Then one of the masked people grabbed it, flung a cloak over its eyes, and expertly led it away into the dark.

There were about ten of them. They were small and slim, and wore feathered helms, all black, except for a jagged lightning flash across the right eye. They held Keiro in a ring of aimed firelocks. But none of them came near Attia.

She stood, poised, the knife ready.

Keiro drew himself up, his blue eyes fierce. His hand dropped to his sword.

"Don't touch that." The tallest raider took the weapon, then turned to Attia. "Is he your slave?"

The voice was a girl's. The eyes in the mask were mismatched—one alive and gray, the other with a pupil of gold, an unseeing stone.

At once Attia said, "Yes. Don't kill him. He belongs to me."

Keiro snorted but didn't move. She hoped he'd have the sense to stay silent.

The masked girls—for Attia was sure they were all girls—glanced at one another. Then the leader made a sign. The firelocks were lowered.

Keiro looked at Attia. She knew what that look meant.

The Glove was in the inner pocket of his coat, and they'd find it if they searched him.

He folded his arms and grinned. "Surrounded by women. Things are looking up."

Attia glared. "Shut up. Slave."

The golden-eyed girl circled him. "He doesn't have the bearing of a slave. He is arrogant, and a man, and he thinks himself stronger than us." She gave a curt nod. "Throw him over."

"*No!*" Attia stepped forward. "No. He belongs to me. Believe me, I'll fight anyone who tries to kill him."

The masked girl stared at Keiro. Her golden eye glittered and Attia realized that it was not blind, that she saw through it in some way. A halfwoman.

"Search him then for weapons."

Two of the girls searched him; he pretended to enjoy it, but when they took the Glove from his pocket Attia knew it took all his self-control not to lash out.

"What is this?" The leader held up the Glove. It lay in her hands, the dragonskin iridescent in the gloom, the claws split and heavy.

"That's mine," Keiro and Attia said together.

"Ah."

"I carry it for her," Keiro said. He smiled his most charming smile. "I am the Slave of the Glove."

The girl gazed at the dragonclaws with her mismatched eyes. Then she looked up. "Both of you will come with us. In all my years taking toll on the Skywalk I've never seen an object of such power. It ripples in purple and gold. It sings in amber."

Attia moved forward cautiously. "You can see that?"

"I hear it with my eyes." She turned away. Attia flicked a fierce glance at Keiro. He had to shut up and play along.

Two of the masked girls pushed him. "Walk," one said.

The leader fell in beside Attia. "Your name?"

"Attia. You?"

"Rho Cygni. We give up our birth names."

At the large hole in the floor the girls were sliding expertly through.

"Down there?" Attia tried not to let the fear into her voice, but she sensed Rho's smile behind the mask.

"It doesn't lead to the ground. Go on. You'll see."

Attia sat, her legs dangling over the edge. Someone caught her feet and steadied her; she slithered through and grabbed the rusty chain. There was a rickety walkway built close under the viaduct, half hidden by ivy. It was as dark as a tunnel and it creaked underfoot, but at its end it divided into a maze of smaller passageways and rope stairs, hanging rooms and cages.

Rho walked behind her, noiseless as a shadow. At the end she guided Attia to the right into a chamber that moved slightly as if beneath it was nothing but sky. Attia swallowed. The walls were of interwoven wattle and the floor was hidden in a deep coating of feathers. But it was the ceiling that made her stare. It was painted a deep, amazing blue and gleaming in it were patterns of golden stones, like the one in Rho's eye.

"The stars!"

"As Sapphique wrote of them." The girl stood beside her and looked up. "Outside they sing as they cross the sky. The Bull, and the Hunter, and the Chained Princess. And the Swan, of whose Constellation we are." She pulled off her feathered helm and her hair was dark and short, her face pale. "Welcome to the Swan's Nest, Attia."

It was stiflingly warm, and lit by tiny lamps. She saw the shadowy figures remove armor and masks and become girls and women of all ages, some stout, some young and lithe. The smell of food rose from cooking pots. Deep divans filled with downy feathers littered the room.

Rho pushed her toward one. "Sit down. You look exhausted."

Anxious, she said, "Where's . . . my servant?"

"Caged. He won't starve. But this place is not for men."

Attia sat. She was suddenly unbearably weary, but she had to stay alert. The thought of Keiro's certain fury cheered her.

"Please eat. We have plenty."

A bowl of hot soup was put in front of her. She sipped at it hurriedly while Rho sat, elbows on knees, watching.

"You were hungry," she said after a while.

"We've been traveling for days."

"Well, your journey's over now. You're safe here."

Attia savored the thin soup, wondering what she meant. These people seemed friendly, but she must be on her guard. They had Keiro, and they had the Glove.

"We've been expecting you," Rho said quietly.

She almost choked. "Me?"

"Someone like you. Something like this." Rho drew the Glove from her coat, laid it reverently in her lap. "Strange things are happening, Attia. Wonderful things. You saw the tribes migrating. For weeks we've watched them down there, always searching, for food, for warmth, always fleeing from the commotion at the Prison's heart."

"What commotion is that, Rho?"

"I've heard it." The girl's strange gaze turned to Attia. "We all have. Late at night, deep in dreams. Suspended between ceiling and floor, we've felt its vibrations, in the chains and walls, in our bodies. The beating of Incarceron's heart. It grows stronger, daily. We're its providers, and we know."

Attia put down the spoon and tore off some black bread. "The Prison is shutting down. Is that it?"

"Concentrating. Focusing. Whole Wings are dark and silent. The Fimbulwinter has begun, and that was prophesied. And still the Unsapient sends out his demands."

"*Un*sapient?"

"So we call him. They say the Prison summoned him from Outside . . . From his chamber in the Prison's heart he is creating something terrible. They say he is making a man, out of rags and dreams and flowers and metal. A man who'll lead us all to the stars. It will happen soon, Attia."

Gazing at the girl's lit face Attia felt only weariness. She pushed the plate aside and said sadly, "What about you? Tell me about you."

Rho smiled. "I think that can wait till tomorrow. You need to sleep." She dragged a thick cover over to Attia. It was soft and warm and irresistible. Attia snuggled into it.

"You won't lose the Glove," she said sleepily.

"No. Sleep well. You're with us now, Attia Cygni."

She closed her eyes. From somewhere far off she heard Rho say, "Was the slave given food?"

"Yes. But he spent most of the time trying to seduce me," a girl's voice laughed.

Attia rolled over and grinned.

Hours later, deep in sleep, between breaths, in her teeth and eyelashes and nerves, she felt the heartbeat. Her heartbeat. Keiro's. Finn's. The Prison's.

17

The world is a chessboard, madam, on which
we play out our ploys and follies. You are the
Queen, of course. Your moves are the strongest.
For myself, I claim only to be a knight, advancing
in a crooked progress. Do we move ourselves, do
you think, or does a great gloved hand place us on
our squares?

—*Private Letter;*
The Warden of Incarceron to Queen Sia

"Were you responsible?" Claudia stepped out of the shadow of the hedge and enjoyed the way Medlicote spun around, alarmed.

He bowed, the half-moons of his glasses flashing in the morning sunlight. "For the storm, my lady? Or the fire?"

"Don't be flippant." She let herself sound imperious. "We were attacked in the forest—Prince Giles and myself. Was it your doing?"

"Please." His ink-stained fingers lifted. "Please, Lady Claudia. Be discreet."

Fuming, she kept silent.

He gazed across the wide lawns. Only peacocks strutted and

squawked. There was a group of courtiers in the orangery; faint giggles drifted from the scented gardens.

"We made no attack," he said quietly. "Believe me, madam, if we had, Prince Giles—if he is Giles—would be dead. The Steel Wolves deserve their reputation."

"You failed to kill the Queen on several occasions." She was scathing. "And you placed a dagger next to Finn . . ."

"To ensure he remembers us. But the forest, no. If I may say so, you were unwise to ride out without an escort. The Realm is full of discontents. The poor suffer their injustices, but they don't forgive them. It was probably a simple attempt at robbery."

She thought it was the Queen's plot, though she had no intention of letting him know that. Instead she snapped a bud from the rosebush and said, "And the fire?"

He looked stricken. "That is a disaster. You know who was responsible for that, madam. The Queen has never wanted the Portal reopened."

"And now she thinks she's won." Claudia jumped as a peacock rustled its magnificent tail into a fan. The hundred eyes watched her. "She thinks that my father is cut off."

"Without the Portal, he is."

"You knew my father well, Master Medlicote?"

Medlicote frowned. "I was his secretary for ten years. But he was not an easy man to know."

"He kept his secrets?"

"Always."

"About Incarceron?"

"I knew nothing about the Prison."

She nodded and took her hand out of her pocket. "Do you recognize this?"

He looked at it, wondering. "It's the Warden's pocketwatch. He always wore it."

She was watching him closely, alert for any glimmer of hidden recognition, of knowledge. In the glasses she saw the reflection of the open watchcase, the silver cube turning on the chain.

"He left it for me. You have no idea then, where the Prison is?"

"None. I wrote his correspondence. I ordered his affairs. But I never went there with him."

She clicked the case shut. He seemed puzzled, had given no sign of knowing what he was looking at.

"How did he travel there?" she asked quietly.

"I never discovered that. He would disappear, for a day, or a week. We . . . the Wolves . . . believe the Prison to be some sort of underground labyrinth, below the Court. Obviously the Portal gave access." He looked at her curiously. "You know more about this than I do. There may be information in his study, at your house in the Wardenry. I was never allowed in there."

His study.

She tried not to reveal by even a blink the shock his words sparked. "Thank you. Thank you."

Hardly knowing what she said, she turned on her heel, but his voice stopped her.

"Lady Claudia. Something else. We have learned that when the false prince is executed you will share his fate."

"*What!*"

He was standing with his glasses in his hands, his dusty shoulders stooped. In the sunlight he seemed suddenly a half-blind, agitated man.

"But she can't . . ."

"She will. I warned you, lady. You are an escaped Prisoner. She would not be breaking any laws."

Claudia was cold. She could hardly believe this. "Are you sure?"

"One of the Privy Council has a mistress. The woman is one of our operatives. He told her that the Queen was adamant."

"Did she hear anything else? Whether the Queen had brought in this Pretender?"

He stared at her. "That interests you more than your own death?"

"Tell me!"

"Unfortunately, no. The Queen professes ignorance as to which of the boys is her true stepson. She's told the Council nothing."

Claudia paced, shredding the rosebud. "Well, I don't intend to be executed, by her or your Wolves or anyone else. Thank you." She had ducked under the rose arch when he took a step after her and said softly, "Master Jared was bribed to stop work on the Portal. Did you know that?"

She stopped still as death, without turning. The roses were white, perfectly scented. Fat bees fumbled in their petals. There was a thorn in the bud she held; it hurt her fingers and she dropped it.

He came no nearer. His voice was quiet. "The Queen offered him—"

"There's nothing"—she turned, almost spitting the words—"*nothing*, that she could offer that he would take. Nothing!"

A bell chimed, then another from the Ivory Tower. It was the signal for the Inquisition of the Candidates. Medlicote kept his eyes on her. Then he put his spectacles back on and bowed clumsily. "My mistake, my lady," he said.

She watched him walk away. She was trembling. She didn't know how much with anger, how much with fear.

━◦○◦━

JARED LOOKED down with a rueful smile at the book in his hand. It had been a favorite of his when he had been a student here, a small red book of mysterious and cryptic poems that languished unread on the shelves. Now, opening the pages, he found the oak leaf he had once placed in it, on page forty-seven, at the sonnet about the dove that would cure the devastation of the Years of Rage, a flowering rose in its beak. Reading the lines now, he let his memories slip back to that time. It had not been so long ago. He had been the youngest graduate of the

Academy since Protocol began, considered brilliant, assured of a great career.

The oak leaf was as frail as cobweb, a skeleton of veins. His fingers trembling slightly, he closed the book and slid it back. He was certainly above such self-pity.

The library of the Academy was a vast and hushed collection of rooms. Great oak cabinets of books, some of them chained, stood in ranks down the galleried halls.

Sapienti sat huddled over manuscripts and illuminated volumes, quill nibs scraping, each stall lit by a small lamp that looked like a candle but was in fact a high intensity personal diode powered by the hidden underground generators. Jared estimated that at least a third of the precious remaining power of the Realm was consumed here. Not just in the library, of course. The apparent quills were linked to a central computer that also ran the lunar observatory and the extensive medical wing. The Queen, though he hated her, had been right. If there had once been a cure for him, this was the only place it might still be found.

"Master?" The librarian had returned, the Queen's letter in his hand. "This is all in order. Please follow me."

The Esoterica was the heart of the library. It was rumored to be a secret chamber, entered only by the First High Sapient and the Warden. Jared certainly had never been there. His heart fluttered a little with excitement.

They walked through three rooms, through a hall of maps

and up a winding stair into a small gallery that ran around above the reading room, under the dusty cornice. In the far corner was a shadowy alcove, containing a desk and a chair, the arms carved with winding snakes.

The librarian bowed. "If you need anything, please ask one of my assistants."

Jared nodded and sat. He tried not to show his surprise and disappointment; he had expected something more secret, more impressive, but perhaps that had been foolish.

He glanced around.

There were no obvious watching devices, but they were here, he sensed that. He put his hand into his coat and slid out the disc he had prepared. He slipped the disc under the desk and it clasped itself on tight.

The desk, despite appearances, was metal. He touched it, and a portion of the wainscoting became a screen that lit discreetly. It said YOU HAVE ENTERED THE ESOTERICA.

He worked quickly. Soon diagrams of the lymphatic and nervous systems rippled over the screen. He studied them intently, cross-referencing with the fragments of medical research that the system still held. The room below was silent, formal busts of ancient Sapienti staring in stiff rigor from their marble pedestals. Outside the distant casement, a few doves cooed.

A librarian padded by, carrying a heap of parchment. Jared smiled gently.

They were keeping a good watch on him.

By three, the time for the brief afternoon rain shower, he was ready. As the light dimmed and the room grew gloomier, he slid his hand under the desk and touched the disc.

At once, under the diagrams of the nervous system, writing appeared. It had taken a long time to find the encrypted files on Incarceron, and his eyes were tired, his thirst a torment. But as the first thunder rumbled, here they were.

Reading one script below another was a skill he had perfected long ago. It needed concentration, and always gave him a headache, but that would be bearable. After ten minutes he had worked out one symbol that unlocked others, then recognized an old variant of the Sapient tongue he had once studied.

As he translated, the words began to form out of the mass of strange glyphs.

Rota of the original Prisoners.

Sentences and Judicial reports.

Criminal Records; Photoimages.

Duties of the Warden.

He touched the last line. The screen rearranged, and under its web of nerves informed him curtly: *This material is classified. Speak the password.*

He swore quietly.

Incorrect, the screen said. *You have two more attempts before an alarm will be sounded.*

Jared closed his eyes and tried not to groan. He glanced around; saw the rain slashing against the windows, the small lights on the desks below brighten imperceptibly. He made himself breathe slowly, felt sweat prickle his back.

Then he whispered, "Incarceron."

Incorrect. You have one more attempt before an alarm will be sounded.

He should withdraw and think about it. If they found out, he'd never get this far again. And yet time was against him. Time, which the Realm had been denied, was taking its revenge.

Pages turned below. He leaned closer, seeing in the screen his own pale face, the dark hollows of his eyes. There was a word in his mind and he had no idea if it was the right one. But the face was both his and another's, and it was narrow and its hair was dark and he opened his mouth and whispered its name.

"Sapphique?"

Lists. Rotas. Data.

It spread like a virus over the page, over the diagrams, over everything. The strength and speed of the information astounded him; he tapped the disc to record it as it rapidly came and went.

"Master?"

Jared almost jumped.

One of the Academy porters stood there, a big man, his dark coat shiny with age, his staff tipped with a white pearl. "Sorry to disturb you at work, Master, but this came. From the Court."

It was a parchment letter, sealed with Claudia's black swan insignia.

"Thank you." Jared took it, gave the man a coin, and smiled calmly. Behind him the screen showed endless medical diagrams. Used to the austere ways of the Sapienti, the porter bowed and withdrew.

The seal snapped as Jared opened it. And yet he knew it would have been read by the Queen's spies.

> *My dearest Master Jared,*
>
> *The most dreadful thing has happened! A fire broke out in the cellars of the East Court, and most of the ground and upper floors have collapsed. No one was hurt but the entrance to the Portal is buried under tons of rubble. The Queen's Majesty assures me everything possible will be done but I am so dismayed! My father is lost to us, and Giles bemoans the fate of his friends. Today he faces the trial of the Inquisitors. Pray search hard, dear friend, for our only alternative lies in silence and secrecy.*
>
> *Your most loving and obedient pupil,*
> *Claudia Arlexa*

He smiled ruefully at the Protocol. She could do much better. But then, the note was not just for him, it was for the Queen. A fire! Sia was taking no chances—first removing him and then sealing the entrance to the Prison.

But what the Queen presumably didn't know and only he and Claudia did, was that there was another entrance to the Portal, through the Warden's study at home in the sleepy manor house of the Wardenry. *Our only alternative lies in silence and secrecy.* She had known he would understand.

The porter, fidgeting at a respectful distance, said, "The messenger returns to Court in an hour. Will there be any answer, Master?"

"Yes. Please bring some ink and paper."

As the man went, Jared took out a tiny scanner and ran it across the vellum. Scrawled in red across the neatly written lines was IF FINN LOSES THEY INTEND TO KILL US BOTH. YOU KNOW WHERE WE'LL BE. I TRUST YOU.

He drew in a sharp breath. The porter, anxious, placed the inkwell on the desk. "Master, are you in pain?"

He sat, white. "Yes," he said, crumpling the paper.

He had never guessed they would kill her. And what had she meant by *I trust you*?

∞

THE QUEEN rose and all the diners stood hurriedly, even those still eating. The summer meal of cold meats and venison pasties, of lavender cream and syllabub lay scattered on the white-clothed tables.

"Now." She dabbed her lips with a kerchief. "You will all retire, except the Claimants."

Claudia curtsied. "I ask permission to attend the trial, Majesty."

The Queen's lips made a perfect red pout. "I'm sorry, Claudia. Not this time."

"Nor me?" Caspar said, drinking.

"Or you either, my sweet. Run away and shoot things." But she was still looking at Claudia, and suddenly, almost mischievously, she took her by the arm. "Oh Claudia! It's such a shame about the Portal! And you know I'm so sorry to have to appoint a new Warden. Your dear father was so . . . astute."

Claudia kept the smile plastered to her face. "As Your Majesty wishes." She wouldn't beg. That was what Sia wanted.

"If only you'd married Caspar! In fact, even now—"

She couldn't stand this. She couldn't pull away either, so she stood rigid and said, "That choice is over, Majesty."

"Too right," Caspar muttered. "You had your chance, Claudia. I wouldn't touch you now—"

"Even for twice the dowry?" his mother said.

He stared. "Are you serious?"

Sia's lips twitched. "You are so easy to tease, Caspar, darling."

The doors at the end of the room opened. Beyond them Claudia saw the Court of Inquisition.

The Queen's throne was a vast eagle, its spread wings forming the back, its raised beak open in a harsh cry. The crown of the Havaarna encircled its neck.

The Privy Council sat in a circle around it, but on either side of the throne were two empty seats, one white and one black. As the Council filed in, Claudia watched a small door in the wall open and two figures emerge. She had expected Finn and Giles. Instead she saw the Inquisitors of Sun and Shadow.

The Shadow Lord wore black velvet lined with sable, and his hair and beard were as jet as his clothes. His face was harsh and unreadable. The other, in white, was graceful and smiling, his robe satin, edged with pearls.

She had never seen either of them before.

"My Lord of Shadow." The Queen went to her throne and turned formally. "And my Lord Sun. Your duty here is to question and draw out the truth, so that we and our Council may come to our verdict. Do you swear to deal faithfully in this inquiry?"

Both men knelt and kissed her hand. Then they walked, one to the black chair, one to the white, and sat. The Queen smoothed her dress, pulling a small lace fan out of her sleeve.

"Excellent. Then let's begin. Close the doors."

A gong rang.

Finn and the Pretender were ushered in.

Claudia frowned. Finn wore his usual dark colors, without ornament. He looked defiant and anxious. The Pretender wore a coat of purest yellow silk, as expensive as could be made. The two stood and faced each other on the tiled floor.

"Your name?" the Lord Shadow snapped.

As the doors slammed in her face Claudia heard their joint response.

"Giles Alexander Ferdinand Havaarna."

She stared at the carved wood, then turned and walked quickly away through the crowd. And like a whisper in her ear her father's voice came to her, coldly amused. "Do you see them, Claudia? Pieces on the chessboard. How sad that only one can win the game."

18

> *What makes a prince?*
> *A sunny sky, an open door.*
> *What makes a prisoner?*
> *A question with no answer.*
> *—Songs of Sapphique*

"Get me out, Attia."

"I can't yet." She crouched by the wooden bars of the cage. "You'll have to be patient."

"Having too nice a time with your pretty new friends?" Keiro sat lounged against the far wall, arms folded, legs stretched out. He looked cool and scornful but she knew him well enough to see that, inside, he was blazing.

"I need to keep in with them. You can see that."

"So who are they?"

"All women. Most of them seem to hate men—they've probably suffered at their hands. They call themselves the Cygni. They each have a sort of number for a name. The number of a star."

"How poetic." Keiro tipped his head. "Now tell me when they're going to kill me."

"They're considering. I've begged them not to."

"And the Glove?"

"Rho's got it."

"Get it back."

"I'm working on it." She glanced at the door of the room warily. "This nest is a sort of hanging structure. Rooms and passages, all woven together. I think there's some way down to the floor of the hall but I haven't found it yet."

Keiro was silent a moment. "The horse?"

"No idea."

"Great. All our stuff."

"All *your* stuff." She pushed her tangled hair back. "There's something else. They work for the Warden. They call him the Unsapient."

His blue eyes stared at her. "They want to take him the Glove!"

He was always so quick, she thought. "Yes, but—"

"Attia, you have to get it back!" He was up on his feet now, gripping the bars. "The Glove is our only way to Incarceron."

"How, exactly? We're outnumbered."

He kicked the bars, furious. "Get me out, Attia. Lie to them. Tell them to throw me over the viaduct. Just get me out."

As she turned he reached out and grabbed her. "They're all halfmen, aren't they?"

"Some of them. Rho. Zeta. A woman called Omega has pincers instead of hands." She looked at him. "Does that help you hate them more?"

Keiro laughed coldly and tapped his fingernail on the bars. It rang, metal against metal. "What hypocrisy that would be."

She stepped away. "Listen. I think we're wrong." Before he could explode she hurried on. "If we give the Prison this Glove, it will carry out its crazy plan of Escape. Everyone here will die. I don't think I can do that, Keiro. I just don't think I can."

He was staring at her, with that cold, intent look that always scared her.

She backed off. "Maybe I should just take the Glove and go. Leave you here."

She got to the door before his whisper came, icy with threat. "That would make you just the same as Finn. A liar. A traitor. You wouldn't do that to me, Attia."

She didn't look back.

⊲◦◦◦⊳

"TELL US once more about the day you remember. The day of the hunt." The Shadow Lord loomed over him, eyes hard.

Finn stood in the empty center of the room. He wanted to pace about. Instead he said, "I was riding . . ."

"Alone?"

"No . . . there must have been others. At first."

"Which others?"

He rubbed his face. "I don't know. I've tried to think, over and over, but . . ."

"You were fourteen."

"Fifteen. I was fifteen." They were trying to trick him.

"The horse was chestnut?"

"Gray." He stared, angry, toward the Queen. She sat, eyes half closed, a small dog on her lap. Her fingers stroked it rhythmically.

"The horse jumped," he said. "I told you, I felt a sort of sting in my leg. I fell off."

"With your courtiers around you."

"No, I was alone."

"You just said—"

"I know! Perhaps I got lost!" He shook his head. The warning prickle moved behind his eyes. "Perhaps I took the wrong path. I don't remember!"

He had to stay calm. To be alert. The Pretender lounged on the bench, listening with bored impatience.

The Shadow Lord came closer. His eyes were black and level. "The truth is that you invented this. There was no ambush. You are not Giles. You are the Scum of Incarceron."

"I am Prince Giles." But his voice sounded weak. He heard his own doubt.

"You are a Prisoner. You have stolen. Haven't you?"

"Yes. But you don't understand. In the Prison—"

"You have killed."

"No. Never killed."

"Indeed?" The Inquisitor drew back like a snake. "Not even the woman called the Maestra?"

Finn's head shot up. "How do you know about the Maestra?"

There was a movement of unease around the room.

Some of the Council murmured to each other. The Pretender sat up.

"How we know is not important. She fell, didn't she, inside the Prison, down a great abyss, because the bridge on which she stood had been sabotaged. You were responsible."

"No!" He was shouting now, eye to eye with the man. The Inquisitor did not back off.

"Yes. You stole a device for Escape from her. Your words are a mass of lies. You claim visions. You claim to have spoken with ghosts."

"I didn't kill her!" He grabbed for his sword but it wasn't there. "I was a Prisoner, yes, because the Warden drugged me and put me in that hell. He took away my memory. I am Giles!"

"Incarceron is not a hell. It is a great experiment."

"It's hell. I should know."

"Liar."

"No . . ."

"You are a liar. You have always been a liar! Haven't you? *Haven't you?*"

"No. I don't know!" He couldn't bear it. His throat was ashes, the blurring of the impending seizure tormenting him. If it happened here he was finished.

He became aware of movement, dragged his head up.

The Sun Lord was standing, beckoning for a chair to be brought, and the Shadow Lord had gone back to his seat.

"Please, sire. Be seated. Be calm." The man's hair was silver, his words sweet with concern. "Bring water, here."

A footman brought a tray. A cool goblet was pressed into Finn's hand and he drank, trying not to spill it. He was shaking, his sight blurred by spots and itches. Then he sat, gripping the padded arms of the chair. Sweat was soaking his back. The eyes of the Council were fixed on him; he dared not look at their disbelief. The Queen's fingers fondled the silky fur of her dog. She was watching calmly.

"So," the Sun Lord mused. "You say the Warden imprisoned you?"

"It must have been him."

The man smiled kindly. Finn tensed. The kind ones were always the most deadly.

"But . . . if the Warden was responsible, he could not have acted alone. Not with the abduction of a royal prince. Do you claim that the Privy Council were involved?"

"No."

"The Sapienti?"

.He shrugged wearily. "Someone with knowledge of drugs must have been."

"So you accuse the Sapienti?"

"I don't accuse . . ."

"And the Queen?"

The room was silent. Sullen, Finn clenched his fists. He was staring right into disaster and he knew it. But he didn't care. "She must have known."

No one moved. The Queen's hand was still. The Sun Lord shook his head sadly. "We need to be absolutely clear, sire. Do you accuse the Queen of your abduction? Of your imprisonment?"

Finn didn't look up. His voice was dark with misery, because they had trapped him into this, and Claudia would despise him for his stupidity.

But he still said it.

"Yes. I accuse the Queen."

～∞∞∞～

"LOOK OVER there." Rho stood on the viaduct and pointed.

Narrowing her eyes, Attia strained to see across the dimness of the hall. Birds were flying toward her, dark flocks of them.

Their wings creaked; in a second they were all around her and she ducked with a gasp under the cloud of plumage and beaks. Then they were streaming far into the east.

"Birds, bats, people." Rho turned, her eye of gold shining. "We have to live, Attia, like everyone else, but we don't steal, or kill. We work for a higher purpose. When the Unsapient asks for things he needs, we get them. In the last three months we've sent him—"

"How?"

"What?"

Attia caught the girl by the wrist. "How? How does this . . . Unsapient tell you what he wants?"

Rho pulled away and stared. "He speaks to us."

A shiver of the world interrupted her. Far below a scream arose; cries of terror. Instantly Attia fell flat, grabbing the rusted girders. Another ripple of movement went right through her body, her very fingernails. Next to her a rivet snapped; ivy slithered over the edge.

They waited until the Prisonquake ended, Rho on hands and knees beside her, both of them breathless with fear. As soon as she could speak Attia said, "Let's get back down. Please."

Through the hole the complex of the Nest hung apparently undisturbed.

"The quakes are getting worse." Rho scrambled in the ivy tunnel.

"How does he speak to you? Please, Rho, I really need to know."

"Down here. I'll show you."

They hurried through the room of feathers. Three of the other women were there, cooking stew in a great cauldron, one mopping spills that had slopped out in the shiver. The smell of meat made Attia swallow in appreciation. Then Rho ducked under a doorway into a small rounded place, a bubble of a room. It contained nothing but an Eye.

Attia stopped dead.

The small red glimmer swiveled to look at her. For a moment she stood there, remembering Finn's tale of how he had woken in a cell containing nothing but this, the silent, curious gaze of Incarceron.

Then slowly, she came and stood below it. "I thought you said the Unsapient."

"That's what he calls himself. He is the heart of the Prison's plan."

"Is he now?" Attia took a breath and folded her arms.

Then, so loud that Rho started, she snapped, "Warden. Can you hear me?"

⊰∘∘∘⊱

CLAUDIA PACED up and down the paneled corridor.

When the door opened and the footman slipped out, an empty goblet on his tray, she grabbed him. "What's happening?"

"The Prince Giles is . . ." He glanced past her, bowed, and scurried away.

"Don't scare the servants, Claudia," Caspar muttered from the doorway to the garden.

Furious, she turned and saw his bodyguard, Fax, carrying archery targets under his brawny arms. Caspar wore a bright green coat and a tricorn hat with a white curling feather. "They'll be talking for hours. Come and shoot some crows."

"I'll wait!" She sat on a chair against the wall, kicking the wooden leg with her foot.

An hour later, she was still there.

⋘∞⋙

"AND YOU planned all this yourself?"

"The Queen had no idea, if that's what you mean." The Pretender sat back in the chair, arms loose. His voice was calm and conversational. "The plan was mine—to disappear absolutely. I would not have burdened Her Majesty with such a conspiracy."

"I see." The Sun Lord nodded sagely. "But there was a dead body, was there not? A boy who everyone believed was Giles, laid in state here in the Great Hall for three days. You arranged even that?"

Giles shrugged. "Yes. One of the peasants in the forest died from a bear's attack. It was convenient, I admit. It covered my tracks."

Finn, listening, scowled. It might even be true. Suddenly he thought of the old man Tom. Hadn't he said something about his son? But the Sun Lord was asking mildly, "So you are indeed Prince Giles?"

"Of course I am, man."

"If I were to suggest you are an imposter, that you—"

"I hope"—the Pretender sat up slowly—"I hope, sir, that you are not implying that Her Majesty somehow had me trained or indoctrinated in any way to play this . . . role?"

His clear brown eyes met the Inquisitor's in a direct stare. "You would not dare suggest such a crime."

Finn cursed silently. He watched the Queen's mouth twitch into a small secret smile.

"Indeed not," the Sun Lord said, bowing. "Indeed not, sire."

He had them. If they accused him of that, they accused the Queen, and Finn knew that would never happen. He cursed the boy's cleverness, his plausibility, his easy elegance. He cursed his own rough awkwardness.

The Pretender watched the Sun Lord sit and the Shadow Lord stand. If he was apprehensive, there was no sign of it. He leaned back, almost negligent, and beckoned for water.

The dark man watched him drink it. As soon as the cup was back on the tray, he said, "At the age of eleven you left the Academy."

"I was nine, as you well know. My father felt it more fitting that the Crown Prince should study privately."

"You had several tutors, all eminent Sapienti."

"Yes. All, unfortunately, now dead."

"Your chamberlain, Bartley—"

"Bartlett."

"Ah yes, Bartlett. He is also dead."

"I have heard. He was murdered by the Steel Wolves, as I would have been, if I had stayed here." His face softened. "Dear Bartlett. I loved him greatly."

Finn ground his teeth. A few of the Council glanced at each other.

"You are fluent in seven languages?"

"I am."

The next question was in some foreign tongue that Finn couldn't even identify, and the Pretender's answer was quiet and sneering.

Could he have forgotten whole languages? Was it possible? He rubbed his face, wishing the prickle behind his eyes would die away.

"You are also an accomplished musician?"

"Bring me a viol, a harpsichord." The Pretender sounded bored. "Or I could sing. Shall I sing, lords?" He smiled and burst suddenly into an aria, his tenor voice soaring.

The Privy Council stirred. The Queen giggled.

"Stop it!" Finn leaped to his feet.

The Pretender stopped. He met Finn's eyes and said softly, "Then let you sing, sire. Play for us. Speak in foreign tongues. Recite us the poems of Alicene and Castra. I'm sure they will sound most alluring in your gutter accent."

Finn didn't move. "Those things don't make a prince," he whispered.

"We might debate that." The Pretender stood. "But you have no cultured arguments, have you? All you have is anger, and violence, Prisoner."

"Sire," the Shadow Lord said. "Please sit."

Finn glanced around. The Councilors watched him. They were the jury. Their verdict would condemn him to torture and death or give him the throne. Their faces were hard to read, but he recognized hostility, bewilderment. If only Claudia were here! Or Jared. He longed most of all for Keiro's harsh, arrogant humor.

He said, "My challenge still stands."

The Pretender glanced at the Queen. In a low voice he said, "And my acceptance."

Finn went and sat by the wall, simmering.

The Shadow Lord turned to Giles. "We have witnesses. Boys who were at the Academy with you. Grooms, maids, the ladies of the Court."

"Excellent. I want to see them all." The Pretender settled back comfortably. "Let them be brought in. Let them look at him and look at me. Let them tell you which is the Prince and which the Prisoner."

The Shadow Lord looked hard at him. Then he raised a hand. "Bring in the witnesses," he snapped.

19

> *The Esoterica are the broken fragments of our knowledge. The Sapienti will spend generations restoring the gaps. Much of it will never be recovered.*
> —*Project report; Martor Sapiens*

"I should punish you. You were the one who told Claudia she was not my daughter."

It was not the Prison's metallic sneer. Attia stared up at the red accusing Eye.

"I did tell her. She needed to know."

"It was cruel." The Warden's voice sounded grave and weary. Quite suddenly the wall of the room rippled, and he was there.

Rho almost screamed. Attia stared, astonished.

A man stood before her in three-dimensional image, his edges frail and rippling. In places she could see right through him. His gray eyes were cold, and she had to make an effort not to flinch, or kneel, like Rho had hastily done.

She had only ever seen him as Blaize. Now he was the Warden. He wore a black silk coat and black knee breeches; his boots were finest leather, his silvered hair caught back in a velvet ribbon. At first she thought that despite his austerity she had never seen anyone so fine, and yet as he stepped closer she caught the wear on his sleeve, the stained coat, the slightly untrimmed beard.

He nodded sourly. "Yes. The conditions of the Prison begin to affect even me."

"Do you expect me to feel sorry for you?"

"The dog-slave grows a little bold, it seems. So where is Sapphique's Glove?"

Attia almost smiled. "Ask my captors."

"We're not your captors," Rhos whispered. "You can go anytime." The girl was gazing furtively up at the Warden with her gray and gold eyes. She seemed both fascinated and appalled.

"The Glove!" the Warden snapped.

Rho bowed, scrambled up, and ran out.

At once Attia said, "They've got Keiro. I want him released."

"Why?" The Warden's smile was acid. He looked around the Nest with interest. "I doubt very much whether he would do the same for you."

"You don't know him."

"On the contrary. I have studied his record, and yours. Keiro is ambitious and ruthless. He will act for himself, without a qualm." He smiled. "I will use that against him."

He adjusted an invisible control; the image wavered and then became clearer. He was so close, she could have touched him. He turned and gazed at her sideways. "Of course, you could always bring the Glove yourself and leave him behind."

For a moment she thought he had read her thoughts. Then she said, "If you want it, tell them to release him."

Before he answered, Rho was back, breathless, the doorway behind her crowded with inquisitive girls. She laid the Glove down carefully before the Warden's image.

He crouched. He reached out for the Glove and his hand passed right through it. The dragonskin scales glittered. "So! It still exists! What a marvel that is."

For a moment he was fascinated. Behind him Attia glimpsed a vast, shadowy place, dimly red. And there was a sound, a pulsing beat that she recognized from her dream.

She said, "If you went Outside, you could tell them about Finn. You could be a witness for him. Don't you see, you could tell them that you took his memory, that you put him here."

He stood slowly and dusted what looked like rust from his gloves.

"Prisoner, you assume too much." He looked at her, a steel-cold gaze. "I care nothing for Finn, or the Queen, or any of the Havaarna."

"You care about Claudia. She could be in danger too."

His gray eyes flickered. For a moment she thought she had stung him, but he was hard to read. He said, "Claudia is my concern. And I fully intend to be the next ruler of the Realm myself. Now bring me the Glove."

"Not without Keiro."

John Arlex did not move. "Don't bargain with me, Attia."

"I won't let him be killed." Her breath came short and it almost hurt to speak. She prepared herself for some great anger.

But to her surprise he glanced aside as if consulting something and then shrugged. "Very well. Release the thief. But hurry. The Prison grows impatient for its freedom. And—"

There was a crack, a spitting of sparks.

Where he had been, only an echo blinded her eyes, a faint smell of burning hung.

Attia was startled, but she moved quickly, stooping and picking up the Glove, feeling again its heaviness, the warm, slightly oily texture of its skin. She turned to Rho.

"Send someone to get Keiro. And show me the way down."

≈≈≈

IT HAPPENED so quickly, Claudia almost thought she imagined it. One minute she was huddled miserably in the chair outside the guarded door, gazing down the gilded corridor, and in the next moment the corridor was a ruin.

She blinked.

The blue vase was cracked. Its marble pedestal was painted wood. The walls were a mess of wires and faded paint. Great damp patches soaked the ceiling; in one corner the plaster had fallen and drips cascaded in.

She stood up, astonished.

Then, with a ripple so subtle she felt it only in her nerves, the splendor came back.

Claudia turned her head and stared at the two soldiers guarding the door. If they had noticed anything strange they weren't showing it, their faces carefully blank.

"Did you see that!"

"I'm sorry, madam." The left-hand one's eyes kept straight ahead. "See what?"

She swiveled to the other. "You?"

He seemed pale. His hand was sweaty on the halberd. "I thought . . . but no. Nothing."

She turned her back on them and walked up the corridor. Her shoes clattered on the marble floor; she touched the vase and it was perfect. The walls were gilt paneling, beautifully ornamented with Cupid masks and wooden swags. Of course she had known that much of the Era here was illusion, but she felt that for a moment she had been granted a vision, a glimmer of the world as it really was. It was hard to breathe. As if, for that instant, even the air had been sucked away.

The power had flickered.

With a crack that made her jump the double doors opened behind her and the Privy Councilors surged out, a grave, chattering straggle. Claudia grabbed the nearest. "Lord Arto. What's happened?"

He disengaged her hand gently. "It's all over, my dear. We are retiring to consider our verdict; it must be presented tomorrow. I must say I myself have no doubts as to . . ."

Then, as if remembering her fate was involved, he smiled and fluttered a bow and was gone.

Claudia saw the Queen. Sia chatted with her ladies and a foppish youth in a gold coat who was rumored to be her latest lover. He looked hardly older than Caspar. The dog had been dumped in his arms; Sia clapped her hands and everyone turned.

"Friends! We have such a tiresome wait for the verdict, and I hate waiting! So tonight there will be a masked ball in the Shell Grotto, and everyone is to attend. Everyone, mind!" Her colorless eyes met Claudia's and she smiled her sweetest smile. "Or I will be very, very displeased."

The men bowed, the women dropped curtsies. As the entourage swept past, Claudia breathed out in dismay, seeing the Pretender follow, surrounded by a group of the most fashionable young men. He was already gaining supporters, it seemed.

He bowed graciously. "I'm afraid there's no doubt about the verdict, Claudia."

"You were convincing?"

"You should have seen me!"

"You don't convince me."

He smiled, a little sadly. Then he took her aside. "My offer still stands. Marry me, Claudia. We were betrothed a long time ago, so let's do what our fathers wanted. Together we can give the people the justice they deserve."

She looked at his earnest face, his perfect confidence, his

concerned eyes, remembering how just for a second the world had flickered around her. Now she had no idea again how much was false.

She removed her arm from his and bowed. "Let's wait for the verdict."

He seemed to draw back, and then he bowed too, coldly.

"I would be a bitter enemy, Claudia," he said.

She didn't doubt it. Whoever he was, wherever the Queen had found him, his confidence was real enough.

She watched him rejoin the courtiers, their silk clothes brilliant in the flashes of sunshine through the casements. Then she turned and went into the empty Council Room.

Finn was sitting on the chair in the center.

He glanced up, and she saw at once what a struggle it had all been. He looked drained.

She sat on the bench.

"It's over," he said.

"You don't know that."

"He had witnesses. A whole line of people—servants, courtiers, friends. They all looked at us both and said he was Giles. He had answers to every question. He even had this." He rolled up his sleeve and stared at the eagle on his wrist. "And I had nothing, Claudia."

She didn't know what to say. She hated this powerlessness.

"But do you know what?" He gently rubbed the faded tattoo with his finger. "Now, when no one else believes me—maybe not even you—now is the first time since I came here that I really know I'm Giles."

She opened her mouth and then closed it.

"This mark. It used to keep me going, in the Prison. I used to lie awake at night and dream of how things would be Outside, of who I really was. I imagined my mother and father, a warm house, having enough to eat, Keiro in all the splendid clothes he wanted. I used to look at this and know it must mean something. A crowned eagle with its wings spread wide. Like it was about to fly away."

She had to snap him out of this. "We needn't wait for their stupid verdict. I've made plans. Two horses will be ready for us, secretly saddled, at the edge of the forest, at midnight. We can ride for the Wardenry, and use the Portal there to contact my father."

He wasn't listening. "The old man in the forest said that Sapphique flew, in the end. Flew away to the stars."

"And the Queen has ordered a masked ball. What better cover!"

His eyes lifted to her and she saw the signs Jared had warned her of: the whitening of the lips, the strangely unfocused gaze. She hurried across to him. "Stay calm, Finn. Nothing is over. Keiro will find my father and—"

The room vanished.

It became a chamber of grime, of cobwebs, of cables. For a second Finn knew he was back in the gray world of Incarceron.

Then the Privy Council chamber gleamed around him.

He stared at her. "What was *that*?"

Claudia pulled him roughly to his feet. "I think that was reality, Finn."

KEIRO SPAT the last wet rag out of his mouth and gasped in air. Breathing was a great relief; he allowed himself a few vicious swear words too. They had gagged him to keep him from talking to them. Obviously, they knew he was irresistible. Quickly, he pulled his chained wrists under him, dragged his feet through them, the muscles in his arms straining. He stifled a groan as his bruises ached. But at least his hands were in front now.

The cell swayed under his feet. If the place really was wicker, he should be able to hack a way through. He had no tools, though, and there was always the chance that there was nothing below but empty air.

He shook the chain and tested it.

The links were the finest steel and it had been elaborately tied. The knots would take hours to undo, and they were bound to hear the chink.

Keiro scowled. He had to get out of here now because Attia had not been joking. The girl was crazy and he should dump her here, with this nest of star-blind devotees.

Another oath-betrayer. He certainly knew how to pick them.

He chose the weakest-looking link and twisted his hands so

that the fingernail of his right forefinger could slide into the thin gap. Then he prised.

Metal against metal, the fine links strained. He felt no pain, and that terrified him, because where did the metal end and the nerves begin? In his hand? In his heart?

The thought made him lever the link open with a swift anger; at once he bent it far enough to slip the next link out. The chain fell from around his wrists.

But before he could get up he heard footsteps, and the swaying of the cage told him one of the girls was coming, so instantly he looped the chain loosely over his hands and sat back.

When Omega came through the door with two others pointing firelocks at him, Keiro just grinned at her. "Hello, gorgeous," he said. "I knew you couldn't keep away."

⋘◯◯◯▷

JARED HAD been given a room at the top of the Seventh Tower. The climb made him breathless, but it was worth it for the view of the forest, dark miles of trees over the twilit hills. He leaned out of the casement, both hands on the gritty sill, and breathed in the warm dusk.

There were the stars, brilliant and unreachable. For a moment he thought a ripple passed over them, that their brightness dimmed. For a moment the nearest trees were dead and white and ghostly. Then the dizziness passed. He rubbed his eyes with both hands. Was this the illness?

Moths danced around the lantern.

The room behind him was stark. It had a bed, a chair and table, and a mirror that he had taken down and turned to the wall. Still, the less there was in the room, the less chance of it being bugged.

Leaning out, he pulled a handkerchief from his pocket, unwrapped the disc, placed it on the sill, and activated it.

The screen was minute, but as yet there was nothing wrong with his eyesight.

Duties of the Warden. The words unraveled quickly. There were dozens of subtitles. Food provision, educational facilities, health care—his hand hovered over that, but he moved on quickly—social care, structural maintenance. So much information—it would take weeks to read it all. How many Wardens had ever done so? Probably only Martor Sapiens, the first. The designer.

Martor.

He searched for design, narrowed it down to structure, found a doubly encrypted entry in the last file. He couldn't decipher it, but he opened it.

The screen showed an image that made him smile, leaning there under the stars. It showed the crystal Key.

—◁◇◇◇▷—

"JOIN US," Rho begged. "Let him take the Glove and you stay with us."

Up on the viaduct Attia waited with the Glove in her hand

255

and a pack of food on her back and watched three armed women push Keiro up through the hole.

His coat was filthy and his bright hair dull with grease. For a moment she was tempted. Meeting his inquiring stare she dreamed for a moment of sidestepping this crazy obsession of his, of finding her own place of warmth and safety. Maybe she could even try to find her brothers and sisters, somewhere far off in the Wing she had lived in before the Comitatus had dragged her away to be their dog-slave.

But then Keiro snapped, "Are you going to stand there all day! Get these chains off me," and something rippled in her that might have been a cold shiver of reality. It made her feel hard and determined. If Incarceron had the Glove its ambition would be complete. It would break free of itself and leave the Prison a dark and lifeless shell. Keiro might Escape, but no one else would.

She took the Glove and held it out.

"I'm sorry, Keiro," she said. "I can't let you do it."

His hands gripped the chains. "*Attia!*"

But she flung the Glove out into the empty air.

AFTER AN hour's work, the moths flitting around the lamp on the sill, the code gave way with a sigh of rippling letters and the word EXITS came up on the screen. Jared's weariness vanished. He sat up and read avidly.

1. There will be only one Key and this will remain in the possession of the Warden at all times

2. The Key is not needed for the Portal but is the only way of return from Incarceron, except for

3. The Emergency exit

Jared drew in a breath. He glanced quickly around the room. It was dim and silent, the only movement his own vast shadow on the wall, and the dark moths, fluttering in the light and over the tiny screen.

Should you lose the Key, there is a secret door. In the Heart of Incarceron a chamber has been constructed to withstand any catastrophic spatial collapse or environmental catastrophe. Do not use this channel unless absolutely necessary. Its stability cannot be guaranteed. To use the exit a mobile neural net has been constructed, to be worn on the hand. It is activated by extremes of emotion, and thus will not work until a time of great danger. We have given the door a codename, known only to you. That name is SAPPHIQUE.

Jared read the final sentence. Then he read it again. He sat back, his breath frosting in the night air, ignoring the moth that landed on the screen, the heavy footsteps up the stair.

Outside, the stars shimmered in the eternal sky.

20

When he was born, silent and alone, his mind was empty. He had no past, no being. He found himself in the deepest place of darkness and loneliness.

"Give me a name," he begged.

The Prison said, "I lay this fate on you, Prisoner. You shall have no name unless I give it to you. And I will never give it."

He groaned. He reached out his fingers and found raised letters on the door. Great iron letters, riveted through.

After hours, he had grasped their shape.

"Sapphique," he said, "will be my name."

—Legends of Sapphique

Keiro leaped.

With a gasp Attia saw him jump high, the chain flung away. He caught the Glove.

And then he was gone.

Attia dived for him; Rho grabbed her. As he fell his hand shot out; grabbing the ivy, he swung and crashed into the side of the viaduct, a concussion that should have stunned him, but somehow he held tight, twisted around, scrabbling in the glossy leaves.

"You fool!" Attia stormed.

Keiro grabbed the ivy. He glanced up at her and she saw the bruised triumph in his eyes. "Now what, dog-slave?" he yelled. "Do you pull me up, or do I fall?"

Before she could answer, movement shook them all.

Under her feet the viaduct was humming. A high, faint vibration trembled in its girders and meshes. "What is it?" she breathed.

Rho turned, her mismatched eyes gazing into the darkness. She drew in a breath; her face was white.

"They're coming."

"What? Another migration? Up here?"

"There!" Keiro yelled.

Attia stared into the darkness, but whatever had terrified them both was invisible to her. The bridge was shivering, as if a great host had set foot on it, as if their massed tramp had set the whole thing moving on a frequency that would make it shudder and rupture into impossible waves.

Then she saw them.

Fist-sized shapes, dark and rounded, they crawled, on the meshes and wires, in the ivy leaves. For a second she had no idea what they were; then with a creeping of her skin she realized they were Beetles, millions of them, the Prison's all-devouring carnivores. Already the viaduct was glistening with them; there was a terrible new sound, the acidic crack and dissolving of metal, the rustle of carapaces and small pincers cutting steel and wire.

Attia snatched a firelock from the nearest girl. "Get your people! Get them down!" But the Cygni were already moving, she could see them unraveling ladders that flipped out far below, the rungs lashing to and fro.

"Come with us," Rho said.

"I can't leave him."

"You have to!"

Firelocks were slashing; looking down she saw that Keiro had hauled himself up and was kicking savagely at one of the Beetles that had reached him. It fell with a sudden high whine.

Two of the things came out of the ivy at her feet; she leaped back, staring, and saw the metal under them begin to smoke and corrode rapidly, its surface dulling to black.

Then it crumbled to dust.

Rho fired at them, and jumped the gap. "Attia! Come on!"

She could have gone. But if she did she would never see Finn again. Never see the stars.

She said, "Good-bye, Rho. Thank the others for me."

Smoke rose between them, blurring the world. Rho said, "I see both dark and gold for you, Attia. I see Sapphique opening the secret door to you." She stepped back. "Good luck."

Attia wanted to say more, but the words seemed to choke in her throat. Instead she raised the weapon and fired a vicious sweep at the Beetles swarming toward her.

They burst into blue and purple flame, a sizzling explosion of circuits.

"That's what I like to see!" Keiro had climbed up the ivy, now he was hauling himself over the side of the viaduct, the Glove tucked in his belt. He grabbed for the weapon.

Attia jerked back. "Not this time."

"What are you going to do? Kill me?"

"I don't need to. They'll do it for me."

He watched the relentless glistening insects devour the viaduct, and his face was bright and hard. Already the bridge was severed; chunks of it fell away into the unguessable distances below. The gap to Rho's empty ladders was too far to jump now.

He turned.

Mesh shuddered; a vibration sent a great crack splitting through girders. With a sound like gunshot, bolts and rivets snapped.

"No way out."

"Only down." Attia glanced over. "Do you think . . . If we climbed . . . ?"

"It would collapse before we were halfway." He bit his lip, then yelled out at the sky, "Prison! Do you hear me?"

If it did, it did not answer. Under Attia's feet the metal began to separate.

"Do you see this?" Keiro pulled out the dragonglove. "If you want it, you have to save it. You have to catch it. And us!"

The road broke open. Attia slid, bracing her feet wide.

Frost fell in showers from girders; a great creaking, straining howl rang through the structure. Metal struts sprang out. Keiro grabbed her by the arm. "Time to take a chance," he hissed in her ear.

And before she could yell in terror he had leaped with her off the bridge.

⸎

CLAUDIA PONDERED the selection of masks. One was a Columbine's upper face with glittering blue sapphires, topped with a blue feather. Another was white silk, a cat with elegant slanting eyes and whiskers of silver wire. Fur trimmed its edge. She picked a red devil from the bed, but it had to be held on a stick, so that was no use. Tonight, she needed to be as secret as she could.

The cat, then.

Sitting cross-legged on the bolster, she said to Alys, "You've packed what I need?"

Her nurse, folding clothes, frowned. "Claudia, are you sure this is wise?"

"Wise or not, we're going."

"But if the Council find that Finn is the Prince . . ."

She looked up. "They won't. You know that."

Far below, in the halls and chambers of the palace, musicians were tuning up. Faint scrapes and screeches and ripples of notes rang through the corridors.

Alys sighed. "Poor dear Finn. I've grown fond of him,

Claudia. Even though he's as moody as you can be."

"I'm not moody, I'm practical. Finn's still trapped in his past."

"He misses this boy Keiro. He told me one day all about their adventures. The Prison sounded such a terrible place, and yet . . . well, he seemed almost sad, looking back. Wistful. As if he was . . ."

"Happier there?"

"No. No, I wouldn't say that. As if his life was more real there."

Claudia snorted. "He probably told you a pack of lies. His stories are never the same twice. Jared says he learned that in order to survive."

The mention of Jared silenced them both. Finally Alys said cautiously, "Have you heard from Master Jared?"

"He's probably far too busy to answer my letter." It sounded defensive, even to her.

Alys did the straps up on the leather bag and pushed a stray hair back. "I hope he's taking care of himself. I'm sure that Academy is a drafty great barn of a place."

"You fuss over him," Claudia snapped.

"Of course I do. We all should."

Claudia stood. She didn't want the worry of this now, didn't want to have to face Jared's loss. And the words Medlicote had spoken burned in her. Jared could never be bought. She would never believe that. "We'll leave the ball at midnight. Make sure Simon is waiting with the horses. Behind the folly near the stream, out beyond the High Meadow."

"I know. And if he's seen?"

"He's just exercising them."

"At midnight! Claudia . . ."

She scowled. "Well, if he has to, he'll just have to hide in the forest." Seeing Alys's alarm she raised a hand. "And that's the end of it!"

Wearing the cat mask would mean the white silk dress, which was annoyingly cumbersome, but under it she would wear dark breeches and if she was hot, she'd have to put up with it. Boots and jacket were in the pack. As Alys fussed about the fastenings of the dress Claudia thought about her father. His mask would have been very simple, of black velvet, and he would have worn it with a faint air of scorn in his gray eyes. He never danced, but he would have stood elegantly at the fireplace and talked, and bowed, and watched her in the minuet and the gavotte. She frowned.

Was she missing him? That would be ridiculous. But there was something that was pulling him into her mind, and as Alys hitched the last lace tight Claudia realized that it was his portrait, there on the wall, looking at her.

His portrait?

"There." Alys stepped back, hot. "That's the best I can do. Oh you do look well, Claudia. White suits you . . ."

There was a tap on the door.

"Come in," she said, and Finn came in, and they both

stared. For a moment she wasn't even sure it was him. His clothes were black velvet, slashed with silver, and his mask was black, and his hair was caught back in a dark ribbon.

But for a moment it could have been the Pretender, until he spoke.

"I look ridiculous."

"You look fine."

He propped himself on a chair. "Keiro would love this place. He would be so flamboyant here, so popular. He always said he'd make a great prince."

"He'd have us at war within a year." Claudia glanced at her nurse. "Leave us now please, Alys."

Alys went to the door. "Good luck, both of you," she said softly. "I'll see you at the Wardenry."

When she was gone, they listened to the tuning fiddles.

Finally Finn said, "Is she going now?"

"Leaving at once, with the carriage. A decoy."

"Claudia . . ."

"Wait."

Surprised, he saw she had crossed to a small portrait on the wall, of a man in a dark coat.

"Isn't that your father?"

"Yes. And it wasn't here yesterday."

Finn stood up and crossed to stand behind her. "Are you sure?"

"Yes!"

The Warden gazed out at them. His eyes had that cold calm certainty that Finn remembered, the slightly scornful air that Claudia often had.

"You're like him," he said.

"How can I be like him!" Her venom startled him. "He's not really my father, remember."

"I didn't mean like that . . ." But it was best not to say any more about it, he thought. "How did it get here?"

"I don't know." She reached up and took the painting down. It looked like oil on canvas, and the frame seemed worm-eaten, but when she turned it over, they saw it was plastiglas, and the painting a clever reproduction.

And tucked into the back of the frame was a note.

⊰∘○∘⊱

THE DOOR of Jared's room opened noiselessly and the big man stepped inside. He was breathless from the climb, and the sword he held was sharp and heavy, but he was fairly certain he wouldn't need it.

The Sapient hadn't even noticed him yet. For a moment the assassin almost felt sorry for him. So young for a Sapient, so gentle. But he had turned his head now and was standing, quickly, as if he knew his danger.

"Yes? Did you knock?"

"Death doesn't knock, Master. Death just walks in, where he wants to."

Jared nodded slowly. He slipped a disc into his pocket.

"I see. You, then, are my executioner?"

"I am."

"Don't I know you?"

"Yes, Master. This afternoon I had the pleasure of bringing your letter to the library."

"Of course. The porter." Jared moved away from the window, so that the old desk was between them. "So that wasn't the only message from Court."

"You're quick, Master, like all these scholars." The porter leaned companionably on the sword. "My instructions came direct from the Queen herself. She employs me, in a . . . private capacity." He glanced around. "You see, she seems to think you've been prying into things you shouldn't. She sends you this."

He held out a sliver of paper.

Jared reached out and took it, over the desk. There was no way past the man to the door, and the drop from the window was suicidal. He unfolded the note.

I am very disappointed in you, Master Jared. I offered you the chance of a cure, but that's not what you've been researching, is it? Did you really think you could fool me? I do feel just a little betrayed. And oh, how very sad Claudia will be.

It was unsigned, but he knew the Queen's hand by now.

He crumpled it.

"I'll have it back if I may, Master. Not to leave any evidence, you see."

Jared dropped the paper on the desk.

"And that clever little gadget, sir, if you please."

He took the disc out and looked at it ruefully, his delicate fingers adjusting it. "Ah, I understand. The moths! I thought they were a little too curious. I believe they are my designs too."

"Insult to injury, sir, I'm sure." The man hefted the sword regretfully. "I hope you know this is not personal at all, Master. I thought you a very kind gentleman."

"So I'm already in the past tense."

"I don't know about tenses and such learning, sir." The man spoke quietly, but there was an edge to his voice now. "Such learning was never for the son of an ostler."

"My father was a falconer," Jared said mildly.

"Then maybe they saw your cleverness early."

"I suppose they did." Jared touched the table with his finger. "I suppose also it's no use to offer money? To ask you to reconsider? To join the cause of Prince Giles . . ."

"Not till I know which Giles is the true one, sir," the man said firmly. "But, as I said, nothing personal."

Jared smiled, surprising himself. "I see." He felt calm and light. "Surely a sword is a little . . . obvious?"

"Oh bless you, sir, I won't need this. Not unless you make me. You see, in view of your illness, the Queen thought a little jump from the tower would look about right. All the learned Sapienti running out into the quad to find your body. Poor

Master Jared. Took the quick way out. So understandable."

Jared nodded. He put the disc down in front of him on the desk and heard a tiny metallic click. He glanced up, and his eyes were green and sad. "I'm afraid I'm going to have to put you to the trouble of a fight. I don't intend to jump."

"Ah," the porter sighed. "Well, as you wish. A man has his pride."

"Yes. He does." As he said it he moved, jerking to one side.

The big man laughed. "You'll not get past me, sir."

Jared came around in front of the desk and stood face-to-face with him. "Then get it over with."

Two-fisted, the man raised the sword and struck. Jared leaped to one side with all his agility as it clanged down, feeling the point whistle past his face, the blade smash across the desk. But he barely heard the scream, the sizzle of blue electrified flesh, because the charge seemed to suck the air out of the room and fling him back against the wall.

Then there was nothing but a singed smell and an echoing that rang in his ears as if he were deafened.

Gripping the stone work, he pulled himself upright.

The man lay in a heap on the floor; he was still, but breathing.

Jared gazed down at him. He felt a dull regret, a shame.

And under that a fierce and surprising energy. He laughed a shaky laugh. So this was how it felt to nearly kill a man.

But of course, there was nothing personal in it.

Carefully he detached the disc from the metal desk, switched its field off, and dropped it into his pocket. Bending over the porter, he felt his pulse and laid him gently on his side. The man was badly shocked and his hands were burned, but he would almost certainly live. Jared kicked the sword under the bed, then grabbed his pack and raced down the stairs. In the dark portico where the sunlight slanted through the stained-glass windows a tire-woman was hauling a basket of laundry from the Senior Sapient's study.

Jared paused. "Excuse me. I'm sorry. I've left a bit of a mess in my room, number fifty-six at the top. Do you think someone could clear it up?"

She looked at him, then nodded. "I'll get someone. Master."

The basket was obviously heavy and he wanted to tell her not to hurry, but the man needed help, so he said, "Thank you," and turned away. He had to be careful. Who knew what other private arrangements the Queen had here?

In the stable the horses were sleepy, snuffling nosebags. He saddled his quickly, and then before mounting took the narrow syringe from its case and injected the medication into his arm, concentrating on breathing, on the ebbing of the pain in his chest.

He closed the case and leaned a moment, giddy, on the animal's warm flank; its long nose came around and nuzzled him.

One thing was sure. There would be no cure now. He had had his only chance, and it was gone.

⊸◦◦◦⊷

"READ IT," Finn said.

She read, her voice shaky. *"My dear Claudia, Just a brief word . . ."*

As she said it her voice faltered and stopped because, as if she had activated it, the portrait came to life. Her father's face turned to her and he spoke, his gaze as clear as if he really saw her . . .

It will be my last chance to contact you, I'm afraid. Incarceron has become rather demanding in its ambition. It has drained almost all the power of the Keys, and awaits only Sapphique's Glove.

"The Glove," Finn muttered, and she said, "Father . . ." but the voice went on, calm and amused and recorded . . .

Your friend Keiro holds that. It will certainly be the final piece of the puzzle. I begin to feel that I have served my purpose, and that Incarceron has begun to realize it does not need a Warden anymore. It's really very ironic. Like the Sapienti of old, I have created a monster, and it has no loyalty.

He paused, and then the smile went, and he looked drawn. He said, *Guard the Portal, Claudia. The terrible cruelty of the Prison must not infect the Realm. If anything tries to come through, any person, any being, whoever it seems to be, you must destroy it. Incarceron is crafty, and I no longer know its plans.*

He laughed a wintry laugh. *It seems you will be my successor after all.*

His face froze.

She looked up at Finn.

Far below, the viols and flutes and fiddles struck up the first merry dance of the Ball.

21

"The fault is yours," the Enchanter said. "How could a Prison know of Escape but through your dreams? It would be best to give up the Glove."

Sapphique shook his head. "Too late. It has grown into me now. How could I sing my songs without it?"

—Sapphique and the Dark Enchanter

As Finn and Claudia walked arm in arm along the terrace the crowding courtiers bowed and murmured. Fans fluttered. Eyes watched through the faces of demons, wolves, mermaids, storks.

"Sapphique's Glove," Finn muttered. "Keiro has Sapphique's Glove."

She could feel the charge of excitement through his arm. As if he had been shocked into some new hope.

Down the steps the flower beds were curves of twilit flowers. Beyond the formal gardens she could already see lit trails of lanterns over the lawns leading to the elaborate pinnacles of the Shell Grotto. Quickly she tugged him behind a vast urn noisily overflowing with water.

"How could he have it?"

"Who cares? If it's real, it might do anything! Unless it's some scam he's playing."

"No." She watched the crowd, thronging under the lanterns. "Attia mentioned a glove. And then she stopped, very suddenly. As if Keiro wouldn't let her say any more."

"Because it's real!" Finn paced the path, brushing phlox that released its sweet, clinging scent. "It really exists!"

Claudia said, "People are looking."

"I don't care! Gildas would have been so horrified. He never trusted Keiro."

"But you do."

"I've told you. Always. How did he get hold of it? How is he going to use it?"

She gazed at the hundreds of courtiers, a mass of peacock dresses, gleaming satin coats, elaborate wigs of piled flaxen hair. They streamed into the pavilions and the grotto, their chatter loud and endless.

"Perhaps this Glove was the power source Jared noticed."

"Yes!" He leaned against the urn, getting moss on his coat. Behind the mask his eyes were bright with hope. Claudia felt only unease.

"Finn. My father seems to think this Glove will complete Incarceron's plan to Escape. That would be a disaster. Surely Keiro wouldn't . . ."

"You never know what Keiro will do."

"But would he do that? Would he give the Prison the means

of destroying everyone in there, just so that he might Escape too?" She had moved to stand right in front of him; he had to look at her.

"No."

"Are you sure?"

"Of course I'm sure." His voice was low and furious. "I know Keiro."

"You just said . . ."

"Well . . . he wouldn't do that."

She shook her head, suddenly losing patience with his stupid, blind loyalty. "I don't believe you. I think you're afraid he will do it. I'm certain that Attia's terrified of it. And you heard what my father said. Nothing—*no one*—must come through the Portal."

"Your father! He's no more your father than I am."

"Shut up!"

"And since when did you do what he says?"

Hot with anger, they faced each other, dark mask to cat face.

"I do what I want!"

"But you'd believe him before Keiro?"

"Yes," she spat. "I would. And before you, too."

For a second there was a hurt shock in his eyes; then they were cold. "You'd kill Keiro?"

"If the Prison was using him. If I had to."

He was very still. Then he hissed, "I thought you were different, Claudia. But you're just as false and cruel and stupid as

275

the rest of them." He walked into the crowd, shoved two men aside, and, ignoring their protests, barged into the grotto.

Claudia stared after him, every muscle scorched with wrath. How dare he talk to her like that! If he wasn't Giles, he was just some Scum of the Prison, and she, despite facts, was the Warden's daughter.

She gripped her hands, controlling the rage. It took a deep breath to get her heartbeat down; she wanted to yell and smash things, but instead she had to plaster on the smile and wait here till midnight.

And what then?

After this, would Finn even come with her?

A ripple moved through the crowd, a flurry of elaborate courtesies, and she saw Sia pass, in a diaphanous gown of flimsy white, her wig a towering construction of woven hair in which an armada of tiny gilt ships tossed and drowned.

"Claudia?"

The Pretender was beside her. "I see your brutish escort just stormed off."

She took the fan from her sleeve and flicked it open. "We had a slight disagreement, that's all."

Giles's mask was an eagle's face, beautifully made with real feathers, its beak hooked and proud. As with everything he did, it was designed to reinforce his image as Prince-in-waiting. It gave him a strangeness, as masks always do. But his eyes were smiling.

"A lovers' tiff?"

"Of course not!"

"Then allow me to escort you in." He offered her his arm, and after a moment she took it. "And don't worry about Finn, Claudia. Finn is history."

Together, they walked across the lawns to the ball.

―◦○◦―

ATTIA FELL.

She fell like Sapphique had fallen. A terrible, flapping, tumbling fall, arms splayed out, with no breath, no sight, no hearing. She fell through a roaring vortex, into a mouth, down a throat that swallowed her. Her clothes and hair, her very skin, rippled and seemed to be torn away so that she was nothing but a screaming soul plunging headlong into the abyss.

But then Attia knew that the world was impossible, that it was a creature that mocked her. Because the air thickened and nets of cloud formed under her—dense springy clouds that tumbled her from one to another—and somewhere there was laughter that might have been Keiro's and might have been the Prison's, as if she couldn't tell them apart now.

In a flicker between gasps she saw the world re-form; the hall floor convulsed, split, rolled away. A river erupted under the viaduct, a black torrent that rose up to meet her so fast that she had hardly snatched a breath before she had plunged into it, deep, deep into a darkness of frothing bubbles.

A membrane of water webbed her wide mouth.

And then her head burst out, gasping, and the torrent was slowing, drifting her under dark girders, into caves, into a dim underworld. Dead Beetles were washed along beside her; the stream was a conduit of rust, red as blood, channeled between steep metal sides, its surface greasy and bobbing with debris, stinking, the outfall of a world. As if it was the aorta of some great being, sick with bacteria, never to be healed.

The conduit tipped her over a weir and left her, sprawled, on a gritty shore, where Keiro was crouched on hands and knees, retching into the black sand.

Wet, cold, unbelievably battered, she tried to sit up, but couldn't. And yet his choked voice was a rasp of triumph.

"It needs us, Attia! We've won. We've beaten it."

She didn't answer.

She was watching the Eye.

⊸⊂◦◦◦⊃⊸

THE SHELL grotto was well named.

A vast cavern, its walls and pendulous roof gleamed with mother-of-pearl and crystal; each shell arranged in patterns that whorled and spiraled. False stalactites, hand-adorned with a million minute crystals, hung from the ceiling.

It was a glassy, dazzling spectacle.

Claudia danced with Giles, with men with fox faces and knights' helms, with highwaymen and harlequins. She felt icily calm, and had no idea where Finn was, but perhaps he could see her. She hoped he could. She chatted, fluttered the fan, made eyes at everyone through the slanted holes of the mask, and told herself she was enjoying it.

When the chimes of the clock formed of a million tiny periwinkles struck eleven, she sipped iced tea from rosy glasses and nibbled on the cakes and cool sorbets handed out by serving girls dressed as nymphs.

And then she saw them.

They wore masks, but she knew they were the Privy Council. A sudden influx of loud, brilliantly dressed men, some in long robes, their voices dry and parched from debate, harsh with relief.

She edged to the nearest, safe behind her mask. "Sire. Have the Council come to a verdict?"

The man winked behind his owl face and toasted her with a glass. "We certainly have, my pretty kitten." He came close, his breath foul. "Meet me behind the pavilion and I might even tell you what it was."

She bowed, flicked the fan, and backed away.

Stupid, simpering fools. But this changed everything!

The Queen wouldn't wait for tomorrow; suddenly Claudia realized they had been tricked, that the announcement would be made here, tonight, and the loser arrested on the spot. Sia had outguessed them. She had to find Finn!

⊰∘∘∘⊱

OUTSIDE, ON the dark lawns beside the lake, Finn stood with his back to the distant Grotto and ignored the silky voice. But it spoke again, and he felt it like a knife between his shoulder blades.

"They've reached the verdict. We both know what it will be."

The eagle face was reflected, hideously swollen, in the glass Finn held. He said, "Then let's finish it now. Right here."

The lawns were deserted, the lake a ripple of boats and torches.

Giles laughed, a low amusement. "You know I accept."

Finn nodded. A great relief surged up in him. He threw down the wineglass, turned, and drew his sword.

But Giles was beckoning to a servant, who came from the shadows with a small leather case.

"Oh no," Giles said softly. "After all, you were the one who challenged me. That means by all the rules of honor I get to choose the weapons."

He flipped the lid open.

Starlight gleamed on two long, ivory-handled pistols.

⊂◦◦◦⊃

FORCING HER way through the crowd Claudia searched the glittering room, was snatched into the dance and squirmed out of it, ducked under curtains into kissing couples, dodged troupes of strolling minstrels. The ball became a nightmare of grotesque faces, but where was Finn?

Suddenly, near the arched entrance a jester in cap and bells sprang out in front of her. "Oh Claudia, is that you? I insist you dance with me. Most of these women are complete clod-hoppers."

"Caspar! Have you seen Finn?"

The jester's painted lips curled in a smile. They came close to her ear and whispered, "Yes. But I'll only tell you where he is if you dance with me."

"Caspar, don't be an idiot . . ."

"It's the only way you'll find him."

"I haven't got time . . ." But he had caught her hands and dragged her into the gavotte, a great stately square of couples pacing and joining hands to the music, their masks forming crazy partnerships of devil and cockercl, goddess and hawk.

"Caspar!" She hauled him out and pinned him against the glittering wall. "Tell me where he is now or you get my knee where it hurts. I mean it!"

He scowled, waving the bells crossly. "You're a total bore about him. Forget him." His eyes went sly. "Because my dear mama's explained it all to me. You see, when the Pretender is chosen, then Finn is dead and after a few weeks we expose the other one as a fake too and so I get the throne."

"So he *is* a fake?"

"Of course he is."

She stared at him so hard, he said, "You look really strange. Don't tell me you didn't know."

"Did you know that when Finn dies, I do?"

He was silent. Then, "My mother wouldn't do that. I wouldn't let her."

"She'll eat you alive, Caspar. *Now where is Finn?*"

The jester's face had lost its mirth. "He's with the other one. They've gone out by the lake."

For a second she stared at him and felt nothing but cold fear.

Then she ran.

—◦◦◦◦—

FINN STOOD in the darkness and watched the muzzle of the pistol as it rose. Giles held it at arm's length, ten paces away across the dark lawn. He held it steady, and the hole that the bullet would fire from was a perfect circle of blackness, the dark eye of death.

Finn stared into it.

He would not flinch.

He wouldn't move.

Every muscle was so tense he felt he would break, that he had become wooden, that the shot would fracture him into pieces.

But he would not move.

He felt calm, as if this was the moment of decision. If he died here he could never have been Giles. If he was meant to live, he would live. Stupid, Keiro would say.

But it made him feel strong.

And as the Pretender's finger clicked back on the trigger, he felt its answer deep in his mind, as if a cascade of images was shifting and unlocking.

"*Giles! No!*"

He didn't know which of them Claudia's scream was for.

But neither of them was looking at her when Giles fired.

⤏⟨○○○⟩⤎

IT WAS a huge Eye and it was brilliantly red.

For a moment Attia thought it was the dragon of the old story, its head low, staring at her, and then she saw that it was the opening of a cave, that outside it a fiery light burned.

She picked herself up, and stared at Keiro.

He looked terrible, just as she must: wet, ragged, bruised. But the water had made his hair yellow again; he slicked it back and said, "I must have been crazy bringing you."

She limped past him, too weary to even care anymore.

The cave was a red velvet chamber, perfectly circular, with seven tunnels leading out of it. In the center of the room, cooking something over a small bright fire, a man sat with his back to them. He had long hair, and wore a dark robe, and he didn't turn.

The meat crackled, its smell fabulous.

Keiro glanced at the hastily rigged tent, the gaudy stripes, the small wheeled cart where a cyber-ox chewed something green and soggy. "No," he said. "Impossible."

He stepped forward, but the man said, "Still with your handsome pal then, Attia?"

283

Her eyes widened with shock.

She said, *"Rix?"*

"Who else? And how did I get here? By the Art Magicke, sweetie." He turned and gave his sly gap-tooth grin. "Did you really think I was just some backstreet conjuror?" He winked and leaned forward, sprinkling some dark dust on the flames.

Keiro sat. "I don't believe this."

"Believe it." Rix stood. "Because I am the Dark Enchanter, and now I enchant you both into magic sleep."

Smoke was billowing from the fire, sweet and cloying.

Keiro jumped up and stumbled, and fell. Darkness entered Attia's nose, her throat, her eyes.

It took her hand and led her into silence.

FINN FELT the bullet pass his chest like a crack of lightning.

Instantly he raised his pistol and pointed it straight at Giles's head. The eagle mask tilted.

From the clock tower the chimes of midnight began; Claudia, gasping for breath, couldn't move, even though she knew the Queen would be announcing the verdict right now. "Finn. Please," she whispered.

"You never believed me."

"I believe you now. Don't shoot him."

He smiled, his eyes dark under the black mask. His finger clicked the trigger steadily back.

Giles stumbled away.

"Keep still," Finn growled.

"Look." The Pretender spread his hands. "We can make a deal."

"Sia chose well. But you're no prince."

"Let me go. I'll tell them. Explain everything."

"Oh, I don't think so." The trigger trembled.

"I swear . . ."

"Too late," Finn said, and fired.

Giles crashed back onto the grass with a speed that made Claudia screech; she ran to him and knelt over him.

Finn came up and stood gazing down. "I should have killed him," he said.

The bullet had struck the Pretender's arm; it hung broken, and the impact had knocked him senseless. Claudia turned. A great hubbub was rising from the lit grotto; dancers were running out tearing off their masks, unsheathing swords.

"His coat," she said.

Finn hauled him up and they stripped the silk coat from him; Finn shrugged his own off and struggled into the other. As he fitted the eagle mask over his face Claudia tugged the dark coat and mask onto the Pretender. "Keep the pistol," she hissed as the soldiers came racing up.

Finn grabbed her and held the pistol to her back as she swore and struggled.

The guard dropped to one knee. "Sire, the verdict has been given."

"What was it?" Claudia gasped.

The guard ignored her. "You indeed are Prince Giles."

Finn gave a hard laugh that made Claudia stare at him.

"I know who I am." His breath came harsh from inside the eagle's beak. "This Scum from the Prison is wounded. Take him and throw him in some cell. Where is the Queen?"

"In the ballroom . . ."

"Stand aside." Leading Claudia like a prisoner he stalked off toward the lights. Once out of earshot he muttered, "Where are the horses?"

"At Shear's Folly."

He dropped her arm, threw the pistol into the grass, and took one look back at his lost, enchanted Palace. Then he said, "Let's go."

WHAT KEY UNLOCKS
THE HEART?

> *. . . deep forests and dark lanes. A*
> *Realm of magic and beauty. A land*
> *like those in legends.*
> —*King Endor's Decree*

Lightning flickered.

It blinked silently across the sky, lighting the underside of the ominous clouds, and Jared pulled the nervous horse to a halt.

He waited, counting the seconds. Finally, when the weight of tension seemed almost too heavy to bear, the rumble broke; it thundered across the sky above the Forest, as if a being of enormous anger raged over the treetops.

The night was close, sticky with humidity. The reins in his hands creaked, the soft leather greasy with sweat. He leaned forward over the horse's neck, breathing painfully, every bone in his body aching.

At first he had ridden recklessly, afraid of pursuit, turning off the road onto obscure forest tracks, anything that led west, toward the Wardenry. But now, after hours, the track had dwindled to this narrow foxtrail, the undergrowth so matted it brushed his knees and the horse's flank, raising a rank smell of trampled weeds and the decay of centuries of leaves.

He was deep in the forest; there was no way of seeing the stars, and though he wasn't really lost—he always carried a small way-finder—there was no way on from here. The ground was broken with streams and slopes, the darkness intense. And the storm was coming.

Jared rubbed the horse's mane. He would have to backtrack to the stream. But he was so tired, and the pain that lived inside him had somehow come out and was wrapping itself around him; he couldn't help thinking he was riding deeper into it, that its thorns were the forest's.

He was thirsty and hot. He would go back to the stream and drink.

The horse whickered as he coaxed it; its ears flickered as the thunder rumbled again. Jared let it find the way; he only realized that his eyes were closed when the reins slid from his fingers and the horse's long neck dipped; there was a quiet slurp of water.

"Good boy," he whispered.

Carefully, he slid down, holding on to the saddlebow. As soon as his feet met the ground he crumpled, as if he had no strength even to stand. Only clinging on kept him upright.

Ghostly umbels of hemlock rose all around, higher than his head, their perfume sickly. Jared breathed deeply; then he slid to his knees and felt in the darkness until his fingers touched water.

Icy cold, it flowed among stems and stones.

He cupped it and drank, and its cold made him cough, but it was better than wine. He drank more, splashing his face and hair and the back of his neck with its freezing shock. Then he unrolled the syringe from his pack and injected the usual dose.

He had to sleep. There was fog in his mind, a numbness that scared him. He wound the Sapient coat around himself and curled up in the scratchy, rustling nettles. But now he could not close his eyes.

It wasn't the forest he feared. It was the thought that he might die here, and never wake again. That the horse would wander away and the leaves of autumn cover him, that he would decay to bones and never be found. That Claudia would . . .

He told himself to stop. But the pain laughed at him. The pain was his dark twin now, sleeping with its arms tight about him.

With a shudder he sat up, pushing back wet hair. This was hysteria. He was quite certainly not about to die here. For one thing, he had information Finn and Claudia needed, about the door in the Prison's heart, about the Glove. He intended to get it to them.

For another, his death was unlikely to be this easy.

Then he saw the star.

It was red, and small. It was watching him. He tried to stop shivering and focus, but the glimmer was hard to see. Either his fever was causing him to hallucinate, or this was some marsh-gas, flickering above the ground. Grasping a branch, he scrambled to his knees.

The red Eye winked.

Jared reached up, caught the reins, and dragged the horse from its grazing, toward the light.

He was burning, the darkness tugging him back, each step a clutch of pain, a shiver of sweat. Nettles stung him; he pushed through low branches, a cloud of metallic moths, a sky where a thousand stars slid and slithered.

Under a vast oak he stopped, breathless. Before him was a clearing, with a fire burning there, and feeding it with kindling a thin, dark-haired man, flamelight playing over his face.

The man turned.

"Come, Master Jared," he said quietly. "Come to the fire."

Jared crumpled, holding the oak bough, its ridged bark powdery under his nails.

Then the man's arms were around him. "I've got you," the voice said. "I've got you now."

⬥

WHEN ATTIA wanted to wake she found she couldn't. Sleep lay heavy on her eyelids like stones. Her arms were behind her and for a moment she was back in the tiny box-bed in the cell her family had once called home, a cramped corridor where six families camped in ramshackle shelters of stolen wire and mesh.

She smelled the damp and tried to turn and something held her still.

She realized she was sitting upright, and a serpent was coiled around her wrists.

Instantly, her eyes snapped open.

Rix was squatting by the fire. He was folding a small wad of ket, and he blurred before her as he slipped it into his cheek and chewed.

She tugged. There was no snake; her hands were tied behind her and she leaned against something warm and slumped. She realized it was Keiro. Rix had trussed them back to back.

"Well, Attia." Rix's voice was cold. "You look a little uncomfortable."

The ropes were cutting her hands and ankles. Keiro's weight was heavy on her shoulder. But she just smiled. "How did you get here, Rix? However did you find us?"

He spread his magician's fingers. "For the Dark Enchanter, nothing is impossible. The magic of the Glove drew me, through the miles of corridors and echoing galleries."

He chewed the ket with red-stained teeth.

Attia nodded. He looked thinner and lankier, his face pocked and scabbed and unwashed, his lank hair greasy.

The crazy look was back in his eyes.

He must already have the Glove.

Keiro was stirring behind her, as if their voices had wakened him. As he moved she glanced quickly around, saw the dark tunnels that led out of the cave, each as narrow as a slot. The wagon would never get through them. Rix grinned his gappy grin. "Don't worry, Attia. I have plans. It's all arranged."

His voice hardened and he leaned over and kicked Keiro. "So, highwayman. Thieving isn't so good for you now, is it?"

Keiro swore under his breath. Attia felt him wriggle and jerk, pulling her painfully as he squirmed around to get a better look at Rix. Reflected grotesquely in a copper pan on the wagon she saw his blue eyes, a smear of blood on his forehead. But being Keiro, his voice was icily cool.

"Didn't think you'd bear such a grudge, Rix."

"Nothing so paltry as a grudge." Rix stared back, his eyes glinting. "This is revenge. Served cold. I swore it, I'll do it."

Keiro's hand felt warm and sweaty. It groped for Attia's fingers while he said, "I'm sure we can come to some arrangement."

"About what?" Rix leaned forward, drawing something dark and shining from his coat. "This?"

She felt Keiro's stillness. His dismay.

Rix spread out the dragonskin fingers, smoothed the cracked and ancient claws. "It drew me. It called me. Through the transitways, through the humming air, I could hear it. See how its static shivers on my skin."

The hairs on his arm were lifting.

He nuzzled his cheek against the gauntlet and its fine scales rippled. "This is mine. My touch, my senses. My magician's art." He watched them slyly, over the dragonskin. "No artist can lose his touch. It called me, and I found it again."

Attia clutched Keiro's fingers, slid along the rope to the knots. *He's crazy*, she wanted to tell him. *Unstable. Be careful.*

But Keiro's answer was quiet and mocking. "I'm happy for you. But Incarceron and I have a deal, and you wouldn't dare—"

"Long ago," Rix said, "the Prison and I also had a deal. A wager. A game of riddles."

"I thought that was Sapphique."

Rix grinned. "And I won. But Incarceron cheats, you know? It gave me its Glove and promised Escape, but what Escape is there for those of us trapped in the mazes of our minds, highwayman? What secret trapdoors are there, what tunnels to the Outside? Because I have seen the Outside, seen it, and it's vaster than you could dream."

Attia felt icy with fear.

Rix grinned at her. "Attia thinks I'm insane."

"No . . ." she lied.

"Oh yes, sweetkin. And you may be right." He straightened his lanky body and sighed. "And here you both are at my mercy, like the babes in the wood in a patchbook I once read."

Attia laughed. Anything to keep him talking. "Not another one."

"Their wicked stepmother left them in the dark forest. But

they found a house all made of gingerbread and the witch that lived there turned them into swans. They flew away linked by a golden chain." He was gazing at the tiny swans pinned to the Glove.

"Right," Keiro said acidly. "And then?"

"They came to a great tower where a sorcerer lived." Rix put the Glove away tidily and went and rummaged in the wagon.

Attia felt the ropes burn her wrists as Keiro tugged at them furiously. "And he released them?"

"I'm afraid not." Rix turned. He had the long sword that he used in his act, and its blade was sharp. "I'm afraid it's not a happy ending, Attia. You see, they had betrayed him, and stolen from him. He was very angry about it. So he had to kill them."

⬥

THREE LEAGUES from the Court Claudia dragged the winded horse to a halt and gazed back. The great complex of towers was brilliantly lit, the Glass Palace a shining splendor. Finn's horse thudded to stillness beside her, its harness clinking. He stared silently.

"Will Jared know we've gone?"

"I sent him a message."

Her voice was taut; he glanced at her. "What's wrong then?"

It took a while for her to answer. "Medlicote told me the Queen had bribed Jared."

"No chance. There's no way he would . . ."

"There's his illness. She'd use that against him."

Finn frowned. Under the perfect stars the Court glittered, as cold and cruel as scattered diamonds. "Will he really die from it?"

"I think so. He makes light of it. But I think so." The desolation in her voice chilled him, but she sat upright and as the wind whipped her hair back, he saw there were no tears in her eyes.

Thunder rumbled, far off.

He wanted to say something comforting, but the horse was restless, stamping its impatience, and in the Prison death had been too familiar to feel strange now. Controlling the horse, he brought it back around to her. "Jared is brilliant, Claudia. He's far too clever to be controlled by the Queen, or anyone else. Don't worry. Trust him."

"I told him I did."

Still she didn't move. He reached out and caught her arm. "Come on. We need to hurry."

She turned and looked at him. "You could have killed Giles."

"I should have. Keiro would despair. But that boy is not Giles. I am." He met her eyes. "Standing there with that pistol pointed at me, I knew. *I remembered*, Claudia. I remembered."

She stared at him, astonished.

Then the horse whinnied, and they saw the lights of the

Court, all its hundreds of candles and lanterns and windows flicker and go out. For a whole minute the Palace was a blackness under the stars. Claudia held her breath. If they didn't come back on . . . If this was the end . . .

Then the Palace was blazing again.

Finn held out his hand. "I think you should give me Incarceron."

She hesitated. Then she drew out her father's watch and handed it to him, and he held up the silver cube, so that it spun on its chain. "Keep it safe, *sire*."

"The Prison is drawing power from its own systems." He glanced down at the Palace, where a clamor of bells and shouts had begun to ring out.

"And from ours," Claudia whispered.

◄००००►

"YOU CAN'T. Rix, you can't." Attia's voice was earnest and low, anything to keep him calm. "It's ridiculous. I worked for you—we went against that gang of bandits together, that mob in the plague village. You liked me. We got on. You can't hurt me."

"You know a few too many secrets, Attia."

"Cheap tricks! Cons. Everybody knows them." It was the real sword, not the collapsible one. She licked sweat from her lip.

"Well, maybe." He pretended to consider, and then grinned. "But you see, it's the Glove. Stealing that was unforgivable.

298

The Glove is telling me to do it. So I've decided you'll go first, and then your friend there can watch. It'll be quick, Attia. I'm a merciful man."

Keiro was silent, as if he was leaving this to her. He had given up on the knots. Nothing would undo those in time.

Attia said, "You're tired, Rix. You're mad. You know it."

"I've walked a few wild Wings." He swept the sword experimentally through the air. "I've crawled a few crazy corridors."

"Talking of which," Keiro said suddenly, "where's that pack of freaks you usually travel with?"

"Resting." Rix was working himself up. "I needed to move fast." He swung the sword again. There was a sly light in his eye that terrified Attia. His voice was slurred with ket. "Behold!" he cried. "You search for a Sapient who will show you the way Out. I am that man!"

It was the patter of his act. She struggled, kicking, jerking against Keiro. "He'll do it. He's off his skull!"

Rix swung to an imaginary crowd. "The way that Sapphique took lies through the Door of Death. I will take this girl there and I will bring her back!"

The fire crackled. He bowed to its applause, to the ranks of roaring people, held up the sword in his hand. "Death. We fear it. We would do anything to avoid it. Before your eyes, you will see the dead live."

"*No.*" Attia gasped. "Keiro . . ."

Keiro sat still. "No chance. He's got us."

Rix's face was flushed in the red light; his eyes bright as if with fever. "I will release her! I will bring her back!"

With a whipping slash that made her screech, the sword was raised, and at the same time Keiro's voice, acid with scorn and deliberately conversational, came from the darkness behind her.

"So tell me, Rix, since you seem to think you're Sapphique. What was the answer to the riddle you asked the dragon? What *is* the Key that unlocks the heart?"

*He worked night and day. He made a coat
that would transform him; he would be more
than a man; a winged creature, beautiful as
light. All the birds brought him feathers. Even
the eagle. Even the swan.*

—*Legends of Sapphique*

Jared was sure he was still delirious. Because he lay in a ruined stable and there was a fire, crackling loudly in the silent night.

The rafters were a mesh of holes above his head, and in one place a barn owl stared down with wide astonished eyes. From somewhere water dripped. The splashes landed rhythmically just beside his face, as if after some great rainstorm. A small pool had formed, soaking into the straw.

Someone's hand lay half out of the blankets; he tried absently to make it move, and the long fingers cramped and stretched. It was his, then.

He felt disconnected, only vaguely interested, as if he had been out of his body on some long and tiring journey.

As if he had come home to find the house cold and comfortless.

His throat, when he remembered it, was dry. His eyes itched. His body, when he moved it, ached.

And he must be delirious, because there were no stars. Instead, through the broken roof of the building a single red Eye hung huge in the sky, like the moon in some livid eclipse.

Jared studied it. It stared back, but it wasn't watching him. It was watching the man.

The man was busy. Over his knees he had some old coat—a Sapient robe, perhaps—and on each side of him rose a great stack of feathers. Some were blue, like the one Jared had sent through the Portal. Others were long and black, like a swan's, and brown, an eagle's plumage.

"The blue ones are very useful," the man said, without turning. "Thank you for them."

"My pleasure," Jared murmured. Each word was a croak.

The stable was hung with small golden lanterns, like the ones used at Court. Or perhaps these were the stars, taken down and propped here and there, hung on wires.

The man's hands moved swiftly. He was sewing the feathers into the bare patches of the coat, fixing them first with dabs of pitchy resin that smelled of pinecones when it dripped on the straw. Blue, black, brown. A coat of feathers, wide as wings.

Jared made an effort to sit up and managed it, propping himself dizzily against the wall. He felt weak and shaky.

The man put the coat aside and came over. "Take your time. There's water here."

He brought a jug and cup, and poured. As he held it out Jared saw that the right forefinger of his hand was missing; a smooth scar seamed the knuckle.

"Only a little, Master. It's very cold."

Jared barely felt the shock to his throat. As he drank he watched the dark-haired man, and the man stared back with a rueful, sad smile.

"Thank you."

"There's a well just near here. The best water in the Realm."

"How long have I been here?"

"There's no time here, remember. Time seems to be forbidden in the Realm." He sat back, and there were feathers stuck to him, and his eyes were steady and obsessive as a hawk's.

"You are Sapphique," Jared said quietly.

"I took that name in the Prison."

"Is that where we are?"

Sapphique pulled plumage from his hair. "This is a prison, Master. Whether it's Inside or Out, I've learned, is not really important. I fear they both may be the same."

Jared struggled to think. He had been riding in the forest. There were many outlaws in the forest, many woodwoses and madmen. Those who couldn't bear the stagnation of Era, who wandered as beggars. Was this one of them? ·

Sapphique sat back, his legs stretched out. In the firelight he was young and pale, his hair lank with the forest damp. "But you Escaped," Jared said. "Finn has told me some of the tales they tell about you in there, in Incarceron." He rubbed at his face and found it rough, faintly stubbled.

How long had he been here?

"There are always stories."

"They're not true?"

Sapphique smiled. "You're a scholar, Jared. You know that the word *truth* is a crystal, like the Key. It seems transparent, but it has many facets. Different lights, red and gold and blue, flicker in its depths. Yet it unlocks the door."

"The door . . . You found a secret door, they say."

Sapphique poured more water. "How I searched for it. I spent whole lifetimes searching. I forgot my family, my home; I gave blood, tears, a finger. I made myself wings and I flew so high, the sky struck me down. I fell so far into the dark that there seemed no ending to the abyss. And yet in the end, there it was, a tiny plain door in the Prison's heart. The emergency exit. Right there all the time."

Jared sipped the cold water. This must be a vision, like Finn had in his seizures. He himself was probably lying delirious now in the dark rainy woodland. And yet could it be so real?

"Sapphique . . . I must ask you . . ."

"Ask, my friend."

"The door. Can all the Prisoners leave by it? Is that possible?"

But Sapphique had gathered the feathered coat and was examining its holes. "Each man has to find it himself, as I did."

Jared lay back. He tugged the blanket around him, shivering and tired. In the Sapient tongue he said softly, "Tell me, Master, did you know Incarceron was tiny?"

"Is it?" Sapphique replied in the same language, his green eyes as he looked up lit by deep points of flame. "To you, perhaps. Not to its Prisoners. Every prison is a universe for its inmates. And think, Jared Sapiens. Might not the Realm also be tiny, swinging from the watch chain of some being in a world even vaster? Escape is not enough; it does not answer the questions. It is not Freedom. And so I will repair my wings and fly away to the stars. Do you see them?"

He pointed, and Jared drew in a breath of awe because there they were, all around him, the galaxies and nebulae, the thousands of constellations he had so often watched through the powerful telescope in his tower, the glittering brilliance of the universe.

"Do you hear their song?" Sapphique murmured.

But only the silence of the Forest came to them, and Sapphique sighed. "Too far away. But they do sing, and I will hear that music."

Jared shook his head. Weariness was creeping over him, and the old fear. "Perhaps Death is our escape."

"Death is a door, certainly." Sapphique stopped threading a blue feather and looked at him. "You fear death, Jared?"

"I fear the way to it."

The narrow face seemed all angles in the firelight. It said, "Don't let the Prison wear my Glove, use my hands, speak with my face. Whatever you have to do, do not allow that."

There were so many questions Jared wanted to ask. But they scuttled away from him like rats into holes and he closed his eyes and lay back. Like his own shadow, Sapphique leaned beside him.

"Incarceron never sleeps. It dreams, and its dreams are terrible. But it never sleeps."

He barely heard. He was falling down the barrel of a telescope, through its convex lenses, into a universe of galaxies.

⊰○○⊱

RIX BLINKED.

He paused, barely for a second.

Then he slashed the sword down. Attia flinched and screamed, but it whistled behind her and sliced the ropes that held her to Keiro, nicking her wrist so that it bled.

"What the hell are you doing?" she gasped, scrambling away.

The magician didn't even look at her. He pointed the trembling blade at Keiro. "*What did you say?*"

If Keiro was amazed he didn't show it. He stared straight back, and his voice was cool and careful. "I said, what's the Key that unlocks the heart. What's the matter, Rix? Can't answer your own riddle?"

Rix was white. He turned and walked in a rapid circle and came back. "That's it. It's you. *It's you!*"

"What's me?"

"How can it be *you*? I don't want it to be you! For a while I thought it might be her." He jabbed the blade at Attia. "But she never said it, never came near saying it!"

He paced another frantic circle.

Keiro had drawn his knife. Hacking at the ropes on his ankles he muttered, "He's crazy."

"No. Wait." Attia watched Rix, her eyes wide. "You mean the Question, don't you? The Question you once told me only your Apprentice would ever ask you. That was it? *Keiro* asked it?"

"He did." Rix couldn't seem to keep still. He was shivering, his long fingers gripping and loosening on the sword hilt. "It's him. It's you." He tossed the sword down and hugged himself. "A Scum thief is my Apprentice."

"We're all scum," Keiro said. "If you think—"

Attia silenced him with a glare. They had to be so careful here.

He undid the ropes and stretched his feet out with a grimace. Then he leaned back and she saw he understood.

He smiled his most charming smile. "Rix. Please sit down."

The lanky magician collapsed and huddled up like a spider. His utter dismay almost made Attia want to laugh aloud, and yet she felt sorry for him. Some dream that had kept him going for years had come true, and he was devastated in his disappointment.

"This changes everything."

"I should think so." Keiro tossed the knife to Attia. "So I'm the sorcerer's Apprentice, am I? Well, it might come in useful."

She scowled at him. Joking was stupid. They had to use this.

"What does it mean?" Keiro leaned forward, his shadow huge on the cave wall.

"It means revenge is forgotten." Rix stared blankly into the flames. "The Art Magicke has rules. It means I have to teach you all my tricks. All the substitutions, the replications, the illusions. How to read minds and palms and leaves. How to disappear and reappear."

"How to saw people in half?"

"That too."

"Nice."

"And the secret writings, the hidden craft, the alchemies, the names of the Great Powers. How to raise the dead, how to live forever. How to make gold pour from a donkey's ear."

They stared at his rapt, gloomy face. Keiro raised an eyebrow at Attia. They both knew how precarious this was. Rix was unstable enough to kill; their lives depended on his whims. And he had the Glove.

Gently she said, "So we're all friends again now?"

"You!" He glared at her. "Not you!"

"Now now, Rix." Keiro faced him. "Attia's my slave. She does what I say."

She swallowed her fury and glanced away. He was enjoying this. He would tease Rix within inches of insanity, then grin and charm the danger away. She was trapped here between them, and she had to stay, because of the Glove. Because she had to get it before Keiro did.

Rix seemed sunk in torpor. And yet after a moment he nodded, muttered to himself, and went to the wagon, tugging things out.

"Food?" Keiro said hopefully.

Attia whispered, "Don't push your luck."

"At least I have luck. I'm the Apprentice, I can twist him around my finger like flexiwire."

But when Rix came back with bread and cheese Keiro ate it as gratefully as Attia, while Rix watched and chewed ket and seemed to recover his gap-toothed humor.

"Thieving not paying well these days then?"

Keiro shrugged.

"All the jewels you carry. Sacks of loot." Rix sniggered. "Fine clothes."

Keiro fixed him with a cold eye. "So which is the tunnel we leave by?"

Rix looked at the seven slots. "There they are. Seven narrow arches. Seven openings into the darkness. One leads to the heart of the Prison. But we sleep now. At Lightson, I take you into the unknown."

Keiro sucked his fingers. "Anything you say, boss."

FINN AND Claudia rode all night. They galloped down the dark lanes of the Realm, clattering over bridges and through fords where sleepy ducks flapped from the rushes, quacking. They clopped through muddy villages where dogs barked and only a child's eye at the edge of a lifted shutter watched them go by.

They had become ghosts, Claudia thought, or shadows. Cloaked in black like outlaws, they fled the Court, and behind them there would be uproar, the Queen furious, the Pretender vengeful, the servants panicked, the army being ordered out.

This was rebellion, and nothing would be the same now. They had rejected Protocol. Claudia wore the dark breeches and coat and Finn had flung the Pretender's finery into the hedge. As the dawn began to break they topped a rise and found themselves high above the golden countryside, the cocks crowing in its pretty farmyards, its picturesque hovels glowing in the new light.

"Another perfect day," Finn muttered.

"Not for long maybe. Not if Incarceron has its way."

Grimly, she led the way down the track.

By midday they were too exhausted to go on, the horses stumbling with weariness. At an isolated byre shadowed by elms they found straw heaped in a dim sun-slanted loft, where dull flies buzzed and doves cooed in the rafters.

There was nothing to eat.

Claudia curled up and slept. If they spoke, she didn't remember it.

When she woke it was from a dream of someone knocking insistently at her door, of Alys saying, "Claudia, your father's here. Get dressed, Claudia!"

And then soft in her ear, Jared's whisper: "Do you trust me, Claudia?"

With a gasp she sat upright.

The light was fading. The doves had gone and the barn was silent, with only a rustle in the far corner that might have been mice.

She leaned back slowly on one elbow.

Finn had his back to her; he slept with his body curled up in the straw, the sword by his hand.

She watched him for a while until his breathing altered, and although he didn't move, she knew he was awake. She said, "How much do you remember?"

"Everything."

"Such as?"

"My father. How he died. Bartlett. My engagement with you. My whole life at Court before the Prison. In snatches . . . foggy, but there. The only thing I don't know is what happened between the ambush in the forest and the day I woke in the Prison cell. Perhaps I never will."

Claudia drew her knees up and picked straw from them.

Was this the truth? Or had it become so necessary for him to know that he had convinced himself?

Maybe her silence revealed her doubts. He rolled over. "Your dress that day was silver. You were so small—you wore a little necklace of pearls and they gave me white roses to present to you. You gave me your portrait in a silver frame."

Had it been silver? She had thought gold.

"I was scared of you."

"Why?"

"They said I had to marry you. But you were so perfect and shining, your voice was so bright. I just wanted to go and play with my new dog."

She stared at him. Then she said, "Come on. They're probably only hours behind."

Usually it took three days to travel between the Court and the Wardenry, but that was with inn stops, and carriages. Like this, it was a relentless gallop, sore and weary and stopping only to buy hard bread and ale from a girl who came running out from a decaying cottage. They rode past watermills and churches, over wide downs where sheep scattered before them, through wool-snagged hedges, over ditches and the wide grass-grown scars of the ancient wars.

Finn let Claudia lead. He no longer knew where they were, and every bone in his body ached with the strain of the unaccustomed riding. But his mind was clear, clearer and happier than he ever remembered. He saw the land sharp and bright;

the smells of the trampled grass, the birdsong, the soft mists that rose from the earth seemed new things to him. He dared not hope that the fits were over. But perhaps his memory had brought back some old strength, some certainties.

The landscape changed slowly. It became hilly, the fields smaller, the hedges thick, untrimmed masses of oak and birch and holly. All night they rode through them, down lanes and bridle paths and secret ways as Claudia became more and more certain of where she was.

And then, when Finn was almost asleep in the saddle, his horse slowed to a halt, and he opened his eyes and looked down on an ancient manor house, pale in the glimmer of the broken moon, its moat a silver sheen, its windows lit with candles, the perfume of its ghostly roses sweet in the night.

Claudia smiled in relief. "Welcome to the Wardenry." Then she laughed ruefully. "I left in a carriage full of finery to go to my wedding. What a way to come back."

Finn nodded. "But you still brought the Prince," he said.

24

People will love you if you tell them of your fears.
—The Mirror of Dreams to Sapphique

"Well?"

Rix grinned. With a showman's flourish he pointed to the third tunnel from the left.

Keiro walked over to it and peered in. It seemed as dark and smelly as the rest. "How do you know?"

"I hear the heartbeat of the Prison."

There was a small red Eye just inside each of the tunnels. They all watched Keiro.

"If you say so."

"Don't you believe me?"

Keiro turned. "Like I said, you're the boss. Which reminds me, when do I start my training?"

"Right now." Rix seemed to have gotten over his disappointment. He had a self-important air this morning; he took a coin out of nowhere before Keiro's eyes, spun it, and held it out to him. "You practice moving it between your fingers like this. And so. You see?"

The coin rippled between his bony knuckles.

Keiro took it. "I'm sure I can manage that."

"You've picked enough pockets to be deft, you mean."

Keiro smiled. He palmed the coin, then made it reappear. Then he ran it pleasantly through his fingers, not as smoothly as Rix, but far better than Attia could have done.

"Room for improvement," Rix said loftily. "But my Apprentice is a natural."

He turned away, ignoring Attia completely, and strode into the tunnel.

She followed, feeling gloomy and a little jealous. Behind her the coin tinkled as Keiro dropped it and swore.

The tunnel was high, its smooth walls perfectly circular. It was lit only by the Eyes, which were placed at regular intervals in the roof, so that the red glow of one was distant before the next made their shadows loom on the floor.

"Are you watching us so closely?" Attia wanted to ask. She could feel Incarceron here, its curiosity, its need, breathing in her ear, like a fourth walker in the shadows.

Rix was far in front, with a bag on his back and the sword, and somewhere, hidden on his person, the Glove.

Attia had no weapons, nothing to carry. She felt light, because everything she knew or owned had been left behind, in some past that was slipping from her mind.

Except Finn. She still carried Finn's words like treasure in her hands. *I haven't abandoned you.*

Keiro came last. His dark red coat was torn and ragged,

but he wore a belt with two knives from the wagon stuck in it and he had scrubbed his hands and face and tied up his hair. As he walked he tipped the coin between his fingers, tossed it and caught it, but all the time his blue eyes were fixed on Rix's back. Attia knew why. He was still smarting at the loss of the Glove. Rix might no longer want revenge, but she was sure Keiro did.

After hours she realized the tunnel was narrowing. The walls were appreciably closer, and the color of them was changing to a deep red. Once she slipped, and looking down, saw that the metal floor was wet with some rusty liquid, running from the gloom ahead.

It was just after that that they found the first body.

It had been a man. He lay sprawled against the tunnel wall, as if washed there by some sudden flood, his crumpled torso barely more than a rag-hung skeleton.

Rix stood over it and sighed. "Poor human flotsam. He came farther than most."

Attia said, "Why is it still here? Not recycled?"

"Because the Prison is preoccupied with its Great Work. Systems are breaking down." He seemed to have forgotten he wasn't speaking to her anymore.

As soon as he had walked on, Keiro muttered, "Are you with me or not?"

She scowled. "You know what I think about the Glove."

"That's a no then."

She shrugged.

"Suit yourself. Looks like you're back being the dog-slave. That's the difference between us."

He walked past her and she glared at his back.

"The difference between us," she said, "is that you're arrogant Scum and I'm not."

He laughed and tossed the coin.

Soon there was debris everywhere. Bones, carcasses of animals, wrecked Sweepers, tangled masses of crumpled wires and components. The rusty water flowed over them, deeper now, and Incarceron's Eyes saw everything. The travelers picked their way through, the water knee-high, and flowing fast.

"Don't you care?" Rix snapped suddenly, as if his thoughts had burst out of him. He was gazing down at what might have been a halfman, its metallic face grinning up through the water.

"Don't you feel for the creatures that crawl in your veins?"

Keiro's hand was at his sword but the words were not for him. The answer came as laughter; a deep rumble that made the floor shake and the lights flicker.

Rix paled. "I didn't mean it! No offense."

Keiro came up and grabbed him. "Fool! Do you want it to flood this and sweep us all away!"

"It won't do that." Rix's voice was shaky but defiant. "I have its greatest desire."

"Yes, and if you're dead when you deliver it, what does Incarceron care? Keep your mouth shut!"

Rix stared at him. "I'm the master. Not you."

Keiro pushed past him and waded on. "Not for long."

Rix looked at Attia. But before she could speak, he hurried on.

All day the tunnel narrowed. After about three hours the roof was so low that Rix could stretch up and touch it. The flow of the water was a river now; objects were washed down in it, small Beetles and tangles of metal. Keiro suggested a torch, and Rix lit one reluctantly; in its acrid smoke they saw that the walls of the tunnel were covered with scum, a milky froth obliterating graffiti that seemed to have been there for centuries—names, dates, curses, prayers. And there was a sound too, thudding softly for hours before Attia was aware she could hear it, a deep, pounding shudder, the vibration that she had felt in her dream in the Swan's Nest.

She came up to Keiro as he stood listening. In front of them the tunnel shrank into the dark.

"The heartbeat of the Prison," she said.

"Shush . . ."

"Surely you can hear it?"

"Not that. Something else."

She kept silent, hearing only the wading sloshes of Rix behind them, weighed down by his pack. And then Keiro swore, and she heard it too. With an unearthly screech a flock of tiny bloodred birds shot out of the tunnel, splitting in panic, so that Rix ducked.

Behind the birds, something vast was coming. They couldn't see it yet, but they could hear it; it scraped and sheared against the sides, as if it was metal, a great tangle of sharpness, a mass forced down by the current. Keiro swung the torch, scattering sparks; he scanned the roof and the walls. "Back! It'll flatten us!"

Rix looked sick. "Back where?"

Attia said, "There's nowhere. We have to go ahead."

It was a hard choice. And yet Keiro didn't hesitate. He raced into the dark, stumbling in the deep water, the torch shedding burning pitch like stars into the torrent.

The roar of the approaching object filled the tunnel; ahead in the darkness Attia could see it now, an enormous ball of tangled wires, red light faceted from its angles as it rolled toward them.

She grabbed Rix and hustled him on, straight into the path of the thing, knowing it was death, huge, a pressure wave building in her ears and throat.

Keiro yelled.

And then he disappeared.

It was so sudden, like a magic trick, that Rix howled in anger and she almost stumbled, but then she was floundering toward the spot, and the rumble of the great mesh ball was on her, over her, above her . . .

A hand shot out.

She was hauled sideways and she fell, deep in the water, Rix crashing over her. Then arms went around her waist and hefted

319

her aside, and the three of them felt the scorching heat as the object sheared past them, its blades scraping sparks from the walls. And she saw there were drowned faces in it; rivets and helmets and coils of wire and candlesticks. It was a compacted sphere of ore and girders, impaling a thousand colored rags, scraps of steel flaking off in its wake.

As it passed she felt the friction, the condensed air imploding in her eardrums. It filled the tunnel fully; it scraped itself by with a million screeches and the darkness stank of scorching.

And then it was wedged tight in the dark, filling the world, and her knee was aching, and Keiro was picking himself up and swearing furiously at the state of his coat.

Attia stood slowly.

She was deafened and stunned; Rix looked dazed. The torch was out, floating in the thigh-high water, and there was no Eye here, but gradually she made out the dim shape of this fork in the tunnel that had saved them.

Ahead was a red glow.

Keiro slicked back his hair.

He looked up at the crushed and tangled surface of the sphere; it shuddered, the force of the water juddering it against the constricting walls.

There was no way back now. Over the noise he yelled something, and though Attia couldn't hear it, she knew what it was. He pointed ahead and waded on.

She turned and saw Rix reaching out to touch something that glared out from the metal, and she saw it was a mouth; the open snarling maw of a great wolf, as if some statue had been swept away in there, and was struggling to get out.

She pulled at his arm. Reluctantly, he turned away.

⋘○○○⋙

"I WANT the drawbridge up." Claudia marched along the corridor shedding her coat and gloves. "Archers in the gatehouse, on every roof, on the Sapient's tower."

"Master Jared's experiments . . ." the old man muttered.

"Pack the delicate things and get them down in the cellars. Ralph, this is F—Prince Giles. This is my steward, Ralph . . ."

The old man bowed deeply, his arms full of Claudia's scattered clothes. "Sire. I am so honored to welcome you to the Wardenry. I only wish—"

"We haven't got time." Claudia turned. "Where's Alys?"

"Upstairs, madam. She arrived yesterday, with your messages. Everything has been done. The Warden's levies have been raised. We have two hundred men billeted in the stableblock and more are arriving hourly."

Claudia nodded. She flung open the doors of a large, wood-paneled chamber. Finn smelled the sweetness of roses outside its open casements as he strode in after her.

"Good. Weapons?"

"You'll need to consult with Captain Soames, my lady. I believe he's in the kitchens."

"Find him. And Ralph." She turned. "I want all the servants assembled in the lower hall in twenty minutes."

He nodded, his wig slightly askew. "I'll see to it."

At the door, just before he bowed himself out, he said, "Welcome back, my lady. We've missed you."

She smiled, surprised. "Thank you."

When the doors were closed, Finn went straight to the cold meats and fruit laid out on the table. "He won't be so pleased when the Queen's army comes over the horizon."

She nodded, and sat wearily in the chair. "Pass me some of that chicken."

For a while they ate silently. Finn gazed around at the room, its white plaster ceiling pargeted with scrolls and lozenges, the great fireplace with the emblems of the black swan. The house was calm, the stillness drowsy with bees and the sweetness of roses.

"So this is the Wardenry."

"Yes." She poured out some wine. "Mine, and staying mine."

"It's beautiful." He put down his plate. "But there's no way we can defend it."

She scowled. "It has a moat and a drawbridge. It commands the land around. We have two hundred men."

"The Queen has cannon." He stood and walked to the window, pushing it open. "My grandfather chose the wrong Era for us. Something a bit more primitive would have kept us equal." He turned quickly. "They will use the weapons of the time, won't they? Do you think they might have things we don't know about . . . relics of the War?"

The thought turned her cold. The Years of Rage had been a cataclysm that had destroyed a civilization; its energies had stilled the tides and hollowed the moon. "Let's hope we're too small a target."

For a moment she crumbled cheese on her plate. Then she said, "Come on."

The servants' hall was a buzz of anxiety. As he walked in beside Claudia, Finn felt the noise subside, but a fraction too slowly. Grooms and maidservants turned; powdered footmen waited in elaborate livery.

There was a long wooden table in the center; Claudia stepped up onto a bench and then onto the tabletop.

"Friends."

They were silent now, except for the doves cooing outside.

"I'm very glad to be back home." She smiled, but he knew she was tense. "But things have changed. You'll have had all the news from Court—you know about the two candidates for the throne. Well, things have come to such a point that we . . . I . . . have had to make a decision about which one I support." She stretched out her hand, and Finn stepped up beside her.

"This is Prince Giles. Our future king. My betrothed."

The last phrase astonished him but he tried not to show it. He nodded at them gravely and they all stared up at him, their eyes taking in every travel-worn detail of his clothing, his face.

He found himself standing tall, steeling himself not to flinch from that examination.

He should say something. He managed, "I thank you all for your support," but it produced not even a ripple. Alys was by the door, her hands gripped tight together. Ralph, near the table, said boldly, "God bless you, sire!"

Claudia didn't wait for any response. "The Queen has declared the Pretender as her candidate. Essentially, this means civil war. I'm sorry to put it so bluntly, but it's important you all understand what is happening here. Many of you have lived at the Wardenry for generations. You were my father's servants. The Warden is no longer here, but I have spoken to him . . ."

That did produce a murmur.

"Is he in favor of this prince?" someone asked.

"He is. But he would wish me to treat you with respect. Therefore I say this."

She folded her arms and gazed out at them. "The young women and all the children will leave immediately. I'll give you an armed escort to the village, though it won't be needed. As for the men and the senior staff, the choice is yours. No one who wants to go will be prevented. There's no Protocol here anymore—I'm saying this to you as equals. You must make up your own minds."

She paused, but there was silence, so into it she said, "Assemble in the courtyard at the midday bell, and Captain Soames's men will take care of you. I wish you well."

"But my lady," someone said. "What will you do?"

It was a boy, near the back.

Claudia grinned at him. "Hello, Job. We'll stay. Finn and I will use the . . . machinery in my father's study to try and contact him in Incarceron. It will take time, but . . ."

"And Master Jared, ma'am." One of the maids' voices, anxious. "Where is he? He would know what to do."

There was a ripple of agreement. Claudia's eyes slid to Finn. She said sharply, "Jared's on his way. But we already know what to do. The true king has been found, and those who once tried to destroy him must not succeed again."

She was in control, but she had not won them over. Finn could sense that. There was a silent discontent, an unspoken doubt. They knew her too well, from a child. And though she was an imperious mistress, they had probably never loved her. She wasn't speaking to their hearts.

So he held his hand out and took hers. "Friends, Claudia is right to give you a choice. I owe everything to her. Without her I would be dead now, or worse, thrown back into the hell of Incarceron. I wish I could tell you what her support means. But to do that I would have to explain the Prison to you, and I won't do that, because I dare not speak about it, it hurts me even to think of it."

They were intent; the word *Incarceron* was like a charm. Finn allowed his voice to tremble.

"I was a child. I was snatched from a world of beauty and

peace to a torment of pain and hunger, a hell where men murder each other without a care, where women and children sell themselves to stay alive. I know about death. I've suffered the miseries of the poor. I know about loneliness, how wretched it is to be alone and terrified in a maze of echoing halls and dark dread. This is the knowledge Incarceron gave me. And when I am King, this is the knowledge I will use. There will be no more Protocol, no more fear. No more being locked in. I will do my best—I swear this to you—my best to make this Realm a true paradise, and a free world for all its people. And Incarceron too. That's all I can say to you. All I can promise you. Except that if we lose, I will kill myself rather than go back there."

The silence was different. It was caught in their throats.

And when a soldier growled, "I'm with you, my lord," another answered at once, and then another, and suddenly the room was a hubbub of voices until Ralph's reedy "God save Prince Giles" had them roaring their approval.

Finn smiled, wan.

Claudia watched him, and when their eyes met, she saw there was a triumph in him, quiet but proud.

Keiro had been right, she thought. Finn could talk his way to a crown.

She turned. A footman was pushing his way through to her, white and wide-eyed. She crouched, and his voice, thin and terrified, silenced the hubbub.

"They're here, my lady. The Queen's army is here."

25

*Some say a vast pendulum swings in the heart
of the Prison, or that there is a chamber there
white-hot with energy, like the core of a star.
For myself, I think that if Incarceron has a heart
it is icy, and nothing could survive there.*

—Lord Calliston's Diary

The tunnel narrowed rapidly. Soon Keiro was on hands and knees in the shallow water, struggling to keep the new torch alight. Behind her Attia heard Rix gasp as he crawled, the pack slung under his belly, the roof bruising his back.

And was it her imagination, or was the air warmer?

She said, "What if it gets too small?"

"Stupid question," Keiro muttered. "We die. There's no way back."

It *was* hotter. And choked with dust. She felt it on her lips and skin. Crawling was painful; her knees and palms sore and cut. The tunnel had shrunk to a tube now, a red pulsing heat that they had to force their way through.

Suddenly Rix stopped dead. "Volcano."

Keiro twisted around. *"What!"*

"Imagine. If the heart of the Prison is in fact a great magma chamber, sealed by terrible compression in the very center of its being."

"Oh for god's sake . . ."

"And if we reach it, if it is pierced by even so much as a needle point . . ."

"Rix!" Attia said fiercely. "This isn't helping."

She heard him breathing hard. "But it may be true. What do we know? And yet we could know. We could understand all things at once."

She squirmed to look back. He was lying full length in the water. He had the Glove in his hand.

"No," she breathed.

He looked up and his face was lit with that sly delight she had come to dread. And then he was shouting, his voice deafening in the confined space.

"I WILL PUT ON THE GLOVE. I WILL BECOME ALL-KNOWING."

Keiro was beside her, knife in hand. "I'll finish him this time. I swear I will."

"LIKE THE MAN IN THE GARDEN . . ."

"What garden, Rix?" she asked quietly. "What garden?"

"The one in the Prison, somewhere. You know."

"I don't." She had her hand around Keiro's wrist, forcing him still. "Tell me."

Rix stroked the Glove. "There was a garden and a tree grew there with golden apples and if you ate one of them, you knew everything. And then Sapphique climbed over the fence and killed the many-headed monster and picked the apple, because he wanted to know, you see, Attia. He wanted to know how to Escape."

"Right." She had wriggled back. She was close to his pocked face.

"And a snake came out of the grass and it said, 'Oh go on, eat the apple. I dare you.' And he stopped then with it to his mouth because he knew the snake was Incarceron."

Keiro groaned. "Let me . . ."

"Put the Glove away, Rix. Or give it to me."

His fingers caressed its dark scales. "And because if he ate it he would know how small he was. How much of a nothing he was. He would see himself as a speck in the vastness of the Prison."

"So he didn't eat it, right?"

Rix stared at her. "What?"

"In the patchbook. He didn't eat it."

There was silence. Something seemed to pass over Rix's face; then he frowned crossly at her and tucked the Glove away inside his coat. "I don't know what you're talking about, Attia. What patchbook? Why aren't we getting on?"

She watched him a moment, then shoved Keiro on with her foot. Muttering, he shuffled back. The moment was over, but it had been too close. Somehow, quickly, she had to get the Glove from Rix before he went too far.

But as she gripped the slimy filth and pulled herself after Keiro she felt his boots ahead and he wasn't moving.

She looked up and saw the torchlight glowing on the end of the tunnel.

It was a rounded vault of corbelled stone, and a single gargoyle leered down at them with its tongue impudently out. The water was pouring from its mouth, a green slime down the walls.

"That's it? The end?" She almost dropped her forehead down into the water. "We can't even turn!"

"End of the tunnel. Not quite the end of the line." Keiro had wriggled over on his back and was looking up, his hair dripping. "Look."

In the roof immediately above him was a shaft. It was circular and around it were letters, strange sigils in some language Attia didn't know.

"Sapient letters." Keiro flinched as the sparks from the torch fell toward his face. "Gildas used to use them all the time. And look at that."

An eagle. Her heart leaped as she saw the sign that Finn wore on his wrist, its wings wide, a crown around its neck.

Down through the center of the hole, its final links just drifting above Keiro's hand, hung a chain ladder. As they watched, it shuddered gently, in the vibrations from above.

Rix's voice was calm in the darkness behind her. "Well, climb it, Apprentice."

◄◦◦◦►

THERE WAS no stable.

Jared stood in the center of the clearing and looked blearily around.

No stable, no feathers. Only, on the floor of the clearing, a scorched circle, that might once have been the blackened scar of a fire. He walked around it. The bracken was deep and curled in the dawn light; spiderwebs, looking like cradles of wool meshed with dew, filled every crack between stem and stalk.

He sucked his dry lips, then ran his hand over his forehead, behind his neck.

He must have been here one, perhaps two days, rolled in that blanket, delirious, the horse snuffling and cropping leaves and wandering aimlessly nearby.

His clothes were sodden with damp and sweat, his hair lank, his hands bitten by insects, and he still couldn't stop shivering. But he felt as if some door had opened inside him, some bridge had been crossed.

Walking back to the horse, he took out his medication pouch and crouched, considering the dose. Then he injected the fine needle into his vein, feeling the sharp prick that always set his teeth on edge. He withdrew it, cleaned it, and put it away. Then he took his own pulse, wiped a handkerchief in the dew, and washed his face and smiled at a sudden memory of one of the maids at home asking him if dew was really good for her complexion.

It was certainly fresh and cold.

He took the horse's reins in hand and climbed up onto its back.

He could not have survived such a fever without warmth. Without water. He should be parched with thirst, and he wasn't. And yet no one had been here.

As he urged the horse to a gallop, he thought about the power of vision; whether Sapphique had been an aspect of his own mind, or a real being. None of it was that simple.

There were whole shelves of texts back in the Library discussing the powers of the visionary imagination, of memory and dreams.

Jared smiled wanly to the trees of the wood.

For him it had happened. That was what mattered.

He rode hard. By midday he was in the lands of the Wardenry, tired, but surprising himself by his endurance.

At a farm he climbed down a little stiffly and was given milk and cheese by the farmer, a stout, perspiring man who seemed on edge, his glance always wandering to the horizon.

When Jared offered money the man pressed it back at him. "No, Master. A Sapient once treated my wife for free and I've never forgotten that. But a word of advice. Hurry on now, wherever you're bound. There's trouble brewing here."

"Trouble?" Jared looked at him.

"I've heard the Lady Claudia is condemned. And that lad with her, the one who claims to be the Prince."

"He is the Prince."

The farmer pulled a face. "Whatever you say, Master. High politics are not for me. But this I do know: The Queen has an army on the march, and they're maybe at the Wardenry itself by now. I had three outlying barns fired by them yesterday, and sheep snatched. Thieving scum."

Jared stared at him in cold terror. Grabbing the horse, he said, "I would be grateful, sir, if you hadn't seen me. You understand?"

The farmer nodded. "In these hard times, Master, only the silent are wise."

He was afraid now. He rode more carefully, taking field paths and bridleways, keeping to deep lanes between high hedges. In one place, crossing a road, he saw the tracks of hooves and wagons; deep ruts of wheels dragging some heavy ironware. He rubbed the horse's coarse mane.

Where was Claudia? What had happened at Court?

By late afternoon he came up a track into a small copse of beeches on a hilltop. The trees were quiet, their leaves brushed only by a faint breeze, full of the tiny whistlings of invisible birds.

Jared climbed down, and stood for a moment letting the ache ease in his back and legs. Then he tied up the horse and walked cautiously through the bronze leaf-litter, ankle-deep in its rustling crispness.

Under the beeches nothing grew; he moved from tree to tree awkwardly, but only a fox confronted him.

"Master Fox," Jared muttered.

The fox paused a second. Then it turned and trotted away.

Reassured, he moved to the edge of the trees and crouched behind a broad trunk. Carefully, he peered around it.

An army was encamped on the broad hillside. All around the ancient house of the Wardenry, there were tents and wagons and the glint of armor. Squadrons of cavalry rode in arrogant display; a mass of soldiers were digging a great trench in the wide lawns.

Jared drew in a breath of dismay.

He could see more men arriving down the lanes; pikemen led by drummers and a fife-player, the reedy whistle audible even up here. Flags fluttered everywhere, and to the left, under a brilliant standard of the white rose, a great pavilion was being raised by sweating men.

The Queen's tent.

He looked at the house. The windows were shuttered, the drawbridge tightly raised. On the roof of the gatehouse metal glinted; he thought there were men up there, and perhaps the light cannon that were kept there had been prepared and moved up to the battlements. His own tower had someone on its parapet.

He breathed out and turned, sitting knees up in the dead leaves.

This was a disaster. There was no way the Wardenry could withstand any sort of sustained attack. Its walls were thick, but it was a fortified manor and not a castle.

Claudia must simply be playing for time. She must be planning to use the Portal.

The thought made him agitated; he stood and paced.

She had no idea of the dangers of that device! He had to get inside before she tried anything so foolish.

The horse whickered.

He froze, hearing the tread behind him, the footsteps through the rustling leaves.

And then the voice, lightly mocking. "Well, Master Jared. Aren't you supposed to be dead?"

—◇◇◇—

"HOW MANY?" Finn asked.

Claudia had a visor that magnified things. She was staring through it now, counting. "Seven. Eight. I'm not sure what's on that contraption to the left of the Queen's tent."

"It barely matters." Captain Soames, a gray, stocky man, sounded gloomy. "Eight pieces of ordnance could shell us all to pieces."

"What do we have?" Finn asked quietly.

"Two cannon, my lord. One authentic Era, the other a mishmash of base metal—it will likely explode if we try to fire it. Crossbows, arquebuses, pikemen, archers. Ten men with muskets. About eighty cavalry."

"I've known worse odds," Finn said, thinking of a few ambushes the Comitatus had tried.

"I'm sure," Claudia said acidly. "And what were the casualties like?"

He shrugged. "In the Prison, no one counted."

Below them, a trumpet rang out, once, twice, three times. With a great grinding of gears, the drawbridge began to creak down.

Captain Soames went to the circular stair. "Steady there. And be prepared to pull it up if I give the order."

Claudia lowered the visor. "They're looking. No one's making any moves."

"The Queen hasn't arrived. A man who came in last night says she and the Council are making a royal progress to show off the Pretender; they're in Mayfield, and will be here in hours."

With a thud, the drawbridge was down. The flock of black swans on the moat skidded noisily down to the weedy end and flapped.

Claudia leaned over the battlements.

The women walked out slowly, with bundles on their backs. Some carried children. Older girls walked hand in hand with their brothers and sisters. They turned, waving at the windows. Behind, on a great wain pulled by the biggest carthorse, the older servants that were leaving sat stoically, rocking with the bumps on the wooden bridge.

Finn counted twenty-two. "Is Ralph going?"

Claudia laughed. "I ordered him to. He said, 'Yes, my lady. And what will you be requiring for dinner tonight?' He thinks this place would fall down without him."

"He, like all of us, serves the Warden," Captain Soames said. "No disrespect to you, my lady, but the Warden is our master. If he's not here, we guard his house."

Claudia frowned. "My father doesn't deserve any of you."

But she said it so quietly, only Finn heard her.

When Soames had gone to supervise the drawbridge being raised Finn stood beside her, watching the girls trudge down into the Queen's camp.

"They'll be questioned. Who's here, our plans."

"I know. But I won't be responsible for their deaths."

"You think it will come to that?"

She glanced at him. "We have to set up talks. Play for time. Work on the Portal."

Finn nodded. She walked past him to the stairs and said over her shoulder, "Come on. You shouldn't stand up here. One arrow from that camp and it would be all over."

He looked at her, and just as she got to the stairs, he said, "You do believe me, Claudia, don't you? I need you to believe that I remember."

"Of course I believe you," she said. "Now come on."

But she had her back to him, and she didn't turn around.

"IT'S DARK. Hold that torch higher."

Keiro's voice came impatiently down the shaft; the echoes made it hollow and strange. Attia stretched up as high as she could, but the torchlight showed her nothing of him. Below her Rix shouted, "What can you see?"

"I can't see anything. I'm going on."

Scrapes and clangs. Muttered swearing that the shaft took and whispered to itself. Worried, Attia called, "Be careful."

He didn't bother to answer. The ladder twisted and jerked as she struggled to hold it still; Rix came and hauled on it with all his weight, and it was easier. She said, "Listen, Rix. While we're alone. You have to listen to me. Keiro will steal the Glove from you. Why not pull a stunt on him?"

He smiled, sly. "You mean give it to you, and carry a fake one? Oh my poor Attia. Is this the limit of your cunning? A child could do better."

She glared at him. "At least I won't give it to the Prison. At least I won't kill us all."

He winked. "Incarceron is my father, Attia. I am born of its cells. It will not betray me."

Disgusted, she gripped the ladder.

And realized it was still.

"Keiro?"

They waited, hearing the thud-thud, thud-thud of the Prison's heart.

"Keiro? Answer me."

The ladder swung easily now. No one was on it.

"*Keiro!*"

There was a sound, but it was muffled and far away.

Hastily she shoved the torch into Rix's hands. "He's found something. I'm going up."

As she hauled herself up the first slippery rungs, he said, "If it's trouble, say the word *problem*. I'll understand."

She stared at his pock-marked face, his gap-toothed grin. Then she swung down and put her face close to his.

"Just how crazy are you, Rix? A lot, or not at all? Because I'm beginning to be very unsure."

He arched one eyebrow. "I am the Dark Enchanter, Attia. *I am unknowable.*"

The ladder wriggled and slid under her as if it were alive. She turned and climbed quickly, soon breathless, hauling her weight up. Her hands slid on the mud Keiro's boots had left; the heat grew as she went up, a murky sulfurous stench that reminded her uneasily of Rix's idea of the magma chamber.

Her arms ached. Each step now was an effort and the torch, far below, was no more than a spark in the darkness. She hauled herself up one more rung and hung, giddily.

And then she realized there was no shaft wall in front of her, but a faintly lit space.

And a pair of boots.

They were black, rather battered, with a silver buckle on one and broken stitching on the other. And whoever wore them was bending down, because his shadow was over her and he was saying, "How very pleasant to meet you again, Attia."

And he reached down and grabbed her chin and jerked her face up, and she saw his cold smile.

26

Watch, be silent, act only when the moment is right.
— *The Steel Wolves*

The study door looked exactly the same; black as ebony, the black swan spitting defiance down at them, its eye bright as a diamond.

"This opened it once before." Claudia waited impatiently as the disc hummed. Behind her, Finn stood in the long corridor, gazing down at the vases and suits of armor.

"A bit better than the Court cellars," he said. "But are you sure it will be the same Portal? How can it be?"

The disc clicked. "Don't ask me." She reached up and snapped it off. "Jared had a theory it was some halfway point between here and the Prison."

"Meaning we lose size in there?"

"I don't know." The door lock chuntered, she turned the handle, and it opened.

When he followed her in through the dizzying threshold, Finn stared around. Then he nodded. "Amazing."

The Portal was the room he had grown to know in the Palace. All Jared's contraptions and wires still trailed from the controls; the huge feather lay curled in a corner, drifting as the breeze took it. The room hummed in its tilted silence, its solitary desk and chair enigmatic as ever.

Claudia crossed the floor and said, "Incarceron."

A small drawer rolled open. Inside he saw a black cushion with an empty key shape in it. "This is where I stole the Key. It seems so long ago. I was so scared that day! So. Where do we start?"

He shrugged. "You're the one who had Jared for a tutor."

"He worked too fast to explain everything to me."

"Well, there must be notes. Diagrams . . ."

"There are." Piled on the desk were pages of writing in Jared's spidery script, a book of drawings, lists of equations. Claudia picked one up and sighed. "We'd better start. This could take all night."

He didn't answer, so she looked up and saw his face. She stood quickly. "Finn."

He was pale; there was a tinge of blue around his lips. She grabbed him and made him sit on the floor, kicking circuits aside. "Be calm. Breathe slowly. Have you got any of those pills Jared made up?"

He shook his head, feeling the prickling agony invade and darken his sight, feeling the shame and sheer anger flood him. "I'll be fine," he heard himself mumble. "I'll be fine."

He preferred darkness. He put his hands over his eyes and sat there, against the gray wall, numb, breathing, counting.

After a while Claudia went; there was shouting, running feet. A cup was pressed into his hand. "Water," she said.

Then, "Ralph will stay with you. I have to go. The Queen has come."

He wanted to stand but couldn't. He wanted her to stay, but she was gone.

Ralph's hand was on his shoulder, the quavery voice in his ear. "I'm with you, sire."

This shouldn't happen. If he remembered, he was cured.

He should be cured.

ATTIA CLIMBED over the top of the ladder and stood upright.

The Warden dropped her hand. "Welcome to the heart of Incarceron."

They eyed each other. He wore a dark suit still, but his skin was grained now with the dirt of the Prison, his hair unkempt and graying. A firelock was thrust into his belt.

Behind him, in the red room Keiro stood, looking as if his temper was under tight control. Three men held weapons on him.

"Our thief friend here does not seem to have the Glove. So you must."

Attia shrugged. "Wrong again." She took her coat off and flung it down. "See for yourself."

The Warden raised an eyebrow. He kicked the coat to one of the Prisoners, who searched it rapidly.

"Nothing, sire."

"Then I must search you, Attia."

He was rough and thorough, and she scorched with anger, but when the muffled cry came up the shaft, he stopped abruptly. "Is that the mountebank Rix?"

She was surprised he didn't know. "Yes."

"Get him up here. Now."

She walked to the edge of the shaft and crouched down.

"Rix! Come up. It's safe. No problems."

The Warden pulled her back and made a sign to one of his men. As Rix made his way noisily up the swinging ladder the man knelt, aiming his firelock directly at the hole. When Rix's head came up, he stared straight into the muzzle of the gun.

"Slowly, magician." The Warden crouched, his eyes gray and ashen. "Very slowly, if you want to keep your head."

Attia glanced at Keiro. He raised his eyebrows and she shook her head, the tiniest movement. They watched Rix.

He climbed out of the shaft and held his hands wide of his body.

"The Glove?" the Warden said.

"Hidden. In a secret place that I will divulge only to Incarceron itself."

The Warden sighed, took out a handkerchief that was still almost white, and wiped his hands. Wearily he said, "Search him."

They were even harder on Rix. A few blows to keep him quiet, his pack ripped apart, his body scoured.

They found hidden coins, colored handkerchiefs, two mice, a collapsible dove cage. They found hidden pockets, false sleeves, reversible linings. But no Glove.

The Warden sat watching, and Keiro lazed defiantly on the tiled floor. Attia took the chance to stare around. They were in a vast hall of black and white tiles. It stretched into the distance, the walls hung with red satin, sagging in great swathes. At the far end, so distant it could barely be seen, was a long table flanked by standing candlesticks, branches lit with tiny flames.

Finally the prisoners stood back. "There's nothing else on him, sire. He's clean."

Behind her, Attia felt Keiro sit up slowly.

"I see." The Warden's smile was wintry. "Well, Rix, you disappoint me. But if you wish to speak to Incarceron, then speak. The Prison hears you."

Rix bowed. He buttoned his ragged coat and summoned his dignity. "Then the Prison's majesty will hear my request. *I ask to speak to Incarceron face-to-face. As Sapphique did.*"

There was a soft laughter.

It came out of the walls and the floor and the roof, and the armed men looked around in terror.

"What do you say to that?" the Warden asked.

"I say the Prisoner is overbold, and that I could devour him now and scour the very circuits of his brain for this knowledge."

Rix knelt humbly. "All my life I have dreamed of you. I

have guarded your Glove, and I have longed to bring it to you. Allow your servant this privilege."

Keiro snorted with scorn.

Rix glanced at Attia.

His eyes flickered to the shaft, then back. It was such a swift movement, she almost missed it, but she looked and saw the string.

It was barely visible, very thin and transparent, the stuff he used in his act for levitating objects. It was looped around a rung of the ladder, and it trailed down into the shaft.

Of course. There had been no Eyes in the shaft.

She made a small step toward it.

The Prison's voice was cool and metallic. "*I am so moved, Rix. The Warden will bring you to me, and yes, you will see me face-to-face. You will tell me where the Glove is and then for your reward I will very slowly and very carefully destroy you, atom by atom, for centuries. You will scream like the prisoners in your patchbooks, like Prometheus eaten daily by the eagle, like Loki as poison drips on his face. When I have Escaped and everyone else is dead, your struggles will still convulse the Prison.*"

Rix bowed, white-faced.

"*John Arlex.*"

The Warden said drily, "What now?"

"*Bring them all.*"

Attia moved. With a yell to Keiro, she jumped for the shaft, was racing down it. The string swung; she grabbed at it, hauled it up, snatched the dry scaly thing it held, thrust it down her shirt.

Then arms grabbed her; she kicked and bit, but the Warden's men hauled her up and she saw Keiro sprawled and the Warden standing over him, weapon in hand.

Claudia's father stared at her in mock dismay. "Escape, Attia? There is no Escape. For any of us."

Morose, he met her eyes and his gaze was bleak. Then he stalked away, down the long hall. "Bring them."

Keiro wiped blood from his nose. He gave her one look.

Rix too.

This time she nodded.

JARED TURNED slowly.

"My Lord of Steen," he said.

Caspar leaned against a tree trunk. He wore a breastplate of such dazzling steel, it hurt to look at it, and his breeches and boots were of finest leather.

"I see my lord is dressed for war," Jared murmured.

"You didn't used to be so sarcastic, Master."

"I'm sorry. I have had a trying time."

Caspar grinned. "My mother will be amazed you survived. She's been waiting for a message from the Academy for days, but none has come." He stepped forward. "Did you kill him, Master, with some Sapient potion? Or do you have secret fighting skills?"

Jared looked down at his delicate hands. "Let's say I surprised even myself, sire. But is the Queen here?"

Caspar pointed. "Oh yes. She wouldn't miss this for the world."

A white horse. It was saddled with the finest white leather fittings, and on it Sia rode sidesaddle, in an austere gown of dark gray. She too wore a breastplate, and a hat with a feather, and around her and before her pikemen marched, their weapons slanted in perfect array.

Jared came to stand by the Earl. "What's happening?"

"It's a parlay. They'll talk each other to death. Look, there's Claudia."

Jared's breath tightened as he saw her. She was standing on the gatehouse roof, and Soames and Alys were with her.

"Where's Finn?" He murmured it to himself, but Caspar heard and snorted.

"Tired out maybe." He grinned sidelong at Jared. "Ah, Master Sapient, she's cast both of us off now. I admit I always had something of an eye for Claudia, but marrying her—that was my mother's plan. She would have turned out far too fierce and bossy, so I don't care. But it must be hard for you. You and she were always so close. Everyone says so. Until *he* came along."

Jared smiled. "You have a poisonous tongue, Caspar."

"Yes. And it stings you, doesn't it?" He turned with negligent ease. "Perhaps we'll go down and hear what they're saying. My mother will be rather proud when I drag you through the ranks and throw you down before her. And I'd love to see Claudia's face!"

Jared stepped back. "You don't seem to be armed, my lord."

"No. I'm not." Caspar smiled sweetly. "But Fax is."

A rustle. It came from the left, and Jared turned very slowly to face it, knowing his freedom was over.

Sitting on a tree trunk, an ax slung between his knees, the huge bulk of his body rippling with chainmail, the prince's bodyguard nodded, unsmiling.

"NOT UNTIL my father returns."

Claudia's voice rang out clearly, so that everyone could hear it.

The Queen sighed daintily. She had dismounted and was sitting in a wicker chair before the gatehouse, so close that even a child could have shot her. Claudia had to admire her complete arrogance.

"And what do you hope to gain, Claudia? I have enough men and arms to batter the Wardenry to pieces. And we both know your father—a man who led a plot to try and kill me—will never return. He is where he belongs—in the Prison. Now, do be sensible. Hand over the Prisoner Finn, and then you and I can talk. Perhaps I was hasty in my decisions. Perhaps the Wardenry can remain in your possession. Perhaps."

Claudia folded her arms. "I'll have to think about it."

"We could have been such friends, Claudia." Sia waved a bee away. "When I told you once we were alike, I meant it. You would have been the next Queen. Perhaps you still could be."

Claudia drew herself up. "I will be the next Queen. Because Finn is the rightful Prince, the real Giles. Not that liar beside you."

The Pretender smiled, took off his hat, and bowed. His right arm was strapped into a black sling and he wore a pistol in his sash, but otherwise he seemed as poised and pleasantly arrogant as ever. He called out, "You don't believe that, Claudia. Not really."

"You think so?"

"I know you won't put your servants' lives at risk on the word of some jailbird. I know you, Claudia. Now come out and let's talk. We can sort this out."

Claudia stared at him. She shivered in the cool wind.

A few drops of rain struck her face. She said, "He spared your life."

"Because he knows I'm his Prince. So do you."

For a desperate moment she almost doubted what Caspar had told her.

And with her instinct for weakness, Sia said, "I do hope you aren't waiting for Master Jared, Claudia."

Claudia's head shot up. "Why? Where is he?"

Sia rose and shrugged her small shoulders. "At the Academy,

I believe. But I have heard rumors that he is in poor health."
She smiled icily. "*Very* poor."

Claudia came forward till she was gripping the cold stones
of the battlement. "If anything happens to Jared," she hissed,
"if you touch a hair of his head I swear I'll kill you myself
before the Steel Wolves even get close."

A commotion behind her. Soames was pulling her back.
Finn was at the top of the stair, pale but alert, Ralph puffing
behind him.

"If I needed more proof of your treachery, those words would
be enough." The Queen signaled hastily for her horse, as if the
mention of the Steel Wolves had alarmed her.

"You would be wise to remember that Jared's life is at stake,
as well as that of every other person in that house. And if I have
to burn it to the ground to end this matter, I will."

Stepping onto the bent back of a soldier, she swung daintily
into the saddle. "You have until exactly seven o'clock tomorrow
morning to hand over the Escaped Prisoner. If he is not in my
hands by then, the bombardment begins."

Claudia watched her go.

The Pretender glared up scornfully at Finn. "If you're really
not Prison Scum you'd come out," he said. "And not hide
behind a girl."

⊸◦◦◦⊸

JARED SAID quietly, "It seems a shame to have escaped one
assassin to be faced with another."

351

Caspar nodded. "I know. But that's war."

Fax lumbered to his feet. "Boss?"

"I think we'll tie him up," Caspar said, "and then I can lead him down. In fact, Fax, once we get to the camp you can keep out of the way." He smiled at Jared. "My mother adores me, but she's never had much confidence in me. This will be a chance to show her what I can do. Hold out your hands."

Jared sighed. He lifted his hands and then a paleness came over him; he staggered, almost fell.

"I'm sorry," he whispered.

Caspar grinned at Fax. "Nice try, Master . . ."

"No. Really. My medication. It's just in my saddlebag . . ."

He crumpled and sat in the leaves shakily.

Caspar pulled a face, then waved impatiently and Fax turned to the horse. As soon as the man moved Jared leaped up and ran, haring between the trees, jumping the sprawling roots, but even as his breath grew to an ache, he heard the footfalls behind him, heavy and close, and then the growling laugh as he tripped and rolled and slammed up against a tree trunk.

He scrambled around. Fax stood over him, swinging the ax. Behind, Caspar grinned with triumph. "Oh go on, then, Fax. One good blow."

The giant raised the blade.

Jared gripped the tree; he felt its smooth trunk under his hands.

Fax moved. He jerked and his smile became glassy, a fixed

rictus that seemed to go through his body, and his arm, and the ax, so that it fell, thudding blade down in the soft earth.

After a frozen pause, eyes wide, he crashed after it.

Jared breathed out, astonished.

An arrow, buried up to its plume, jutted from the man's back.

Caspar let out a howl of rage and fear. He grabbed at the ax, but a voice from the left said quietly, "Drop the weapon, Lord Earl. Now."

"Who are you? How dare you . . . !"

The voice sounded grim. "We're the Steel Wolves, lord. As you already know."

27

*Once he had crossed the sword-bridge he came to a
room with a banquet of fine food spread on a table.
He sat down and picked up a piece of bread, but
the power of the Glove turned it to ashes. He picked
up water but the glass shattered. So he traveled on,
because he knew now that he was close to the door.*

—*Wanderings of Sapphique*

"This is my kingdom now." The Warden waved at the table.
"My seat of judgment. And here, my private suite." He
flung the doors open and walked through. The three Prisoners
shoved Rix, Attia, and Keiro after him.

Inside, Attia stared.

They were in a small room hung with tapestries. There were
windows in the walls, high stained-glass images impossible to
see in the dimness, a few hands and faces lit by flamelight from
the vast fire in the hearth.

The heat was fierce and welcome. The Warden turned.
"Please sit."

There were chairs of carved ebony, their backs formed by
pairs of black swans with entwined necks. Heavy beams spread
in intricate patterns in the roof; chandeliers splatted wax on the

tiled floor. From somewhere nearby the throb of the vibrations echoed.

"You must be tired after your terrible journey," the Warden said. "Bring them food."

Attia sat. She felt weary and filthy; her hair was matted with the slime of the tunnel. And the Glove! Its claws scratched against her bare skin, but she dared not move it, in case the Warden noticed. His gray eyes were sharp and watchful.

The food, when it came, was a tray of bread and water, dropped down on the ground. Keiro ignored it, but Rix had no scruples; he ate as if he was famished, kneeling and cramming the bread into his mouth. Attia reached down and picked up a crust; she chewed it slowly, but it was dry and hard.

"Prison fare," she said.

"That is where we are." The Warden sat, flicking out the tails of his coat.

"So what happened to your tower?" Keiro asked.

"I have many boltholes in the Prison. I use the tower as my library. This is my laboratory."

"I don't see any test tubes."

John Arlex smiled. "You will, all too soon. That is, if you want to be part of this wretch's crazy plan."

Keiro shrugged. "I've come this far."

"So you have." The Warden put the tips of his fingers together. "The halfman, the dog-slave, and the lunatic."

Keiro didn't show his feelings by a flicker.

"And do you think you will Escape?" The Warden picked up the jug and poured himself a goblet of water.

"No." Keiro gazed around.

"Then you're wise. As you know, you personally cannot leave. Your body contains elements of Incarceron."

"Yes. But then, this body the Prison has made itself is completely formed of such *elements*." Keiro leaned back, mocking the Warden's pose, steepling his own fingers. "And it fully intends to leave. Once it has the Glove. So I have to assume there is a power in the Glove itself that makes this possible. And might even make it possible for me."

The Warden stared at him and he stared back.

Behind them, Rix coughed as he tried to eat and drink at the same time.

"You're wasted as a sorcerer's Apprentice," the Warden said quietly. "Perhaps you would do better working for me."

Keiro laughed.

"Oh, don't dismiss it so easily. You have the temperament for cruelty, Keiro. The Prison is your environment. Outside will disappoint you."

Into the silence of their mutual gaze Attia snapped, "You must miss your daughter."

The Warden's gray eyes slid to her. She had expected some anger, but all he said was, "Yes. I do."

Seeing her surprise, he smiled. "How little you inmates

understand of me. I needed an heir and yes, I stole Claudia as a baby from this place. Now she and I can never escape each other. I do miss her. I'm sure she misses me." He drank from the goblet, a fastidious sip. "We have a twisted love. A love that is part hate and part admiration and part fear. But love all the same."

Rix belched. He wiped his mouth with his hand and said, "I'm ready now."

"Ready?"

"To face it. Incarceron."

The Warden laughed. "You fool! You have no idea! Don't you see that you've been facing Incarceron every day of your miserable, scavenging, trick-playing life? You breathe Incarceron, you eat and dream and wear Incarceron. It's the scorn in every eye here, the word in every mouth. There is nowhere you can go to Escape from it."

"Unless I die," Rix said.

"Unless you die. And that is easily arranged. But if you have any crazy plan about the Prison taking you with it . . ."

He shook his head.

"But you'll go with it," Keiro murmured.

The Warden's smile was wintry. "My daughter needs me."

"I don't understand why you haven't gone before. You have both the Keys . . ."

The smile went. John Arlex stood, and he was tall and imposing. "Had. You'll see. When the Prison is ready it will call for us. Until then you stay here. My men will be outside."

He walked to the door, kicking aside the empty plate. Keiro did not move or look up, but his voice carried a cool insolence.

"You're just as much a Prisoner here as we are. No difference."

The Warden stopped, just for a moment. Then he opened the door and let himself out. His back was rigid.

Keiro laughed, softly.

Rix nodded, approving. "You tell him, Apprentice."

⌐◦◊◦⌐

"YOU'VE KILLED him." Jared straightened from the body and stared at Medlicote. "There was no need . . ."

"Every need, Master. You would not have survived a blow from that ax. And you have the knowledge we all want."

The secretary looked strange holding the firelock. His coat was as dusty as ever, his half-moon glasses catching the setting sun. Now he glanced around at the men blindfolding Caspar. "I'm sorry, but the prince too must die. He has seen us."

"Yes I have." Caspar sounded terrified and furious all at once. "You, Medlicote, and you, Grahame, and you, Hal Keane. All of you are traitors and once the Queen knows . . ."

"Exactly." Medlicote's voice was heavy. "Best if you stand aside, Master. You need have no part of this."

Jared didn't move. He eyed Medlicote through the dusk.

"You would really kill an unarmed boy?"

"They killed Prince Giles."

"Finn is Giles."

Medlicote sighed. "Master, the Wolves know that Giles is truly dead. The Warden of Incarceron was our leader. He would have told us if the Prince was placed in the Prison."

The shock rocked Jared. He tried to recover. "The Warden is a man of great depth. He has his own plans. He may have misled you."

The secretary nodded. "I know him better than you, Master. But that doesn't concern us now. Please stand aside."

"Don't, Jared!" Caspar's voice was a sharp cry. "Don't leave me! Do something! I would never have killed you, Master! I swear!"

Jared rubbed his face. He was tired and sore and cold. He was worried sick about Claudia. But he said, "Listen to me, Medlicote. The boy is no use to anyone dead. But as a hostage he is immensely valuable. As soon as the moon sets and the night is dark enough I intend to use a secret way I know to get into the Wardenry . . ."

"What way?"

Jared jerked his head at the listening gentlemen. "I can't say. You may have spies even in your Clan. But there is a way. Let me take Caspar with me. If the Queen sees her precious son paraded on the battlements she'll stop the bombardment instantly. You must see that this will work."

Medlicote gazed at him through the glasses. Then he said, "I will talk to my brothers."

They walked aside and made a small group under the beeches.

Blindfolded and tied, Caspar whispered, "Where are you, Master Sapient?"

"Still here."

"Save me. Untie me. My mother will load treasure on you. Anything you want. Don't leave me to these monsters, Jared."

Jared sat wearily in the beech leaves and watched the monsters. He saw grave, bitter men. Some he recognized—a gentleman of the King's Chamber, a member of the Privy Council. Was his life any safer than Caspar's now that he knew who they were? And why was he so tangled in this web of murder and intrigue when all he had ever wanted was to study the ancient writings and the stars?

"They're coming back. Untie me, Jared. Don't let them shoot me like Fax."

He stood. "Sire, I'm doing my best."

The men approached in the twilight. The sun had gone, and from the Queen's camp a trumpet rang out.

Laughter and the ripple of viols came from the royal tent.

Caspar groaned.

"We've made up our minds." Medlicote put the firelock down and gazed at Jared through the mothy evening. "We agree to your plan."

Caspar gasped and slumped a little. Jared nodded.

"But. There are conditions. We know what you were researching in the Academy. We know you decoded files, and we assume you learned secrets there, about the Prison. Can you find a way Out for the Warden?"

"I believe it's possible," Jared said cautiously.

"Then you must swear to us, Master, that you will do everything you can to restore him to us. He must be held against his will. If the Prison is not the paradise we thought, he would never have abandoned us. The Warden is faithful to the Clan."

They really were deluded, Jared thought. But he nodded. "I'll do my best."

"To make certain, I will enter the Wardenry with you."

"No!" Caspar turned his head blindly. "He'll kill me, even in there!"

Jared gazed at Medlicote. "Don't fear, sire. Claudia would never let that happen."

"Claudia." Caspar nodded in relief. "Yes, you're right. Claudia and I were always friends. My fiancée once. Could be again."

The Steel Wolves looked down at him in bitter silence. One of them muttered, "The heir of the Havaarnas. What a future we face."

"We will overthrow all of them, and Protocol too."

Medlicote turned. "The moon sets in a few hours. We'll wait till then."

"Good." Jared sat, pushing damp hair from his face. "In that case, my lords, if you have anything a poor Sapient could eat, he would be grateful. And then I'll sleep, and you can wake me." He glanced up, through the branches of the trees. "Here. Under the stars."

—◁◦◦◦▷—

CLAUDIA AND Finn sat opposite each other at the table.

Servants poured wine; Ralph ushered in three footmen carrying tureens and then supervised the dishes, removing covers and placing utensils next to Claudia.

She sat, brooding over the melon on her plate. Beyond the candles and piled centerpiece of fruit Finn drank silently.

"Will there be anything else, madam?"

She looked up. "No, Ralph, thank you. It looks wonderful. Please thank the staff."

He bowed, but she caught his surprised glance and almost smiled. Maybe she had changed. Maybe she was not quite the same haughty little girl anymore.

When he had gone and they were alone, neither of them spoke. Finn piled some food on his plate and then poked at it listlessly. Claudia couldn't face anything.

"It's strange. For months I've wanted to be here, at home, with Ralph fussing." She looked around at the familiar dark-paneled room. "But it's not the same."

"Maybe that's because of the army outside."

She glared at him. Then she said, "It got to you. What he said."

"About hiding behind a girl?" He snorted. "I've heard worse. In the Prison Jormanric hurled insults that would freeze that idiot's blood."

She picked at a grape. "He *did* get to you."

Finn threw down his spoon with a clatter and jumped up. He strode angrily around the room.

"All right, Claudia, yes, he did. I should have killed him when I had the chance. No Pretender, no problem. And he's right in one thing. If we haven't cracked the Portal by seven, then I will walk out, alone, because there's no way I'm having any of your people die for me. A woman died once before because I could only think about my own Escape. I saw her fall screaming down a black abyss and it was my fault. It won't happen again."

Claudia pushed a pip around her plate. "Finn, that's exactly what he wants you to do. Be noble, give yourself up. Be killed." She turned. "Think! The Queen doesn't know about the Portal here—if she did, this place would be rubble by now. And now that you remember who you are . . . that you're really Giles, you can't just sacrifice yourself. You're the King."

He stopped and looked at her. "I don't like the way you said that."

"Said what?"

"Remember. *Remember.* You don't believe me, Claudia."

"Of course I do . . ."

"You think I'm lying. Maybe to myself."

"Finn . . ." She stood, but he waved her away.

"And the fit . . . it didn't happen, but it was coming. And it shouldn't be. Not anymore."

"They'll take time to go. Jared told you that." Exasperated, she stared at him. "Stop thinking about yourself for a minute, Finn! Jared is missing—god knows where he is. Keiro—"

"Don't talk to me about Keiro!"

He had turned, and his face was so white it scared her.

She was silent, knowing she had touched a raw nerve, letting her anger simmer.

Finn stared at her. Then, quieter, he said, "I never stop thinking about Keiro. I never stop wishing I'd never come here."

She laughed, acid. "You prefer the Prison?"

"I betrayed him. And Attia. If I could go back . . ."

She turned, snatched up her glass, and drank, her fingers trembling on the delicate stem. Behind her the fire crackled over its logs and plasticoals.

"Be careful what you wish for, Finn. You might get it."

He leaned on the fireplace, looking down. Beside him the carved figures watched; the black swan's eye glittered like a diamond.

In the heated room nothing moved but the flames. They made the heavy furniture shimmer, the facets of the crystals glint like watchful stars.

Outside, voices murmured in the corridor. The rumble of cannonballs being stacked came from the roof. If Claudia listened very hard she could hear the revelry from the Queen's camp.

Suddenly needing fresh air, she went to the window and opened the casement.

It was dark, the moon hung low, close to the horizon. Beyond the lawns the hills were crowned with trees, and she wondered how many artillery pieces the Queen had brought up behind them. Sick with sudden fear she said, "You miss Keiro and I miss my father." Sensing his head turn, she nodded. "No, I didn't think I would, but I do . . . Maybe there's more of him in me than I thought."

He said nothing.

Claudia pulled the window shut and went to the door. "Try and eat something. Ralph will be disappointed otherwise. I'm going back up."

He didn't move. They had left the study a mess of papers and diagrams and still nothing made sense. It was hopeless, because neither of them had any idea what they were looking for. But he couldn't tell her that.

At the door she paused. "Listen, Finn. If we don't succeed and you walk out like some hero, the Queen will destroy this house anyway. She won't be content now without a show of force. There's a secret way out—a tunnel under the stables. It's a trapdoor, under the fourth stall. The stable boy, Job, found it one day and showed Jared and me. It's old, pre-Era, and it comes up beyond the moat. If they break in, remember it, because I want to be sure you'll use it. You're the King. You're the one who understands Incarceron. You're too valuable to lose. The rest of us are not."

For a while he couldn't answer her, and when he turned, he saw she'd gone.

The door clicked slowly shut.

He stared at its wooden boards.

28

*How will we know when the great Destruction is
near? Because there will be weeping and anguish
and strange cries in the night. The Swan will sing
and the Moth will savage the Tiger. Chains will
spring open. The lights will go out, one by one like
dreams at daybreak.*

Amongst this chaos, one thing is sure.

*The Prison will close its eyes against the sufferings
of its children.*

—Lord Calliston's Diary

*T*he stars.

Jared slept beneath them, uneasy in the rustling
leaves.

From the battlements Finn gazed up at them, seeing the
impossible distances between galaxies and nebulae, and thinking they were not as wide as the distances between people.

In the study Claudia sensed them, in the sparks and crackles
on the screen.

IN THE Prison, Attia dreamed of them. She sat curled on the
hard chair, Rix repacking his hidden pockets obsessively with
coins and glass discs and hidden handkerchiefs.

A single spark flickered deep in the coin Keiro spun and caught, spun and caught.

And all over Incarceron, through its tunnels and corridors, its cells and seas, the Eyes began to close. One by one they rippled off down galleries where people came out of their huts to stare; in cities where priests of obscure cults cried out to Sapphique; in remote halls where nomads had wandered for centuries; above a crazed Prisoner digging his lifelong tunnel with a rusty spade. The Eyes went out in ceilings, in the cobwebbed corner of a cell, in the den of a Winglord, in the thatched eaves of a cottage. Incarceron withdrew its gaze, and for the first time since its waking the Prison ignored its inmates, drew in on itself, closed down empty sections, gathered its great strength.

In her sleep Attia turned, and woke. Something had changed, had disturbed her, but she didn't know what it was. The hall was dark, the fire almost out. Keiro was a huddle in the chair, one leg dangling over its wooden armrest, sleeping his light sleep. Rix was brooding. His eyes were fixed on her.

Alarmed, she felt for the Glove and touched its reassuring crackle.

"It was a pity you weren't the one to say the riddle, Attia." Rix's voice was a whisper. "I would have preferred to work with you."

He didn't ask if she had the Glove safe, but she knew why. The Prison would hear.

She rubbed her cricked neck and answered, equally quietly, "What are you up to, Rix?"

"Up to?" He grinned. "I'm up to the greatest illusion anyone has ever performed. What a sensation it will be, Attia! People will talk about it for generations."

"If there *are* people." Keiro had opened his eyes. He was listening, and not to Rix. "Hear that?"

The heartbeat had changed.

It was faster, the double-thump louder. As Attia listened, the crystals in the chandelier above her tinkled with it; she felt the faintest reverberation in the chair she sat on.

Then, so loud it made her jump, a bell rang.

High and clear it pierced the darkness; she jammed her hands to her ears in a grimace of shock. Once, twice, three times it rang. Four. Five. Six.

As the last chime ended, its silvery clarity almost painful, the door opened and the Warden came in. His dark frockcoat was strapped with a belt and two firelocks. He wore a sword, and his eyes were gray points of winter.

"Stand up," he said.

Keiro lounged to his feet. "No minions?"

"Not now. No one enters the Heart of Incarceron but myself. You will be the first—and last—of its creatures to see Incarceron's own face."

Attia felt Rix squeeze her hand. "The honor is beyond expression," the magician muttered, bowing.

She knew he wanted the Glove from her, right now. She stepped away, toward the Warden, because this decision would be no one's but hers.

Keiro saw. His smile was cool, and it annoyed her.

If the Warden noticed anything he made no sign. Instead he crossed to the corner of the room and tugged aside a tapestry of forest trees and stags.

Behind it rose a portcullis, ancient and rusted. John Arlex bent and with both hands turned an ancient winch. Once, twice, he heaved it around, and creaking and flaking rust, the portcullis rose, and beyond it they saw a small, worm-eaten wooden door. The Warden shoved it open. A draft of warm air swept out over them. Beyond, they saw darkness, pounding with steam and heat.

John Arlex drew his sword. "This is it, Rix. This is what you've dreamed of."

—◁○○○▷—

AS FINN came into the study Claudia glanced up.

Her eyes were red-rimmed. He wondered if she had been crying. Certainly she was furious with frustration.

"Look at it!" she snapped. "Hours of work and it's still a mystery. A total, incomprehensible mess!"

Jared's papers were in chaos. Finn set down the tray of wine Ralph had insisted he bring and stared around. "You should take a rest. You must be making some progress."

She laughed harshly. Then she stood so quickly the great

blue feather propped in the corner lifted into the air. "I don't know! The Portal flickers, it crackles, sounds come out of it."

"What sounds?"

"Cries. Voices. Nothing clear." She snapped a switch and he heard them, the distant, faintest echoes of distress.

"Sounds like frightened people. In some big space." He looked at her. "Terrified, even."

"Is it familiar?"

He laughed, bitter. "Claudia, the Prison is full of frightened people."

"Then there's no way of knowing which part of the Prison that is, or . . ."

"What's that?" He stepped closer.

"What?"

"That other sound. Behind . . ."

She stared at him, then went to the controls and began to adjust them. Gradually, out of the chaos of hissing and static, emerged a deeper bass, a repeated, double pounding motif.

Finn kept still, listening.

Claudia said, "It's the same sound we heard before, when my father spoke to us."

"It's louder now."

"Have you any idea . . . ?"

He shook his head. "In all my time Inside I never heard anything like that."

For a moment only the heartbeat filled the room. Then from

Finn's pocket came a sudden pinging that startled them both. He pulled out her father's watch.

Startled, Claudia said, "It's never done that before."

Finn flicked open the gold lid. The clock hands showed six o'clock; the chimes rang out like tiny urgent bells. As if in response the Portal chuntered and went silent.

She came closer. "I didn't know it had an alarm. Who set it? Why now?"

Finn didn't answer. He was staring gloomily at the time. Then he said, "Perhaps to tell us there's only an hour left till the deadline."

The silver cube that was Incarceron spun slowly on its chain.

⚊◦◦◦⚊

"TAKE CARE here, both of you." Jared climbed over the roof-fall.

He turned and held up the lantern so that Caspar could manage. "Perhaps we should untie his hands?"

"I wouldn't advise it." Medlicote prodded the Earl with the firelock. "Quickly, sire."

"I could break my neck!" Caspar sounded more irritable than worried. As Jared helped him over the pile of stones he slid and swore. "My mother will have both of you beheaded for this. You do know that?"

"Only too well." Jared peered ahead. He had forgotten the state of the tunnel; even when he and Claudia had first explored it, it had been in a state of collapse, and that had been years

372

ago. She had always meant to have it repaired, but had never gotten around to it. There was nothing false about its age or the frequent crumbling of its walls. A brick vault loomed over him, green with dripping slime and infested with mosquitoes that whined around the lantern.

"How much farther?" Medlicote asked. He looked worried. "I think we're under the moat."

Somewhere ahead an ominous plopping noise told them of a leak.

"If this roof comes down . . ." Medlicote muttered. He didn't finish. Then he said, "Perhaps we should go back."

"You may go back any time you wish, sir." Jared ducked through hanging webs into the dark. "But I intend to find Claudia. And we would do well to be out of here before the cannon start firing."

But as he pushed on into the stinking darkness he wondered whether they had started already, or whether the pounding in his ears was just his own heartbeat.

ATTIA WALKED through the small door and staggered, because the world was tilted. It straightened itself under her feet, so that she almost fell, and had to grab Rix to keep her balance.

He, staring upward, did not even notice.

"My god!" he said. "We're Outside!"

The space had no roof, no walls. It was so vast it had no ending, nothing but steamy mist through which they couldn't see.

In that instant she knew she was tiny in the face of the universe; it terrified her. She edged close to Rix and he grasped her hand, as if he, too, was moved by that sudden giddiness.

Swirls of steam curled miles above them like clouds. The floor was made of some hard mineral, the squares of it enormous. As the Warden led them forward their footsteps were loud across the shining black surface. She counted. It took thirteen steps to reach the next white square.

"Pieces on a chessboard." Keiro voiced her thoughts.

"As Outside, so within," the Warden murmured, amused.

And there was silence. That was what scared her most. The heartbeat had stopped as soon as they passed the door, as if they had somehow entered its very chambers, and here, so deep within itself, no sound lived.

A shadow flickered on the clouds.

Keiro turned quickly. "What was that?"

A hand. Enormous. And then, a beam of light moving over feathers, vast feathers each taller than a man.

Rix stared up, bewildered. "Sapphique," he gasped. "Are you here?"

It was a mirage, a vision. It hung in the clouds and rose like a colossus into the sky, a great being of white shimmers and drifts of steam; a nose, an eye, the plumage of wings so wide they could enfold the world.

Even Keiro was awed. Attia couldn't move. Rix muttered under his breath.

But the Warden's voice, behind them, was calm.

"Impressed? But that too is an illusion, Rix, and you don't even spot it?" His scorn was rich and deep. "Why should mere size impress you so much? It's all relative. What would you say if I told you that the whole of Incarceron is actually tinier than a cube of sugar in a universe of giants?"

Rix tore his eyes from the apparition. "I'd say you were the madman, Warden."

"Perhaps I am. Come and see what causes your mirage."

Keiro pulled Attia on. At first she was unable to stop staring back, because the shadow on the clouds grew as they moved away from it, rippling and fading and reappearing. Rix, though, hurried after the Warden, as if he had already forgotten his wonder. "How tiny?"

"Tinier than you could imagine." John Arlex glanced at him.

"But in my imagination, I am immense! I am the universe. There's nothing else but me."

Keiro said, "Just like the Prison, then."

Ahead of them the steam cleared. Alone in the center of the marble floor, pinpointed by a ring of spotlights, they saw a man.

He was standing on a platform reached by five steps, and at first they thought he was winged, the plumage black as a swan's. Then they saw he wore a Sapient's robe of darkest iridescence and it was threaded with feathers. His face was narrow and beautiful, shining with radiance. Each eye was perfect, the lips held in a smile of compassion, his hair dark. One hand was lifted, the other hung at his side. He did not move, or speak, or breathe.

Rix stepped up onto the lowest step, staring up.

"Sapphique," he murmured. "The Prison's face is Sapphique's."

"It's just a statue," Keiro snapped.

All around them, as close as a caress against their cheeks, Incarceron whispered, *"No, it isn't. It's my body."*

THE PORTAL said something.

Finn turned and stared at it. Wisps of gray, like curls of cloud, were moving over its surface. The hum in the room modulated and changed. All the lights flickered off and on.

"Get back." Claudia was already at the controls. "Something's happening inside."

"Your father, he warned us . . . about what might come through."

"I know what he said!" She didn't turn, her fingers playing on the controls. "Are you armed?"

He drew his sword slowly.

The room dimmed.

"What if it's Keiro? I can't kill Keiro!"

"Incarceron is cunning enough to look like anyone."

"I can't, Claudia!" He moved closer.

Suddenly, without warning, the room tipped. It spoke. It said, *"My body . . ."*

Finn staggered, slamming against the desk. The sword clattered out of his hand as he grabbed at Claudia, but she slid back with a gasp, missing her footing, crashing into the chair, falling back into its seat.

And before she could stand up, she was gone.

⊰◦◦◦⊱

RIX MOVED. He snatched the sword from the Warden's belt and swung it to Attia's neck. He said, "It's time to give me my Glove back."

"Rix . . ." Beside her was the right hand of the statue. Small red circuits rippled at its fingers ends.

"Do what you have to, my son," the Prison said eagerly.

Rix nodded. "I hear you, Master." He pulled Attia's coat open and snatched out the Glove. He held it up in triumph and from all sides the beams of light swiveled and focused on it, throwing swollen replicated shadows not only of the statue now but of all of them, great cloudy Keiros and Attias on the clouds.

"Behold," Rix murmured. "The greatest illusion the Prison has ever seen."

The sword tip whipped away from Attia's neck. She moved, but Keiro was quicker. Diving forward he batted the blade aside and punched Rix hard in the chest.

But it was Keiro who cried out. He was flung back jerking with shock, and Rix laughed, his gap-tooth grin wide.

"Magic! How powerful it is, my Apprentice! How it guards its master!"

He turned to the image, lifted the Glove toward its sparking fingers.

"No!" Attia cried. "You can't do this!" She turned to the Warden. "Stop him!"

The Warden said quietly, "There is nothing I can do. There never has been."

She grabbed at Rix, but even as she touched him the shock burned into her nerves, an electric spark of recoil that screamed in her own voice. Then she was on the floor and Keiro was standing over her. "Are you all right?"

She crouched over her burned fingers. "He's wired up. He's beaten us."

"*Rix.*" Incarceron's order was urgent. "*Give me my Glove. Give me my freedom. Do it NOW.*"

Rix turned and Attia rolled. She shot out her foot and the magician tripped and fell, crashing on the white floor, the Glove falling from his hand and skidding over the shiny marble, Keiro diving after it and grabbing it with a whoop of joy.

He scrambled back, out of reach. "Now, Prison, you get your freedom. But from me. And only if you do what you promised. Tell me I'm the one who gets to Escape with you."

The Prison laughed, ominous. "*Do you really think I keep such promises?*"

Keiro circled, gazing up, ignoring Rix's howls of anger. He showed no disappointment. "Take me or I wear the Glove."

"*You would not dare.*"

"Watch me."

"The Glove will kill you."

"Better than living in this hell."

Their stubbornness made them equal, Attia thought.

Keiro turned, a slow circle. He slid his metal fingernail toward the Glove's opening.

"I will torment you." Incarceron's voice was a high metallic whine. *"I will make you pray for death."*

"Keiro, don't," Attia whispered.

For a second he hesitated. And then from behind her the Warden's cool voice cut the air. "Wear it. Put it on."

"What?"

"Put it on. The Prison won't risk destroying its only way Out. I think the result will surprise you."

Keiro stared at him in surprise and the Warden stared back. Then Keiro slipped his fingers deeper.

"Wait." Incarceron's voice thundered. The cloud flickered with invisible lightning. *"I will not allow that. No. Stop. Please."*

"You stop me," Keiro breathed. A spark leaped between his metal nail and the Glove. He gasped with the pain. And then he was gone.

⊲◦◦◦⊳

THERE WAS no light, no blinding brilliant flash. Instead, as Finn stared at Claudia he saw she was no longer there. She had become a vacuum of herself, a shadow, a negative image. And as he watched she re-emerged from the darkness, pixel by pixel, atom by atom, the reassembly of a fragmented being, all its thoughts and limbs and dreams and features, and it wasn't Claudia, it was someone else.

He groped for the sword, his eyes blinded by what might be tears, the blade whipping up to the face that stared at his, the amazed blue eyes, the dirty blond hair.

For a long moment Finn was still, both of them were, face-to-face, and then Keiro reached forward and took the sword from him and turned the point to the ground.

The door burst open. Jared took one look around the Portal and stood stock-still. His heart was hammering so hard he was breathless, and he leaned back against the wall.

Behind him Medlicote pushed Caspar in, and they stared.

They saw, facing Finn, a stranger in a filthy red coat, his eyes blue with triumph, his muscled hand tight around the hilt of a sharp sword. There was no one else in the room.

"Who are you?" Caspar demanded.

Keiro turned and gazed at the shining breastplate and splendid clothes.

He leveled the blade an inch from Caspar's eyes.

"Your worst nightmare," he said.

THE WINGED MAN

29

Did he Escape? For there is a rumor that is whispered in the dark, a rumor that he remains, trapped deep in the Prison's heart, his body turned to stone; that the cries we hear are his cries, that his struggles shake the world.

But we know what we know.

—The Steel Wolves

Jared stepped forward and grabbed the Glove from Keiro's hand, flinging it down on the floor as if it were alive. "Did you hear its dreams?" he said. "Did it control you?"

Keiro laughed. "Does it look like it?"

"But you wore it!"

"No. I didn't." Keiro was too amazed to think about the Glove. He flicked Caspar's coat-collar with the sword tip. "Nice material. And just my size."

He was glowing with delight. If he felt sick or dazzled by the room's white light he didn't show it. He took in everything— the four of them, the cluttered Portal, the huge feather—with one avid sweep of his eyes. "So this is Outside."

Finn swallowed. His mouth felt dry. He glanced at Jared and almost felt the Sapient's dismay.

Keiro tapped Caspar's breastplate with the sword. "I want that too."

Finn said, "It's different here. There are wardrobes full of clothes."

"I want his."

Caspar looked terrified. "Do . . . do you know who I am?" he stammered.

Keiro grinned. "No."

"*Where's Claudia?*" Jared's agonized question cut the tension.

Keiro shrugged. "How should I know?"

"They changed places." Finn kept his eyes on his oathbrother. "She was sitting in the chair and she just . . . dissolved. Keiro appeared. Is that what the Glove does? Is that the power it has? Can I put it on now, and . . ."

"No one puts it on until I say." Jared moved past him. He went to the chair and gripped it, leaning on its back. His face was pale with weariness and he looked more anxious than Finn had ever seen him. Quickly, Finn said, "Master Medlicote, pour some wine please."

The fragrant smell filled the air. Keiro sniffed it. "What is that?"

"Better than the Prison muck." Finn watched him. "Try some. And you, Master."

As the drink was poured he watched his oathbrother prowl around the room, exploring everything. It was all wrong. He should be happy. He should be so elated to have Keiro here. And yet there was a deep dread inside him, a shivery, sickening terror, because this wasn't how it should have happened. And because Claudia was gone, and suddenly there was a hole in the world.

He said, "Who was with you?"

Keiro sipped the red liquid and his eyebrows rose. "Attia. The Warden. And Rix."

"Who's Rix?" Finn said, but Jared turned from the screen instantly. "The Warden was with you?"

"He told me to do it. He said, *'Put the Glove on.'* Maybe he knew . . ." Keiro stopped instantly. "That's it! Of course he knew. It was his way of getting the Glove out of the Prison's reach."

Jared turned back to the screen. Placing his fingers on it, he stared sadly into its darkness. "At least she's with her father."

"If they're still alive." Keiro glanced at Caspar's tied wrists. "What's going on here, anyway? I thought this was where people were free." Turning, he saw them all staring at him.

Medlicote whispered, "What do you mean, if they're still alive?"

"Use your brain." Keiro sheathed the sword and went to the door. "The Prison is going to be very, very angry about this. It may have killed them all already."

Jared stared at him. "You knew that might happen, and you still—"

"That's how it is in Incarceron," Keiro said. "Every man

for himself. As my brother will tell you." He turned and faced Finn. "So. Are you going to show me our kingdom? Or are you ashamed of your jailbird brother? That is, if we're still brothers."

Finn said quietly, "We're still brothers."

"You don't seem so pleased to see me."

He shrugged. "It's the shock. And Claudia . . . she's in there . . ."

Keiro raised an eyebrow. "So that's how it is. Well, I suppose she's rich, and enough of a bitch to make a good Queen."

"That's what I've missed about you. Your tact and courtesy."

"Not to mention my quicksilver wit and devastating looks."

They stood face-to-face. Finn said, "Keiro—"

A sudden explosion rumbled over their heads. The room shook, a plate sliding to the floor and smashing.

Finn swung to Jared. "They've opened fire!"

"Then I suggest you get the Queen's beloved son up to the battlements," Jared said quietly. "I have work to do here."

He exchanged one swift look with Finn, and Finn saw the discarded Glove was in his hand. "Be careful, Master."

"Just stop them firing. And Finn." Jared came over and gripped his wrist. "Do not, on any account, leave this house. I need you here. Do you understand me?"

After a moment Finn said, "I understand."

Another rumble. Keiro said, "Tell me that's not cannon fire."

"A whole regiment of it," Caspar said, smug.

Finn pushed him away and turned to Keiro. "Look. We're besieged. There's an army out there and we're outgunned and outmanned. Things are not good. I'm afraid you haven't come into some paradise. You've come into a battle."

Keiro had always been an expert at taking things in his stride. Now he looked curiously up the sumptuous corridor. "In that case, brother, I'm exactly what you need."

⸺⸻◦◦◦◦⸻⸺

CLAUDIA FELT as if she had been broken apart and reassembled, badly, piece by piece. As if she had been forced through some barrier of mesh, a matrix of collapsing dimensions.

She was standing on a great bare floor of black and white tiles.

Facing her father.

He seemed utterly dismayed. "No!" he breathed. And then, almost like a cry of pain, "*No!*"

The floor rippled. She steadied herself, arms out, and then breathed in, and the stink of the Prison overwhelmed her, the stench of endlessly recycled air and human fear.

She gasped and put both hands over her face.

The Warden came toward her. For a moment she thought he would take her hands in his cold fingers, print her cheek with his icy kiss. Instead he said, "This shouldn't have happened. How could this happen!"

"You tell me." She glanced around, saw Attia staring at her, and a tall ragged man who seemed utterly astounded, his hands knotted and his eyes deep hollows of awe.

"Magic," he breathed. "The true Art."

It was Attia who said, "Keiro's vanished. He vanished and you appeared. Does that mean he's Outside?"

"How am I supposed to know?"

"You have to know!" Attia yelled. "He has the Glove!"

The floor rippled again, a wave of cracking tiles.

"No time now for this." The Warden pulled out a firelock and gave it to Claudia. "Take this. Protect yourself against whatever the Prison sends."

She held the weapon limply, but then she saw that behind them the whole vast space was flooding with clouds that swirled and blackened and sparked lightning. One flash cracked into the floor beside the Warden. He swung around, staring up. "Listen to me, Incarceron! This is not our fault!"

"Then whose fault is it?" The voice of the Prison seethed with fury. Its words were crackled and raw, dissolving into hisses of static. *"You told him to do it. You betrayed me."*

The Warden said coldly, "Not at all. It may look that way, but you and—"

"Why should I not burn you all into ash?"

"Because you would damage your delicately made creation." The Warden stepped close to the statue; Claudia stared up at it in awe as he pulled her after him. "I think you are too astute to do that." He smiled. "It seems to me, Incarceron, that things have changed now between us. For years you have done what you wanted, ruled as you liked. You controlled yourself. I was Warden only in name. Now the one thing you want is beyond your grasp."

Claudia felt Attia jump up on the step behind her.

"Listen to him," the girl whispered. "This is all about him and his power."

The Prison laughed, a sinister chuckle. *"You think so?"*

John Arlex shrugged. He looked at Claudia. "I know so. The Glove has been taken Outside. It will be returned to you only by my orders."

"Your orders? Indeed?"

"My orders, as Clanlord of the Steel Wolves."

He was bluffing, Claudia thought. She said aloud, "Do you remember me, Prison?"

"I remember you. You were mine and you are mine again. But now, unless I have my Glove, I will close down the lights and the air and the heat. I will leave millions to suffocate in darkness."

"You will not," the Warden said evenly, "or you will never have the Glove." He spoke as if to a child, with a clear severity. "Instead, you show me the secret door that Sapphique used."

"So that you and your so-called daughter can release yourselves, and leave me trapped here?" The voice was clotted with sparks. *"Never."*

The Prison convulsed. Claudia staggered and fell against Rix. He grabbed her arm, grinning.

"My father's anger," he whispered.

"I will destroy you all now."

The black squares of the floor rolled back and were holes. Out of them rose cables with open mouths of venom. They kinked and curled like snakes of power, cracking and spitting.

"Up the steps." The Warden climbed quickly to the feet of the winged man, Rix shoving Claudia after him. Attia came last, glancing around.

White vivid shocks split the darkness.

"It won't harm the statue," the Warden murmured.

Attia glared. "You can't be sure . . ."

High in the roof, a great rumble silenced her. The clouds were storm black. Tiny hard pellets of snow were falling from them. In seconds the temperature was below zero and dropping fast, and Rix's breath steamed as he breathed out. "It won't have to damage it. It'll just freeze us here to its feet."

And each of the tiny flakes whispered as it fell, in million-fold anger.

Yes.

Yes.

Yes.

◁◦◦◦▷

THE FIRST shot had just been a warning. The ball had sailed right over the roof and crashed somewhere in the woods beyond. But Finn knew the next one would smash through; as he ran up the last stair and out onto the battlements he saw

390

through the acrid smoke the Queen's artillerymen adjusting the angles of the five great cannon they had ranged across the lawns.

Behind him, Keiro gasped.

Finn turned. His oathbrother stood transfixed, gazing out at the pale dawn sky slashed with gold and scarlet.

The sun was rising. It hung like a great red globe above the beechwoods, and rooks rose in clouds to meet it from the branches.

The long shadow of the house stretched over lawns and gardens, and on the moat light glimmered on the ripples the swans made as they woke.

Keiro walked to the battlements and gripped the stonework, as if to make sure it was all real. He gazed for a long moment on the perfection of the morning, at the scarlet and gold pennants flapping over the Queen's pavilions, the lavender hedges, the roses, the bees that hummed in the honeysuckle flowers under his hands.

"Amazing," he breathed. "Totally amazing."

"You haven't seen anything yet," Finn muttered. "When the sun gets high, it'll dazzle you. And at night . . ." He stopped. "Go inside. Ralph, get him some hot water, the best clothes . . ."

Keiro shook his head. "Tempting, brother, but not yet. First we deal with this enemy Queen."

Medlicote came up behind them, a little breathless, and

behind him the soldiers pushed Caspar, red in the face and furious.

"Finn, get these ropes off me. I insist!"

Finn nodded and the nearest guard sliced the knot swiftly. Caspar made a great show of rubbing his chafed wrists, staring haughtily around at everyone except Keiro, whose eyes he seemed too terrified to meet.

Captain Soames stared at him in disbelief.

"Isn't that . . . ?"

"That's a miracle." Finn said. "Now. Can we get their attention before they blast us to pieces?"

The flag was raised; it flapped loudly. In the Queen's camp a few men pointed; someone ran into the large tent.

No one came out.

The guns were a row of dark muzzles.

"If they fire . . ." Medlicote said nervously.

Keiro said, "Someone's coming."

A courtier was galloping toward them on a gray horse. He spoke to the artillerymen as he passed, then galloped cautiously over the lawns to the edge of the moat.

"You wish to surrender the Prisoner?" he called up.

"Shut up and listen to me." Finn leaned over. "Tell the Queen if she fires on us she kills her son. Understand?"

He grabbed Caspar and hauled him to the battlements.

The courtier stared up in horror, his horse prancing under him. "The Earl? But . . ."

Keiro stepped up to Caspar, one arm around his shoulders. "Here he is! With both ears, both eyes, and both hands. Unless you'd like some proof to take the Queen?"

"No!" the man gasped.

"Shame." Keiro held a knife carelessly against Caspar's cheek. "But I suggest you tell the Queen that he's in my hands now and I'm not like the rest of you. I'm not playing any games."

He tightened his grip and Caspar stifled a gasp.

Finn said, "No."

Keiro smiled his most charming smile. "Run along now."

The courtier turned his horse and raced for the tents. Clods of earth were flung up by the hooves. As he passed he yelled urgently at the men by the cannons; they backed away, obviously puzzled.

Keiro turned. He pushed the point of the knife very slightly into Caspar's white skin. A small red spot swelled with blood.

"A little souvenir," he whispered.

"Leave him." Finn came and tugged Caspar away and pushed the half-fainting Earl at Captain Soames. "Put him somewhere safe and have a man stay with him. Food and water. Anything he needs."

As they took the boy away he turned on Keiro angrily. "This is not the Prison!"

"So you keep telling me."

"You don't need to be so savage."

Keiro shrugged. "Too late. This is me, Finn. This is what the Prison has made me. Not like all this, no." He waved at the manor house. "This pretty world, those toy soldiers. I'm real. And I'm free. Free to do whatever I want."

He headed for the stairs.

"Where are you going?"

"That bath, brother. Those clothes."

Finn nodded to Ralph. "Find him some."

Seeing the consternation in the old man's face, he turned away.

He had forgotten. In three months he had forgotten the wildness in Keiro, his arrogance, his utter willfulness. How he had always been scared of what Keiro would do.

A woman's scream of fury jerked his head up. It cut the morning like a knife, and it came from the Queen's pavilion.

Well, at least that was one message that had gone home.

30

As the Beast I took your finger.
As the Dragon I give you my hand.
Now you have crawled and clambered into my heart.
I can't see you anymore.
Are you still here?

—*Mirror of Dreams to Sapphique*

The very air was freezing.

Huddled at the feet of the winged Sapphique, Attia could not stop shivering. Knees up, arms wrapped around herself, she suffered the numbing agony of cold. Her shoulders were white, her arms, her back. Snow made the miserable heap that was Rix into an albino wizard, his straggly hair glistening with half-melted slush. "We'll die," he croaked.

"No." The Warden had not stopped pacing. His footsteps made a complete circle about the base of the statue. "No. This is a bluff. The Prison is computing a solution. I know how its mind works. It's trying out every plot and plan it can devise, and in the meantime it hopes to force us to give it the Glove."

"But you can't!" Rix groaned.

"Do you think I can't speak to the Outside?"

Claudia was standing right behind him. She said, "Can you? Or are you bluffing too? Is this part of the game you've spent your life playing?"

Her father stopped and turned to her. Pinched with cold, his face was deathly pale against the high dark collar. "You still hate me then?"

"I don't hate you. But I can't forgive you."

He smiled. "For rescuing you from a life in hell? For giving you everything you could ever want—money, education, great estates? Betrothal to a prince?"

He always did this to her. Made her feel foolish and ungrateful. But still she said, "All that, yes. But you never really loved me."

"How do you know?" His face was close to hers.

"I would have known. I would have felt . . ."

"Ah, but I play games, remember?" His eyes were clear and gray. "With the Queen. With the Prison. It has taught me to be careful what I show to the world." He took a slow breath, the snow catching on his narrow beard. "Perhaps I loved you more than you knew. But if we come to accusations, Claudia, I might say this. You love only Jared."

"Don't bring Jared into this! You wanted your daughter to be Queen. Any daughter would do. I could have been anyone."

The Warden stepped back, as if her anger was a wave that pushed him away.

Rix chuckled. "A puppet," he said.

396

"What?"

"A puppet. Carved perfectly by a lonely man from wood. And yet the puppet comes alive and torments him."

John Arlex frowned. "Keep your stories for your act, magician."

"*This is my act, sire.*" For a moment the voice was changed; it became the soft voice of Sapphique, so that they all stared at him through the falling snow. But Rix just grinned his gap-toothed grin.

The Prison howled. It gusted the snow against them in an angry scream. Attia glanced up and saw that the statue was crusted with icicles. Snow whitened the crevices of its hand, clogged the plumage of its coat. Sapphique's eyes were glinting with ice; over his face a frost spread almost as she looked, stars of crystal joining up like some inhuman virus. She was too cold to bear it. She jumped up. "We'll freeze here. And god knows what's happening elsewhere."

Claudia nodded gloomily. "Putting Keiro in the middle of a siege is a recipe for disaster. If only I knew where Jared is."

"*I have come to my decision.*" The Prison's venomous whisper was all around them.

"Excellent." The Warden glared up into the snowfall. "I was sure you'd come to your senses. Show me the Door. I'll ensure the Glove is returned to you."

Silence.

Then, with a snigger that sent shivers down Attia's spine,

Incarceron said, *"I am not such a fool, John. The Glove first."*

"We leave first."

"I don't trust you."

"Very wise," Rix muttered.

"I was made by the Wise."

The Warden smiled coldly. "Nor do I trust you."

"Then you will not be surprised at what I do next. You think I cannot reach the Glove. But I have spent centuries investigating my own power and its sources. I have discovered things that astonished me. I assure you, John, I can suck the life out of your pretty Realm."

Claudia said, "What do you mean? You can't . . ."

"Ask your father. How pale he looks now. I will show all of you who is the true Prince of the Realm."

The Warden seemed shaken. "Tell me what you mean to do. Tell me!"

But only the snow fell, icy and relentless.

Attia said, "You're scared. It's scared you."

They all saw his consternation. "I don't understand what it means," he whispered.

Dismay struck Claudia like a blow. "But you're the Warden . . ."

"I have lost control, Claudia. I told you, we're all Prisoners now."

It was Attia who said, "Do you hear that?"

A low thudding. It came from across the hall, and as they

stared out they realized that the snow had stopped falling.

The electric snakes slid silently into the black tiles of the floor, which clicked across and became solid again.

"Hammering," Rix said.

Attia shook her head. "More than that."

Blows against the door, far off in the suddenly frosty air of the great hall. Blows of axes and sledgehammers and fists.

"Prisoners," the Warden said. And then, "A riot."

⊸◦◦◦▻

WHEN JARED walked into the Great Chamber Finn turned in relief. "Any progress?"

"The Portal is working. But the screen shows only snow."

"Snow!"

Jared sat, wrapping his Sapient coat around him. "It seems to be snowing in the Prison. The temperature is five degrees below zero and dropping."

Finn jumped up and paced in despair. "It's taking its revenge."

"So it seems. For this." Jared took the Glove out and placed it carefully on the table. Finn came and touched its scaly skin.

"Is it really Sapphique's?"

Jared sighed. "I have tried every analysis I know. It just seems to be what it looks like. Reptile skin. Claws. Much of it is recycled matter." He looked baffled and anxious. "I have no idea how it works, Finn."

They were silent. The shutters had been drawn back and

sunlight slanted in. A wasp murmured in the windowpanes. It was hard to believe a besieging army was encamped outside.

"Have they made any move?" Jared said.

"None. It's a standoff. But they may attack and try to rescue Caspar."

"Where is he?"

"In there." Finn nodded at the door to the next chamber. "It's locked, and that's the only way in."

He leaned against the empty fireplace. "I'm lost without Claudia, Master. She'd know what to do."

"You have Keiro instead. As you wanted."

Finn smiled, wan. "Not instead. As for Keiro . . . I'm beginning to wish—"

"Don't say that." Jared's green eyes watched him. "He's your brother."

"Only when it suits him."

As if the words had summoned him like a spell, a soldier flung the door open and Keiro walked in.

He was breathless and exhilarated and looked every inch a prince. His coat was deepest midnight blue, his blond hair shone clean. Rings glinted on his fingers. He sprawled on the bench, admiring his expensive leather boots. "This place is fantastic," he said. "I can't believe it's real."

"It's not," Jared said quietly. "Keiro, tell us about the situation Inside."

Keiro laughed and poured some wine. "I can only guess that

the Prison is furious, Master Sapient. I suggest you destroy your machines and nail up the door that leads there and forget all about it. No one can save the Prisoners now."

Jared watched him. "You sound just like its builders," he said.

"Claudia," Finn said.

"Oh yes, well I'm sorry about the Princess. But it was me you wanted to rescue, wasn't it? And I'm here. So let's win our little war, brother, and enjoy our perfect kingdom."

Finn stood over him. "Why did I ever make an oath with you?"

"To survive. Because without me you couldn't." Keiro stood lightly, gazing at Finn. "But something's changed in you, Finn. Not just all this. Something inside."

"I've remembered."

"Remembered!"

"Who I am," Finn said. "I remembered that I am a prince and that my name is Giles."

Keiro said nothing for a moment. His eyes flickered to Jared's and back. "Well. So will the Prince ride into the Prison with all his men and all his horses?"

"No." Finn took the watch out and set it down on the table beside the Glove. "Because this is the Prison. This is where you came from. This is the vast edifice that had us all fooled." He grasped Keiro's hand and put the watch in it, lifting the silver cube close to his eyes. "This is Incarceron."

Jared expected awe, or astonishment. He saw neither.

Keiro burst into a fit of laughter. "You believe that?" he managed to gasp. "Even you, Master?"

Before Jared could answer, the door opened and Ralph came in with a guard at his back.

"What?" Finn barked.

"Sire." Ralph was pale and breathless. "Sire . . ."

The soldier stepped out from behind him and he had a drawn sword in one hand and a pistol in the other.

Two more men slipped around the door. One slammed it shut and put his back to it.

Jared stood, slowly.

Keiro didn't move, his eyes alert.

"We've come for the Earl. One of you open that door and get him. If anyone else moves, I fire."

The pistol was raised and pointed directly at Finn's eyes. Ralph gasped, "I'm sorry, sire, so sorry! They made me tell them . . ."

"It's all right, Ralph." Finn stared at the Queen's man. "Jared?"

Jared said, "I'll fetch him. Don't shoot. There's no need for violence."

He moved to the door, out of Finn's eye line, and Finn was left staring at the gun. He smiled, wan. "This is the second time this has happened to me."

"Oh come on, brother." Keiro's voice was light and sharp.

"It was an odd day in the Prison when such things didn't happen."

A door was unlocked behind them. Jared's voice spoke, low and quiet. Then there was a laugh of pure glee. That must be Caspar.

"How did you get in here?" Finn said.

The soldier's aim did not waver. But he said, "We captured one of the Steel Wolves out there in the woods. He was . . . persuaded to talk. He showed us the tunnel the Sapient used."

Sweating, Finn said, "Do you really think you'll get out the same way?"

"No, Prisoner. I think we'll go out through the front door."

Instantly, one of the other men swiveled his weapon.

"Keep still!"

Keiro must have moved. Finn could only see his shadow on the floor.

Finn licked dry lips. "You are overconfident."

"I don't think so. Have they harmed you, sire?"

"They wouldn't have dared." Caspar stalked into the room and stared around. "Well, this is better, don't you think, Finn? Now I'm the one in command." He folded his arms. "What if I told these men to cut off a few ears and hands?"

Finn heard the threat in Keiro's low laugh. "You wouldn't have the guts, little boy."

Caspar glared. "No? I might do it myself."

"Sire," Jared said. "We brought you here to stop the siege, not to harm you. You know that."

"Don't try to fool me with words, Jared. These two cut-throats would have killed me anyway, and maybe you as well, later on. This is a nest of rebels. And I don't know where Claudia is hiding, but she won't get any mercy from us either."

His eye fell on the Glove and he stared at it curiously. "What is *that*?"

"Please don't touch that," Jared said, his voice edged with nerves.

Caspar took a step nearer to the table. "Why not?"

Keiro's shadow had edged close. Finn tensed himself.

"It's a magical object of great power." Jared's reluctance was just right. "It may give access to the Prison."

Greed lit Caspar's face. "She'll be thrilled if I take that back for her."

"Sire." The guard's eyes wavered. "Don't . . ."

Caspar ignored him, took one step forward, and in that instant Jared grabbed him, locked his arms behind him, and held him in a tight grip.

Keiro whooped. Jared said, "Lower the gun. Please."

"You won't hurt the Earl, Master," the soldier said. "And my orders are clear. The Prisoner dies."

His finger twitched and Finn crashed as Keiro shoved him aside. The blast detonated with an explosion that threw him against the side of the table and stunned him, so that the shouts and smashing cups as Ralph and Jared heaved the table over and dragged him behind it seemed like objects inside his own head falling and breaking, the pool of wine like his own blood, trickling along the floor.

And then as the door was flung open, in all the stamping and shouts, he knew the blood was not his but Keiro's, because his brother lay still and crumpled beside him in the uproar.

"Finn! Finn!" Jared's hands raised him. "Can you hear me? Finn?"

"I'm all right," he said. But the words came out thick and groggy and he dragged himself out of Jared's grip.

"Our men heard the shot. It's all over."

Finn's hand touched Keiro's arm. His heart was thudding; he gripped the blue velvet sleeve.

"Keiro?"

For a moment there was nothing, no movement, no answer, and he felt all color drain away from the world, his life shrivel to a terrible fear.

And then Keiro jerked and rolled and they saw that his hand was wounded, a slashed burnmark across the palm. He lay on his back and his body convulsed.

"You're laughing?" Finn stared. "Why are you laughing?"

"Because it hurts, brother." Keiro pulled himself upright and there were tears of agony in his eyes. "It hurts, and that means it's real."

It was his right hand, the metal thumbnail stark in the scorched flesh.

Finn shook his head and croaked out a laugh with him. "You're mad."

"Indeed he is," Jared said.

But Keiro looked up at him. "It's worth knowing, Master. Flesh and blood. It's a start, anyway."

As they helped him up Finn looked around and saw Caspar under guard, the other men being hustled out.

"Get that tunnel sealed," he hissed, and Soames bowed. "Immediately, my lord." But as he turned he stopped dead, and in that second something terrible happened to the world.

The bees stopped buzzing.

The table dissolved into worm-eaten dust and collapsed.

Patches fell off the ceiling.

The sun went out.

31

My Realm will last forever.
—*King Endor's Decree*

Finn lurched to the casement and stared out.

He saw a darkening sky, clotted with clouds that built up and blotted out the daylight. The wind had risen, and the day was far, far colder than it should have been.

And the world was transformed.

He saw horses in the courtyard collapsing into twitching cybernetworks of limbs, their skin and eyes shriveling and shredding. He saw walls crumbling into holes, a stinking moat where nothing grew, parched acres of arid grassland.

Flowers withered as he gazed on them; the swans rose and flapped away. All the glorious beauty of the honeysuckle and clematis was dried into spindly crisp vines, the few weak petals blown away by the wind.

Doors were flung open; a guardsman came running down the steps, his fine livery a mismatched moth-eaten suit of gray.

Pushing in next to Finn, Keiro stared. "What's happening to it all? Are we still in the Prison? Is this one of Incarceron's clean-ups?"

Finn's throat was dry. He couldn't answer.

It was like a spell dissolving. All around him Claudia's paradise of the Wardenry was coming apart, the house a slipshod ruin, its golden-stoned splendor fading even as he watched, color washing from the mews and the stables, even the maze twisting to a dank thicket of brambles.

Jared murmured, "Perhaps the Prison is in us."

Finn turned. The room was a shell. The fine velvet hangings were rags, the once-white ceiling a mass of cracks. Jared bent over the wreck of the table, searching in its dust.

The fire was out, every bust and portrait showed patches and crude repairs. And worst of all, on every wall, their illusory holoimages dead, hundreds of cables and wires were revealed in all their naked, ugly uselessness.

"So much for Era." Finn grasped the red curtain and it fell to shreds in his fingers.

"This was how it was all the time." Jared straightened, the Glove in his hand. "We fooled ourselves with images."

"But how . . . ?"

"The power is gone. Completely." Jared gazed around, calm. "This is the true Realm, Finn. This is the kingdom you've inherited."

"So you're telling me this whole place is a trick!" Keiro kicked a vase over and watched it smash. "Like one of Rix's tacky stage routines? And you *knew*? All along?"

"We knew."

"Are you all mad?"

"Perhaps we are," Jared said. "Reality is hard to bear, so Era was invented to shield us from it. And yes, most of the time it was easy to forget. After all, the world is what you see and hear. For you that is the only reality."

"I might just as well have stayed Inside." Keiro's disgust was complete. Then he turned, caught by the truth. "This destruction is the Prison's work!"

"Of course it is." Finn rubbed his sore shoulder. "How else—"

"Sire." The guard captain burst in, breathless. "Sire! The Queen!"

Finn shoved him aside and raced up the corridor, Keiro close behind. Jared paused to slip the Glove in his robe and then followed, quickly. He climbed the great staircase as fast as he could, over rotten treads and mice-gnawed wainscots, gusted at by the wind whipping through the windows where plastiglas had vanished. He dared not think about his Tower—but at least all the scientific equipment there was genuine.

Or was it?

Stopping with one hand on the banister, he realized that he had no way of knowing. That nothing he had taken for granted could now be trusted.

And yet this disintegration didn't devastate him, as it had Finn and his wayward brother. Perhaps it was because he had always felt his own illness to be a tiny flaw in the

Realm's perfection, a crack that could not be patched up or disguised.

Now everything was as marred as he was. In the unsilvered mirror he caught a slant of his own delicate face, and smiled gently at himself. Claudia had wanted to overthrow Protocol. Perhaps the Prison had done it for her.

From the battlements, though, the terrible vista drained his smile away.

The Wardenry was a wasteland. All its meadows were scrub, all its rich woodlands mere naked branches against the gray winter sky.

The world had turned old in an instant.

But it was the enemy camp that held everyone's eyes. All the gaudy pennants, the flimsy pavilions were wrecked, their poles snapped. Horses neighed in confusion, men's armor rusted and fell from their bodies in the turmoil, their muskets suddenly useless antiques, their swords so brittle that they snapped in the hand.

"The cannon." Finn's voice was hard with joy. "They'll never dare fire the cannon now, in case they explode. They can't touch us."

Keiro glanced at him. "Brother, this ruin doesn't need cannon. A good shove would knock it down."

A trumpet rang out. From the Queen's pavilion a woman came out. She was veiled, and she leaned on the arm of a boy in a gaudy coat who could only be the Pretender. Together they walked through the camp, almost unnoticed in the panic.

"Is she surrendering?" Finn muttered.

Keiro turned to a guard. "Get Caspar up here."

The soldier hesitated, glancing at Finn, who said, "Do as my brother says."

The man ran. Keiro grinned.

The Queen came to the edge of the moat and looked up through her veil. Jewels glinted at her throat and ears. At least those must be real.

"Let us in!" the Pretender yelled up. He looked shaken, all his composure lost. "Finn! The Queen wants to speak with you!"

There was no ceremony, no Protocol, no heralds, no courtiers. Just a woman and a boy, looking lost. Finn drew back. "Lower the drawbridge. Take them to the Great Chamber."

Jared was staring down. "It seems it's not just me then," he murmured.

"Master?" Finn looked at him. The Sapient was gazing down at the veiled Queen with a great sadness in his eyes.

"Best leave this to me, Finn," he said softly.

⚬◦⚬

"THERE MUST be hundreds of them out there!" Attia stared across at the juddering door.

"Stay here," the Warden snapped. "I'm the Warden. I'll face them."

411

He stepped down onto the snowy floor and trudged quickly toward the hammering. Claudia watched.

"If they're Prisoners, they're desperate," Attia said. "Conditions must be impossible."

"They'll be looking for anyone to tear apart." Rix stared, his eyes glinting with the crazy brilliance Attia dreaded.

Claudia shook her head with fury. "This is all your fault. Why did you have to bring that evil Glove here!"

"Because your dear father ordered me to, sweetkin. I, too, am a Wolf of Steel."

Her father. She turned and ran down the steps, across the floor, after him. Locked in with madmen and thieves, her father was the only familiar presence here. Just behind her Attia gasped, "Wait for me."

"Doesn't the Apprentice want to stay with the sorcerer?" Claudia snapped.

"I'm not his Apprentice. Keiro is." Attia caught up with her. Then she said, "Is Finn safe?"

Claudia glanced at her thin face and short, hacked hair.

"His memory has come back."

"Has it?"

"So he says."

"And the fits?"

Claudia shrugged.

"Does he . . . think about us?" It was a whisper.

"He thought about Keiro all the time," Claudia said acidly.

"So I hope he's happy now." She didn't say what else she thought—that Finn had barely mentioned Attia's name.

The Warden had reached the small door. Outside it, the noise was terrible. Blades whacked into wood and metal; with one almighty smash the corner of an ax glinted through the ebony. The door shook to its foundations.

"Silence out there!" the Warden yelled.

Someone called out. A woman howled. The blows were redoubled.

"They can't hear you," Claudia said. "And if they get in . . ."

"They don't want to listen to anyone." Attia went around and stood before the Warden's face. "Least of all you. They'll blame you."

Through the tumult he smiled coldly at them. "We'll see. I'm still the Warden here. But perhaps before we start we should take a few precautions." He drew out a small disc of silver. On its lid was a wolf, the snarling mouth wide. He touched it and it lit.

"What are you doing?" Claudia jumped back as another blow sent wood splinters into the snow.

"I told you. Making sure the Prison doesn't win."

She held his arm. "What about us?"

"We are expendable." His eyes were gray and clear. Then he said into the device, "It's me. What's the situation Out there?"

As he listened his face darkened. Attia moved away from the

door; it was buckling now, the hinges straining, rivets crack-ing. "They're coming through."

But Claudia was watching her father as he said harshly, "Then do it now! *Destroy the Glove.* Before it's too late."

⊰◦◦◦⊱

MEDLICOTE SLIPPED the receiver shut, dropped it into his pocket, and gazed up the ruined corridor. Voices echoed from the Great Chamber; he walked quickly toward it, through a crowd of scared footmen, past Ralph, who caught his arm and asked, "What's happening? Is this the end of the world?"

The secretary shrugged. "The end of one world, sir, perhaps the beginning of another. Is Master Jared in there?"

"Yes. And the Queen! The Queen herself!"

Medlicote nodded. The half-moons of his spectacles were empty, the lenses gone. He opened the door.

In the ruined chamber someone had found a real candle; Keiro had made a flame and lit it.

The Prison had taught survival, at least, Finn thought. They would all need those skills now. He turned. "Madam?"

Sia stood just inside the door. She had not spoken since crossing the drawbridge, and her silence scared him.

"I presume our war is at a standstill?"

"You presume wrong," the Queen whispered. "My war is over."

Her voice was broken, a faint quaver. Through her veil her eyes, pale as ice, watched him. She seemed bent, even bowed.

"Over?" He glanced at the Pretender. The boy who had claimed to be Giles stood grimly before the empty hearth, his right arm still bandaged, his fine armor tarnishing even as they watched. "What do you mean?"

"She means it's finished." Jared came forward and stood before the Queen, and Finn was shocked at how she had shrunk. Jared's voice was gentle. "I'm sorry this has happened to you," he said.

"Are you?" Sia whispered. "Maybe you are, Master Jared. Maybe only you can know something of what I feel. I once taunted you with your own death. You would be justified now in doing the same to me."

He shook his head.

"I thought you said the Queen was young?" Keiro muttered in Finn's ear.

"She is."

But then her fingers caught at Jared's sleeve, and Finn swallowed a gasp because they were the fingers of an ancient woman, mottled and sagging with wrinkled skin, the nails dry and splintered.

"After all, of us both I will be the one now to die first." She glanced aside, with a trace of her old coquettish manner. "Let me show you death, Jared. Not these young boys. Only you, Master, will see what Sia really is."

Hands trembling, she moved before him and raised her veil. Over her shoulder, Finn saw how Jared was caught between horror and pity, how he gazed silently on the Queen's ruined beauty without lowering his eyes.

The room was silent. Keiro glanced back at Medlicote, standing humbly inside the door.

Sia dropped her veil. She said, "Whatever else I was, I have been a Queen. Let me die like a Queen."

Jared bowed. He said, "Ralph. Light a fire in the red bedroom. Do the best you can."

Uncertain, the steward nodded. He took the old woman's arm and helped her out.

32

The dove will rise above destruction
With a white rose in her beak.
Over storm
Over tempest.
Over time and the ages.
And the petals will fall to the ground like snow.
    —Sapphique's Prophecy of the World's End

As soon as the door closed Keiro said, "I don't get it."

"She tried to preserve her youth." Jared sat, as if the moment had weakened him. "They called her a witch, but she almost certainly used skinwands and some sort of ongoing genetic implants. Now all her stolen years have come crashing down on her at once."

"It sounds like one of Rix's fairy tales," Keiro said calmly.

"So she'll die?"

"Very soon."

"Fine. That just leaves him." Keiro jabbed his injured hand at the Pretender.

Finn lifted his head and he and the Pretender gazed at each other. "You don't look so much like me now," Finn said.

The boy's appearance had altered too, his lips thinner, nose longer, hair too dark. There was still a resemblance, but it had no real substance anymore. It had died with the Era.

"Look," the Pretender said. "It wasn't my idea. They found me. They offered me a kingdom! You would have done it—anyone would! They promised my family enough gold to keep my six brothers fed for years. I had no choice." He drew himself up. "And I was good, Finn. You have to admit it. I had everyone fooled. Maybe I even fooled you." He glanced down at his wrist, where the eagle tattoo had vanished. "Another piece of Protocol," he murmured.

Keiro found a chair and lounged in it. "I think we should put him in that tiny cube you call the Prison."

"No. He writes a confession and admits publicly that he was an imposter. That the Queen and Caspar were behind a plot to place a false Giles on the throne. And then we let him go." Finn looked at Jared. "He's no threat to us now."

Jared nodded. "I agree."

Keiro looked less than convinced, but Finn stood. "Take him away."

But as the Pretender reached the door Finn said softly, "Claudia never believed in you."

The Pretender stopped and laughed. *"No?"* he whispered. He turned his head and gazed back at Finn. "I think she believed in me more than she ever believed in you."

The words stabbed Finn, a breathtaking pain. He whipped his sword out and advanced on the Pretender, wanting only to run him through, to destroy this venomous infuriating image of all he had never been. But Jared was in his way, and the Sapient's green gaze held him still.

Without turning, Jared said, "Get him out," and the guards hustled the Pretender away.

Finn threw the sword down on the wrecked floor.

"So we've won." Keiro picked it up and examined the blade. "A ruined kingdom, maybe, but all ours. We're Winglords at last, brother."

"There's a greater enemy than the Queen." Finn stared at Jared, still sore. "There always was. We have to save ourselves and Claudia from the Prison."

"And Attia." Keiro looked up. "Don't forget your little dog-slave."

"You mean you're concerned about her?"

Keiro shrugged. "She was a pain. But I got used to her."

"Where's the Glove?" Finn snapped.

Jared drew it from his coat. "But I told you, Finn, I don't understand . . ."

Finn came and took it. "This hasn't changed." His fingers crumpled the soft skin. "Not at all, while everything around falls into dust. It brought Keiro Out, and Incarceron wants it more than anything in the Realm. It's our only hope now."

"Sire."

Finn turned. He had forgotten Medlicote was there. The thin man had stood just inside the door all this time, his slightly stooping posture more obvious in his faded coat. "Might I suggest that it is also our only danger?"

"What do you mean?"

The secretary came forward, hesitant. "It's clear the Prison will destroy us all if it can't have this object. And if we hand it over, then Incarceron will leave its Prison and all the inmates will be left to die. It is a terrible choice you face."

Finn frowned.

Jared said, "But you have a suggestion?"

"I do. A radical one, but it might work. *Destroy the Glove.*"

"No." Finn and Keiro said it together.

"Sirs, listen to me." He seemed scared, Finn thought, and not of them. "Master Jared admits he is puzzled by this device. And have you thought that it might be the very presence of the Glove here that is draining the Realm of its power? You only believe that to be caused by the Prison's malice. You do not truly know!"

Finn frowned. He turned the Glove over, then glanced at Jared. "Do you think he's right?"

"No, I don't. We need the Glove."

"But you said—"

"Give me time." Jared rose and came over. "Give me time and I'll work it out."

"We don't have time." Finn looked at the Sapient's frail face. "You don't, and neither do those in the Prison."

Medlicote said, "You are the King, sire. No one—not even the Privy Council—will doubt that now. Destroy it.

This is what the Warden would want us to do."

Jared said sharply, "You can't know that."

"I know the Warden. And do you think, sir, that the Steel Wolves will stand by and allow this new danger, now that Protocol is gone?"

As the candle guttered Finn said, "Are you threatening me?"

"How could I, sire?" Medlicote kept one eye on Keiro, but his voice was meek and anxious. "You must decide. Destroy it, and the Prison is trapped forever in its self. Allow it access to Sapphique's power, and you will unleash its horrors on us. Where do you think Incarceron will come, when it is free? What sort of tyrant will it become Out here? Will you allow it to make us all its slaves?"

Finn was silent. He glanced at Keiro, who just gazed back. More than ever he wished that Claudia would open the door and stalk in. She knew her father. She would know if this was what they should do.

In the shattered room a broken casement banged in the wind. A gale was howling around the house, and rain began to patter hard against the cracked glass. "Jared?"

"Don't destroy it. It's our last weapon."

"But if he's right, if—"

"Trust me, Finn. I have an idea."

Thunder rumbled. Medlicote shrugged. "I am loath to say this, sire, but Master Jared may not be the one to listen to. Perhaps his reasons are not ours."

Finn said, "What do you mean?"

"Master Jared is a sick man. Perhaps he feels such an object of power could be his cure."

They stared at him.

Jared was pale; he seemed both astonished and confused. "Finn . . ."

Finn held up a hand. "You don't have to justify yourself to me, Master." He advanced on Medlicote as if his anger had found its outlet. "I would never, *never* believe that you would put your own life before the safety of millions.".

Medlicote knew he had gone too far. He stepped back. "A man's life is everything to him."

A great crash echoed in the house, as if some part of the structure had fallen.

"We should get out." Keiro stood, restless. "This place is a deathtrap."

Jared had not taken his gaze from Finn. "We need to find Claudia. The Glove will help us. Destroy it and the Prison has no reason to keep her alive."

"If they are still alive."

Jared glanced at Medlicote. "I would suggest that the Warden certainly is."

Finn took a moment to understand. Then with a speed that made Keiro turn, he threw Medlicote back against the wall, one arm jammed under his throat. "You've spoken with him, haven't you?"

"Sire . . ."

"Haven't you!"

The secretary gasped for breath. Then he nodded.

⌾⟩⟨⌾

CLAUDIA SAID, "Who were you talking to?"

"Medlicote." Her father turned to face the door. "One of the Steel Wolves. A good man. He'll deal with the Glove. Now we'll see who commands here."

But the roar of the angry Prisoners almost drowned his words. Claudia glared at him, infuriated by his pride and his stubbornness. Then she said, "They'll trample you down. But there's another thing we can do to stop Incarceron. We can burn the statue."

Her father stared. "It will never allow us."

"It's preoccupied. You said so yourself." She turned to Attia. "Come on!"

The two of them raced across the snowy waste of the hall. On the walls the hangings were frozen in their folds. Claudia grabbed the nearest and tugged, dust and shards of ice crashing around her. "Rix! Help us!"

The magician sat on the pedestal, all knees and elbows. He was rippling coins through his hands, muttering to himself. "Heads, they kill us. Tails, we Escape."

"Forget him." Attia jumped up and heaved the tapestry down. "He's crazy. They both are."

Together they dragged down all the hangings. Close to, the

423

tapestries were holed and ragged under their film of ice, and on them Attia recognized all the old legends of Sapphique—his crawling over the sword-bridge, offering his finger to the Beast, stealing the children, conversing with the King of the Swans. With a clatter of rings the woven scenes crumpled into clouds of fibers and icy mildew, and she and Claudia dragged them to the statue, piling them around its feet, while its beautiful face gazed out at the howling mob behind the door.

The Warden watched. Beyond him, blow by blow, the last panels were shattered. A hinge smashed; the door jerked down.

"Rix!" Attia yelled. "We need a flame!"

Claudia raced back across the floor, grabbing the Warden's hand. "Father. Come away! Quickly!"

He stared at the broken door, the arms thrusting through, as if he would stop them with only his authority.

"I'm the Warden, Claudia. I'm in charge."

"NO!" She hauled him back and pulled him, and as she did the door collapsed.

They saw a mass of Prisoners, those in front crushed and trampled by others behind. They hammered with fists and flailing chains. Their weapons were manacles and iron bars. They howled the cries of the desperate millions of Incarceron, the lost descendants of the first Prisoners, the Scum and the Civicry and the Ardenti and the Magpies and all the thousands of gangs and tribes, Wingtowns and outlaws.

As they poured into the hall Claudia turned and ran, her

father at her back, both of them fleeing over the trampled snowfield that the floor had become, and in its mockery the Prison picked them out in intense spotlights that crossed and recrossed from its invisible roof.

⊂⌀⌀⌀⊃

"HERE IT is." Keiro tugged the receiver out of Medlicote's pocket and tossed it to Finn, who let the man go and flicked it open.

"How does this work?"

Medlicote crumpled onto the floor, half choked. "Touch the dial. Then speak."

Finn looked at Jared. Then he jabbed his thumb down on the small disc at one edge.

"Warden," he said. "Can you hear me?"

⊂⌀⌀⌀⊃

RIX STOOD.

Attia grabbed a piece of wood as a weapon and tested it. But she knew that before the sweeping anger of that mob nothing would be strong enough.

On the steps the Warden turned.

A tiny bleep sounded inside his coat; he reached for the disc, but as he brought it out Claudia grabbed it, her eyes widening as the Prisoners poured in, a jostling, stinking, roaring host.

A voice said, "Can you hear me?"

"Finn?"

"Claudia!" The relief was clear in his voice. "What's happening?"

425

"We're in trouble. There's a riot here. We're going to burn the statue, Finn, or try." She caught, out of the corner of her eye, the flicker of flame in Rix's hand. "Then Incarceron has no way out."

"Is the Glove destroyed?" the Warden hissed.

A murmur. A blur of static. And then, in her ear, Jared's voice. "Claudia?"

She felt only a stab of joy.

"Claudia, it's me. Listen to me please. I want you to promise me something."

"Master . . ."

"I want you to promise me that you will not burn the image, Claudia."

She blinked. Attia stared.

"But . . . we have to. Incarceron . . ."

"I know what you think. But I'm beginning to understand what is happening here. I have spoken to Sapphique. Promise me, Claudia. *Tell me you trust me.*"

She turned. Saw the crowd reach the bottom step, the front runners flinging themselves up.

"I trust you, Jared," she whispered. "I always did. I love you, Master."

—◁◦◦◦▷—

THE SOUND rose to a screech that made Jared jerk away; the disc fell and rolled on the floor.

Keiro pounced on it and yelled, "Claudia!" but there was

only a hissing and spitting that might have been the noise of a multitude or the chaos of interstellar static.

Finn turned on Jared. "Are you crazy? She was right! Without its body . . ."

"I know." Jared was pale. He leaned against the fireplace, the Glove tight in his hand. "And I ask you what I asked her. I have a plan, Finn. It may be foolish, it may be impossible. But it might save us all."

Finn stared at him. Outside the rain lashed, flinging the casement open, snuffing the last flicker of the candle out.

He was cold and shaken, his hands icy. The fear in Claudia's voice had infected him like a taste of the Prison, and for a moment he was back in that white cell where he had been born, and was no prince but a Prisoner with no memory and no hope.

The house shivered around them as lightning struck.

"What do you need?" Finn said.

⊰∞⊱

IT WAS Incarceron that stopped them. As the Prisoners surged to the second step its voice rang out in power through the vast hall.

"I will kill anyone who comes closer."

The step pulsed with sudden light. Currents of power ran along it and rippled in blue waves. The crowd convulsed. Some pushed on, others stopped, or squirmed back. It became a vortex of movement, and the spotlights circled lazily over it, stabbing down to show a terrified eye, a flailing hand.

Attia snatched the kindling from Rix.

She moved to thrust it into the rotten fibers, but Claudia grabbed her hand. "Wait."

"For what?"

She turned, but Claudia jerked her wrist savagely and the tiny burning scrap fell, flaring in the air. It landed on the tapestries but before the *whoof* of flame took hold Claudia had stamped it out.

"Are you mad? We're finished!" Attia was furious. "You've finished us . . ."

"Jared . . ."

"Jared is wrong!"

"I am very pleased to have you all here for this execution." The Prison's sarcasm echoed through the freezing air, tiny, icy snowflakes drifting from its heights. *"You will see my justice and understand that I have no favorites. Behold, the man before you. John Arlex, your Warden."*

The Warden was gray and grim, but he drew himself up, his dark coat glistening with snow.

"Listen to me," he yelled. "The Prison is trying to leave us! To leave its own people to starve!"

Only the nearest heard him, and they howled him down.

As she closed up beside him Claudia knew that only the Prison's proclamation kept the mob back, and that the Prison was playing with them.

"John Arlex, who hates and detests you. See how he cowers under this image of Sapphique. Does he think it will protect him from my wrath?"

They needn't have bothered with the tapestries. Claudia realized that Incarceron would burn its own body, that its anger at the Glove's loss, at the end of all its plans, would be their end too. The same pyre would consume them all.

And then, beside her, a sharp voice said, "Oh my father. Listen to me."

The crowd hushed.

They stilled as if the voice was one they knew, had heard before, so that they quieted to hear it again.

And Claudia felt in her bones and nerves how Incarceron zigzagged closer, moved in, its reply murmured in her ear and against her cheek, a quiet, fascinated question of secret doubt.

"Is that you, Rix?"

Rix laughed. His eyes were narrowed, his breath stank of ket. He opened his arms wide. "Let me show you what I can do. The greatest magic ever performed. Let me show you, my father, how I will bring your body to life."

33

*He raised his hands. They saw his coat was
feathered like the wings of the Swan when
it dies, when it sings its secret song. And
he opened the door that none of them had
seen until now.*

—*Legends of Sapphique*

As Finn moved out into the corridor he saw that Keiro was
right. The very antiquity of the house was against them
now; all its true decay, like the Queen's, had come upon it at
once.

"Ralph!"

Ralph came hastening up, stepping over lumps of fallen
plaster. "Sire."

"Evacuate. Everyone is to leave."

"But where will we go, sire?"

Finn scowled. "I don't know! Certainly the Queen's Camp
is in no better shape. Find what shelter you can in the stables,
the outlying cottages. No one must stay here but us. Where's
Caspar?"

Ralph tugged off his decaying wig. Underneath, his own
hair was shaved close. His chin was stubbled, and his face

unwashed. He looked weary and lost. "With his mother. The poor lad is devastated. I think even he had no idea of her reality."

Finn glanced around. Keiro had Medlicote in an armlock. Jared, tall in his Sapient robe, carried the Glove.

"Do we need this scum?" Keiro muttered.

"No. Let him go with the rest."

Giving the secretary's arm one last painful jerk, Keiro shoved him away.

"Get outside," Finn said, "where it's safe. Find the rest of your people."

"Nowhere is safe." Medlicote ducked as a suit of armor beside him suddenly crashed into dust. "Not while the Glove exists."

Finn shrugged. He turned to Jared. "Let's go."

The three of them ran past the secretary and along the corridors of the house. They moved through a nightmare of dissolving beauty, of fragmented hangings and paintings lost under grime and mold. In places chandeliers of white candles had fallen; the crystal droplets lay like tears in the broken wax. Keiro moved ahead, heaving wreckage aside; Finn kept near Jared, unsure of the Sapient's strength. They struggled to the foot of the great stairway, but as Finn looked up he was appalled at the destruction on the upper floors. A silent blink of lightning showed him a vast crack running right down the outside wall. Debris of vases and plastiglas crunched under their feet; potpourri and fungal spores and the dust of centuries blurred the air like snow.

The stairs were ruined. Keiro climbed two, his back flat against the wall, but on the third tread his foot plunged through, and he tugged it out, swearing. "We'll never get up this."

"We must get to the study, and the Portal." Jared looked up anxiously. He felt utterly weary, his head light and dizzy. When had he last taken his medication? He leaned against the wall and tugged out the pouch and stared at it in despair.

The small syringe had broken into pieces, as if the glass had brittled and aged instantly. The serum had congealed to a yellow crust.

Finn said, "What will you do?"

Jared almost smiled. He replaced the pieces and tossed the pouch out into the corridor, and Finn saw his eyes were remote and dark. "It was only ever a stopgap, Finn. Like everyone else, I must now live without my little comforts."

If he dies, Finn thought, if I let him die, Claudia will never forgive me. He glared up at his oathbrother. "We have to get up there. You're the expert, Keiro. Do something!"

Keiro frowned. Then he tugged off his velvet coat and tied back his hair in a scrap of ribbon. He tore away some of the hangings and bound them rapidly around his hands, swearing as he touched his scorched palm.

"Rope. I need rope."

Finn snatched down the thick tasseled ties that held the curtains and knotted them firmly together—bizarre cables of gold and scarlet. Keiro looped them over his shoulder.

Then he set off up the stairs.

The world had inverted, Jared thought, watching his inching progress, because a staircase he had climbed every day for years had became a treacherous obstacle, a deathtrap. This was how time transformed things, how your own body betrayed you. This was what the Realm had tried to forget, in its deliberate elegant amnesia.

Keiro had to ascend the stairs as a mountaineer climbs a scree slope. The whole central section was gone, and as he grabbed at the higher treads their edges crumbled away in his hands.

Finn and Jared watched, anxious. Above the house thunder rumbled; far off in the stableyard they heard the shouts of the guards, ushering everyone out, the neighing of horses, the screech of a hawk.

Finally, at Finn's elbow, a breathless voice said, "The drawbridge is down, sire, and everyone across."

"Then you go too." Finn didn't turn, willing Keiro on as he balanced precariously between a banister and a fallen panel.

"The Queen, sire." Ralph wiped his smeared face with a filthy rag that might once have been a handkerchief. "The Queen is dead."

The stab of shock was so distant that Finn almost missed it. And then the news sank in, and he saw that Jared had heard it too. The Sapient bowed his head sadly.

"So you are King, sire."

Was it that simple? he wondered. But all he said was, "Ralph, go now."

The old steward didn't move. "I would like to stay and help. To rescue the Lady Claudia and my master."

"I'm not sure there are any masters now."

Jared drew in his breath. Keiro had slithered to one side; now all his weight was on the curved banister, and it was bending, the wood snapping out, dry and brittle.

"Be careful!"

Keiro's reply was inaudible. Then he heaved himself up, leaped two steps that cracked under him, and flung himself at the landing.

He grabbed it with both hands, but as he did so the whole staircase collapsed behind him in a thunderous crashing of dust and worm-ridden timber, tumbling down on the hall, choking the stairwell.

Keiro swung, dragging himself up, every muscle in his arms straining, blinded by dust. Finally he got one knee over and crumpled on the landing in cold relief.

He coughed until the tears made tracks down his smudged face. Then he crawled to the edge and looked down. Below was a black swirling vortex of dust and debris.

"Finn?" he said. He stood, his legs aching. "Finn? Jared?"

⋖◦◦◦⋗

HE WAS either completely crazy or off his head on ket, Attia thought.

Rix stood before his audience in perfect confidence, and the people stared up at him, bewildered, excited, thirsting for truth. But this time the Prison was in the audience too.

"Are you mad, Prisoner?" it said.

"Almost certainly, Father," Rix said. "But if I succeed, you will take me with you?"

Incarceron spat a laugh. *"If you succeed, you really would be the Dark Enchanter. But you're just a fraud, Rix. A liar, a mountebank, a conman. Do you think to con me?"*

"I wouldn't dream of it." Rix glanced at Attia. "I'll need my old assistant."

He winked, and before she could stammer an answer he had turned to the crowd and stepped forward to the edge of the pedestal.

"Friends," he said. "Welcome to my greatest wonder! You think you will see illusions. You think I will fool you with mirrors, with hidden devices. But I am not like other magicians. I am the Dark Enchanter, and I will show you the magic of the stars!"

The crowd gasped. So did Attia.

He raised his hand, and *he was wearing a glove.* It was made of skin, dark as midnight, and flickers of light sparked from it.

Behind Attia, Claudia said, "I thought . . . Don't tell me Keiro had the wrong one."

"Of course not. This is a prop. Just a prop."

But the doubt had slid into Attia too, like a cold knife, because how could you know, with Rix, what was real and what was not?

He waved his hand in a great arc, and the snow stopped falling. The air grew warmer, lights in every color rainbowing from the high roof. Was he doing this? Or was Incarceron amusing itself at his expense?

Whatever the truth, the people were transfixed. They stared upward, crying out. Some fell on their knees. Some moved back, afraid.

Rix was tall. Somehow he had brought nobility to his craggy face, made the wildness in his eyes a holy glimmer.

"There is much sorrow here," he said. "There is much fear."

It was the patter of his act. And yet it was fragmented, changed. As if in the kaleidoscope of his mind it was falling into new patterns. Quietly he said, "I need a volunteer. One who is willing to have its deepest fear revealed. Willing to bear its soul to my gaze."

He looked upward.

The Prison flickered white lights over its statue. Then it said, "*I volunteer.*"

⸺◦◦◦⸺

FOR A moment all Keiro heard was his own heart thudding and the echoes of slithering wood. Then Finn said, "We're all right."

He stepped out of an alcove in the wall, and from the shad-

436

ows behind him Ralph said in despair, "How do we get up now? There's no way . . ."

"Of course there is." Keiro's voice was brisk. From the darkness a red and gold tassel came down and hit Finn on the shoulder.

"Is it safe?"

"I've tied it to the nearest column. It's the best I can do. Come on."

Finn looked at Jared. They both knew that if the column gave way or the rope fell apart the climber would fall to his death. Jared said, "It has to be me. With respect, Finn, the Portal is a mystery to you."

It was true, but Finn shook his head. "You won't manage . . ."

Jared drew himself up. "I'm not so weak."

"You're not weak at all." Finn glanced up into the dimness. Then he grabbed the rope and tied it fiercely around Jared's waist and under his arms. "Use it to abseil. Use all the footholds you can find and try not to put all your weight on it. We'll—"

"Finn." Jared put a hand on his chest. "Don't worry." He braced the rope, then turned his head. "Did you hear that?"

"What?"

"Thunder," Ralph said doubtfully.

They listened a moment, hearing the terrible storm rage across the Realm, the atmosphere loosed from its long control.

Then Keiro yelled, "Move!" and Jared felt the rope jerk him up the first stairs.

The climb was a nightmare. Soon the rope was burning his hands, and the effort of clambering and hauling himself up left him breathless. The old pain burned in his chest, and the ache of his back and neck as he groped from splintered step to panel, grabbing at cobwebbed sills and shifting timbers, exhausted him.

Above, Keiro's face was a pale oval in the shadows. "Come on, Master! You can do it."

Jared gasped. He had to stop, just for breath, but as he did the small notch into which he had jammed his boot gave way, and with a crash and a cry he fell, the rope bringing him up short in a bone-cracking agony of wrenched muscles.

For a moment he saw nothing.

The world was gone and he was hanging weightless in a black sky, and around him, silently, galaxies and nebulae were icily turning. The stars had voices; they were calling his name, but still he circled, slowly, until the star that was Sapphique leaned close and whispered, "I'm waiting for you, Master. And Claudia is waiting."

He opened his eyes. Pain flowed back like a wave, filling his veins, his mouth, his nerves.

Keiro said, "Jared. Climb. Climb!"

He obeyed. Like a child, without thinking, he tugged himself up, hand over hand. Climbing through the pain, through the dark fire of his breathing, while far below Finn and Ralph were two glimmers in the black hall.

"More. A bit more."

Something grabbed above him. His sweat-soaked hands slid on the ropes, the skin raw, his knees and ankles knots of rubbed flesh. A warm grip caught on his. A hand hauled under his elbow.

"I've got you. I've got you."

And then a strength that seemed miraculous to him heaved him upward and he crouched on all fours over the pain, coughing and retching.

"He's safe." Keiro's yell was calm. "Move, Finn."

Finn turned to Ralph. "Ralph, you're not coming. Do this for me. Get out and find the Privy Council. They have to take charge now. Tell them I . . ." He paused and swallowed. "Tell them the King orders it. Food and shelter for everyone."

"But you . . ."

"I'll be back. With Claudia."

"But sire, do you mean to re-enter the Prison?"

Finn wound the rope around his hands and swung upward. "Not if I can help it. But if I have to, I will."

He climbed quickly and fiercely, pulling himself up with jerks of energy, disdaining Keiro's hand and rolling over the edge swiftly. The landing was dark. The whole gable-end of the house must have gone, because down at the far end he could see the sky against rafters and half a chimney.

"The Portal may be wrecked," Keiro muttered.

"No. The Portal isn't even in this house." Finn turned. "Master?"

The landing was empty.

"Jared?"

Then they saw him. He was far down the corridor, at the study door. "I'm sorry, Finn," he said gently. "This is my plan. I have to do this on my own."

Something clicked.

Finn ran, Keiro at his back, and when he reached the door he flung himself at it, the black swan arched defiantly over him.

But it was locked from the inside.

34

The Prison was a being of beauty once. Its program was love. But perhaps we were too hard to love. Perhaps we asked too much of it. Perhaps we drove it mad.
                                    —Lord Calliston's Diary

Rix reached out with his gloved hand, and from above, a tiny pencil-thin light beam came down to touch him. It rippled softly over his palm, and after a while he nodded.

"I see strange things in your mind, my father. I see how they made you in their own image, how you woke in the darkness. I see the people that inhabit you, I see all the corridors and cells and dusty dungeons where they live."

"Rix!" Attia's voice was sharp. "Stop this."

He smiled, but he didn't look at her. "I see how lonely you are, and how crazed. You have fed on your own soul, my master. You have devoured your own humanity. You have fouled your own Eden. And now you want to Escape."

"You see a beam of light in your hand, Prisoner."

"As you say. A beam of light." But the smile was gone now, and Rix raised the glove so that the light caught a glitter of silver dust that fell through his open fingers.

The crowd gasped.

The dust fell and fell. There was too much of it. It became a cascade of tiny sparkles in a black sky.

"I see the stars," Rix said, his voice tight. "Beneath them lies a ruined palace, its windows dark and broken. I peep at it through the keyhole of a tiny doorway. A storm roars about it. It is Outside."

Claudia gripped Attia's wrist. "Is he . . . ?"

"I think it's a vision. He's done this before."

"Outside!" She turned to the Warden. "Does he mean the Realm?"

His gray eyes were hard. "I fear so."

"But Finn . . ."

"Hush, Claudia. I need to understand this."

Furious, she stared at Rix. He was shivering, his eyes thin slits of white. "There is a way," he whispered, rapt. "Sapphique found it."

"*Sapphique?*" Incarceron's voice hummed and rumbled around the hall. And then it spoke again, and there was sudden fear in it, and wonder. "*How are you doing this, Rix? How are you doing this?*"

Rix blinked. For a moment he seemed shaken. The people were silent.

Then he moved his fingers, and the shower of silver became gold.

"The Art Magicke," he breathed.

JARED STOOD back from the door. If Finn was beating on it, as he suspected, the sound did not come through.

He turned.

The Realm might be ruined, but nothing in this room had changed. As the Portal straightened itself he felt the quiet hum of its mystery calm him, the gray walls and single desk focus his vision. He raised a shaking hand to his mouth and licked blood from the grazed skin.

Suddenly, fatigue rippled through him. All he wanted to do was sleep, and he slumped in the metal chair before the snowy screen and fought the desire to lay his head on the desk and close his eyes and forget everything.

But the snow held his gaze. Behind its mystery Claudia was trapped, and the Prison and the Realm were caught in that destruction.

He made himself sit up, wiped his face with a grubby sleeve, brushed the hair from his eyes. He took the Glove out and laid it on the gray metal surface. Then he made a few adjustments to the controls and spoke.

He used the Sapient tongue. He said, "Incarceron!"

The snow still fell, but its patterns changed, to a swirl of wonder. It answered him, its voice amazed. "*How are you doing this, Rix? How are you doing this?*"

"I'm not Rix." Jared spread his fine hands on the desk and stared at them. "You spoke to me once before. You know who I am."

"I knew a voice like this, long ago." The Prison's murmur hung in the still air of the room.

"Long ago," Jared whispered. "Before you were old, and evil. When the Sapienti first created you. And many times since, in my endless journeying."

"You are Sapphique."

He smiled wearily. "I am now. And you and I, Incarceron, have the same problem. We are both trapped in our bodies. Maybe we can help each other." He picked up the Glove and fingered its fine scales. "Perhaps the hour has come that all the prophesies tell of. The hour that the world ends, and Sapphique returns."

⬦⬦⬦

CLAUDIA SAID, "They're out of their minds with terror. They'll rush us and kill him."

The crowd was increasingly disturbed. She could feel their panic, sense the urgency in the way they pushed forward, craning to see, their hot sweaty stench rising toward her. They knew if Incarceron Escaped it was the end for them. If they began to believe Rix could do this, they would have nothing left to lose.

Attia grabbed Rix's knife. Claudia lifted the firelock and looked at her father. He didn't move, his eyes fixed in fascination on Rix.

She pushed past him, Attia with her, and together they edged around to stand on the steps between Rix and the

444

crowd, even though it was futile, a mere gesture of defense.

"*I knew a voice like this, long ago,*" the Prison murmured. Rix laughed harshly. The words of his act seemed charged now, like prophecy.

"There is a way Out. Sapphique found it. The door is tiny, tinier than an atom. And the eagle and the swan spread their wings to guard it."

"*You are Sapphique.*"

"Sapphique returns. Did you ever love me, Incarceron?"

The Prison hummed. Its voice was hoarse. "*I remember you. Out of them all, you were my brother and my son. We dreamed the same dream.*"

Rix swung to the statue. He gazed up at its calm face, its dead eyes. "Keep very still," he whispered anxiously, as if for only the Prison to hear. "Or the danger is extreme."

He turned to the crowd. "The time has come, friends. I will release him. I will bring him back!"

⊸⊂◯◯◯⊃⊷

"AGAIN!" FINN and Keiro threw themselves at the door, but it didn't even shudder. There was no sound from inside. Breathless, Keiro turned his back to the ebony swan and said, "We could get one of those planks and—" He stopped.

"Hear that?"

Voices. The clamor of men in the house, men swarming up the rope in the stairwell, shadowy figures crowding the fragmenting corridor.

Finn stepped forward. "Who's there?"

But he knew who they were even before the flickering lightning showed him. The Steel Wolves had come in a pack of silver muzzles, their eyes bright behind the masks of assassins and murderers.

Medlicote's voice said, "I'm sorry, Finn. I can't leave it like this. No one will be surprised if you and your friend perish in the ruins of the Wardenry. Then a new world will begin, without kings, without tyrants."

"Jared is in there," Finn snapped. "And your Warden . . ."

"The Warden has given his orders."

Pistols were raised.

Beside him, Finn felt Keiro's arrogant defiance, that odd way he had of making himself taller, every muscle taut.

"Our last stand, brother," Finn said bitterly.

"Speak for yourself," Keiro said.

The Steel Wolves advanced, a tentative line across the corridor.

Finn tensed, but Keiro seemed almost languid. "Come on, my friends. A little closer, please."

They stopped, as if his words made them nervous. Then, just as Finn had known he would, he attacked.

❖

JARED HELD the Glove in both hands. Its scales were curiously supple, as if the centuries had worn them. As if only Time had worn the Glove.

"Aren't you afraid?" Incarceron asked, curious.

"Of course I'm afraid. I think I've been afraid a long time now." He touched the ridged and heavy claws. "But what would you know about that?"

"The Sapienti taught me to feel."

"Pleasure? Cruelty?"

"Loneliness. Despair."

Jared shook his head. "They wanted you to love too. Your Prisoners. To care for them."

Its voice was a wistful draft, a crack of sound. *"You know you were the only one I ever loved, Sapphique. The only one I cared for. You were the tiny crack in my armor. You were the door."*

"Was that why you let me Escape?"

"Children always escape from their parents, in the end." A murmur came through the Portal like a sigh down a long, empty corridor. *"I am afraid too,"* it said.

"Then we must be afraid together." Jared slipped his fingers into the Glove. He pulled it on firmly, and as he did he heard far off a pounding, maybe on a door, maybe in his heart, maybe of a thousand footsteps crowding close.

He closed his eyes. As the Glove enfolded it, his hand chilled, became one with the skin. His neurons burned. The claws curled as he clenched them. His body became icy, and vast, and crowded with a million terrors. And then his whole being collapsed, shriveling inward and inward down an endless vortex of light. He bent his head and cried aloud.

"*I AM afraid too.*" The Prison's murmur rang through all its halls and forests, over its seas. Deep in the Ice Wing its fear snapped icicles, sent flocks of birds flapping over metal forests no Prisoner had ever crossed.

Rix closed his eyes. His face was a rigor of ecstasy. He flung out his arms and cried, "None of us need to be afraid ever again. *Behold!*"

Claudia heard Attia's gasp. The crowd gave a great roar and surged forward, and as she jumped back she turned her head and saw her father staring intently at the image of Sapphique. Its right hand was wearing the Glove.

Amazed, she tried to say, "How . . . ?" but her whisper was lost in the tumult.

The statue's fingers were dragonskin, its nails were claws. *And they were moving.*

The right hand flexed; it opened and reached out as if groping in the dark, or searching for something to touch.

The people were silent. Some fell on their knees, others turned and fought their way back through the packed rabble.

Claudia and Attia stood still. Attia felt as if her amazement would burst through her, as if the wonder of what she saw, of what it meant, would make her scream aloud with fear and joy.

Only the Warden watched calmly. Claudia realized that he knew what was happening here.

"Explain," she whispered.

Her father gazed at the image of Sapphique and there was a grim appreciation in his gray eyes.

"Why, my dear Claudia," he said in his acid voice. "A great miracle is happening. We are so privileged to be here." And then, quieter, "And it seems I have underestimated Master Jared yet again."

━━◁◦◦◦▷━━

A FIRELOCK slashed the roof. One man was already down, crumpled and moaning. Back to back, Finn and Keiro circled.

The ruined corridor was a breathless tangle of light, slanted with darkness. A musket fired, the ball splintering wood at Finn's elbow. He struck out, sweeping the gun aside, crashing the masked man back.

Behind him, Keiro fought with a snatched foil until it was broken, then threw it down and went in with bare hands. He moved with accuracy, savage and fast, and for Finn, beside him, there was no longer any Realm and no Incarceron, only the hot violence of blows and pain, a stab at the chest desperately fended off, a body flung against the paneling.

He yelled, sweat in his eyes, as Medlicote lunged at him, the secretary's foil whipping double as it struck the wall, and instantly they were both grappling for the blade, and Finn had the man in a tight hold around the chest, forcing him down. Lightning flickered, showed Keiro's grin, the steel flash of a wolf muzzle. Thunder growled, a low, distant rumble. A burst

449

of flame. It shot up, and by its light Finn saw the Wolves dive, breathless and bloodied as it slashed over them.

"Throw your weapons down." Keiro's voice was breathless and raw. He fired again, and they all flinched as plaster crashed in a white snow. "*Throw them down!*"

A few thuds.

"Now lie down. Anyone still standing dies."

Slowly they obeyed him. Finn tore off Medlicote's mask and flung it away. Sudden fury burned in him. He said, "I am King here, Master Medlicote. Do you understand?" His voice was a rasp of wrath. "The old world has ended and there will be no more plotting and no more lies!" He hauled the man up like a limp rag and slammed him against the wall. "*I am Giles. Protocol is over!*"

"Finn." Keiro came and took the foil from his hand. "Leave him. He's half dead anyway."

Slowly, Finn let the man go, and he slumped in relief.

Finn turned to his oathbrother, gradually bringing him into focus, as if anger had been a rippling in the air.

"Keep calm, brother." Keiro surveyed his captives. "As I always taught you . . ."

"I am calm."

"Right. Well, at least you haven't grown as soft as the rest of them out here." Keiro swung around and raised the weapon. He blasted it, once, twice, at the study door, under the angry swan, and the door shuddered and burst inward.

Moving past him, Finn strode in through the smoke, stumbling as the Portal rippled its welcome.

But the room was empty.

⊲◦◦◦⊳

THIS WAS DEATH.

It was warm and sticky and there were waves of it, washing over Jared like pain. It had no air to breathe, no words to speak. It was a choking in his throat.

And then it was a gray brightness and Claudia stood in it, and her father, and Attia. He reached out to her and tried to speak her name, but his lips were cold and numb as marble and his tongue too stiff to move.

"Am I dead?" he asked the Prison, but the question murmured through hills and corridors and down cobwebbed galleries centuries old, and he realized that he was the Prison, that all its dreams were his.

He was a whole world, and yet he was a tiny creature. He could breathe, his heart was beating strongly, his eyesight was clear. He felt as if a great worry had fallen from him, a great weight from his back, and maybe it had, maybe that was his old life. And inside him there were forests and oceans, high bridges over deep crevasses, spiral staircases down to the empty white cells where his illness had been born. He had journeyed through it, explored all its secrets, fallen into its darkness.

Only he knew the riddle's answer, and the door that led Out.

Claudia heard it. In the silence the statue rippled and it spoke her name.

As she stared at it she stumbled back, but her father gripped her elbow. "I've taught you never to be afraid," he said quietly. "And besides, you know who this is."

It came alive, even as she watched. His eyes opened and were green, that intelligent, curious gaze she knew so well.

The delicate face lost its ivory and was flushed with life.

The long hair darkened and swung, the Sapient robe glimmered in iridescent grays. He spread his arms and the feathers shimmered like wings.

He stepped down from the pedestal and stood before her. *Claudia*, he said. And then, "Claudia."

Words choked in her throat.

But Rix was leaping in the roaring adulation of the crowd; he caught Attia's hand and made her bow with him in the storm of applause that went on and on, the howls of joy, the screaming cries that greeted Sapphique as he returned to save his people.

35

He sang his last song. And the words of that have never been written down. But it was sweet and of great beauty, and those that heard it were changed utterly.

Some say it was the song that moves the stars.

—Sapphique's Last Song

Finn walked slowly to the screen and stared at it. It was no longer snowy, but clear and brilliant, and he could see a girl staring straight at him.

"Claudia!" he said.

She didn't seem to hear him. Then he realized he was looking at her through someone else's eyes, eyes that were very slightly blurred, as if the Prison's gaze had tears in it.

Behind him, Keiro came close.

"What in hell is going on in there?"

As if his words had triggered it, the sound snapped on, a burst of roaring and applause and howls of joy that made them wince.

CLAUDIA REACHED out and took the Gloved hand. "Master," she said. "How have you come here? What have you done?"

He smiled his calm smile. "I think I have undertaken a

new experiment, Claudia. My most ambitious research project yet."

"Don't tease me." She clenched her fist on his scaled fingers.

"I never betrayed you," he said. "The Queen offered me forbidden knowledge. I don't think this was what she meant."

"I never once thought you would betray me." She stared at the Glove. "These people all think you're Sapphique. Tell them it's not true."

"I am Sapphique." The noise that greeted his words was tremendous but he didn't take his eyes off her. "He's what they want, Claudia. And Incarceron and I will give them their safety." The dragon fingers curled around hers. *"I feel so strange, Claudia.* It's as if you are all inside me, as if I've shed my skin and underneath is a new being, and I can see so much and I hear so many sounds and touch so many minds. I am dreaming the dreams of the Prison, and they are so sad."

"But can you come back? Do you have to stay here forever?" Her dismay sounded weak, but she didn't care, not even if her selfishness stood in the way of all Incarceron's Prisoners. "I can't do without you, Jared. I need you."

He shook his head. "You will be Queen, and queens don't have tutors." He reached out and put his arms around her and kissed her forehead. "But I'm not going anywhere. You'll carry me on your watchchain." He looked beyond her, at the Warden. "And from now on there will be freedom for us all."

The Warden's smile was narrow. "So, my old friend, you have found yourself a body after all."

"Despite all your efforts, John Arlex."

"But you haven't Escaped."

Jared shrugged, an odd, slightly alien movement. *"Ah, but I have. I've Escaped myself, but I won't be leaving. That is the paradox that is Sapphique."*

He made a small movement with his hand, and all the people gasped. Behind them, all around them, the walls lit and they saw the gray room of the Portal, its door crowded with watchers, and Finn and Keiro jerking back in surprise.

Jared turned. "Now we're all together. Inside and Outside."

"Do you mean the Prisoners can Escape?" Keiro snapped, and Claudia realized they had heard everything.

Jared smiled. "Escape to what? To the ruin of the Realm? We will make this their paradise, Keiro, just as it was supposed to be, just as the Sapienti always planned it. No one will need to Escape; I promise you that. But the door will be open, for those who wish to come and go."

Claudia stepped back from him. She knew him so well, and yet he was different. As if his personality and another had intersected, two different voices fragmenting into one, like the black and white tiles on the floor of the hall, forming a new pattern, and that pattern was Sapphique.

She glanced around, saw Rix transfixed, edging closer, Attia still and pale, staring up at Finn.

People murmured, echoing his words, passing them from one to another. She heard the promise reverberate through the Prison's landscapes. But she felt desolate and sick, because once she had been the Warden's daughter, and now she would be the Queen, and without Jared it would be another role to play, another part of the game.

Jared edged past her and walked down to meet the crowd. They held out their hands and touched him, grasped the dragonglove, fell at his feet. One, a woman, sobbed, and he touched her gently, his hands around hers.

"Don't worry," the Warden said softly in Claudia's ear.

"I can't help it. He's not strong."

"Oh, I think he is stronger than all of us."

"The Prison will corrupt him." Attia said it, and Claudia turned on her angrily. "No!"

"It will. Incarceron is cruel, and your tutor is too gentle to control it. It will all go wrong just like it did before." Attia was cold; she knew her words hurt, but she still said them, and a bitter misery made her add, "And you and Finn won't have much of a kingdom either, by the looks of things."

She looked up at Finn and he gazed back. "Come Out," he said. "Both of you."

Behind her Rix said, "Shall I open you a magic door, Attia? And will I get my Apprentice back?"

"No chance." Keiro flickered a blue glance at Finn. "The pay's better out here."

At the edge of the steps, Jared turned. "Well, Rix," he said. "Shall we see more of the Art Magicke? Make us a door, Rix."

The sorcerer laughed. He took a small piece of chalk from his pocket and held it up, and the crowd stared. Then he bent over and drew with it on the marble floor where the statue had once stood. Carefully he drew the door of a dungeon, ancient and wooden, with a barred grille and a great keyhole and chains looped across it. On it he wrote SAPPHIQUE.

"They all think you're Sapphique," he said to Jared, straightening. "But of course you're not. I won't tell them, you can trust me." He came close to Attia and winked at her. "It's all an illusion. There's a patchbook like it. A man steals fire from the gods and saves the people with its warmth. They punish him by binding him with a great chain forever. But he struggles and squirms, and at the world's end he will come back. In a ship made of fingernails." Then he smiled at her sadly. "I'll miss you, Attia."

Jared reached out and touched the chalked door with the tip of a dragonclaw. Instantly it became real, and opened, the door falling inward with a great clang, leaving a rectangular darkness in the floor.

Finn stepped back, bewildered. At his feet too the floor had swung down. The pit was black and empty.

Jared led Claudia gently to its edge. "Go on, Claudia. You'll be there, and I here. We'll work together, just as we always have."

She nodded, and looked at her father. The Warden said,

"Master Jared, may I have a word with my daughter?"

Jared bowed and moved away.

"Do as he says," the Warden said.

"What about you?"

Her father smiled his cold smile. "My plan was for you to be Queen, Claudia. That was what I worked for. Perhaps it is time I did some work here, in my own realm. This new regime will need a Warden. Jared is far too lenient, and Incarceron too harsh."

She nodded. Then she said, "Tell me the truth. What happened to Prince Giles?"

He was silent a while. He stroked his narrow beard with his thumb. "Claudia . . ."

"Tell me."

"Does it matter?" He looked at Finn. "The Realm has its king."

"But is he?"

His gray eyes held her. "If you are my daughter, you will not ask me."

She was silent too. For a long moment they looked at each other. Then, formally, he lifted her hand and kissed it, and she gave him a low curtsy.

"Good-bye, Father," she whispered.

"Rebuild the Realm," he said. "And I will come home at intervals, as I used to do. Perhaps from now on you will not dread my coming so much."

"I won't dread it at all." She walked to the edge of the trap-door and glanced back at him. "You must come to Finn's coronation."

"And yours."

She shrugged. Then, with one last look at Jared, she walked down the steps of darkness inside the door, and they saw her climb up into the room of the Portal, Finn catching her hand and helping her Out.

"Go on, girl," Rix said to Attia.

"No." She was watching the screen. "You can't lose both your Apprentices, Rix."

"Ah, but my powers have grown. Now I can conjure a winged being into life, Attia. I can bring a man from the stars. What a show I'll take on the road! I'm made, forever. However, it's true I can always use an assistant . . ."

"I could stay . . ."

Keiro said, "So you're scared then?"

"Scared?" Attia glared up at him. "Of what?"

"Of seeing Outside."

"What do you care?"

He shrugged, his eyes blue and cold. "I don't."

"Right."

"But Finn needs all the help he can get. If you were in any way grateful . . ."

"For what? I was the one who got the Glove. Who saved your life."

Finn said, "Come Out, Attia. Please. I want you to see the stars. Gildas would have wanted that."

She stared up at him, silent, and made no move, and whatever she was thinking, there was no trace of it on her face. But Jared, with the eyes of Incarceron, must have seen something, because he came over and held her hand, and she turned and stalked down the steps of darkness, and into a strange shiver of space that twisted so that suddenly the steps were leading upward, and as Jared's hand left hers another came down and hauled her up, a scarred, muscular hand with a scorched palm and a steel fingernail.

Keiro said, "Not so difficult, was it?"

She stared around. The room was gray and calm; it hummed with a faint power. Outside the door in a ruined corridor a few bruised men watched, sitting slumped against the wall. They looked at her as if she were a ghost.

In the screen on the desk the Warden's face was fading. "Not only will I come to the coronation, Claudia," he said. "But I will expect an invitation to the wedding."

And then the screen was dark, and it whispered in Jared's voice, *So will I.*

THERE WAS no way down, so they climbed up the remains of the stairs to the roof.

Finn took out the watch; he looked at the cube a long moment, then he gave it to Claudia. "You keep this."

She let the silver cube lie on her palm. "Are they really there? Or have we never known where Incarceron is?"

But Finn had no answer, and holding the watch tight, she could only climb after him.

The damage to the house horrified her; she fingered hangings that fell to pieces and touched the holes in walls and windows uncomprehendingly. "It can't be possible. How can we ever put all this together again?"

"We can't," Keiro said brutally. He led them up the stone steps, his voice echoing back. "If Incarceron is cruel, Finn, so are you. You show me a glimpse of paradise and then it's gone."

Finn glanced at Attia. "I'm sorry," he said quietly. "To both of you."

She shrugged. "As long as the stars haven't gone."

He stood aside for her on the final step. "No," he said. "They haven't."

She stepped out onto the stone battlements and stopped, and he saw it come into her face, the shock and the wonder he remembered for himself, and she gasped as she stared upward. The storm had swept the sky clear. Brilliant and fiery, the stars hung in their splendor, in their secret patterns, their distant nebulae, and Attia's breath frosted as she gazed at them. Behind her Keiro's eyes were wide; he stood still, transfixed by magic.

"They exist. They really exist!"

The Realm was dark. The distant army of refugees huddled

around campfires, flickers of flame. Beyond them the land rose in dim hills and the black fringes of forest, a realm without power, exposed to the night, all its finery as shriveled and battered as the silk flag with its black swan that fluttered, shredded, over their heads.

"We'll never survive." Claudia shook her head. "We don't know how to anymore."

"Yes we do," Attia said.

Keiro pointed. "So do they."

And she saw, faint and far, the candlepoints of flame in the cottages of the poor, the hovels where the Prison's wrath and fury had brought no change.

"Those are the stars too," Finn said quietly.